PASSION'S AWAKENING

"You are a remarkable woman, Lacy Flemming," Jared murmured.

"Thank you," she replied lamely. Lacy wished she could think of some light repartee or witty rejoinder to his comment, but none was forthcoming. Her cheeks flaming, she turned on her heel and started off toward the ice house.

Jared's hand closed lightly about her upper arm. "Don't run away from me."

Shivers raced out from the spot where his fingers touched her. "I am not running away . . . from you."

"Little liar," Jared accused.

Rooted to the spot, Lacy watched him lower his head toward hers. Some part of her mind told her to step back, but for the life of her she couldn't move. His mouth captured hers in a tender assault, and Lacy felt her insides melt. Against her lips, his moved persuasively, coaxing and teasing until her trepidations evaporated like the morning dew beneath the hot sun.

She knew the improprieties of the moment were too numerous to count. Jared Steele was little more than a stranger. Yet somehow she had no desire but to surrender to the bliss he was evoking as he deepened the kiss and crushed her tightly against him. Shocked, thrilled, she gave herself up to the headiness that made reality disappear. . . .

Virginia Embrace

Elizabeth Sherwood

PINNACLE BOOKS
WINDSOR PUBLISHING CORP.

PINNACLE BOOKS

are published by

Windsor Publishing Corp.
475 Park Avenue South
New York, NY 10016

First Printing: December 1992

Printed in the United States of America

For Joshua
My hero

Special thanks go to

Joyce A. Flaherty
for having enough faith in me
to make this book possible

Mary Bullard and Lisa Robinson
for unwavering support

The Faculty and Staff of Poquoson High School
for years of friendship

Prologue

Isle of Wight County, Virginia
November 1839

The putrid stench of impending death clogged the room with a nauseating vehemence. Sweltering heat from the fire blazing in the hearth only intensified the effect, making those surrounding Stewart Flemming's deathbed press handkerchiefs to their noses in silent self-defense.

Lacy Flemming braved the fetor of her father's wasting body and stepped closer to tenderly take his shaking hand in her own. In solemn reverie, she studied the fingers that had once been so strong and capable. Now, they were little more than gnarled bone and tightly stretched flesh.

"Can I get you anything, Papa?" she asked, swallowing the aching tightness in her throat.

The hollow cavity of Stewart Flemming's chest collapsed briefly before it rose and drew in a strained breath. His eyes fluttered open to search out the room and his mouth worked long before rasping words were uttered.

"Where are Travis and Marriette?"

Lacy's gaze shifted to the chairs at the foot of the bed where her brother and sister sat. "They're both here, Papa," she reassured him.

Hearing his name, Travis came forward to stand beside Lacy. "Yes, Father."

Stewart squinted through blurry eyes to make out the form of his son. "And Marriette?"

Slowly, reluctantly, Marriette rose and came to stand beside her siblings, her grimace hidden by the swath of scented linen she held to her nose.

"I'm here, too, Papa," she muttered.

The presence of all his children was a temporary balm to Stewart. His grating breath evened out and a smile touched his lips. "You've all been good children to me and your mother, God rest her soul." His gaze rested briefly on each of his offspring. "I can go to my grave a contented man."

"You mustn't talk this way, Papa," Lacy pleaded, clasping his hand more tightly. "You can get better."

Stewart's smile broadened ruefully. "Ah, Lacy, your optimism always was your most endearing quality." He squeezed her hand gently. "Don't change after I'm gone. And don't waste your time with useless tears, either. You . . . all of you . . . will be too busy with the Watch to squander your energy on mourning."

Travis took a step closer to the bed, his face drawn into lines of remorse. "Don't worry yourself about the plantation, Father. It's stood for five generations. I'll make sure it remains for those that follow."

8

As though his son's avowal wasn't enough, a desperate look gleamed Stewart's eyes. They didn't know, none of them understood how it really was with Swan's Watch.

His voice rose, anxious and slightly breathless. "She's a demanding mistress, the Watch is. She'll take all you have and still not be satisfied." His sight turned inward, examining the past fifty years of his life, years he had offered up in loving sacrifice to his family's plantation. "There isn't a day that goes by that she won't need your attention, your loving care. She can be as helpless as a newborn babe, and as selfish as any two-bit whore. Mind me, your sweat won't be enough for Swan's Watch, she'll want your blood, too."

In the wake of his vehement words, only silence ensued. And Stewart wouldn't have had it any other way. These were his last moments in life and it was his duty to forewarn them.

Gripping Lacy's hand with surprising strength, he uttered, "The Watch is yours now, passing to the three of you equally. Take care of her and she'll take care of you. Be true to her and she'll not fail you."

His eyelids drooped slightly, his fingers loosened. The last breath he drew was a hollow rasp. "In the end, she'll decide who's most worthy to have her . . . the Watch will choose her own mistress or master."

Stewart stared sightlessly at the high ceiling, his hands sagged limply. And all about the room hung the sound of his last words.

Chapter One

May 1840

Cloying afternoon humidity beat down on a graying shack, bathing two strained bodies in a sheen of glistening sweat. Limbs entwined and mouths clung as the steady bed-creaking rhythm increased. A discordant harmony of labored gasps filled the stagnant, musty air with an urgent song that intensified and finally crescendoed. From nearby, a solitary cicada added its piercing voice to the finale that echoed along the nearby Pagan River.

Travis Flemming flung himself off the soft, young body beneath him, and face down, drew in a series of deep breaths. As an afterthought he threw an arm around the figure beside him.

"I ain't goin' nowhere." The girlish voice held a note of laughter.

Turning his blond head just enough to open one eye, Travis stared at Rose's smile. A sated, purely feminine smile that fed his ego and made him want to climb right back on top of her. A grin of his own grew. It was always this way with Rose. His Rose.

"What you grinnin' at?" his Rose asked smugly.

There was no need for an answer. They both knew how good it had been, how good it always was between them, but he wasn't about to dish out compliments every time he spilled his seed. Not any more than he could let on just how special Rose was to him. His grin made a quick transition into a frown. He hated admitting it, but the truth was, this little fifteen-year-old was the best thing ever to come his way.

He thought about that. It didn't make an ounce of sense. She wasn't the most beautiful woman he'd bedded, nor the most experienced. Hell, she was still practically a kid. Yet she had gotten into his blood like a fever that had no cure. Damn, he should want a medicine for the kind of effect she had on his body.

Mentally, he shook his head. It might be understandable if he was some poor white trash who counted his blessings when a woman so much as looked his way. But he was Travis Flemming, for Christ's sake, Stewart Flemming's only son. He'd had more than his share of women and now at twenty-eight, ought to be out looking for a wife. Instead, the only woman he seemed to want was Rose. He mouthed another silent curse.

Annoyed with the futility of the issue, he flipped over onto his back then gave her a light shove. "Get my clothes, Rosie."

Without so much as a blink, Rose gathered his garments that had been dropped and scattered about the dingy shack. Handing them over, she waited for

12

Travis to rise. Then still naked, she lay down once again on the narrow bed.

Silently, she watched Travis hurry into his pants, then reach for his shirt. "You're in a rush," she remarked, careful to keep her tone casual. She couldn't help but wonder at his haste. He always lingered through this part of their visits, taking his time getting dressed while he stared at her body. He said looking at her was almost as good as having her. And she liked having his blue eyes on her almost as much as his tanned hands. Yet now he hadn't even glanced up to see whether her knees were spread the way he liked.

"Yeah, I'm in a hurry," he said, stomping a boot into place. "A shipping king from up north is sailing in today. I'm supposed to meet him at the wharves and I don't want to be late."

Inwardly, Rose sighed. For a moment, she had feared she might have done something to displease Travis. Or worse, his sisters had found out about these trysts. Travis wanted as few people as possible to know he was bedding her, and that definitely included his sisters.

Reassured, she relaxed back against the flattened pillows and brazenly studied him. Travis Flemming was a fine-looking man with those blue eyes and blond hair that marked him as a true Flemming. His resemblance to his dead daddy was uncanny, one had only to glance at Travis to remember Stewart Flemming. The squared jaw and clefted chin were identical, as was the tall, stocky build. Travis still had that lean look of youth, though, that his father had lost years ago. Rose rather appreciated that. She didn't think she would enjoy being diddled by some man with folds of fat.

"You goin' to want me again tomorrow?" she asked.

Working his other boot on, Travis answered distractedly. "If I do, you'll know."

Rose wasn't offended by his offhand manner. Hardly a day went by that they didn't end up in this shack and she saw no reason to think tomorrow would be any different. There was a certain headiness to be found in that knowledge and it prompted her to tease him boldly.

"What if I got me other plans?"

About to step to the door, Travis's head snapped around and in that second before he saw her flirting grin, his eyes glazed over with ice. Almost immediately, however, he recognized her ploy, all wrapped up in a seductive display of charms. His momentary tension dissolved, to be replaced by a surge of self-indulgence. He could take a few minutes to play her game.

"You don't have plans," he assured her.

"How do you know?" Her taunting words were accompanied by a wicked gleam in her eyes.

"When it comes to you, I know everything there is to know."

"Maybe, maybe not."

Sauntering back to the bed, Travis raked his gaze over her generous contours with an intensity that stripped away any secrets she pretended to have. Beneath that stare, Rose felt her insides quiver until she wanted to melt. Finally, Travis placed a hand on either side of her shoulders and lowering his head, crushed his mouth against hers. When he drew back,

14

his lips hovered the slightest fraction over hers and his words came out as a tender endearment.

"Don't get uppity with me, nigger."

In as gentle a voice, Rose answered, "No, sir, massa Travis."

Jared Steele braced himself against the forward rail of his ship and took his first good look at the Pagan River. As rivers went, it was modest, a narrow tributary of the mighty James. Still, it was deep enough to navigate into the heart of some of the richest farmland in all of Virginia and that was all that mattered.

He scanned the forested shores at both sides. Greedy marsh grass, unwilling to confine itself to solid ground, spread out from the soggy banks, obliterating the river's edge. The forest itself was choked with underbrush, bayberry and vines forming a seemingly impenetrable wall. Soft pines grew out of the brushy tangle, straight and towering, yet lacking any branches for most of their height. Only the tops possessed limbs covered with dark green needles.

Jared's brows rose as he scrutinized the flat landscape. This corner of Virginia was a far cry from his home in Connecticut, where the rushing river cut cleanly through rolling hills of stone and the air possessed a permanently cool edge. Here, there was an abundant lushness, where a luxurious profusion of greens mingled with earthy browns, and pungent odors of murky water combined with the scent of forest decay. And it was all encompassed by a humid moisture that seemed to hang in the air. Like a thin fog, it glazed everything with an opaque film, giving the scene a slightly unreal quality.

"Smithfield port off the starboard bow."

At the bosun's call, Jared glanced off to the right. The town of Smithfield came into view, a collection of waterfront warehouses and ships of every description. The wharf, even at this distance, could be seen teeming with activity.

Again, Jared's brows arched. From everything he had heard, the port was small, but what it lacked in size it more than made up for in the magnitude of its operation. Daily, ships left for all corners of the world laden with lumber, tobacco, hams, and peanuts. A healthy profit was made as each of those ships left this deceptively modest town, a profit that benefited both planter and shipper alike. It was the prospect of that profit that had brought him south.

Yet, it wasn't the sole reason, he admitted honestly. True, he wished to expand the operations of his shipping firm, but he couldn't deny that for months he had been plagued by a restlessness. Life had become mundane, almost stagnant. He found little challenge in the day-to-day routine of shipping. He needed to break new ground, discover new opportunities.

Pushing away from the rail, he crossed to the quarterdeck and descended to his cabin, considering the business ahead of him. There were sources here that had yet to be fully tapped. That very sentiment had been most glowingly recounted in several letters from one Travis Flemming of Swan's Watch.

Jared opened his cabin door and stepped into the

cool interior, but drew up slightly at the sight of his cabin boy just finishing with the packing.

"Just about done, are you?" Jared inquired, crossing to his bunk and the gray jacket laid out for him.

Tommy Little spun on his heel, and eyed his employer with open admiration. "Yes, sir, Mister Steele. Got everything stowed just like you asked. Got you enough clothes here to last you a month at least." He fastened the last of the leather bindings on the trunk. "You want me to take these topside now?"

Jared shrugged into his jacket with smooth, lithe movements. "There's no hurry, Tom. From the feel of things, we're only just about to dock."

Tommy's young face scrunched up. He wasn't certain how Jared Steele could tell such a thing, but sure enough, the ship pitched with all the telltale signs of mooring up. In a matter of seconds, the sounds of heavy footsteps could be heard from the above decks as deckhands scrambled to secure the two hundred-ton Baltimore clipper.

As always, the process drew Tommy to the upper decks, some youthful fancy being satisfied by the seemingly impossible feat of maneuvering the vessel to a complete standstill. Wry laughter plainly evident in the curve of his lips, Jared watched the boy dash off.

"Youth," he uttered on a dry chuckle. But he had to admit that he had been no different when he had begun sailing with his father. At the age of ten, he had found excitement in every aspect of seafaring life. Now, twenty-five years later, his enjoyment was tempered only by the responsibilities of owning his own fleet. The thrill of the sea was still a heady lure.

He gave into that lure now and joined most of the

17

men on deck as the last of the mooring lines were tied off and the gangplank was lowered. In no short amount of time, a tall blond man separated himself from the crowd milling about the dock and boarded the ship. With the assistance of one of the ship's hands, the man made his way to Jared's side.

"Mister Steele?"

Jared nodded, detecting a slight drawl in the man's words.

Travis extended his hand with a hearty smile. "Sir, Travis Flemming at your service. We have been anticipating your arrival, sir."

Jared extended his own hand, mildly taken aback by the fact that Travis Flemming would extend the welcome in person. More times than not, a foreman or secretary saw to such matters. Jared was pleasantly surprised.

"It is a pleasure, Mister Flemming."

"Travis, please," he insisted with a cordial smile. "After all, you shall be a guest at my house for some time. We hope to make your stay as agreeable as possible, and formality does tend to trip one up."

Virgina hospitality was something of which Jared had only heard. In the ensuing minutes, he discovered quite quickly that the saying was more than mere words. With supreme graciousness, Travis escorted him to a waiting carriage, but not before making certain that Jared's trunks were sent on via a second wagon.

Throughout the ride up the steep hill of Smithfield, past the old brick courthouse and out of town, Travis made certain of Jared's comfort. He entertained his guest with an informative and amusing

18

account of the county news and local interests. By the time the carriage turned onto the long, crushed-shell drive through Swan's Watch, Jared felt thoroughly welcomed to Virginia.

His gaze more than curious, he viewed the plantation. Acres of fields boasted young crops of corn and peanuts. Beyond those, against the horizon, hardwood forests formed a perimeter of grayish-green.

"What do you think of her, sir?" Travis asked, noting Jared's keen regard of the land.

Jared pulled his attention from the far-off trees and turned to his companion. "Her?"

Waving a hand in an all-encompassing gesture, Travis explained, "Swan's Watch. She seems to have caught your eye, and I was interested in what you thought?"

Behind the query, Jared detected a note that went beyond simple interest. Travis Flemming's voice harbored a certain pride, but also an odd expectancy.

"The land is very impressive," Jared admitted honestly.

A sigh mixed with the smile that broadened Travis's face. "You have yet to see the best of her. The house from the riverside, the dependencies, the formal terraces and gardens."

"How many acres?"

"Just over fifteen hundred, all original property from the 1620 land grant."

Jared found that last bit of information surprising. He knew it was no easy task owning that much land, for there were too many factors involved that could affect that status. Taxes alone more often than not saw one's property sold off or divided. The fact that Swan's Watch had remained intact for over two hundred years was silent proof that the plantation had been prosperous.

Genuinely impressed, he tipped his head in salute to Travis. "You and your grandfathers are to be commended. And I look forward to a full tour of the grounds."

"You needn't wait much longer," Travis averred. Their carriage rounded a bend in the drive and the house came into view for the first time. "Welcome to Swan's Watch."

Jared's gaze was captured by the brick Georgian structure, and he conceded Flemming's earlier pride. The manor was indeed magnificent. Surrounded by spreading willows, the five-bay house was a tribute to the craftsmanship of artisans dead some hundred and fifty years. The basic cube of the design was enhanced by pavilions projecting from either side. The extra corners were a unique feature, as was the elegant entrance with its glass transom and sculpted pilasters. The roofline was edged with a dentiled cornice while intricate masonry patterns bordered each window.

A flash of pink shone from one of those second-story windows. Squinting slightly, Jared detected the figure of a woman as she moved within.

Lacy Flemming crossed before one of her bedroom windows as she swept her hair off her shoulders. With practiced fingers, she divided the silver-blond mass into three equal parts and plaited the length into a single braid.

Distractedly, her gaze fell to the ring of keys that lay on her dresser. That heavy ring held the key to every lock on every door on the entire plantation from attic to cooperage. The collection usually rested in the pocket of her skirt or apron as she went about her daily chores. But tonight, it would remain beside her collection of brushes and combs.

Still, just the sight of the keys was a reminder that tomorrow she needed to see that the raw wool was brought down from the storehouse. The weavers needed to tend to that chore soon if there was to be warmer cloth for winter.

The sound of her door opening pulled her from her thoughts. Turning, she found her sister practically dancing into the room in a swirl of red-striped muslin.

"You should see him, Lacy," Marriette declared, her face aglow with ill-concealed excitement. "He's so deliciously handsome, it makes me want to throw up my skirts and forsake my virtue."

At the bold remark, Lacy flushed as bright as her fair skin could tolerate and stared at her older sister. "Marriette, I wish you wouldn't talk in that manner," she managed to get out in a miserable voice.

Ignoring Lacy's embarrassment, Marriette shut the door she had thrust open and twirled her way across the room. "He's enough to take a girl's breath away."

"Marriette . . ."

"I wasn't able to see the color of his eyes, but I imagine they might be green."

Realizing this was going to be a very one-sided conversation, Lacy turned to her mirror again and continued to braid her hair. "I assume you are referring to Mister Steele?"

Marriette paused in exasperated wonder. "Well, of course I'm talking about Mister Steele. Who else have we been expecting?" Sighing, she gave her cluster of yellow curls a toss and searched the ceiling for divine providence. How in Heaven's name she and Lacy could be sisters, she would never know. The girl was just too obtuse.

Catching Marriette's piqued expression in the mirror, Lacy shrugged. "You didn't take the time to mention a name when you burst in here to expound on Mister Steele's physiognomy . . . and your chastity."

Although the note of reproach in Lacy's voice was subtle, it annoyed Marriette to no end. Thrusting out her lower lip, she flounced to a cushioned chair and lounged back, her crinolined skirts flaring out around her.

"Oh, peanuts to that. You were just afraid Travis would hear. But don't worry, he's downstairs this very minute sipping bourbon with Mister Steele." The contours of her mouth took on a devilish curve and her cobalt eyes glinted with wicked delight. "Just wait until you see him. I chanced to see him step from the carriage . . ."

"Most likely hanging out your window," Lacy interrupted wryly.

If Lacy hadn't been so near the truth, Marriette would have protested. But the elder sister could not deny her preoccupation with men, although she did credit herself with having the discretion to limit her interest to those who were young and wealthy. But that, she reasoned, was just the natural way of things. She was twenty years old, in her prime and God had seen fit to bless her with a comely face and the type of rounded figure men seemed attracted to. Who was she to question the Lord's ways? And besides, if He hadn't meant for her to return a man's regard, He would have made certain she was blind.

"Don't be snide, Lacy," she quipped, looking down her elegant nose, "it isn't becoming. As I was saying, there is nothing sedate about Mister Steele. He stands inches over Travis and I would swear there is no padding in the shoulders of his jacket. And his hair is black, if you can imagine that. No, no, it's more like pitch. No . . . his hair is like midnight." Marriette closed her eyes and hugged her arms to her waist. "He is truly the most magnificent man I have ever beheld."

Confusion stilled Lacy's fingers. "I thought you believed that of Carter."

Pulled from the throes of her poetic reverie, Marriette's eyes snapped open to glare accusingly across the room. "That's just like you, Lacy, to snatch me out of the clouds that way."

"That was never my intention," Lacy replied levelly. "I simply do not understand how you can have ecstasies about a man you've only just glimpsed from your window, when you have been proclaiming your devotion to Carter James these past months. You are nearly betrothed to the man."

"An engagement has yet to be decided upon," the elder sister remarked airily, then added with a shrug, "And after seeing Mister Steele, I may not want Carter."

Stunned, Lacy turned to stare at her sister. "You are jesting."

"No, I don't believe so."

Lacy could hardly believe it. Marriette had set her sights on Carter James ever since he had inherited Bellehaven plantation from his father a little over a year ago. He was the catch of the entire Tidewater and Marriette had brought him to the point of proposing marriage. Now, on a whim, she might just snub her nose and disregard the entire matter.

"What of Carter?"

Momentarily distracted by her manicure, Marriette paused to frown at a fingernail. "What of him?" she asked, as she nibbled on a ragged cuticle.

"You can't possibly treat him this way."

Marriette found only one thing more boring than her fingernail, and that was Lacy prattling on about Carter. She dropped her hand limply into her lap. "You are going on about trivialities."

"Trivialities?" Fresh color tinted Lacy's cheeks. She was appalled at her sister's attitude. "You have claimed to love him. How can you say that is nothing?"

Marriette's chin came up defensively. "I don't see why you're in such a tizzy about this, you don't even like Carter."

"Whether I like him or not makes no difference."

The last thing Marriette wanted was to be taken to task, especially by a sister two years her junior. Irritated, she came to her feet. "I don't know why I even bothered to come in here and discuss this with you. You don't know anything about the ways of the heart, Lacy, yet you stand there and pronounce judgment on me like the very voice of experience. Why, you haven't even had a serious suitor yet and you've been out an entire year."

If Marriette had shown the slightest sensitivity toward the matter, Lacy might have yielded the discussion. As it was, Lacy believed her sister deserved nothing better than scorn for her complete lack of consideration.

"I may be without a suitor and I may be inept at the social intricacies of flirtation, but at least others can rest easy at night knowing I would not tread upon their feelings."

The barb pricked Marriette's temper. "I'm going to have to speak to Reverend Thomas about you," she retorted, then sniffed disdainfully. "We should have you canonized as soon as possible."

In sheer self-defense, Lacy's chin came up. "If honest emotion, compassion and caring signifies sainthood, then I will gladly polish my halo."

Marriette's dark eyes narrowed maliciously. She should have known Lacy would turn all self-righteous and noble. It was too detestable for words. Disgusted, she stalked to the door, then paused in the hall for one last comment.

"Look to that holier-than-thou attitude of yours the next time you see the back of a suitor." Smiling in satisfaction, she made her way to the stairway in search of Mr. Steele.

In Marriette's wake, Lacy resisted the urge to slam the door. Gritting her teeth, she quietly secured the shutter before leaning back in a bid for self-control. Behind tightly closed eyes, the nasty scene replayed in her mind and she wondered if she and Marriette would ever go for more than an hour without coming to incivility. Sadly, she didn't think so. The differences between them were too great.

Dispiritedly, she considered those contrasts. They seemed epitomized by the fact that she was closeted in her room, mourning a sisterly affection that did not exist, while Marriette had shrugged off their disagreement and was now downstairs engaged in a gay rapport with Mr. Steele.

Sighing, Lacy admitted that was her sister's way. Marriette was, by nature, a gregarious changeling. She molded her temperament to suit the occasion. In a social setting, she used her beauty and wit with flamboyant style that charmed even the most sober character. Ancient widows as well as young gallants were drawn to her enchanting disposition, the charm that Marriette reserved exclusively for anyone other than her family. Add to that, a buxom figure, ready smiles and an infectious laugh, and it was no secret why Marriette Flemming was the toast of the county.

It was also no secret, least of all to Lacy, that she herself was deemed of questionable character. To the casual acquaintance, her reserved demeanor and serious bent denoted a cool temperament. Lacy gave a wry laugh, knowing the unjust impression was the furthest thing from the truth.

Pushing away from the door, she stepped before the full-length mirror. As though to verify the differences between her and Marriette, she studied her image with exacting scrutiny. The glass showed a young woman, delicately boned and of average height. Above the full flare of her skirt, the snug-fitting, pale pink bodice revealed a slim figure, gently curved.

Her oval face presented a marked defiance to the

standard Flemming visage. The hue of her eyes was more turquoise than blue, her mouth more subtly sculpted than the generous curves possessed by her siblings. And while the Flemming women from one end of Virginia to the other prided themselves on their camelialike complexions and wavy golden curls, Lacy had to content herself with a scattering of freckles across her nose and silver-blond hair that stubbornly defied the curling irons.

Giving into the last remnants of frustration, she stuck her tongue out at her reflection. The absurdity of her action brought a smile to her lips and, with a pragmatic shrug, she moved to the window seat.

The personal critique was unnecessary. She had learned long ago to be satisfied with the realities of herself. And in all honesty she did not wish for more. Despite the fact that since childhood others had seen fit to compare her to Marriette and judge her lacking, Lacy was not discontent with her appearance or her disposition.

She was pleased that the use of her corset was due to fashion and not necessity. It did not discomfit her that she had no interest in gossip. And she did not yearn for a score of beaux. In her heart, there was room for only one man. Unlike Marriette with her penchant to impatiently gather as many admirers as possible, Lacy was content to bide her time patiently and wait for the one man she would love.

A quick glance to the clock on the mantel brought her to her feet. It was past six. Dinner in honor of Mr. Steele's arrival was set for seven, and she should have been in the parlor by now. She adjusted the pink and green plaid bertha into a becoming drape over her shoulders, puffed up the short, bouffant sleeves to lay at her elbows, nudged any remaining disquietudes to the back of her mind, and went below to meet Mr. Steele.

A mingling of voices reached her ears as she neared the foot of the stairway. Her hand resting on the polished mahogany banister, she stood in the paneled great hall for a moment, then followed the laughter down the hall to the parlor.

At the doorway, Lacy scanned the blue and yellow room and immediately felt chagrined at her tardiness. Travis and Marriette were present, seated in a cozy setting before the marble fireplace. And sitting in a wing-back with his back toward the door was Mr. Steele. Disconcertingly, Lacy admitted her association with the man would have to begin with an apology.

"I beg your pardon, all, for my delay," she said, as she came forward.

The tall form of Jared Steele rose as Lacy approached. Travis also came to his feet and eyed his younger sister with an affectionate smile.

"No harm, Lacy." Stepping to her side, he made the introductions. "Jared Steele, may I present my younger sister, Lacy."

Lacy's first glance at Jared Steele pushed all thoughts but one from her mind. Marriette had been right. Jared Steele *was* the most magnificent man she had ever seen. He was dressed in shades of gray; a charcoal-hued jacket that defined the broad width of his shoulders, a silver cravat over a crisp white shirt, and snugly fitting gray pants that delineated the long muscular length of his legs.

Marriette had likened his hair to midnight, but the evening sky had no claim on the blue highlights that glinted in the thick strands. In looking up, Lacy decided he had to be three inches over six feet, which helped explain why she felt overwhelmed by his presence.

On only one count could Lacy fault her sister's sentiments. The man's eyes; they were not green, but a rich, smoky gray, surrounded with thick lashes and capped by dark brows. Together with his straight nose, strongly molded lips and lean-edged jaw, his face was handsome enough *to make her want to throw up her skirts and . . .*

"Welcome to our home, Mister Steele!" she blurted out as she shoved Marriette's proclaimed intention of forsaking virtue out of her mind. In agonizing embarrassment, she felt her face flush scarlet.

His appreciative gaze laced with speculation, Jared looked down at the silver-blond beauty before him and was jarred by the impact created by the sight of her. Like a blow in the dark, the effect was sudden and unexpected, but in this instance, heartily welcomed. Lacy Flemming was the loveliest of creatures, radiating a serene elegance he found irresistible. Conscious of the assembled group, he was hard-pressed not to let his eyes stray along every delightful curve and plane. It was by force of will alone that he kept himself from staring.

"Miss Lacy, it is an honor," he averred. "Swan's Watch has welcomed me most warmly."

Marriette's smooth voice intervened. "Mister Steele, you have such a gracious way of putting things."

His attention reluctantly shifted to Marriette.

"The results of being in such cordial company, Miss Flemming."

"Oh, dear," she replied on a laugh. "You simply must call me Marriette." She gave him an outrageously engaging smile, complete with a calculated glance out of the corners of her eyes. "After all, we wish to make your stay a pleasant one."

Jared suppressed the urge to raise his brows at Marriette's effusive cordiality. Instead, he gave her a courtly smile. "A first-name basis suits me well, Marriette."

Glad for the diversion the discourse provided, Lacy sat beside Travis on the Chippendale settee, hoping to become as inconspicuous as possible. Unfortunately, her desire to blend into the intricate pattern work on the sofa dissolved as Jared took his seat directly opposite her. In a short amount of time, she realized that his gaze wandered to her with amazing frequency.

By the time the party adjourned to the dining room and had finished their peanut soup, Lacy was a bundle of raw nerves. Jared Steele had the most unimaginable effect on her. Despite the length of table that lay between them, she was acutely aware of him, of the deep timbre of his voice, the smoothly controlled movements of his hands and the subtle, but thorough glances he sent her way.

With studied deliberateness, she paid great attention to her food and wondered what in the world was the matter with her. She had never been so conscious of any man. Ever. It was as though every fiber of her being was excruciatingly attuned to him, inexorably urging her to lift her eyes and openly stare at him.

Surreptitiously, she chanced a look his way, and was struck by the pure masculinity of him. He seemed to radiate an undercurrent of strength that dominated the room.

Without warning, he turned his attention from Travis and looked her way. Caught staring, Lacy smiled weakly, blinked rapidly and looked to her plate.

The second course of boiled chub with clam sauce, greens with ham and *vol-a-vent* of oysters sat in Lacy's stomach like a brick. It was all she could do to swallow one mouthful after another and endure through dessert. It was to her vast relief that dinner finally concluded and the men rose to adjourn to the library for the remainder of the evening.

Marriette left her seat and came forward, her hand extended to Jared with languid grace. "Good night, Jared," she murmured sweetly. "I do hope you have a pleasant first night here at Swan's Watch."

His movements a study of polished ease, Jared raised her fingers for a token brush of his lips. "Thank you, Marriette. Already my stay has been more than agreeable."

Lacy watched her sister bestow a dazzling parting smile on Jared before gliding from the room with perfect aplomb, and she gave a sigh. If she could have only an ounce of Marriette's sangfroid at this moment, she would be eternally grateful. Unfortunately, the thought of having Jared Steele kiss her hand, no matter how circumspectly, drove rioting shivers down her spine. But there were no options left open to her. It was only polite to offer her hand; to do otherwise would be insulting.

Gathering her wits, she scolded herself for carrying on like a ninny, and forced her legs to carry her from the end of the table to stand before Jared Steele. She could only hope that her face bore none of the inner confusion she felt.

"Good night, Mister Steele," she murmured quietly, extending her hand.

Jared gathered her cold fingers in his warm grasp. At the chill touch of her hand, his brows lowered.

"Lacy, I thought we decided that it was to be first names?" he commented with a lightness that belied the intensity in his eyes.

Her fingers still held firmly in his strong hand, Lacy swallowed hard, his name stuck neatly in her throat. "Yes . . . yes you are quite right . . . Jared."

If Jared could feel her tension, he made no notice of it. Instead, he gave her a heartwarming smile and slowly raised her hand to his lips.

"Good night to you, Lacy."

The pressure of his lips on her hand was brief, but it was anything but casual, and Lacy's eyes widened. The touch was electrifying, alarmingly so, shooting quivers up her arm and then straight to the pit of her stomach. Helplessly, her lips parted, but before she could even draw a steadying breath, he relinquished her hand and stepped back, the very picture of gentlemanly decorum.

Free of the hold he seemed to have over her, Lacy gave him a weak smile before nodding to Travis. Then she hurried across the room. Once in the haven of her own bedroom, she laid a shaking hand over her stomach, and wondered what in the world had happened to her.

Chapter Two

Enough was enough! Lacy mentally scolded herself as she left her room the next morning. Thoughts of Jared Steele had chased her through the night, making sleep almost impossible. The image of his ruggedly chiseled face had created the most peculiar ache in her stomach, forcing her to toss and turn in self-defense. Now she found herself anticipating seeing him at breakfast.

Well, she was going to have to get a hold of her wayward emotions and concentrate on her morning chores. To that end, she pushed Jared Steele to the farthest corner of her mind and descended the stairs, her serviceable gown of pale blue muslin with its single petticoat beneath making only the barest hint of a sound.

The clock in the main entrance hall chimed five and out of habit, Lacy glanced to the transom over the front door letting in the new light of the dawn. This was her favorite hour of the day, when the house was still and hushed. As usual, she was the only one in the house awake. Travis normally slept until six and Marriette . . . well Marriette emerged from her room at any time that suited her. Not for the first time, Lacy shook her head in amazement, thinking her brother and sister were missing the best part of the day.

Her step light, she made her way to the back door and out onto the brick landing, but she halted abruptly at the sight of Jared leaning casually against one of the pilasters. At the sound of her approach, he straightened and turned to face her.

Unexpectedly, her limbs were assailed by an onslaught of nerves, and she was helpless in trying to still the sudden shaking of her hands. She had hoped to have some respite from the hold he seemed to have over her. Instead, she was faced with the very source of her disquietude, a man who looked more devastatingly handsome in the dawn light than in her dreams.

She couldn't help but notice the powerful figure he cut. Dressed casually in a loose-fitting white shirt tucked into black riding pants, the width of his shoulders was as starkly evident as the narrow tapering of his waist and hips. And underlying the virility of him, was a powerful sense of command.

"Good morning, Mister Steele," she remarked carefully, glad that her voice did not betray any of her inner turmoil.

Jared smiled, baring even white teeth, but he shook his head in mock dismay. "Ah, Lacy, I thought we settled the matter of my name last evening."

Self-consciously, she shoved her hands into her

34

pockets, grateful for the reassuring feel of her ring of keys.

"Yes, you're right of course, Jared."

At the sound of his name from her lips, Jared's smile grew. She was a beautiful sight to behold. Her silver-blond hair was fastened in a simple knot atop her head, allowing an alluring view of the slim column of her neck. The blue of her dress complemented the hue of her eyes, and her skin held a rosy glow as though she had just climbed from her bed. It was a fascinating thought, to think of Lacy Flemming in bed. *His* bed.

His smile grew, becoming increasingly more charming and gracious by the second. The effect it had on Lacy was disarming and all she could do was blink and blush profusely.

"You are up rather early this morning, sir," she commented quickly, feeling the heat on her cheeks. "I hope your sleep was comfortable."

"Very much so." He studied her heightened color. "But what of you?" The gray of his eyes took on a devilish tint. "I would have thought you'd be lingering in your own bed."

She tilted her head to one side at his comment. Apparently this Yankee shipper wasn't familiar with plantation life. For some reason, that knowledge eased a good portion of her tension and brought a genuine smile to her lips.

"The Watch does not run herself. She needs careful tending everyday."

"Even at this hour?" he asked, all too aware of the dimples her smile produced.

"Most especially at this hour. If breakfast is to be

35

served on time, if fresh laundry is to be expected, if there is to be enough hot bath water by the end of the day, if . . . if . . . if. The list is endless."

"And these duties fall to you."

Shrugging slightly, Lacy slowly made her way down the steps, Jared by her side. "Yes," she replied simply. Gazing off toward the smokehouse, she missed the speculative glance Jared leveled on her. As it was, her mind was already thinking ahead to the day's menu.

"Are we off to anywhere in particular?" His question brought her gaze back to him.

"We?"

"Exactly," he insisted. "I find I am supremely ignorant of your way of life." He braced his arms akimbo. "Educate me."

It was not quite an order, but much more than a request. Skeptically, Lacy looked up at his undaunted expression and felt her insides twist. Surely he couldn't mean to accompany her on her morning rounds.

"Sir, I . . ."

"Jared," he interjected smoothly.

She blinked several times before gathering her wits. "Jared, I hardly think my morning routine would be of any interest to you." But more than that, she didn't think she could bear up under his close and overwhelming presence.

"Then you should think again, Lacy."

If the implacable note of his voice didn't convince her, then the unwavering determination reflected in the gray depths of his eyes did. Jared Steele meant to escort her on her way.

Truly baffled and not a little discomposed, she spread her hands wide and glanced helplessly about her. Why on earth would he wish to do such a thing?

"I can hardly refuse your request, sir, since you are our guest. But I must tell you that I find it most . . . unusual. Are you certain you wouldn't wish to wait for Travis to show you about the fields?"

Jared's gaze was unwavering. "Most certain."

Faced with that declaration, Lacy had no choice but to acquiesce gracefully. Shrugging with her hands, she turned and led the way toward the dependencies, but the normalcy of her routine had been stripped away.

Jared fell into step beside her, an extremely satisfied smile twitching at his lips. "You never did answer my question," he commented, gazing down at her as they crossed the lawn to a row of small white buildings.

"What question?" she returned. In all honesty, she couldn't remember his asking anything, especially with his disturbing closeness making a jumble of her thoughts.

"My question as to where we are going?"

Glad to be able to focus her thoughts on something less distracting than Jared Steele, she replied, "The kitchen." Lifting her hand she indicated the first of the outbuildings they had reached.

The kitchen was already alive with activity as the two stepped within. Before the huge fireplace ablaze with glowing coals, a tall, rotund black woman stood stirring one of the kettles that hung from the ironworks. Behind her at the worn worktable, one young girl cracked eggs while another sliced ham from its bone. In the far corner, beneath one of the windows, an even younger boy shelled peanuts.

"Good morning," Lacy greeted.

The black woman turned from her kettles, her dark eyes glittering with serious intent, and when she spoke, her words came out in a harried rush. "Mornin', Miz Lacy. I wondered when you wuz goin' to git here. We just 'bout out of cornmeal and I'm goin' to need more ice right soon."

Lacy considered the problems at hand and nodded calmly. "All right, Besha, I'll get Eustis to help with the flour and I'll send Gabe for the ice." In deference to the kitchen's heat, she rolled back her sleeves. "Is everything else all right?"

"Not exactly." She nodded to the sack of peanuts the young boy was working on. "Most of dem nuts Johnny been crackin' got de worms."

The curves of Lacy's lips pulled into a squeamish moue. Rotten peanuts were bad enough, but infested nuts turned her stomach. Nonetheless, she crossed the room and knelt down beside the boy.

"Let's have a look, Johnny." Gingerly, she peered into the burlap sack and removed several of the light brown shells. From all appearances they seemed normal, but with a quick snap she discovered that at least two of the husks contained small white worms.

"Heavens, what a mess," she declared, unable to keep the repugnance from her voice.

Little Johnny silently agreed with a nod of his head. Wide-eyed, he stared at Lacy, hoping she would rescue him from his odious task.

"Johnny, go dump this mess down the old well," she ordered gently. She gave him a conspiratorial

38

wink and added, "We'll forget about peanuts for today."

As though he had been granted his fondest wish, Johnny jumped to his feet and ran from the kitchen, the nasty sack clenched in one of his hands.

Coming to her own feet, Lacy scrubbed her palms against her skirt and returned to Jared's side. "Is there anything else, Besha?"

Now that her problems were soon to be solved, Besha relaxed. "Right as rain. Breakfast is goin' to be fine, just fine." Expectantly, she eyed Jared, her open curiosity impossible for Lacy to miss.

"This is Mister Steele," Lacy explained. "He will be our guest at the Watch for a while."

The cook gave Jared a smile as wide as her ample stomach. "Hope you like good cookin', Mister Steele, cuz you goin' to have some of de best food you done ever ate dis side of de James."

Jared took the audacious statement in stride. "If the meal last evening was anything to judge by, then you will get no arguments from me."

His compliment elicited a crowing laugh from the cook. "A man after my own heart, yes, sir. I'll see if I can't mix you up some of my special cracklin' biscuits."

"Cracklin'?" The term was new to Jared.

"Yes, sir. Cracklin's. Mixed right into de biscuits, and covered wid my special red-eye gravy."

Needing some clarification, Jared turned to Lacy, inquiry plainly etched on the tanned planes of his face.

"Cracklin's are the crispy pieces of fat left over after the last of the lard has been rendered," Lacy explained. "They're quite tasty."

Jared had no great desire to eat hog fat, delicious or otherwise. "I can only trust to your better judgment in the matter."

His skepticism amused Lacy. Smiling up into his doubt-filled eyes, she said, "Sir, on this plantation we use every part of pig except the oink."

Jared's gaze traveled the lilting curve of Lacy's lips, the smile distracting him from any thoughts of cracklin's. Her dimples alone were enough to urge his thoughts to sweeter diversions.

Miss Lacy Flemming of Swan's Watch was as intriguing a morsel as he had ever encountered. One moment she was a flustered young miss, blushing profusely at his regard. And by the next turn, she was all cool beauty, serene and elegant, fully capable of handling the domestic chores of the plantation without the blink of an eye. He surmised that somewhere deep within her there was a perfect blending of both sides of her nature. Fascinated, he determined to discover just who this woman was.

A prolonged silence fell between them as Jared's gaze lingered. Lacy felt the weight of his all-too discerning stare and once again she was besieged by a wave of self-consciousness. His look sent tremors skipping over her nerves to collect in her stomach. The effect was most unsettling and the brief ease of the moment vanished, taking with it her smile.

Turning, she left the kitchen, silently hoping that Jared Steele would not accompany her further. To her dismay, he joined her as she strolled away toward a row of whitewashed log cabins.

"Do I make you nervous?" came his deep-voiced query.

Lacy's head snapped toward him, her eyes rounded in shock. "No," she replied too quickly. Immediately, she gazed away, knowing that her reply sounded false even to her own ears.

"I won't bite," he promised, laughter underscoring his words.

Inwardly, Lacy cringed. This was worse than worse. Beside her was the most disturbing man she had ever encountered. He had the most startling effect on her and she suspected that he knew as much. She could not deny it, yet how could she possibly admit such a thing to him?

"I am not accustomed to company this early in the morning, sir, least of all when I am engaged in chores." That, she hoped, would suffice as an explanation.

It didn't. Jared's smile stretched wide as he cast her a knowing look. Fortunately for Lacy's sake they had reached the slave dwellings and he was forced to keep his teasing comment to himself.

Lacy stepped before the second cabin and knocked on the door. From within came the muted sounds of grumbling before the door was opened.

A withered elderly man, his white hair offering a startling contrast to his dark skin, peered at Lacy through eyes glassed over. At the sight of Lacy, a toothy grin split his face, wrinkles folding in upon wrinkles.

"Mornin' Miz Lacy," he announced, shuffling forward.

Lacy extended a hand to aid the man's passage

41

down the single wooden step to the path. "Good morning, Oliver," she nearly shouted. "How are you today? How are you feeling?"

Oliver cupped a hand behind one ear and squinted. "No, ma'am, I twernt sleepin'."

Nodding, Lacy tried again, enunciating carefully. "There never was any keeping you down, Oliver. How are you today?"

"Fine, fine."

"Are your bones giving you any trouble?"

"No more dan usual, but I got me my cure here." He shoved a gnarled hand into one of his pants pockets and removed a new potato. "You know Besha says dis here tater will cure de rheumatism."

Lacy was all too aware of Besha's "cures." Most were based on superstitions, but if they helped even the slightest bit, Lacy was not about to interfere.

"I'm glad Besha is able to help you. Are you up to lending a hand?"

Oliver's glassy eyes widened. "You know I more dan able, Miz Lacy. What you need doin'?"

Reaching into her dress pocket, Lacy pulled out her heavy ring and removed two wrought-iron keys from the collection.

"Besha needs ice and a sack of meal," she instructed loudly. "Will you find Gabe and Eustis and send them to take care of that?"

"No one better for de task, no, ma'am."

"Thank you, Oliver." She pressed the keys into his palm and then with a departing smile, watched him scuffle away, making sure he didn't lose his balance and fall. It wasn't until she herself turned that she became aware of Jared's intimate inspection. His

42

gray eyes searched her features with an unwavering intensity that made her heart skip a beat.

"Mister Steele?"

It was a long, quiet moment before he said anything. In that time, Lacy felt as though he had stripped away her outer layer of clothing to discover all her innermost secrets.

"You are a remarkable woman, Lacy Flemming," he finally murmured.

A rosy blush flooded her cheeks and it was all she could do to draw a normal breath. She had no idea what had prompted his flattery, but it made her very uncomfortable.

"Thank you," she replied lamely. Instantly, she chastised herself for her weak-sounding voice. For the first time, she wished she possessed an ounce of Marriette's flirtatious gaiety to see her through this ordeal. And an ordeal it was. To have Jared Steele so near at hand, his handsome face gazing down at her, his powerful frame exuding raw masculine strength, was positively unnerving. She wished she could think of some light repartee or witty rejoinder to his comment, but none was forthcoming.

Her cheeks flaming, she turned on her heel and started off through the copse of trees leading to the ice house. She managed several steps before Jared's hand closed lightly about her upper arm and drew her to a halt.

"Don't run away from me."

Shivers raced out from that spot where his fingers touched her and she swallowed. "I am not running away . . . from . . . you."

A smile softened Jared's lips. "No?"

"No. I . . . I have to meet Oliver at the ice house, that's all."

"Little liar," he accused affectionately. "You've been running from me all morning, since last night to be more specific. I come near you, even look in your direction and you get all flustered."

Lacy was beyond speech. It was true. Every word he spoke was the absolute truth. And he was abominable to make an issue of it.

Her chin came up, the blue and green in her eyes warring for dominance as her inner turmoil grew. "Let me go, Mister Steele," she declared heatedly.

"Not until we get this settled."

"I don't . . . know what you're talking about."

"Yes, you do." His hand slid down the length of her arm to gently grasp her hand. "I offered you a simple compliment, nothing more, yet you behave as though I have insulted you."

She stared into his fathomless eyes, trying to sort through her jumbled thoughts. How could she tell him that she wasn't accustomed to compliments, simple or otherwise, especially from a man such as himself? It was Marriette who received accolades from handsome men, and it was Marriette who knew how to deal with them.

"I'm sorry if you misinterpreted my actions, sir. I did not take offense by your comments."

But she was highly discomfited by them, Jared surmised, and he wondered why. She was a beautiful, gracious, warmhearted woman. Compliments by the dozens must have come her way, yet she behaved as though the opposite was true.

Running his fingers along the back of her hand, he

44

sought to make amends. "You'll have to forgive my forthright tongue, Lacy, but the fact is, I'm used to speaking my mind. I cannot help it if I find you fascinating . . ."

"Please . . ." She tried to extricate her hand from his.

". . . and I will not pretend otherwise." His gaze touched the gentle curves of her lips, and when he spoke his voice was a low, mesmerizing murmur that enveloped her as surely as did the warm, humid air. "You have no cause to flee from me."

Held rooted to the spot, Lacy watched him close the distance between them and lower his head toward hers. Some part of her mind told her to step back, but for the life of her she couldn't move. In reality, she wasn't sure if she wanted to.

His mouth captured hers in a tender assault, and Lacy felt her insides melt. Against her lips, his moved persuasively, coaxing and teasing until her trepidations evaporated like the morning dew beneath the hot sun.

She knew the improprieties of the moment were too numerous to count. Jared Steele was little more than a stranger, their association practically nil. Yet somehow she had no desire to do more than remain as she was, and surrender to the bliss he was evoking as he deepened the kiss and crushed her tightly against him.

His tongue traced the contours of her lips before plunging into the sweetness of her mouth. Shocked, thrilled, she gave herself up to the headiness that made reality disappear. Helplessly, her hands slid up the hard wall of his chest to grasp the fine white fabric of his shirt.

Her response was more than Jared could have hoped for, far more than he was prepared for. The feel of her softness against him sent his blood pounding through his veins with a shocking intensity that urged him to strip away every last article of her clothing, lay her down on the soft forest ground and plunge himself deep within her.

He had been captivated by her from the first moment he had laid eyes on her, but he hadn't expected his body to react so fiercely to her. Breathing heavily, he yanked his mouth from hers. "What have you done to me, Lacy?" he ground out against the rapidly beating pulse in her neck.

Lacy was too caught up in her newfound passion to reply. His words were a distant murmur, barely penetrating the sensual fog in which she found herself. Unaware that she did so, she let her yearning gaze seek his, desire sparkling in the turquoise depths.

"Jared?" was all she could manage.

Her throaty whisper skimmed over his raw nerves, adding to the desire that already threatened his self-control. Groaning at the slumberous look in her eyes, he trailed a line of kisses over her jaw, then without warning, thrust her away from him. His move caught her off guard and at the startled look on her face, he exhaled deeply and explained.

"You tempt me beyond all that is sane, Lacy."

Reality crashed down on Lacy like one huge tidal wave. With it came a chorus of conflicting emotions, each vying for control.

"Why did you kiss me?" she asked, her face stained

with color.

He gave her a rueful smile. "Because I was going to lose my mind if I didn't."

"I don't understand. You hardly know me."

"True, but what I do know, appeals to me . . . greatly."

Lacy's eyes filled with awe and Jared quickly jumped on the unspoken disclosure.

"Does that surprise you?"

It more than surprised her. She was stunned, stunned by the fact that he would seek her out and pursue her to the extent that he had. She wasn't used to men reacting to her in that manner. They normally fawned over Marriette, not herself.

"Yes, I am surprised," she admitted.

A lopsided smile came to her lips, but anything she might have said fell by the wayside as Oliver and Gabe made their way toward them. Nonetheless, a strange sense of intimacy encompassed her, even long after the men had seen to the ice and she and Jared headed back to the house to be greeted by Travis.

Standing in the doorway, he watched their progress across the lawn to the steps. "Jared, good morning. I hope you had a pleasant night."

"Yes, very," Jared replied, but it was nothing to compare with his morning. A hand at the small of Lacy's back, he ushered her to the landing.

"Good. And how are you today, Lacy?" Travis's smile was as usual broad and genuine.

At any other time, Lacy wouldn't have thought twice about her brother's innocent inquiry. But the events of her day thus far lent a strain to her reply.

"I'm quite all right." But she wasn't. Her lips still tingled from the pressure of Jared's mouth, and her bones had yet to solidify. Now, with Jared and Travis regarding her, she felt as far from "all right" as she ever had. Hastily, she sought refuge in privacy.

"If you two will excuse me. I . . . breakfast will be ready soon. I'll go see that everything in the dining room is in order."

Jared watched her retreat, seeing it for what it was, and a half smile pulled at his lips. She was definitely a most fascinating woman.

"After breakfast, I thought I would show you around the Watch," Travis offered, interrupting Jared's sublime thoughts. "I think you will find her impressive."

"Thank you, I'd like that." If Swan's Watch was even a tenth as remarkable as Lacy Flemming, Jared was prepared to be impressed.

Chapter Three

Swan's Watch lay basking in the sun, a succulent hedonist luxuriating in the late morning warmth. In self-seeking pursuit, her crops angled toward the brilliant light, while stooped workers nurtured the heated sienna soil. Furrows were dug along the rows of corn, and peanut plants were freed of choking weeds.

From his vantage point astride a bay gelding, Jared surveyed the endless fields with an appreciative eye. Everything he had seen thus far had been most impressive. The peanut was the major cash crop on the plantation, with corn and wheat as the secondary yield. Enough land had been utilized to insure a substantial harvest.

"Very impressive," he told Travis, speaking his thoughts aloud.

Atop his own mount, Travis gloried in the compliment. Never having established a crop without the guidance of his father, he was proud of his accomplishment. He was also greatly relieved that

49

his efforts had begun to pay off, for he had never truly realized how arduous a task it was to be a planter.

"Thank you. We've had a mild spring, although it's been wetter than all hell."

Jared studied an arm of the river on the far side of the fields where he could detect work of some nature in progress. "Any problems with flooding?"

"Not yet, but only because the creek's been dammed." Noticing Jared's interest in the inlet just beyond the peanut fields, he offered, "I've got men fortifying the bulwarks now. Would you care to take a look?"

"Definitely." Any crop that bordered that close to a salt river was in danger of ruination. The mechanics of controlling the water were of special interest to Jared.

An easy gallop brought the men to the far side of the acreage. They reined in where the fields gave way to a tranquil pond bordered by a grove of trees. On the opposite side of the pond, half a dozen black men were in the process of adding stones to a massive, lengthy embankment. The structure divided the creek in two, and kept the river from encroaching any farther onto the land.

"My great-grandfather had the dam built when the river flooded and swept through the north fields. Destroyed everything in its path that year. Nearly bankrupted him."

Jared turned his attention from the architecture of the land to his host. "What saved him?"

"Luck. As it so happened, he had married earlier that year and his wife brought him a sizable marriage settlement. As the story goes, his bride was sorely abused over the matter." Travis had always found the story humorous, and the smile he turned on Travis was both wry and telling. Shrugging he added, "Pride be damned, you don't question fate in these instances. You just thank providence that you can keep the land for another year."

Jared examined the land once more. Vast, teeming, it had the bearing of timelessness. Yet beneath its semblance of enduring abundance, it was but a fragile, tenuous dependent, subject to the whims of nature. And it was left to people like Flemming to deal with those whims. Curious, Travis wondered how well Flemming was coping.

"How much tonnage do you expect these fields to produce?" he asked, nudging his mount toward the dam. Already, he was trying to gauge how sizable a venture he could expect should he decide to ship Flemming's crop.

Travis urged his horse to follow suit, quoting the yields he anticipated from corn, wheat, and peanuts. The figures were enough to raise Travis's brows. But as the sight of the dam reminded him, the capricious elements could drastically alter those figures.

"Mornin'," the plantation's overseer called from beside a wagon full of stones.

"Michael," Travis returned. "How are things going?"

Michael Spruill spread his brawny calloused hands in a shrug. "All right," he replied, then lifted a forefinger to his wide brow when Travis saw to the introductions. "We should have another two feet added by the end of the week."

Jared estimated that another two feet would put

the dam at close to five feet in height. It would take a tidal surge of enormous proportions for the river to flood through the barrier. It would seem that Travis Flemming was leaving nothing to chance.

"Well, get it done before that if you can," Travis remarked. "I want that stand of red oaks felled as soon as possible and every hour spent on this wall is one more hour we're behind with those trees. At this rate, I won't have a decent barrel ready by season's end."

"Yes, sir, Mister Flemming." The burly overseer lifted his hat and scrubbed his forearm over his brow. "But I got to tell you that Syphron there's been actin' up again."

Travis's gaze shot to a tall, broad-shouldered slave helping to unload stones from the wagon. "What's it this time?"

Michael replaced his hat. "I come back from the dry bed with another load of rock and he was gone. Found him hangin' around over at the weaving shop with Taloila and Rose."

The blue of Travis's eyes darkened and his voice took on an uncompromising edge. "What was he doing there?"

"Damned if I know. But my guess is he weren't there for no cloth and he didn't want to see old Taloila."

Travis's jaw tightened. "Keep an eye on him, Michael."

"You got it, Mister Flemming."

"Do you understand me? I don't want him anywhere near Rose."

Squinting slightly, Michael slowly nodded. "Yes,

sir, Mister Flemming."

"You tell him he's to stay clear of her."

Adjusting the brim of his hat, Michael nodded again and moved back to the dam.

Travis stared at Syphron's tall, muscular build for a long moment before he turned back to Jared. When he did, it was to find himself the recipient of the man's scrutinizing gaze.

Jared had viewed the exchange with a fascinated eye. At the mention of this Rose, Flemming had bristled with a vehement intensity that had taken his overseer unawares.

"Problems?" he asked, careful to keep his voice neutral.

The very complacency of Jared's voice brought a heat to Travis's face. Silently cursing his lack of control where Rose was concerned, he headed back for the fields, uncomfortably aware that he owed Jared a reasonable explanation for his behavior. It wasn't until they were well past the trees that he managed an excuse.

"Some of these slaves can be a damned nuisance."

"I wouldn't know," Jared replied levelly. "I don't own slaves."

The censure was there. Travis opened his mouth to come to his own defense, but something about the glinting edge in Jared's eyes forestalled his words. He shoved thoughts of Rose away and chose a more prudent means of discussing the issue of slavery. After all, he could not afford to offend Jared Steele, especially with a bargain yet to be struck between them.

"You should talk with Lacy," he said with a forced

lightness. "If she had her way, we wouldn't have even one slave."

"And you disagree," Jared commented evenly.

"It's a matter of economics. The plantation would never survive if we had to pay for labor. Up until now, we have managed quite well, but the Watch does not turn enough of a profit to do more than maintain."

Jared would have liked nothing better than to have debated the issue for he was adamantly opposed to slavery. But he knew little would be accomplished by such a discussion. In the interest of continued accord between them, he moved the topic to one he found infinitely more appealing.

"Do you and your sister disagree on many things?"

"Lacy?" Travis's voice reflected his relief to be conversing on something less controversial. "No, actually, Lacy and I see eye to eye on most ideas, especially concerning the Watch. Although I will grant you that she can be opinionated as all hell at times."

That didn't surprise Jared. If he had learned nothing else about Lacy Flemming it was that she was a remarkable woman, both intriguing and enticing.

His thoughts settled insistently on the kiss of that morning. His reaction to her artless passion still amazed him. His blood had been ignited by the very naïveté of her manner, and with no effort at all, he could still recall the feel of her soft curves against him. Most surprising, since his tastes usually ran to experienced women, not untried virgins. And he was dead certain that she was a virgin. His every instinct

54

confirmed that.

"I thought we might ride down to the river," Travis said, pulling Jared from his intimate thoughts. "There is a location I have in mind for a pier that I would like you to see."

Jared would have preferred returning to the house. He had an eager, exorbitant desire to find Lacy Flemming.

"By all means," he returned easily. Still, he sent his gaze toward the house in the distance. He cautioned himself to be patient, but he keenly felt the constraint of time.

Time was a matter that weighed heavily on Lacy's mind at that moment. Looking up from the stack of linen that needed mending, she noted that the grandfather clock proclaimed it was just past noon.

Her smooth brow furrowed in annoyance. "Gaye, has Miss Marriette risen yet?"

The young black house girl halted in her mending to reply. "No, Miz Lacy. I don't think so. Would you like me to run upstairs and check for you?"

Lacy heaved a vexed sigh. "No, no, it's all right." But it truly wasn't. She had planned to check on several children who had taken ill that week and then begin work on the estate ledgers. Instead, she was in the sitting room off the front parlor, sorting through the linen, something Marriette had promised to do.

She picked up a newly laundered canopy and inspected the stitching that had unraveled along the hem. "You'll need to use a delicate stitch along this border, Gaye. And secure with a knot every three stitches so we won't have to rework this again."

"Well, there you are," Marriette declared, breezing into the room.

Lacy spun about in her seat. One look at her sister and her eyes rounded incredulously.

Marriette floated forward in a shimmering expanse of pale green taffeta. The five flounces of her skirt, trimmed out in forest green lace, matched her *fanchon* bonnet. A ridiculously small reticule swung jauntily from one of her arms and the scent of her perfume surrounded her. From all appearances, it was apparent that she intended an outing.

"I had begun to think that everyone had deserted me," she commented lightly, tugging on the cuff of her white glove.

"I could say the same of you, Marriette," Lacy returned. "Why are you dressed for church?"

Marriette lifted one shoulder in an indolent shrug. "Jeanne Gail LaRue is having a picnic this afternoon. A small affair, actually, only a few friends, but of course I told her I would be there."

The frown in Lacy's brow deepened. "You didn't say anything about attending a picnic."

"Didn't I? It must have slipped my mind."

"But you promised to see to the mending today."

Marriette pursed her lips into a condescending smile. "You seem to be taking care of that already."

"Only because I couldn't wait for you any longer."

"Why ever not? The house will not come tumbling down about our heads if I don't attend to the linens. Life as we know it will not be forever devastated if I fail to pick up needle and thread."

"No, but now I'm behind in my chores."

The smile dropped from Marriette's lips. "Oh, Lacy, will you please stop badgering me! I don't know what you are going on about, but if you continue, I swear you'll be the cause of a headache."

Lacy gritted her teeth. It was always this way with Marriette, her making every and any excuse to avoid her share of the responsibilities. "Sometimes I think you don't care about the Watch at all."

"Of course I care. Now, where is Mister Steele?"

Lacy's spine stiffened at the mention of his name. "Why?"

"Because I thought I would invite him to join me. It would be a marvelous way to introduce him about."

Lacy could not prevent the rush of disappointment that swamped her at the idea of Marriette and Jared Steele off together for the afternoon. Nor could she explain the sinking feeling that settled in the pit of her stomach, but it was there nonetheless, tugging at her composure.

"He is out with Travis riding the plantation," she replied in clipped tones, telling herself she had no business feeling proprietary toward Jared Steele. Even as inexperienced as she was, she knew that one stolen kiss was not terribly significant. Unfortunately, her heart disagreed.

"*What?*" Marriette exclaimed.

"Travis is taking Mister Steele on a tour of the property."

"Well, peanuts to that."

"I'm sorry if that doesn't suit your social calendar," Lacy got out past stiff lips. She was having a hard time summoning any pity for her sister.

Marriette huffed and plopped her hands on her hips. "There's no need to get snippy about it. After all, it's my afternoon that has been completely ruined." She rolled her eyes in a deprecating glance. "Now, I'll just have to go by myself."

Lacy kept her comments to herself. There was nothing she could say about Jared Steele and there would be no dissuading her sister from doing as she pleased.

Lifting a sheet from the stack, she quietly asked, "Do you need to have a carriage hitched up?"

An inordinately pleased smile came back to Marriette's face. "No, I already had that taken care of. Thomas should be waiting for me."

She sauntered to the mirror set between the two French windows and checked her reflection one last time. It wasn't as though she hadn't thoroughly inspected every last detail of her appearance a dozen times, but as far as she was concerned, one could never be too certain.

Finding every strand of blond hair exactly where it should be, and satisfied that the light rosy powder she had applied to her cheeks gave her face a fresh glow, she turned away for the door. Her spirits revived by the fetching picture she made, she gaily announced, "I'll be certain to return in time for the evening meal."

Minutes later, she was seated in the small, open carriage as it sped away from Swan's Watch, anticipating the afternoon ahead.

The ride to Oakely, the LaRue plantation on the Pagan River, took no longer than twenty minutes. Still, by the time Thomas was handing Marriette down she was more than ready to socialize.

Across the rolling lawn that swept toward the river, she spotted Jeanne Gail and several other friends gathered beneath one of the live oaks. Among those friends was Carter James.

Marriette pursed her lips. She hadn't known that Carter would be present. Having thought to be accompanied by Jared Steele, she hadn't even considered Carter. But now that her plans had gone awry, she wasn't about to ignore the man who could very easily be her future husband.

She mulled that notion over in her mind. Mrs. Carter James. The name did have a nice ring to it, but then, so did Marriette Steele.

Making her way toward the gathering, she fixed her gaze on Carter, inspecting his figure as one might examine a stallion for stud. He was a handsome man, with his almond-shaped eyes and wavy brown hair. His face was lean, as were his chest and legs, but she didn't think he was as tall as Jared Steele. And his voice wasn't nearly as smooth or mellow as the Yankee shipper's, but he *was* enormously wealthy. And while she suspected that Mr. Steele was also extremely affluent, that was a status she had yet to confirm.

It was an amusing dilemma, to be considering two such worthy men for her husband. And the process of choosing was ripe with fascinating possibilities. She wasn't sure how she wanted to play this situation, but it was imperative that she hold both men enthralled until she made up her mind.

"Hello, everyone," she called when she was close enough to be heard.

Petite, round-faced Jeanne Gail left off her gossiping at Marriette's approach and glided forward in greeting. "Marriette, how good to see you. I was saying that I hoped you would arrive soon."

They met and exchanged a brief hug before linking arms.

"If I am late, you'll just have to blame Lacy," Marriette explained. Sighing in exaggerated misery, she whispered, "You know how she can go on about chores and such. But then, she is so devoted to the Watch."

Jeanne Gail shook her head in sympathy, setting her mousy brown curls to bouncing. "She always was the most dutiful person I know."

Marriette affected a long-suffering expression. "She certainly is and to the distraction of all else. I try my best with her, Jeanne, I really do, but there is just no talking to her."

"Don't you worry yourself about that now, Marriette," Jeanne Gail advised. "You just have a good time."

There was never any doubt in Marriette's mind that she intended to do just that. Quickly surrounded by her acquaintances, she didn't give another thought to Lacy or duty or Swan's Watch. Her attention was riveted on Carter James.

"Carter, dear, how have you been?" She lifted her startling blue eyes to his as he took her hand for a kiss that stretched the boundaries of decorum.

"Fine, now that you are here," he murmured silkily. The brown of his eyes shone with a sultry promise, a paltry hint of his more private inclinations. His gaze dropped to her bodice.

The glance was not lost on Marriette. She knew exactly what Carter James was after, and it suited her purposes perfectly to have him looking his fill.

"You have such a way with words, Carter." Feigning a politeness she was far from feeling, she made a show of pulling her hand from his and greeted a mutual lifelong friend.

"N. Douglas," she declared, practically ogling his pleasantly round face, thinning brown hair and broad chest. "I swear I haven't seen you in ages."

Norman Douglas Winston bowed awkwardly from his less than average height, his nerves never quite steady in Marriette Flemming's beautiful company. "It has been some months," he confirmed on a diffident chuckle.

"And how is your mama? I've been meaning to pay her a visit since she took ill."

Nearly mesmerized by Marriette's attention, he exhaled slowly, but there was no defense against the twin spots of color that stained his cheeks. "Mother is recovering nicely. I'll be sure to tell her that you were asking." Unable to help himself, he let his eyes stray along her figure. "And I'll . . . I'll tell her that you're looking as ni . . . as pret . . . lovely as ever."

Marriette accepted the compliment with practiced graciousness, her smile still in place as N. Douglas reticently moved off to another group.

"I don't think I've ever seen you looking anything but beautiful," Carter stated with the polished ease N. Douglas had struggled for.

Marriette's blue gaze flew back to Carter. "Why, Carter," she breathed softly in a perfect blending of embarrassment and delight. Liking the possessive set of his features, her eyes filled with a coy yearning. She dropped her hand lightly on his forearm, and murmured, "Thank you, Carter. You don't know what it does to me to have you find me beautiful."

Catching her lower lip between her teeth, she flicked her glance to his mouth. Her gaze lingered for the briefest second, then she strolled over to one of the blankets spread out on the grass and gracefully sank to her knees, her green skirts billowing about her. As though totally unaware of his gaze adhered to her breasts, she tilted her head to one side and exchanged pleasantries with the ladies already seated.

It didn't surprise her in the least when Carter sat beside her moments later.

The meal progressed well into the afternoon. The warm air and soft river breeze helped create an indolent, good-natured mood that lingered through every course. Laughter complimented the atmosphere even when the gentlemen strolled off to enjoy their cigars and the ladies departed for the house to freshen up.

"You were so clever to have thought of a picnic," Marriette said with a sigh as she and Jeanne Gail followed the other ladies up the front steps.

Jeanne Gail preened under the flattery. "I so hoped that you would enjoy yourself."

"I did, I . . ." Marriette pressed a delicate hand to her chest and stopped. "Jeanne, I've left my reticule."

Acting the perfect hostess, Jeanne offered, "Would you like me to get it for you?"

"Oh, no, I'll just run back and get it. You go on and I'll join you in a minute."

Jeanne Gail gave a naughty smile and shook her

finger in mock disapproval. "If I didn't know you better, Marriette, I would say that you just want to take a peek at Carter James."

Marriette looked absolutely astonished. "Jeanne Gail, you are just awful."

"You wouldn't be saying that if you had seen some of the glances Carter has given you today." Her plain features flushed. "It takes my breath away to just think about it."

Marriette had been very aware of every gaze Carter had directed her way, but she was not going to admit that to anyone. "Oh, peanuts, Jeanne Gail." She laughed. "Go attend to your guests."

As soon as Jeanne entered the house, the smile dropped from Marriette's face. The last thing she wanted was to appear too eagerly enamored of Carter. But her ploy to leave her reticule was the only thing she could think of to gain herself a respite from the women. Their insipid giggling had been enough to drive her to distraction.

Suppressing a shudder, she leisurely retraced her steps toward the setting under the live oak. Rounding a huge boxwood hedge, she was temporarily out of view of both the house and the river, when without warning an arm shot out, clamped about her waist and hauled her behind the thicket.

The startled cry that came to her lips was snatched away by a demanding mouth crushed to hers. Her hands came up to push against the solid chest, but the instant she realized that it was Carter who held her, she let her hands flutter about uselessly.

He had never kissed her before and in high expectation, she eagerly awaited some thrilling excitement to overcome her. But all she felt was the slick wetness of his lips grinding against hers and his fingers biting into her flesh.

"Carter, you mustn't," she avowed weakly, turning her head away.

Carter ignored her protest as well as her feeble attempt to escape. Marriette Flemming was the most audaciously beautiful woman in the commonwealth, possessing a body that could tease the eyeballs right out of a man's head. And for months, she had been flaunting those tantalizing curves before him.

"Just a kiss or two, Marriette." He roughly captured her mouth again, tightening his arms about her.

Marriette's breath caught in her chest, and her eyes flew open. It suited her purposes just fine to have him panting after her, but she did not appreciate being mauled, especially when his kisses were leaving her wholly unaffected.

Freeing her lips once more, she murmured, "What if someone should come this way?"

"They won't," he insisted, fastening his mouth to her neck.

"I shouldn't let you do this."

"Yes, you should."

"But we're not married, we're not even betrothed." She allowed his lips to explore, but only until his hands joined in. When his fingers closed about one of her breasts, she offered another objection.

"Carter, please," she demurred, tugging ineffectually at his hand.

As far as Carter was concerned, he had sat through a lunch made in hell. Marriette's teasing, sedately erotic manner today had taken him to the brink. Sitting next to her had been an agony and he'd be damned if he was going to walk about, rampant with desire and not even sample her goods.

He lowered his arm to her hips and yanked her against his hardness. A strangled groan worked its way up from his throat and he slanted his mouth over hers again, abruptly thrusting his tongue past her lips and into her mouth. One hand grabbed a fistful of her dress and wrenched the fabric up along her thigh. With an ease denoting vast experience in disrobing women, his hand slid along her drawers to search out the drawstring.

The move shocked Marriette's sensibilities. Levering her arms between their bodies, she pushed away with a force that took Carter by surprise.

"You have to stop," she insisted curtly. She stepped back to arrange the folds of her skirt, but Carter reached out and jerked her back against him.

"Marry me," he demanded, his face drawn into tight lines.

"What?" She truly didn't know if she had heard correctly.

"Marry me."

Her lips parted on a startled exclamation. A proposal was not what she had expected when she had plied her wiles today. Nor was it necessarily what she wanted. At least not until she had a chance to discover more about Jared Steele.

"Carter, this is so sudden," she exclaimed.

"It's been coming for months." And now that he had had a taste of her, he was not about to let her go to someone else.

"But I didn't know your feelings ran in that vein. You never hinted toward marriage." She blinked rapidly, seeking an explanation that would pacify him. "Please, I need time to consider this. I can't even think clearly with your kisses still making my heart pound."

Apparently she had said the right thing, for his hands loosened their hold, and the tension drained from his face. For an endless moment, he held her at arm's length, then he released her and stepped back.

"I can do more than make your heart pound, Marriette," he assured her in a husky drawl. "Remember that when you think about becoming my wife."

It was by sheer willpower alone that Marriette kept her sense of relief from showing. She had managed to placate him without offending him into withdrawing his offer.

Her eyes displaying precise amounts of devotion and maidenly confusion, she avowed, "I will think only of you, and about becoming your wife. I simply need time to become adjusted to the idea. After all, becoming Mrs. Carter James is an honor like no other."

The flattery raced straight to his ego, and went far in restoring his obliging disposition. Smiling, he caught her chin between his thumb and forefinger. "You and I will get on well together." He snatched another kiss, letting his tongue glide over her lips, then sauntered off, his mood buoyant.

Marriette exhaled her pent-up breath and pressed a trembling hand to her chest. She needed to become acquainted with Jared Steele as quickly as possible.

Chapter Four

Rose tried to concentrate on winding the cotton thread around a bobbin, but her gaze wandered through the open window of the weaving cottage. In fascination, she watched a group of men carting bales of cotton from a wagon to the cottage storehouse next door.

One man in particular held her regard. Syphron. Tall, with a muscular build, he had come around numerous times, flashing his wide grin, winking at her like the very devil himself. She watched him now, his broad chest stretching the thin fabric of his shirt as he bent and lifted the cotton onto one of his shoulders. He was a powerful man and it showed in the hard edge of his jaw and the steady gait of his walk.

She yanked in her wayward thoughts, jerking her attention back to her task. She had no business thinking about Syphron or any other man, not when there was Travis.

"Rose."

Startled, she looked up to find Syphron standing by the window, smiling broadly. Dismayed, she looked over her shoulder to the door, expecting someone to enter and discover Syphron away from his duties, again.

"Get away from here," she ordered, paying great attention to winding the cotton thread. The last time he had come by to see her, the overseer had caught him and there had been hell to pay. "Mister Spruill told you to leave me be. Didn't that mean nothin' to you?"

"No more than horse manure."

She scoffed in disgust. "You're a fine one to talk, but you're goin' to get us both in trouble." She gave him a fierce look. "Now get."

Syphron's deep-set eyes took on a purposeful gleam. "Come on over here, Rose."

"No."

He laughed deeply. "What you 'fraid of?"

"I ain't afraid of nothin', and that includes you."

"Then leave that mess you foolin' with an' talk with me a spell."

His words were like thick, rich honey, tempting her for a brief second. She raised her gaze to study him and she had to admit that he was a handsome man. But that was as far as she would allow herself to think.

"I ain't gettin' in no trouble for the likes of you," she declared hotly. "Now if you don't leave, I'll get Mister Spruill myself."

The smile left Syphron's face, but only for a moment. He wasn't going to let her refusal get the better of him. He had big plans for little Rose, and it would only be a matter of time before he made her listen.

"All right, I'm goin'." He turned away, then added over his shoulder, "But I ain't goin' far."

She watched him return to his work, more conscious of him than she wanted to be. It was annoying the way he came around, looking at her like he could see through her clothes. But damn if that very notion didn't put butterflies in her stomach.

"Keep yo' mind on yo' work," Taloila warned, scuffling into the room and taking her place at the great four-harness loom.

Rose yanked her gaze from the sight of Syphron to find Taloila steadily watching her. "Oh, hush up, Old African," she mumbled.

The ancient weaver ignored the sullen order and took up her shuttle with an ease born of years of experience. In just seconds, she had the loom working in an intricate operation that never failed to amaze Rose.

Like thin, long fingers, the warp threads of the loom laced and unlaced with the old woman's nimble footwork on the treadles. The pattern was always the same; throw the shuttle, beat the weft, step the treadle, throw the shuttle. Only the fiber ever changed, wool for winter, cotton for summer. The task was tedious, but row after row, hour after hour, yard upon yard, Taloila never complained.

The subtle sound created by the shifting harnesses barely reached the corners of the weaving house. Nonetheless, Rose found the cadence irritating. Sighing, she glanced back to the bobbin on her lap. She hated winding threads, and didn't understand why she had to do it. She was being trained to take Taloila's place as the plantation weaver, but so far, all Rose ever found herself doing was the drudgery work. Miz Lacy wouldn't even let her near a flax wheel, let alone the looms. She was always going on about straight selvedges and tensions. None of that made any sense to Rose.

Shrugging, she dismissed the matter. She didn't want to learn to weave anyway. If she had any choice, she'd be up at the great house, working as a maid or a body servant. Just the idea brought a smile to her pretty, young face.

Her fingers paused in their work as she pictured herself as a maid. She would wear a real dress, the kind Gaye wore, made out of that book muslin Taloila had woven last spring. She'd have a white apron, a cap, and under it all, a petticoat and a real pair of shoes. She'd look as fancy as they came, walking up and down the stairs, carrying linens or trays. And when she turned a corner, the skirt and petticoat would swish about her legs.

"Don' you make no mess out o' my threads, girl." Taloila's cracked voice interrupted Rose's daydream.

Rose blinked. The bobbin and shuttle were still there in her lap, as though proof of her discontent. Throwing Taloila a resentful look, she said, "Your threads are just fine."

"Make sure dey is. No one got time to undo yo' work, if dat's what we callin' what you doin' dese days."

"I do my work," Rose declared, making a great show of slipping a bobbin into a shuttle.

"I call it sittin' an smilin' at de air. You waitin' on

70

dat Syphron to come sniffin' round here again?"

"No."

"So you says."

Rose sneered. "So I know. I ain't got nothin' to do with Syphron."

"Good, cuz Massa Travis won't like no one messin' wid you, girl."

"I ain't worried 'bout Massa Travis."

Taloila gave a crowing laugh. "You should be. You ain't got nothin' else to think 'bout 'cept bein' his concubine."

Bending low, Rose picked another bobbin from her basket. "I got me plenty to think 'bout." Rose thrust her lower lip out. "Like bein' up to the house, maybe workin' as a maid."

A dusty snort preceded the old woman's words. "You better keep yo' mind on threads. You ain't never goin' to be anywhere but here." Depressing a treadle, she slid her shuttle from one gnarled hand to the other. "Especially if Massa Travis puts a baby in yo' belly."

Rolling her eyes, Rose shook her head. "It's a good thing you're gettin' near your time, old woman, 'cause no one so stupid should live so long." She scrunched up her face. "I ain't havin' none of his babies 'cause Besha cook fixes me a potion to take every night."

It was Taloila's turn to smirk. "I lived dis long 'cause I *is* so smart. And I know dat Besha cook ain't God. One day, you is goin' to get wid child. Den how long you think you goin' to be able to keep your secret from Miz Lacy?"

Rose bit the inside of her lip. She didn't give a hoot

71

if everyone on earth knew that she shared the master's bed. But Travis himself was as private as they came and he would not like proof of their goings-on. There was no telling how he might react, but her worst fear was that he would sell her off.

Her eye caught Taloila's and the knowing look in the rheumy gaze made her bristle. "I ain't makin' no trundle bed trash with Massa Travis," she insisted. "So you can stop your preachin' at me." She snatched another skein of thread from her basket. "I swear you're so cantankerous because you been without a man for so long."

"At least de man I had loved me," Taloila shot back.

Rose fell silent. The barb had struck home, close to private dreams of love and children. She wondered often what it would be like to marry a man and be free to raise their family.

Quietly, her voice little more than a whisper, she asked, "Did you ever think of runnin'?"

Taloila studied the girl's young face, then set back to work. "No."

"Never?"

"Weren't no use in tryin'. De only place I wanted to be was back in Africa and I had me no way of gettin' dere. 'Sides, my babies was here. Massa was good 'bout not sellin' babies away from de mamas." She shook her head sadly. "I couldn't leave 'em and dere was too many of us to run."

"I think 'bout it sometimes," Rose confessed.

Without missing a beat, Taloila glanced to Rose and changed treadles. "It ain't good to be talkin' of dat."

Chagrined, Rose lowered her head. "I know," she

mumbled. "I never say anythin' to nobody 'bout it, but . . ." Her voice dwindled and her eyes came up, as though searching the room for help. "I been on this plantation since my first day. I never even been to the town. I think I'd like to go there, or that other place called Norfolk."

"Dose is white folks' places. You'd still be someone's property."

"But I heard of others what run off and never come back. Where do they go?"

All movement of the loom stopped abruptly. Sitting back, Taloila stared straight ahead. Her sight, however, was turned inward. The old muscles of her face worked in a rickety fashion, twisting her lips into a sad line.

"When I was a young girl, wid my first baby, my man tol' me 'bout a place. It's up north, not in dese United States, but way up. Black folks dere is free. Dere ain't no slaves, just people livin' and dyin', comin' and goin' as dey please."

"Is it a long way to get there?"

"Too long." Taloila's hands resumed their work as suddenly as they had stopped.

Curiously, Rose regarded Taloila's somber face. "Old African, what happened to your man?"

The harnesses raised and lowered twice before the old woman spoke. "Dere's a stack of towels over dere on de bench," she snapped. "You take dem up to de house."

The shift in temper was too fast for Rose. At a loss, she slowly set her basket on the floor, then crossed to the bench. Gathering the linens in her arms she turned to leave, but hesitated, her troubled gaze

73

resting on Taloila. The woman sat as rigid as her ancient bones would allow and Rose wondered why the question had caused such upset.

Her bundle pressed to her chest, she moved to the door, but Taloila's voice stopped her on the threshold.

"My man dead. He drowned in de river when he tried to run to dat place up north."

Unmoving, Rose stared at Taloila. The aged one was knee deep in her weaving; throw, beat, step, throw. But down her worn face, a single tear trickled a crooked path.

Steps lagging, Rose made her way up the lane to the manor house. She hoped no one there was in a hurry for the towels, because she didn't think she could move any faster if she tried. Taloila's story had wearied her body as well as her spirit. Not even the approach of the horse behind her was enough to quicken her pace.

A careful hand on the reins, Jared maneuvered his horse around Rose. He found it odd that she didn't step from the middle of the path, but from the look of her, she was in her own world.

Once he was certain the girl was safely behind, he rode back onto the drive and gazed about. The sight was beautiful. In the three days that he had been there, he hadn't had much time to fully appreciate that. But today, he had spent the better part of the morning riding at will, exploring while Travis attended to business matters at the court house.

Much more accustomed to the varying hues of the ocean and its vast space, Jared nonetheless admitted to a certain appreciation of the plantation's verdant design. Ahead, with the river as backdrop, lay the house. Bordered on one side by a formal garden, it was fringed by a copse of trees on the other. The barn and grazing pasture, stable and paddock lay to his immediate right while to the left of the lane were the slave quarters, the dependencies and the household garden. The setting was a tightly ordered arrangement, functional as well as striking. And somehow welcoming.

A flash of yellow moving from the pasture drew his attention. It took only a second for him to recognize the silver-blond hair and graceful pace of the woman as she walked away from several men. The gray of his eyes darkened.

A well-placed heel sent his mount into an easy canter, quickly eating up the ground between himself and Lacy. "Out for a walk?" he asked, reining in beside her.

At his approach, Lacy lifted a hand to shade her eyes against the brilliant sun. She had known that he had been riding the grounds, and a quick glance to his white shirt, black pants and boots confirmed his morning spent in the saddle.

A hesitant curve pulled at her lips. She had not been alone with him since their moments together at the icehouse the day before. Now, as during her restless night just past, she was extremely conscious of all that had transpired between them.

"No, actually, I'm on my way back to the house. I came down here because a calf was found dead this morning. I needed to see to that."

Jared looked to the two men dragging off the dead carcass. He would have thought this a job better suited to Travis, and he couldn't keep the note of surprise from his voice. "Do I take it that you are not squeamish about this sort of thing?"

Lacy's restrained grin grew into a full-fledged smile. "I don't have the option to give into qualms."

The sparkle of the blue and green in her eyes danced along his nerves. "Well, then, let me make your task easier." He leaned toward her and extended a hand down in invitation.

Lacy stared at the firm hand reaching for her and qualms of another sort inundated her. Her gaze dashed to his sculpted thighs gripping the saddle and she pictured herself riding there. Before she could draw another breath, a fine trembling assailed her hands and the curve of her lips straightened.

"I . . . I don't mind the walk," she commented lamely, trying not to imagine herself snuggled against his hard legs, her back resting along his chest, his arms about her.

At her faltering refusal, Jared propped his hand on his thigh, his brows lowered fractionally. Modesty was at play here. He found that inconvenient, but for Lacy he would tolerate it. For a while.

His movements lithe, he swung down from his high perch. "You don't leave me any choice but to join you."

Unnerved by her mental images, Lacy watched him with dismayed awe. The memory of his kisses was still playing havoc with her composure. To have him so close at hand was only marginally better than being seated before him.

"That isn't necessary."

He gave her a purely masculine look filled with

gentle mockery. "These may be modern times, Lacy, but chivalry is not dead. You can't expect me to ride while you walk."

"I didn't really expect you to escort me at all."

Some of the humor left his face. Solemnly, he averred, "You don't expect a great deal from men, do you?"

Any color that had ridden Lacy's cheeks washed away. Not for the first time, he had hit upon an awkward truth. His ability to do that was uncanny, and vexing, especially when she was left to make explanations.

"Mister Steele . . ."

"Jared."

She sighed. "Jared, please feel free to walk with me if you wish."

His head cocked to one side. "You do that quite frequently."

"Do what?"

"Ignore a matter in hopes of not discussing it."

Lacy's back straightened. "I do no such thing."

"Yes, you do. Just now, you slipped right past my remark about your expectations of men. And yesterday, you sidled around the fact that I find you extremely beautiful."

A panic born of embarrassment swept through her. He was so accurate as to be frightening, and she did not know how to deal with that. She wasn't used to men of Jared Steele's ilk, dauntless men who spoke so directly and probed a woman's mind to such an exacting degree.

Feeling helpless in any sort of encounter with him, she implored, "You spoke of chivalry, Mister Steele.

77

Please utilize some now and leave me in peace." Not giving him another glance, she started back for the house.

She knew it would be too much to hope that he grow roots and remain fixed where he was. So she wasn't surprised when his stride brought him beside her, his horse firmly in tow. What did confuse her was that for the rest of the walk to the stable he did not utter a single word. As forthright as he was, she fully anticipated his having a great deal to say.

The silence stretched, and it wasn't until they were on the far side of the stable, removed from curious eyes, that the hush was broken.

Reaching out, Jared clasped her by the arms and backed her up against the stable wall. "You may be in the habit of walking away from others," he announced in a low, intractable voice, drilling his gaze into hers. "But you had best understand something right now, Lacy Flemming. I'm not about to let you walk away from me."

Less than a hand's length separated them and Lacy's breath lodged in her throat. He was too close, too overpowering. Like a physical caress, she could feel the heat of him penetrating the thin layer of her muslin dress, piercing her skin and warming her nerves. Every sensation he had instilled in her yesterday rose up greedily now, robbing her limbs of strength. Nervously, she swallowed, as shaken by her reaction as she was by his tall body looming over her.

"I . . . I . . ."

His face inched closer to hers. "You what?" But he didn't need to ask. Even if she hadn't hinted at it yesterday, he could see her thoughts written all over her face. She was completely overwhelmed by, and unprepared for, his attentions.

He placed a hand on the wall beside her shoulder. "The men in Virginia are either blind"—His other hand, still holding the reins, pressed to the wood by her other shoulder—"or stupid." He closed the small distance separating their mouths. "I am neither."

Lacy's world tilted at the feel of his warm, firm lips upon her own. The contact was searing, demanding in its eloquence as his tongue urged her lips to part. On a sigh, she yielded what he sought and for the second time in as many days, she felt her blood racing.

For the second time in as many days, Jared felt undiluted desire rip through him. He was touching her with nothing more than his mouth, but that caress alone was enough to churn his insides with a potent yearning.

Relaxing the bend of his arms, he brought his weight to bear against her. Her soft curves bore into him, imprinting the shape of her on his mind and senses, impaling him with a need for more. He dragged his mouth from hers, but only as far as that spot just below her ear.

"Did you think I was lying when I told you yesterday that I found you fascinating?" he murmured thickly, nibbling a molten path down her neck.

He expected her to talk? *Now* . . . when his lips were creating the most shocking tingles, now when she could do nothing more than float on this new desire he had brought to her? And she recognized that desire for what it was, for she hadn't ever experienced

79

it before she had set eyes on Jared Steele.

She turned her head slightly to gaze at this man who had so boldly stridden into her life, and who was so effortlessly turning it upside down. But before she could utter the first word, his mouth sought hers again. The kiss was deep, penetrating, a mingling of labored breaths and urgent tongues. Her head swirled, but when his hand gently caressed her breast, stroking the nipple to a stiffened peak, she jumped in shock against the pleasurably aching sensations that raced to the core of her.

It was all too sudden. He was taking her beyond herself with a speed that was frightening. "Jared." His name escaped her lips on an alarmed gasp.

The tone of her voice brought his head up. His own eyes glittering, he stared into the turquoise depths of her eyes and saw the confusion that mingled so freely with the passion. The innocence would have been impossible for him to miss.

Ruefully, he shook his head, exercising all of his control to rein in his desires. She acted on him like the most robust wine and it was difficult for him to temper his need.

"You affect me so thoroughly that I forget just how guileless you really are." He skimmed her heated cheeks with his knuckles. "I'm right, aren't I? There haven't been any other men."

Wondering how he could tell, she whispered, "No."

He smiled, a possessively male smile. It was as though she had been kept safely hidden away, like a rare treasure, waiting for him.

Reveling in the satisfaction he garnered from that

thought and from the feel of her body still pressed intimately to his, he asserted, "I'm of a mind to continue on like this all day."

Lacy's eyes rounded, uncertain if he was teasing or stating fact. "You wouldn't . . ."

"Wouldn't I?" But as much as his body demanded that he assuage the burning need, he wanted time to explore and learn what there was to know about this woman who affected him as no other ever had.

Placing a chaste kiss on her passion-reddened lips, he assured her, "Calm your innocent fears, Lacy." He pushed away from her and stepped back, but the look he leveled on her was ripe with promise.

Lacy took a steadying breath, feeling as though she had just stepped out of the winds of a hurricane. She was conscious of an odd vulnerability in the region of her heart, but she was also acutely aware of an inner joy that permeated her entire being.

She cast a veiled glance to Jared. He was commanding as no other man could be, like some daring conqueror, out to lay claim to her serenity. Yet somehow, she didn't mind. Poise and tranquility were paltry triflings compared to the newfound inspirations that made her feel so alive.

For the walk back to the house, she was blissfully content to have him beside her. Leaving the horse with one of the stable hands, they strolled in each other's company as though it were an everyday occurrence, as though only moments ago, neither had been bound by passion.

They reached the boxwood-lined path leading up to the door, and as always, Lacy's gaze rested on the mansion. And as always, she smiled for the pure pleasure the sight brought her.

"Are you going to share your humor?" Jared inquired, seeing the upward tilt of the corners of her mouth.

"I can't help but love it," she admitted, nodding to the house.

He studied the darkened color of her eyes. "It shows."

"Does it?"

"Definitely." To the point that Jared wished himself to be the recipient of such a look.

One of her shoulders lifted in a shrug. "I suppose I can't help myself. Everything about the Watch, its history, the generations that have lived here, its future, are all very dear to my heart."

Instantly, she bit her lip. She rarely confided such thoughts to anyone, and she wasn't certain why she had done so with Jared. Perhaps it was because he had kissed her. Or maybe it was because of the intensity with which he was watching her. "I suppose that sounded rather silly to you."

It was as far from silly as Jared could imagine. It was, he decided, extremely admirable.

"I've never heard a woman speak so devotedly about her home."

"Does that surprise you?"

"Yes, I admit it does."

A teasing light tinted her eyes as she tossed a paraphrase of his earlier words at him. "You don't expect a great deal from women, do you?"

Her humor caught him off guard, but when it did overtake him, he threw back his head and laughed outright. "Ah, *touché*, Lacy." Around his chuckles, he added, "I deserved that."

"Yes, you did," she averred, liking the sound of his laughter. Its effects were highly contagious. "But I shan't hold it against you. In fact, just to prove that I bear no ill will, I will take you to the very spot for which this plantation was named."

"Where is that?" he asked, hoping it was some place private.

"The spit on Flemming's Creek."

"A rare honor, I take it."

"Indeed. For it is from that location that the roosting swans can be watched each year."

To have named a plantation for that occurrence was a poetic notion, rife with all manner of even more poetic prospects. But before he could properly examine any one of them, Gaye interrupted from the house.

"Miz Lacy?"

From the bottom of the steps, Lacy and Jared looked to the housegirl framed in the doorway.

"Yes, Gaye," Lacy replied.

The girl stepped out onto the landing. "Did you want the beds draped with netting now or did you want me to wait?"

Lacy's merriment gave way to confusion. "I thought Marriette was going to get you started on that?"

Gaye tried not to look chagrined. "Well, I thought so, too, Miz Lacy, but she told me she couldn't bother with the beds. I wouldn't have mentioned it to you except that you told me direct this morning to get to it today."

Lacy couldn't contain her sigh. She might have

expected Marriette to overlook the chore, but that didn't make it any easier to tolerate. She started to ask herself why her sister was so neglectful, but mentally held up a pausing hand, and endured the inevitable.

Pressing her fingertips to her forehead, she once again readjusted her schedule for the day. Three more children had become ill during the night and she needed to see to them, and the week's menu still had to be checked with Besha. "All right, Gaye, we'll leave off waxing the floors in the parlor until tomorrow and tend to the beds now."

Gaye reentered the house, taking with her the light mood that had prevailed minutes earlier.

"I'm sorry, Jared," Lacy murmured. She regretted having to abandon him to his own devices once more, but she was even more sorry that their shared moment had to be cut short. "If you'll excuse me."

Jared's speculative gaze shifted from Lacy to the doorway and back again. For a long second, he didn't say anything.

"I understand only too well the obligations associated with managing an enterprise," he replied graciously. "But I will hold you to your promise to show me the swans from Flemming's Creek."

A slight flush pinkened Lacy's cheeks. It was a promise she anticipated keeping.

Jared climbed the steps, slowly following in Lacy's wake. But while her hurried path took her to the attic, his took him only as far as the second floor and his room. Intending to strip out of his dusty clothes and wash, he opened his door, and stopped dead in his tracks.

"Jared," Marriette declared. "I didn't expect you."

Chapter Five

"You gave me such a start, Jared," Marriette exclaimed, pressing a hand to the opulent fullness of her breasts. "I thought you would still be riding and I came to see if everything in here was in order."

Jared remained by the door, his expression blank. "No, I'm finished for the day. I've come up to wash."

"Well, the pitcher is full. And I made certain that you have plenty of clean towels." She moved to the washstand with an exaggerated swish of her skirts, calculated to draw a man's attention. "Gaye can sometimes be lax about these things and I constantly have to run after her."

She glanced expectantly to Jared. But rather than his being impressed by her efforts, he nonchalantly crossed his arms over his chest and leaned against the door frame.

"How was your ride?" she asked, shaking out a perfectly folded towel.

"Rewarding." One side of his mouth quirked upward.

"Thank goodness. I would be mortified if you were disappointed."

Jared seemed to find some humor in her words. "I wasn't."

His amusement pleased her to no end. "I wouldn't want you to find our hospitality lacking, especially with you such a long way from your home." Bringing the corners of the towel together, she pursed her lips into a pretty moue. "I suppose you miss Connecticut."

He shrugged with his brows. "I haven't been gone all that long. And I am used to traveling."

Looking up from her task, she remarked, "Yes, I suppose in your business, you do roam a great deal." She placed the towel on the washstand. "But that makes the coming home that much more pleasant, wouldn't you say?"

Jared's gaze followed her movements. "That depends on what you are coming home to."

"One's house and property." She turned back to face him. Belatedly, she remembered to add, "And a family, of course."

"Of course." He pushed off from the door frame, but did not advance into the room. Instead, he planted his feet wide in an intimidating stance.

Her steps meandering, Marriette made her way toward the door. "I would think that it would be very sad coming home to a big empty house at the end of each of your journeys. All those huge rooms perfectly quiet." A beguiling laugh escaped her lips. "There I go, assuming that you live in a mansion of sorts."

Jared neither corrected nor denied her assumption. "I don't mind the solitude," was all he offered.

It wasn't nearly enough and a slight frown marred the perfection of her brow. "Well, where is your house?"

"In the town of Wethersfield."

She tested the name. It had an interesting quality to it. "Is that where your shipping firm is located?"

Again, a slow nod preceded his words. "For the most part."

"That must be a grand sight, to see all those ships. How ever do you manage? I mean, one ship going and another coming, having to keep track of barrels and crates and all that." Her steps came to a halt and she blinked as though struck by a sudden revelation. "Why, Jared Steele, you must be a most successful man . . ."

The hint hung in the air like a ponderous stone, just waiting for Jared to grasp it up. But he didn't. And when he did nothing more than coolly stare at Marriette with sharp, gray eyes, she felt an unexpected jolt of uneasiness.

Studying his face, she realized he was not going to give her the answers she sought. But more important, it became apparent that he was annoyed with her. Stunned, she frantically wondered what had gone wrong? She was definitely looking her best. And she had been everything that was polite, but not once had he followed the logical course of their conversation.

Her temper flared, but she clamped down on it before even the slightest inkling could be detected. She had lost valuable ground in this exchange. Instead of learning if he was a rich man, she had only succeeded in irritating him, and that could be extremely detrimental to her cause.

Putting forth her most engaging smile, she vowed, "I truly didn't mean to keep you, Jared. And you must forgive my curious tongue. But I must confess to a certain inquisitiveness where you are concerned." Moving to stand directly before him, she leaned forward slightly and raised luminous, adoring blue eyes to his. "I don't think I have ever met a man quite like you before, Jared Steele."

Instantly, she slipped past him into the hall. Let him ignore *that* hint, she mentally declared, letting free the reins of her temper. Stalking off toward the stairway, her ire mounted with each step she took.

Stubborn, disagreeable man. He had been provoking, evasive, and neglectful. When it came to the particulars of his life, his mouth was as tightly closed as a virgin's legs. And he had not paid the slightest attention to the fact that they had been alone in his room. It had been a provocative setting, one that a man should have reacted to, one that she had anticipated using to her advantage. But it had been for naught.

Twirling on her heel at the bottom of the stairway, she marched the length of the hall to the back door. Frustration accompanied her down the path and away from the house.

Jared Steele had ruined her day. And to make matters only worse, she now had to tend to her chores or she'd never hear the end of it from Travis. Her brother wanted oysters at dinner tonight, and as always, whatever Travis wanted, Travis got. So here she was, having to go down to the river and oversee the selecting of the shellfish, as if no one else on the entire plantation was capable of doing so.

She despised watching the men rake the soft river bottom. Her hair was bound to curl crazily, and the sun was going to freckle her face. And the fishy odor hanging in the air always made her want to press her hand to her nose.

And what of Travis? Well, he was busy in town, most likely enjoying himself, while Lacy was off doing God only knew what.

It was all too vexing, as vexing as Jared Steele himself. But she would be damned if she would let him thwart her efforts. She would just have to find some other means of learning what she wanted to know.

"Then we have an agreement?" Travis asked.

Jared nodded to Travis sitting behind his desk. "Yes, we have an agreement."

Exhilarated, Travis stood and extended his hand. "Good." But it was better than good, it was wonderful, and he had a difficult time not crowing at the top of his lungs. This was the first bargain he had arranged solely on his own, and he was extremely pleased with the terms.

Steele Shipping would be the sole conveyor of the Watch's peanuts and corn. True, the price they'd agreed upon had been more than he would have liked. But as Jared had pointed out, the Watch would make up any difference in monies by the profit incurred from the increased market his firm would make available. Swan's Watch produce would be shipped to parts of the world Travis had never considered.

Jared came to his feet and completed the handshake by clasping Travis's hand. "I'll have my solicitor draw up the papers when I return to Connecticut."

"You can't be thinking of leaving yet." Travis was loathe to part company so soon, especially in the wake of a compromise that was so flattering to both his pocket and his pride. "After all, you've only been with us a short while and I want to introduce you to several other planters in the area. I think they might be interested in doing business with you also."

It was a sound idea that appealed to Jared. He had been fully prepared to remove to his ship while seeking out other possible contracts. But the comfort to be found at Swan's Watch could not be denied, even if he had to contend with Marriette as he had three days earlier. That particular prospect did not sit well with him. Still, he appreciated Travis's hospitality and he also welcomed the opportunity to acquaint himself further with Lacy.

"Thank you. You've convinced me already to send my ship and crew back to Connecticut."

"Then, it's settled, sir."

"Definitely. But I will need to remain on board for several days in preparation for its departure."

They concluded their meeting on the promise that Jared would return to stay at Swan's Watch for as long as he wished. Toward that end, he took his leave to inform his captain of his change in plans.

Travis's own plans were of a more personal nature. Ebullient over his accomplishment, his blood pounded with self-satisfaction and power. It was a heady mixture that went far in stirring up his desires.

His step purposeful, he strode from the study, already anticipating an impassioned hour spent with Rose. But he had no sooner gained the brick path behind the house when Michael Spruill approached from the opposite direction.

"We got problems, Mister Flemming," the stocky overseer began.

"What problems?" Travis countered, thinking nothing could spoil this day.

Michael shook his head. "Five of the men working in the south fields are down."

"What do you mean 'down'?"

"Burning with fever. And another three men I had felling those red oaks are real sick."

Travis scrubbed a hand across his forehead. His day suddenly lost some of its glorious edge. "How bad are they?"

"Bad enough that I sent them back to their quarters."

The breath left Travis in one exhalation. Michael rarely dismissed anyone from the fields for any reason. "Yes, well, I suppose if they're too sick to work, then you did right to dismiss them."

"Yes, sir," Michael avowed. He waited for a moment, his expression expectant. Finally, he prompted, "That leaves us shorthanded."

"Shorthanded?" Travis repeated.

Michael cocked his head away from the house. "That's right. Only half the corn's been irrigated, but it's already taking all our manpower to keep up with the peanuts."

A slight flush stained Travis's cheeks. He hadn't immediately seen the significance of the situation, and it was embarrassing as all hell that his overseer had to explain it to him.

"Damn," he muttered, the curse directed at both himself and the circumstances. No one liked looking stupid, but he feared that was exactly how he looked, like an incompetent idiot incapable of grasping the obvious details and making some kind of decision. And he did now realize that *that* was what Michael wanted, why he had come to him. The man wanted orders on how to handle the matter.

Travis swore again, only this time his denunciation was issued in pure frustration. "Well, do we have anybody we can spare?"

"I thought you might want to pull the men off the trees for a while."

Which, Travis *did* know, would put their lumber production behind. Considering this new agreement with Jared, they would need every bit of lumber as soon as possible if they were going to have enough barrels for shipment.

He sent his gaze out toward the green fields, and scoffed. If they didn't have a crop to ship, there wouldn't be a need for lumber or barrels.

"All right," he said, sighing, "shift the crew from the trees to the fields."

Michael lifted a finger to his brow in a quick salute. "Sure thing, Mister Flemming."

Travis watched the foreman walk away a satisfied man. Turning, he looked back at the house. Inexplicably, he felt the encumbrance of five generations bearing down on him, scrutinizing his every move, charging him to uphold the past and preserve the future. True, his sisters shared in the responsibility, but he felt the weight of his share like some massive shroud. And at times like now, he admitted that it was a burden he wasn't certain he could bear.

The answer always remained the same; what choice did he have? He was a Flemming and no Flemming had ever forsaken the Watch. He would not, could not be the first.

What little remained of his exuberance gave way to cold reality. The contracts to which he had agreed today would go far toward developing the Watch. But meeting the terms of those contracts meant months of hard work.

It was a daunting thought.

One that in some small part of him he resented . . . highly.

His mind no longer set on an afternoon of pleasure, he made his way toward the peanut fields. Rose would have to wait. Swan's Watch was never so acquiescent.

Chills and fever swept through the slave quarters with frightening speed. By noon the following day, only half of the forty-two workers assigned to the fields were well enough to pick up their hoes.

The doctor was summoned at Lacy's insistence. Her concern was of a strictly humanitarian nature. Travis, too, felt concerned, but his major consideration was for the fields left untended, the cooperage standing idle and even the barnyard operations reduced to a bare minimum.

Dr. Gill diagnosed the ailment as the ague. The only treatment was a regimen of camphor for the lungs and arsenicum for the shakes and fever. Beyond that, there was no telling how long the sickness would last, or to what degree it would fester.

It was a declaration that Travis could very well have done without. Sitting astride his horse in the lane leading from the house, he watched the doctor's carriage rumble away, but he could still hear the physician's parting words.

"I've done all I can do, Travis. The rest is in God's hands."

Deep in his gut, Travis prayed that God's hands were indeed benevolent. Every hour that passed saw another slave collapse . . . and one more acre overrun with choking weeds, one more tract drying out. Every available hand had been moved into the fields, but at the expense of all other operations.

Old Oliver, with his nearly deaf ears, had been put to work sharpening plow blades, a task usually performed by the blacksmith, Humphrey. Humphrey had been sent to help out in the south fields. Besha continued to cook, but two of her three helpers had been assigned to carry drinking water to the workers. Even Rose had been given the temporary duty of tending the family's vegetable garden until Jane recovered from the illness.

The blue of his eyes reflecting his inner turmoil, Travis turned his mount and headed for the cattle pens behind the barn. Swan's Watch could survive for only so long under these conditions before she herself would succumb. Her only chance lay in the hope that the illness would run its course quickly.

Until then, Travis expected he would be occupied with more jobs than he had ever thought to undertake. Caring for the cattle was not in his daily routine, but that was only a portion of what he would be doing before the day was out. Whether he liked it or not.

Shepherding the sheep out to the pasture proved to be a relatively painless task, as did feeding the hogs. But mucking out the horse stalls tested his forbearance to its limits. Ever since he had been a child, he had seen someone shoveling out the manure and laying in new hay, and he had never thought twice about the entire matter. But that someone had never been him and by the end of the day, the only opinion he had about horses was that he'd rather they were all dead.

Back protesting, arms aching, Travis trudged back to the house, wanting nothing more than to soak in a tub of steaming water. For a matter of an hour, he wished to set physical labor, Swan's Watch and never-ending responsibility aside and luxuriate in mindless relaxation.

At the back entrance, he shucked off his encrusted boots, then paused to study the once fine leather.

"Shit," he mumbled to himself. "What a waste."

He tossed the pair back out the door, thinking to give them to one of the slaves later. Turning, he strode through the hall and up the stairs, calling for his manservant as he went.

"Henry, I need a bath."

His only answer was a prolonged silence. He gave the name another shout.

The boisterous tone of his voice did elicit a

response, but not from Henry. Marriette emerged from her room, carrying an arm load of rags.

"What are you yelling about?" she snapped, her face pinched tight.

"Where's Henry?" Travis asked.

"How should I know." Coming forward with her words, her skirt swishing militantly in a replica of her agitated frame of mind. "Lacy has me ripping up my old shifts for facecloths. I swear, Travis, she has taken this business of personally nursing the slaves much too seriously for . . . *Lord above, you stink!*"

Despite the bundle, she covered her nose and mouth with a hand, and backed away to an odorless distance. "What have you been doing? You smell like a pig."

Travis halted in his steps and ground his fists onto his hips. This was the absolute last straw. It was bad enough to have to toil like one of the slaves. He did not need to be reminded of it.

In an exaggerated movement that would have done his courtly forefathers proud, he bowed, sweeping his arm in a grand arc before him. "Excuse me if I have offended you, my lady," he professed with a lethal load of sarcasm. "But unlike you, who have had nothing better to do than rip and tear, and I would warrant bitch the entire while, I have been engaged in matters of a more strenuous nature."

"Oh, shut up, Travis," Marriette retorted, stung by his mockery. "I don't have to put up with your nonsense."

"That's typical." He slowly shook his head on a bitter laugh. "I might have expected that of you, sister." Tired enough to be perversely stubborn, he

96

refused to relinquish his acerbity. "You don't ever put up with anything, do you? Not a worn-out hair ribbon, or tea that isn't quite to your liking. And saints preserve us if you're expected actually to help out around here."

Marriette stiffened, her hands clenching about the rags. "What are you talking about? I share in all the chores."

"I'm sure you think you do."

"What does that mean?"

The absurdity of the situation became overwhelming. Throwing up his hands, he spun on his heel and retraced his steps. "Hell, Marriette, go figure it out."

Down the stairs, and out the door, he followed an instinctive urging that took him around to the back of the house. A bath. Was it too much to ask for? Instead, he had to listen to Marriette's shrewish rantings.

His stride punctuated by mounting irritation, he made his way past the kitchen to the slave quarters. Three rows deep, ten cabins to a row; he stalked to the last dwelling in the third row. Without knocking, he shoved open the door, not even certain why he was there.

"I've been told I stink."

Rose looked up from her plate of greens and ham, her young face reflecting her amazement at Travis's disgruntled, filthy appearance. The breeze wafting through the doorway with the fading sun quickly replaced her surprise with amusement.

"You sure have smelled better," she said, her soft voice laced with gentle humor. Her gaze dropped to his stockinged feet and one side of her mouth

97

twitched with a smile.

Travis glared at her and found temperate indulgence in the face of intolerable chaos. She offered tender irreverence served up with a hint of a smile. They were a balm that took the sting from Travis's temper and helped ease his nerves enough to cut the worst of his anger.

His head dropped back and he stared at the crude ceiling, mentally calling himself ten kinds of a fool. He was behaving like an ass, and the only excuse he had was that he hadn't known . . . not when he had been a child, not when he had ridden the grounds with his father. Not even yesterday. He hadn't known the demands the Watch would make of him. How she, for all of her glorious splendor and beauty, could sap his strength and usurp his identity.

His father had tried to warn them. With his dying words he had called her a demanding mistress, as selfish as a two-bit whore. His father had been right, he had known that she could reduce a proud man to a common, stinking drudge. And still, he had gone to his grave in servitude to her.

It was a somber realization, but it was also cathartic, purging Travis of a certain naïveté. *This* was the truth, this day-to-day, hour-by-hour commitment of mind and body to the land. It took more than rain and sun and sturdy backs and hands. Swan's Watch required a person's very life.

"I need a bath," he murmured, his voice wearied.

Rose strained forward to hear his whisper. Rising from the small plank table, she crossed to Travis's side and searched his face. "Are you all right?" she asked, wondering at the sadness she saw in his eyes.

"I'm tired."

She tilted her head to one side. "You sure that's all there is to it?"

A small grin actually broke the straight line of Travis's mouth. His little Rose. She had a wisdom beyond her years. "No," he admitted, "I'm not sure of anything at the moment."

"Other than you be wantin' a bath." Smiling, she added delicately, "And that you smell real bad."

If there was one thing Travis would always be sure of, it was that her smile was like no other. His gaze lingered on the full curve of her lips and the empty hollow of his chest swelled with emotion.

"Yes, and that I smell bad," he repeated.

Seeing the subtle signs of his internal struggle, Rose laid a hand on his chest. She didn't understand what ate at him, but she responded to his need nonetheless. "Smellin' bad don't make no never mind." Her other hand slipped up over his shoulder. "Just proves you been workin' hard."

And suddenly Travis knew why he was there. In the arms of this girl, he would always be assured of acceptance. Regardless of how he looked or what he did, Rose would welcome him exactly as he was.

His arms circled her supple form and pulled her into a tight embrace. Taking her had been the last thing on his mind when he had left the house. Now, it was all he could think of.

His mouth found hers, his tongue parting her lips and thrusting forward with an urgency that bespoke his need. He captured her sigh, made it his own, just as he molded every line and curve of her against him.

He knew the feel of her by heart. Yet her breasts

boring into him sent his blood pounding. Desire combined with necessity, passion with compulsion. A wave of profound desperation engulfed him, and whether it was expedient or not, he could not wait.

In one sure move, he lifted her, kicked the door shut and took two steps to the bed. Quick work saw his pants unfastened and her skirt raised. Unerringly, his body found hers and he thrust into her welcoming warmth as if lingering would have been the end of him. He didn't doubt that it could have been, for nothing had ever felt so right as being encompassed by his little Rose.

His body strained against her in a driving rhythm. Immoderate pleasure, grounded in a fealty of the hearts, surged unrestrained. His senses, rubbed raw from duty and obligation, reveled in the passion that was only short breaths away from fulfillment.

It burst upon him in nearly painful waves, fierce, blazing, tightening every muscle. And then . . . repose. Sweet languorous tranquility of the mind and soul.

His body cushioned by her softness, he dropped his head into the crook of her shoulder, unable to deny the truth of it all. The Watch taxed him beyond his endurance . . . Rose gave him back his strength.

Chapter Six

A wave of dizziness assailed Lacy, forcing her to shut her eyes briefly. Pressing one hand to her forehead, she clung to the wrought-iron door latch with the other, breathing deeply to restore her equilibrium. The cool interior of the laundry helped to some degree, but only enough to prevent her knees from buckling. Her vision remained blurred and a slight buzzing sounded in her ears.

She gave a low groan of frustration. She could not afford to get sick, she simply couldn't. Between nursing the sick and trying to keep up with as much of the normal routine as possible, there was no time available for her to lie in bed.

Squaring her shoulders, she willed the faintness away, opened the laundry door and stepped out into the late afternoon sunlight. But the abrupt transition from the shadows strained her already fatigued senses and she had to pause to collect herself.

Just one more stop, she told herself. She had to check on little five-year-old Sam. He was feeling particularly bad with the fever and she had promised him yesterday that she would visit him again today. Then, she would be able to return to the house.

"For a cup of tea," she promised herself aloud. "Mint tea."

"I prefer mine with lemon," Jared remarked from just beyond the kitchen.

Startled, Lacy looked across the dirt lane to the corner of the kitchen and found Jared standing with one shoulder propped against the whitewashed building. Of its own accord, her heart warmed.

He had been gone six days. And she had missed him, terribly. Seeing him now was an unexpected delight and she took the time to drink in the sight of him.

She had not forgotten how handsome he was, but she had to marvel at the fact that every time she looked at him, it was like seeing him again for the first time. Just as it had at their first introduction, her pulse once again quickened.

Gray eyes, heavily lashed and staring straight at her, high cheekbones and firm lips; the combination of features was dynamically virile, something that was, quite illogically, only enhanced by his casual stance. His arms crossed over his chest, he gave the appearance of grand nonchalance, but she knew only too well that beneath the insouciant façade was a powerful man.

Her gaze skimmed over his white shirt, buff-colored vest, and black pants. She distinctly remembered the feel of his strength.

Through her weariness, she smiled. "Welcome back. I didn't realize that you had returned."

102

"Only a few moments ago," Jared clarified. He pushed off the wall and strode forward, his gaze no less scrutinizing than Lacy's. For nearly a week, the image of her beautiful face had filled his days while the treasured feel of her in his arms had tormented his nights.

For the first time ever, he had found the routine aboard ship to be less than inspiring. Making arrangements for its return home had been frustratingly tedious, and he had had to fight his own impatience to return to Lacy.

A struggle of an entirely different sort, however, was waging inside him just then. Coming to stop within arm's reach of her, he wanted very much to take her in his arms.

"The house was deserted," he offered, wishing they were some place private.

Lacy pressed her hand to her temple again. "I'm sorry. Things have been rather hectic around here." Her shoulders sagged slightly. "There's no telling where Gaye is."

Jared saw her fatigue, and wondered how he could have missed it on first seeing her. Her normally sparkling turquoise eyes were listless and her cheeks were void of any color.

"What's wrong?" His black brows slashed into diagonal lines.

She looked about, not knowing where to start. "Most of the slaves are ill." That was a meager explanation, but it was almost too much of an effort to elucidate in full detail.

"Are you all right?"

"Yes. Just tired."

"Because you've been racing in three directions at once, no doubt."

She gave him a quizzical look. "I have only done what needed to be done. Everyone who is able is doing the same."

Jared seriously doubted that. If he had learned anything in his abbreviated stay thus far, it was that Lacy shouldered a major portion of the responsibilities. He trailed his gaze over the contour of her neck and down her arm. She was a fragile woman to possess such strength.

"I think you should have that tea right now." Before she could even begin to protest, he took her elbow and guided her back toward the house.

Lacy knew she was being manipulated, but she could not for the life of her offer any resistance. With each passing minute, she was feeling increasingly devoid of energy and the thought of sitting for more than five minutes . . . especially with Jared . . . sounded wonderful.

"I will let you get away with this high-handed maneuver this time," she quipped with a dash of her old spirit. "But only because you are our guest."

She meant to add that she would need to look in on little Sam later, but without warning, her world shifted before her eyes. All the blood seemed to drain from her head and her steps faltered.

"Oh, dear." Her words came out as a distant whisper.

The next thing she knew, she was being swung up into strong arms and held securely. She thought she heard Jared's muttered curse and she had a vague impression of being carried . . . then nothing until she opened her eyes and found herself being lowered to her bed.

"Jared?" she queried weakly, trying to understand what had happened and how she came to be in her room.

"Yes, love," he said, easing her head to the brace of pillows.

"What . . ."

"You fainted."

"Fainted?" She pressed a hand to her brow, trying to clear her mind. "Are you sure? I've never fainted in my entire life."

"Well, you just did. Now, lie still."

His stern order sounded logical to Lacy. Struggling to gain her wits, she didn't think to question him. Or to take note of his hands quickly releasing the row of buttons running down her bodice. It wasn't until he had the front of her dress spread wide that she became completely conscious of what he had done.

"*Jared.*" Mortified, she tried to pull her bodice together. Her gaze flew from his hands to the opened door then up to his face. "What are you doing?"

But he proved her efforts useless. Brushing her weak hands aside, he unfastened the front hooks of her corset. "Why you women insist on wearing these things is beyond me."

Her face flaming, Lacy grasped his hands. "You can't do this."

"I can if I want you to breathe properly," he told her, his fingers continuing their work despite her grip. Brooking no interference, he separated the two halves of her corset before Lacy could protest further.

Lacy didn't know which was worse. The feeble

105

sensation swirling about her head or the utter embarrassment that engulfed her. Both combined to render her helpless, all she could do was lie there in confusion, exposed down to her chemise under Jared's all too discerning gaze.

What little fortitude she had retained was sapped by her chagrin, and the strain of the last days finally descended on her full force. Of their own accord, her eyes shut, and suddenly, decorum and modesty were just trivialities, too insignificant to tolerate.

What did it matter that she had let a man undress her? What did it matter that with the door standing wide anyone could come upon them at any moment? She surrendered propriety to exhaustion and gave herself up to Jared's tender regard. Unfortunately, such capitulation did not come without a price and helpless tears rose up behind her closed lids.

Her distress did not go unnoticed by Jared, and he ground his teeth. If she wasn't ill herself, then she was completely worn out. As far as he was concerned, she needed to be stripped naked and put under the covers with a cool cloth across her forehead.

The image danced through his mind, despite the immediacy of the situation. It was a tempting idea to consider slipping beneath the same covers to lie beside her, flesh to flesh, and hold her close while he soothed the strain from her muscles.

He stifled his untimely thoughts. Swallowing a pithy oath, he left her for a moment and returned with a glass of cool water. Carefully, he sat beside her, and eased an arm around her shoulders. "Take a sip." When she had done as she was told, he levered her back against the pillows, then set the glass on the bedside table.

"Better?" he asked.

Lacy nodded. The water did help wash the clog of tears from her throat. But her hold on her composure was only tenuous, especially when she felt Jared take one of her hands in his own.

"How are you feeling?" came his low voice.

The warmth of his touch and the gentleness of his tone drew her eyes open. She could have fabricated a reply that would have sounded adequate, but the discerning glint in his eyes prompted her to the truth.

"I'm feeling very foolish."

"Why?"

She shrugged one shoulder. "Because I'm lying here when I should be tending to the sick. I told little Sam that I would visit him."

With his free hand, he brushed an errant strand of hair away from her cheek. "I'm sure he'll understand if you can't."

"But he's so young. He'll be disappointed."

"Then I'll look in on him."

She blinked in surprise. "You?"

He answered with a lopsided grin. "Won't I do?"

"Well, yes. But you don't have to inconvenience yourself."

"There's no inconvenience." Her hesitation pulled his grin into a straight line. "Lacy, you can't help anyone if you're not well yourself. How long have you been feeling like this?"

"I don't know for sure. Since yesterday, I suppose."

"You suppose." He scoffed in disgusted disbelief. "And you've been going about as usual. Any fever?"

"No."

"When did you last eat?"

Knowing he was not going to like her answer, Lacy held her tongue. Instead, she gave him a question of her own. "Are you always this autocratic?"

"When I need to be."

"You sound like a doctor."

"Don't change the subject."

"I am feeling much better."

"Lacy . . . *when* did you last eat?" Capturing her chin, he held her still for his penetrating stare, demanding that she reply.

Defenseless against the silent dictate, she sighed. "I remember having breakfast yesterday."

This time he didn't bother to smother his curse. "Damn it, Lacy, no wonder you're dropping to your knees." He shoved off the bed and headed for the doorway. "I'm going to get you something to eat right now."

"No, Jared, don't," she called after him. "It will only make more trouble for Besha and she's already overworked as it is." Stretching out a hand, she implored, "Please, Jared."

Her earnest appeal stopped him and he turned to look back at her.

She lifted her hand higher, the blue and green of her eyes softening into a velvet turquoise hue. "Besha will have dinner ready in an hour. I promise I will eat then."

He stood immobile, clearly debating whether to relent or not.

"I promise," she reiterated.

Whether it was her vow or the mellow cast to her gaze that decided for him, Jared didn't know. Nonetheless, he returned to the bed.

"In an hour," he pressed, sitting close beside her.

"I promise." She offered a conciliatory smile, hoping to coax away the last of his temper.

Shaking his head, he conceded, "All right." He studied her at length, marveling at her mettle. "I'm beginning to think that I was lucky to have negotiated contracts with Travis rather than you."

She sensed that somewhere in the compliment there was a criticism. But she let it pass, inexplicably content just to have him near.

"I didn't thank you for coming to my rescue."

"You make me sound like a knight in shining armor."

To some extent, that was how she viewed him. But she didn't think he would appreciate her telling him so. "Still, I am grateful."

His gaze toured her features. "My pleasure."

She felt his look like a physical caress, stroking over her cheeks and lips. Her breath surged into her lungs too quickly and her voice lowered to accommodate her breathlessness.

"Did you finish up with your ship?"

He nodded. "She'll return to Connecticut with the morning tide."

"Won't you be needed in some official capacity when the ship docks?"

"No, my captain normally deals with the harbor master. But I've sent word on ahead to my brother to handle any paper work there might be, and to keep an eye on my house while I'm away."

"Your brother?"

"Stephen. He's my business partner."

Until that moment, she hadn't considered that portion of Jared's life that included a family. But the mention of a brother sparked her curiosity and it showed all over her face.

"Is there a problem with that?" Jared asked, reading her interest.

"Oh, no," she assured him. "I just realized that I know so little about you. I was wondering what your family is like."

Jared exhaled on a chuckle, reaching out to take one of her hands again. "Large enough. Two brothers and four sisters. Both Stephen and Eric are married with families of their own. And my oldest sister, Anna, is betrothed."

"Are you the eldest?"

"Definitely."

For some reason, that delighted Lacy. She pictured him as a child, at least a head taller than any of his siblings. "I suppose you were abominable to your youngest sister when you were growing up," she teased.

That earned her a wry look, but when he spoke his voice was laden with affection. "My youngest sister is a consummate flirt. In her short sixteen years, she has made certain that my father does not have a black hair left on his head. And she is the cause of my mother's penchant for continuously offering up prayers."

"They sound wonderful," she exclaimed, unable to suppress her laugh.

The rippling sound floated between them to dance along Jared's nerves. "I believe they are," he averred, his gaze dropping to her curving lips.

110

The darkening of his eyes and the warmth of his hands stirred her senses with a restive headiness, and it was all she could do not to run her tongue along her lips in a nervous reaction. "I suppose you will miss them."

The broad line of his shoulders rose in a shrug. "Somewhat, but I have other matters here that are far more important." He stared straight into her eyes.

"Yes, Travis did say something about . . ."

"I'm not talking about contracts, Lacy."

Her eyes widened in question.

Running his fingers over the backs of her knuckles, he murmured, "I missed you while I was gone."

"You did?"

His eyes narrowed. "That can't surprise you."

Privately, Lacy admitted that it did. For every day of his absence, she had wished for his return, but she had been afraid to hope that he had felt similarly.

A hesitant smile broke over her face. "I'm glad you've returned. I . . . I missed you, too."

Inordinate pleasure surged through him, and had she been feeling well, he would have followed his natural impulse to sweep her into his arms and show her just how pleased he was by her declaration. Still, there was a great deal to be said for subtle finesse.

He closed the meager distance between them and covered her mouth with his own for a short but very thorough kiss.

"This is not how I envisioned my return," he murmured thickly against her lips.

Feeling as though she was floating away, Lacy choked out, "No?"

"No," he assured her, remembering the nights on

111

board ship when he had pictured her lying soft and yielding beneath him. Unable to help himself, he kissed her again, molding the soft contours of her lips to his own until he forced himself to remember the reason for her being in bed. Regretfully, he lifted his head and sat back, having to satisfy himself with her closeness.

"I should let you rest until dinner."

It would be the wisest thing for him to do, Lacy knew, but she clung to his hand, wanting him to stay, wanting him to kiss her once more and make her feel that wonderful euphoria. Wanting.

"We'll dine at seven," she commented lamely.

He made no move to rise. "I expect to see you there."

Unable to find words, she nodded.

"I don't want you up until then." Like all of his commands, it left no room for disregard.

"All right."

Reluctantly, he stood, and for long moments he did nothing but stare down at her, the gray of his eyes resolute as though he was silently coming to some decision. Finally, he bent and brushed his lips across hers one last time. Then he turned and strode from the room, quietly closing the door before he went in search of little Sam.

In the shadows of the recessed alcove in the hall, Marriette stood rigidly, her chest heaving in anger. Eyes narrowed to malicious blue slits, she watched Jared make his way down the hall and descend the stairs before she turned her gaze to Lacy's door.

"Why you little slut," she whispered. "Who do you think you are?"

Incensed by all she had overheard, she whirled out of her hiding place and stalked to her bedroom. Riding her anger, she snatched open the door and threw it closed, the reverberating sound assuaging only a tiny part of her wrath.

She paced to the window, as though moving across the room would somehow take her away from the words riffling through her head. But she could still hear Jared's low voice, asking if Lacy had a fever. And though she hadn't actually seen, she knew the eloquent silence of a kiss when she heard it.

She swung about and headed back to the door. This was not supposed to be happening. Lacy was not supposed to be involved in any way with Jared Steele, yet her *sweet*, harmless sister had become familiar enough with him to let him undress her. Oh, she had come down the hall in time to hear *that* little scenario unfolding like some sordid farce. It had stopped her cold.

At the door, she spun and retraced her path to the window, calling herself a naive fool for so blindly overlooking Lacy's schemes. Apparently, her reticent little sister wasn't such a prig after all. Damn her. *And* Jared Steele! Was the man blind? What on earth would he want with Lacy?

Her steps halted abruptly. Well, she was not going to stand for this. Until she decided if she wanted to marry Jared, she would not tolerate any interference from anyone, most especially her sister.

She turned to her mirror, already anticipating how best to achieve her goal. Running a hand back over her mussed curls, her gaze dropped to the reflection of her dirtied dress. She looked like some poor white

113

trash. And from the way she had had to carry on today, she felt no better. Every odd job on the entire plantation had come her way, from gathering eggs to paddling the laundry clean in the vats full of boiling water.

Her face creased with a sneer. She needed a bath, she needed her hair washed and curled, she needed a clean dress. But her maid was sick and there was no help to be expected from Gaye. The house girl was helping out in the kitchen.

Temper flaring, she threw herself onto her bed, burying her face in the crook of her bent arm. She could not go down to dinner as she was, and she was not going to present herself to Jared unless she was looking decent. That was not going to happen tonight for she couldn't ready herself by dinner.

She was going to have to wait until tomorrow. But oh, come morning, would she make up for lost time.

Chapter Seven

"I want to know what Jared's finances are, Travis. As part owner of this plantation, I have a right to know who we're becoming involved with."

Standing with her hands braced on her hips, Marriette stated her demands in imperious tones that made Travis glance away from the horse he had been saddling.

"I don't see why you're suddenly so interested in the Watch's monetary affairs, Marriette. You've never cared one way or the other as long as you have enough money to suit your own purposes." He led his mount from the stall out to the stable yard.

"I already told you," she returned, following in her brother's wake. "If we're going to do business with Jared Steele, then I think we have a right to know if his shipping company is sound. After all, it affects the Watch."

Travis gave her a shrewd look. He couldn't fault her for her question. He was just surprised that she had actually thought of it.

Laying a hand on the fine leather saddle, he turned and faced her squarely. "As it happens, Marriette, I have already ascertained that Jared is a wealthy man."

"How wealthy?"

"Very. His shipping company turned more profit in the last two years than the Watch made in the last ten." It was a sobering thought. His blond brows arched as he pursed his lips. Solemnly, he added, "He could buy the Watch outright if he wanted to and still have money to burn."

Marriette's eyes glistened. She might not have ever been all that interested in what went on around the Watch, but she had listened carefully when it was prudent for her to do so. The peanut fields were worth up to a hundred dollars per acre, the rest of the land closer to twenty-five. The fifty or so slaves they owned represented a cost that was close to the going price of the land itself.

Quickly, she ran the numbers through her head and, considering the value of all the buildings and livestock, she arrived at a figure close to a quarter of a million dollars.

"So you see," Travis went on, "you don't have anything to worry about. Now, are you satisfied?"

"Yes," Marriette replied. She was definitely satisfied. Having discovered all she needed to know, she gave Travis a blinding smile and sped off toward the house.

Travis watched her hasty retreat, wondering what maggot of an idea she had taken into her head this time. He never could figure her out. Her moods swung like the pendulum of a clock.

116

He looked at the sun directly overhead. It was nearly noon already and he needed to check on the progress in the south fields. That was almost a laughable notion. Every available man, woman, and child had been shifted to the peanuts, which left the corn standing idle. But there was nothing that could be done about that until the sickness had run its course.

When that was to be, he could only guess. For the sake of the plantation and his own sanity, he fervently hoped that it would be soon.

He mounted and sent his horse out of the paddock. Knowing Rose was working in the kitchen, he glanced to the outbuildings on the far side of the rolling lawn. With the distance separating them, he didn't see the tall, muscular figure hasten into the whitewashed building.

A subtle sound from the doorway of the kitchen made Rose look up from the chicken she was plucking. At the sight of Syphron's solid form her heart lodged in her throat. He stood there plain as day for all to see, calloused hands propped on his lean waist, smiling that broad grin of his as though he didn't have a care in the world.

"What are you doin' here?" she whispered urgently. Her dark gaze darted from his ruggedly chiseled face with its deep-set eyes to the open window where she could see Travis astride his horse.

"I come to see how you was doin'," Syphron replied, stepping into the cool interior of the kitchen. "With everybody catchin' the sickness, I was worried 'bout you."

117

"You goin' to be worryin' 'bout a whole lot more if the massa finds you here." Wiping her hands on her apron, she hurried forward pushing Syphron out of plain view. Quickly, she poked her head out the door and glanced up and down the lane, looking for anyone who might have seen his entrance.

"You're out of your mind, comin' here like this," she scolded as she eased the door to stand ajar. "Mister Spruill told you not to come nosin' around me no more."

Syphron's jaw tightened. "I don't care what he said."

"You should." Wringing her hands, she warned, "Lord, there ain't no tellin' what he'll do if he catches you again."

At her fearful look, Syphron smiled again, his high-sculpted cheekbones rounding into prominence, his heavy brows arching. "You worried 'bout me?" Before Rose had time to answer, he reached out and gathered her into his arms.

Rose gasped, finding herself held intimately against the steely, broad-shouldered frame. "You crazy fool," she squeaked. Frantically she pushed at his immovable chest. "Besha's goin' to be back in a lick."

Her struggles only widened Syphron's smile. The feel of her was all that he had imagined it would be. For months he had had his eye on her as she came and went about the place, her smile as wide as the river, her laughter like some bird singing in the trees. And night after night, he had lain awake on his narrow, straw mattress and dreamt about her lithe body and full, ripe breasts.

118

"Shit on Besha." He laughed. "She ain't goin' to tell no one." His hands settled low on her back, urging her against his rapidly tightening length. "Least of all if you got yourself a proper man."

Rose quieted in his arms. Uncertainly, she looked into his eyes, feeling trapped. "Massa Travis is my man."

Syphron's humor died instantly. Dark eyes heating to a scorching blaze, he yanked his hands away. "He ain't your man."

His deadly voice made the flesh on her arms prickle. "He is, Syphron. Not like Besha got her a married man, but . . ."

"But he's usin' you like he uses one of his horses." Disgusted, he swung away, slapping a hand on the bricks of the fireplace. "Only difference is when he rides you, he don't need to use no harness."

His words speared straight into her and every nerve in her spine jerked. "Who do you think you are, comin' in here, belittlin' me? You ain't got no say-so in what I do."

Syphron turned back to glare accusingly at her. "You think you're in love with him, don't you?"

What she felt was all tangled up in the consuming passion that her fifteen-year-old body felt every time Travis took her. It was combined with a headiness that came with the knowledge that Travis favored her over all others. If that was love, then so be it. Drawing herself up proudly, she vowed. "I'm somebody special to the massa."

"You ain't nothin' but his whore."

"That's a fact, and there ain't nothin' I can do to change that. But he treats me good, and he ain't

119

puttin' it to no other girls on the plantation. Just me."

"And you goin' to be satisfied with that? Damn." He scanned her face, wishing he could see what was in her heart. "Don't you want more, Rose? Don't you want some kind of a life other than spreadin' your legs for him?"

She twirled from the earnest look on his face and returned to the chicken at the worktable. Frostily she said, "I got me the best life I can have."

"No, you don't."

"Yes, I do," she avowed, shoving away secret hopes of raising free children.

"For how long?"

"What?"

"How long you goin' to be his favorite? He wants you now while you're young. But you think he's goin' to look at you when you're no longer prime? He'll find him another girl to diddle and put you aside like some tired old sow that he's done with."

"He wouldn't do that," she declared heatedly, brutally yanking the white feathers with a vengeance.

"You can't know that."

"He won't treat me like that."

"All right, what if he don't?" He stepped to the table with his heated, ruthless words. "He's still goin' to take him a wife someday, and it sure as hell ain't goin' to be you. And you can bet no wife of his is goin' to want you 'round. She ain't goin' to stand to have her husband's whore livin' under her nose, and you'll be gone from here before you even knew what happened."

If he had slapped her in the face, she couldn't have felt more pain. Her fingers stilled and her gaze flew to his. He had stated plain, hard facts, and as much as she didn't want to, she had to face them.

She hadn't ever given any thought to Travis's getting married, but she did now and the prospect was discouraging. Her shoulders slumped as she moved to a wooden stool and sat down in a suddenly wearied heap. She had been foolish to feel so smug about her place in Travis's life. No matter that he came to her . . . alone, at the bottom of everything else, she was still his property, some owned piece of flesh and blood that could be sold on a whim. Or at a wife's urging.

"You see now that I'm talkin' sense?" Syphron persisted when she didn't say anything for long minutes.

Her voice laden with a heavy disillusionment, she returned, "I see only that nothin's changed."

"Only if you let it go on."

She gave him a resentful look. "How can I stop it? You said yourself, I'm only his whore."

"But you don't have to be." Closing the space between them, he came down on his haunches before her. "You don't have to be his whore."

"You're talkin' crazy."

Taking up one of her hands in both of his, he stared intently into her wary eyes. "I ain't talkin' nonsense. I'm talkin' 'bout you and me leavin' this place."

Rose's eyes went wide, filling with fear. Quickly, she laid a hand over his mouth, her gaze darting apprehensively to the door and then the windows.

"Hush up."

Twisting his head aside, he dislodged her hand. "Why? Ain't you ever thought of runnin'?"

She had, but thinking about it and actually doing it were two different things. "You got to put this notion out of your head. Massa will track you down with the dogs for certain."

"That don't mean he'll catch us."

"No one's ever made it, Syphron."

"But that don't mean we can't try."

"Taloila's man tried and he never even came back." Pulling her hand from his she shook her head emphatically. "No, no, I ain't goin' to listen to this."

At her stubborn refusal, he set his jaw and surged to his feet. Frustration riding him hard, he paced to the far corner, jamming a hand to the back of his neck to scrub away a building tension.

"I can't do this no more, Rose," he said quietly, his back toward her. "I got to live as a free man, with my own land and my own wife and children. I want to get up each mornin' and know that whatever I do that day, it's because it's what *I* want to do and not because some man is standin' over me makin' me do it. I want to go to bed each night feelin' proud that I done my best."

A wealth of determination and bitterness was evident in his low voice, and Rose clenched her eyes shut against the powerful feelings his words inspired inside her. Hadn't she wanted those very same things? Hadn't she longed to have a life somewhere else?

"I can't be a slave no more, Rose," he continued. "I got to leave here . . . or die tryin'." He abruptly crossed the room to pull her up from the stool, his hands holding her firmly by her forearms. "And I want you to go with me. To be my woman."

"Marry you?"

"And have my babies."

"But where . . . how . . . ?"

"Ohio, or maybe north of there to Canada."

Despire the fear that swamped her, Rose found herself asking, "Aren't you 'fraid of what might happen if you get caught?"

"I'm more 'fraid of stayin'. Say you'll go with me."

Lines of distress marred the young beauty of her face, indecision clouding the liquid brown of her eyes. "Oh, Syphron, I don't know."

"Say yes, Rose."

"I got to have time to think." There was so much she had to consider. Running was of itself an enormous idea, but there was also the matter of becoming Syphron's wife. She hardly knew him . . . but did that matter in comparison to gaining her freedom? "Let me think on it, Syphron."

A satisfied smile split his face. She hadn't said no. "Don't take too much time."

Out of the corner of her eye, Rose caught the movement of a figure and she looked toward the doorway. She nearly choked on her breath at the sight of Besha silently watching them.

Syphron jerked around, becoming aware of the rotund cook at nearly the same instant. The smile dropped off his face and his brow drew into a fierce scowl.

"You sneakin' round, silent as a cat, Besha," he stated defensively.

Besha looked at the pair. Even if she hadn't heard them making their plans, she would have guessed that something was in the air from the guilt on their faces.

"And you too sly for a fox," she returned. Her eyes narrowed angrily and when she spoke, her voice was thick with fury. "Get on out o' here. I got me no mind to get in trouble for the likes o' you."

A spurt of apprehension stiffened Syphron's back. "You heard what we was sayin'?"

"I don't know nothin', you hear? But you keep clear o' my kitchen from now on. You come back 'gain and I'll take my iron skillet to your head." She jabbed a menacing finger at the air before her. "I don't want none o' your trouble at my door."

It was the best Syphron could expect. She would keep her silence, but that was all. He gave Rose a sidelong glance then hastened out of the kitchen.

As soon as he was away, Besha stalked to the fireplace and slammed a heavy kettle into place on its trivet. "Get that hen cleaned 'fore I take my skillet to you, too."

Rose jumped at the first word and did as she was told. But as she prepared the chicken, she could feel Besha's heavy disapproval lingering on her back.

"Besha?" she began hesitantly.

"What?"

But Rose could barely put her thoughts into words. What she was contemplating could very well see the end of her life. How did you go about discussing *that?*

Her mind besieged by confusion and doubt, she didn't say anything more.

124

*   *   *

Two children were dead. Two children, and thirteen adults. Lacy could hardly believe it. The sickness had finally run its course and, in its vengeful path, had snatched too many precious lives. It was the loss of the little girls that Lacy felt the most keenly.

Standing at the grave site for their burial, she let the tears flow freely as Reverend Burcher offered up prayers for their souls. Sorrowfully, she watched the hastily made pine boxes lowered into the ground to take their places beside the other thirteen newly dug graves.

From her place between Marriette and Travis, she watched the grieving families move off toward their cabins, their lives blighted by tragedy. In her heart, she wished she could ease their suffering, but all she could do was offer her condolences, a meager solace, to be sure.

A warm, steady hand grasped her elbow, and she didn't need to turn to know that it was Jared who was there just behind her. Although he hadn't been obliged to attend the service, he had chosen to do so out of respect for all concerned. Throughout the somber ceremony, she had felt his presence and had relished it just as she now relished the comfort she derived from the contact of his hand.

Turning to face him was as natural as breathing and, had they been somewhere private, she would have followed her inclination to step forward and lay her head against his chest. But Marriette and Travis were both within arm's reach and a few of the slaves

125

who had gathered still lingered. She had to content herself with merely looking into the unwavering strength of his gray eyes.

"Thank you for being here, Jared," she murmured.

Jared's only reply was a gentle tightening of his fingers. Beyond that, he let silence carry the moment.

As a group, they quietly walked back to the house, no one saying anything until they ascended the brick steps to the central hall. Then it was Travis's cheerless voice that broke the hush.

"I for one am in need of a bourbon. Anyone care to join me?" Not waiting for a reply, he strode into the parlor leaving the others to follow in his wake.

"Well, I am glad that this entire affair is finally over," Marriette declared once everyone was seated with their choice of drink. "It has been extremely trying, and I'll be glad to finally have things back to normal."

Travis stared morosely at the amber liquid in his glass and scoffed. "It will be a while yet before we have reestablished any normalcy around here, Marriette."

"Why do you say that?"

Her question pricked his temper and added an acerbic tinge to his voice. "If you hadn't noticed in the past weeks, sister, this plantation has come to a halt. It isn't a matter of simply picking up where we left off and going on as though nothing has happened."

His voice carried just enough sting to make Marriette pause and raise a delicate brow. Her brother's words sounded too much like a chastisement and she resented that, especially in front of Jared.

Sweetly, she returned. "Perhaps you might want to discuss any problems with the Watch later, Travis. We wouldn't want to bore Jared with all the sordid little details."

Travis came to his feet and crossed back to the side table and its collection of liquor decanters. "No, I think Jared is entitled to know the status of things as they stand right now." It galled him to no end that the plantation had come to its present deplorable circumstances under his direction. Pouring himself another dose of whiskey, he raised his glass in a self-mocking salute. "After all, we have business together and what affects the Watch affects Jared's company as well."

From his place beside Lacy on the settee, Jared narrowed his eyes, his assessing gaze following Travis's every gesture. "I think that is a wise decision."

No censure, Travis noted, no criticism or blame cast. Just a straightforward statement of fact. He had to admire Jared's sense of impartiality. It would make it easier to relate the plantation's state of affairs.

Striding to the fireplace, he leaned an elbow against the mantel and sighed before he began. "These past weeks have cost us dearly. It will take considerable time to get the fields in condition again, especially since we've lost so many workers."

Shrugging, Marriette suggested, "The answer is obvious, Travis. We'll just have to buy more slaves, that's all."

Lacy could barely contain her gasp at her sister's nonchalance. Buy a person, sell a person . . . with nary a thought given to the people involved. Slavery was abhorrent enough without having to listen to such contemptuous opinions.

Although Travis did not share Lacy's antislavery sentiments, he, too, was struck by Marriette's flippancy. At any other time, he might have let it pass, but his anxiety forestalled such tolerance. "No, I'm afraid that's not all, Marriette. Thirteen adult slaves." He tapped a finger to the side of his head. "Can you comprehend the kind of expense I'm talking about?"

Lacy knew the account books as well as Travis did and she fully understood how such a transaction would strain the Watch's operating budget. "We can't afford that, Travis," she advised.

"Precisely."

Suddenly feeling very ignorant and not liking that, Marriette retorted, "Well, how many can we afford?"

Travis and Lacy exchanged a long look, before he said, "Five, six at the most. Which means the workers are going to have to work harder just to keep pace with our past schedule, harder still to increase our production to meet the terms of our agreement with Jared."

Jared kept all expression from his face as he addressed Travis. "Do you anticipate problems in that area?"

The easy answer would have been no, but in all honesty, Travis couldn't be certain that they were going to be able to ship the agreed upon tonnage of peanuts. It was a matter of wait and see. "I'd like to think not. At this point, I'll be hopeful and say that we'll manage, but it won't be an easy task."

Marriette shrugged prettily, although behind her congenial smile, she thought her brother an idiot for proclaiming his worries so freely. "I'm sure everything will turn out just fine. The Watch has always stood, and I don't imagine it will not continue to do so. Now, I refuse to discuss this any longer. We've had enough worry and despair around here to last us quite a while."

Rising, she smoothed an errant strand of hair back into place. "Did you all know that the LaRues are having a ball two nights from now? It's to celebrate the official end of the planting season. The invitation arrived several days ago, only we were all too busy to take notice."

Conversation in the room came to a stilted halt, as everyone was surprised by this remark. "Marriette," Travis exclaimed when he mentally shook off his amazement, "I hardly think this is the right time to be talking about parties. We're in the middle of important business."

"It is the perfect time," she countered. "You may have forgotten that Jared is our guest, but I have not. I think he is entitled to a pleasant diversion." She extended her hand his way. "I've been meaning to show you about the gardens, Jared."

Travis relented, but only because Marriette did have a point. In the chaos of the past days, Jared had been treated more like a familiar family member rather than the honored guest that he was.

Staring into the last of the bourbon in his glass, he said, "You are right, of course, Marriette. Jared and I can continue this discussion later."

Jared would have preferred the discussion to continue now, but he couldn't very well insist. He glanced to Marriette's hand raised in invitation. Their last encounter in his room was still a vivid picture in his mind and skeptically he wondered what she considered a pleasant diversion. He could readily guess, and fervently wished to have no part of whatever amusements she had in mind. Still, to refuse her obvious request would be insulting.

Coming to his feet, he accepted with a nod. "I would be glad to accompany you, Marriette." Turning back for Lacy, he added, "Would you care to join us, Lacy?"

But before Lacy could reply, Marriette said, "Yes, why don't you, Lacy. We'd love to have you. Oh, no." She pressed fingertips to her chin, her blond brows lowering over seemingly sincere eyes. "You were supposed to go out to the kitchen, weren't you?" Her disappointment plain for all to see, she aimed a charming sigh at Jared. "As wonderful as Besha is, she does need guidance every now and then and that task falls to Lacy more often than not."

It was in Jared's mind to ask why that was so, but he tactfully kept silent on the subject. Given no choice, he placed a polite hand to Marriette's elbow and escorted her from the room, but with each step he took, he could feel Lacy's disappointment increase.

"I must apologize if we have been ill-mannered." Marriette sighed. She peered up at his set features as she led him from the house to the side garden with its formal arrangements of boxwoods and hollies. "My only excuse is that things have not been normal

130

around here." Her smile was a study in devotion as she queried, "You will forgive us, won't you?"

Jared knew that limpid-eyed look and melted-bone posture well. He had seen it often enough on any number of women who had hoped to snare him into marriage . . . or bed. His jaw tightened as he ground his teeth.

"There is nothing to apologize for, Marriette. Circumstances being what they have been, it is perfectly understandable that conventions have given way to informality."

"You are being very gracious about this, Jared." She slipped her hand into the crook of his elbow. "I can't tell you how much I appreciate your understanding."

"Your apology is accepted, even though it isn't warranted."

A trill of melodious laughter floated from Marriette's lips. "You do say the most charming things, sir. You'll be turning my head if I'm not careful." She lifted one shoulder in a teasing shrug, causing the side of her breast to lightly graze his arm. "But then again, I think you are the most charming man I have ever met."

As flirtations went, Jared was wholly unimpressed. However, he had to give her credit for presentation. If he had the slightest interest in her, he might be moved by her coyly smitten manner and seemingly accidental caress. But he did not find her appealing in the least.

As she took a seat on a stone bench, he scanned her beautiful face. To the eye, she was picture perfect, with her large blue eyes and artfully arranged blond curls. And her body possessed an exotic lushness that irresistibly drew a man's attention. Her smile could at one moment be as innocent as a babe's and in the next be as seductive as any whore's, and when she laughed, the sound was nearly musical in quality.

Yet, none of it rang true. Beneath her perfect façade, he detected a selfishness that he found offensive and a falseness he could never abide. He had witnessed her using both to her own advantage, usually at Lacy's expense.

"It's a shame that Lacy couldn't join us," he remarked casually, although the gray of his eyes had taken on a brittle cast.

Marriette caught her frown in midexpression and remembered to smile. "Yes . . . Lacy . . . she is such a dear, but to be quite honest with you, she isn't much for idle moments." Languidly she shook her head. "She is so devoted to the Watch that I'm afraid she has little time for life's simple pleasures. I doubt she would have enjoyed this quiet interlude."

Jared's brow arched innocently. "Don't you think so? I seem to have garnered another impression of her entirely."

"Really?" This time Marriette couldn't prevent her brow from furrowing. She had Jared all to herself and the last thing she wanted to do was talk about Lacy. "Well, no matter. But I must confess that I am glad for this time alone with you." Her face fell into a shy, maidenly mask and when she spoke, her voice was a sultry whisper. "You are a fascinating man, Jared. I don't think I have ever met anyone quite like you."

Jared chuckled around a scoff. "I'm sure that isn't true."

"Oh, but it is," Marriette insisted, coming to her feet. "Why you've sailed about the world and seen sights that most men only dream of. You're successful and witty and the perfect gentleman." She stepped closer. Her gaze locked with his, but she was fully aware that the fullness of her skirt brushed his legs. "And to look at you snatches my breath away."

Jared's tolerance of the situation evaporated. "Marriette."

"Oh, please forgive my impetuousness," she implored, spotting a figure out of the corner of her eye. "But you must be aware of how you affect me." Before Jared could reply, she rose to her toes and pressed her mouth to his, her body melting along his in a graceful line.

From the end of the path, Lacy stood immobile, eyes wide, her bottom lip clenched between her teeth.

On a dismayed gasp, she turned and fled back to the house.

Chapter Eight

Head lowered, Lacy hurried along the brick path, her vision burning with the picture of Marriette pressed to Jared's body, his head lowered to hers. An anguished sob worked its way up from her chest, constricting her throat. Silently, she prayed that no one was about, for all she wanted to do was reach the sanctuary of her room, sink down on her bed and cry.

Silent footsteps carried her up the flight of stairs to her door. Hands shaking, she rushed into her room, turning instinctively to secure the lock just as bitter tears traced silvery paths down her cheeks.

For long moments she stood unable to move. Squeezing her eyes shut, she tried to block the image of Jared and Marriette from her mind, but her efforts were useless. The picture of them together tore at her insides, making her call herself ten kinds of a fool.

She was as ridiculously naive as a child to have believed that Jared would desire her over Marriette.

Yet right from the start, she had let herself be swayed by his words and persuasive charm. Even the first time he had kissed her by the icehouse, she had allowed herself to be tempted into thinking that she held some unique attraction for Jared.

Barely containing her sobs, she pressed a cold hand to her lips and pushed away from the door. Sinking down on the bed, she hugged a pillow to her chest, helpless against the agony consuming her. In the past weeks, Jared had captured her heart with the same ease with which he had captured her lips. Now, to see him with another woman . . . worse yet, her sister . . . was a torment unlike any she had ever known.

She loved Jared. If she hadn't faced that truth before, she openly acknowledged it now. From the first moment she had looked up into his compelling gray eyes, she had been stirred to the depths of her being. He smiled and shivers raced up her spine. He kissed her and her insides turned to liquid.

And it didn't help to have him pursuing her about the place, escorting her on her morning rounds, catching her in his arms when she was faint. He had been everything that was solicitous, gentle, and kind, and she had helplessly responded to that compassion. Just as she had responded to the desire he kindled within her.

Rolling over onto her back, she stared unseeing at the ceiling, her lips thinned by a bitter pain. It was obvious that she was patently ignorant when it came to men. In her ignorance, she had presumed that Jared's feelings ran in the same vein as her own. From his actions, she had thought that he held her in special regard. But it would seem that *that* wasn't the case if he was kissing Marriette for all to see.

How could she have been so mistaken? There was a simple enough answer that pulled at her conscience. She wanted Jared to love her as she did him. And in so wanting, she had left herself open to this kind of hurt. But he had never claimed to love her. He had simply behaved as a polished man of the world. Unfortunately, she had interpreted his actions to mean so much more. The result was that she had proven herself to be a fanciful simpleton, and she realized now just how unsophisticated she truly was.

Her tears depleted, she sat up feeling drained and dispirited. Eyes red, her gaze drifted about the room, touching on each piece of furniture. It wasn't until she spotted the heavy ring of keys on her dresser that she sighed deeply.

She drew a measure of strength from the sight of the keys. They represented every ordinary and mundane aspect of the Watch, a constancy and permanency as lasting as the plantation itself. There was comfort to be found in such familiarity.

Twining her fingers together, she collected her thoughts and abused emotions and considered how best to go on.

With dignity and a calm, polite façade. There was no other way.

Bright morning sunshine escorted Jared into the dining room. A deep smile suffused his face at the sight of Lacy already seated.

"Good morning, Lacy." His day was off to an

estimable start. The room was empty save for the two of them and he welcomed the privacy.

Lacy looked up from her eggs, her blue-green gaze focused somewhere in the middle of his forehead. "Good morning." She quickly glanced back to her plate, but it was only a matter of seconds before she laid her fork aside and rose.

He gave her a discerning look. "Won't you stay and keep me company?"

Her face a careful blank, she pushed her hands into the pockets of her yellow cotton dress. "I have a thousand things to tend to. I really . . . can't."

Her too rigid bearing gave him pause. "Are you all right?"

"Yes," came her rapid reply. She stepped away from her chair, steadfastly refusing to look directly at him. "I . . . I'm sorry, I have so much to do." With that, she hurried from the room.

The gray of Jared's eyes darkened as he followed her hasty passage. There was something amiss, but he would be damned if he knew what. At dinner last night, she had all but ignored him, her manner as reserved as he had ever known it to be. He might have been able to attribute her restraint to an emotional letdown in the wake of all that had occurred. But there was a coolness about her and she would not look directly at him. And this coolness precluded more than the most polite dialogue on her part.

And now this excuse of pressing chores. Something did not make sense. This was not the Lacy he had come to know over the past weeks. Gone was the warm vibrant woman he knew her to be. Instead, she was a formal study in civility, without a smile or a

137

frown. Even her customary blushes were absent and she had nearly been at a loss for words. In thinking back, he realized that she had barely uttered more than one word to him since he had escorted Marriette about the boxwood garden the day before.

A scoffing grunt strangled his throat at the thought of Marriette. He couldn't say that she was the most forward woman he had ever come across, but she was certainly the most obvious. She had thrown herself into his arms for the sole purpose of being caught and taken to a marriage bed. Suffice it to say, he had shoved her at arm's length almost instantly, and had stalked off to leave her standing alone among the bushes.

His jaw tightened. She grated on his nerves like rusty hinges on a weathered door. Her sister, on the other hand, acted on his senses like the most heady of wines.

His gaze sliced to the doorway where Lacy had disappeared from view. He would get to the bottom of whatever was bothering her. If his time were his own, he would do so this second. But his day was already promised to Travis and together they were headed for town.

Much to his annoyance, he was forced to put his private musings aside. Travis joined him shortly for a quick breakfast and within the half hour the two men were comfortably seated in a carriage on their way toward Smithfield.

"I'd like to introduce you to several planters today," Travis offered. "I have already spoken quite highly of our business dealings to several of my closer neighbors. They've been anxious to meet with you."

138

Jared was genuinely pleased. "Thank you."

Travis held up a hand in mock protest. "Don't thank me too soon. Word of mouth undoubtedly will have spread the news of your presence all over the county. You may find yourself swamped with more business than you care to handle."

It was an interesting notion, one that captured Jared's attention for the better part of the ride. The area, he had come to learn, was an untapped source of wealth. True, trading in and out of the port was brisk, but nowhere near its full capacity. Transporting pork alone from this county could keep ships busy night and day all year.

The coach made its way south toward the center of town, turning east onto Main Street to pull up before the Inn. There, Jared and Travis descended and entered the whitewashed structure.

"More deals have been struck at these tables than in all the offices in the county, I would wager," Travis commented quietly as they were shown to a table by one of the windows. "It's a meeting place without rival."

Confirmation of this appeared shortly in the stocky form of N. Douglas Winston. In town to see his attorney about selling a piece of property, he stopped by the establishment not only to take lunch, but also to mingle with other planters.

"How are things up your way, Travis?" N. Douglas asked, running a hand along his thinning brown hair. "Heard that you had a bout of illness."

"Unfortunately, that was the case," Travis confirmed. "We lost several workers."

"Damn shame." A grimace pulled at N. Douglas's

139

round face. "I suppose you'll be looking for replacements, then."

"Just as soon as I can."

N. Douglas tipped his head to one side as he suggested, "Why don't you ride on out next week and see if we can't work something out between us."

Travis had always known N. Douglas to be a fair and honest man. He wouldn't mind dealing with him. "I'll do that," he promised, then quickly moved from the sore subject of slaves and the resulting expenses to introduce Jared. "N. Douglas has a place on the James," Travis continued once names and handshakes had been exchanged. "Raises the finest hogs anywhere in the entire county."

"I've heard that Virginia hams are without equal," Jared commented.

N. Douglas preened under the compliment. "You'll get no argument from me, sir."

Travis waved a hand at a vacant chair at the table. "Why don't you join us, N. Douglas. I've mentioned Jared's shipping firm to you. Perhaps you might want to talk some business."

Lunch and business lasted well into the afternoon. As Travis had stated, the common room saw more than its share of bargaining. Jared was quick to note that there was a steady stream of patrons, at least a dozen of whom made a point of being introduced. By the time dusk was approaching, he had arranged to meet with no fewer than six planters in the coming weeks, all extremely interested in broadening their shipping base.

"This day will more than likely prove to be most profitable for you," Travis averred on the ride back to

Swan's Watch.

Jared's brows flicked upward appreciatively. "It should prove profitable for all concerned."

From there, the two fell into an easy discussion of shipping, their conversation touching on various routes as well as foreign ports. It was only as the coach entered the plantation lane that Jared lost his interest in the subject.

His thoughts shifted rapidly from business to Lacy. He had had precious little time during the past hours to consider her strangely cool manner, but he contemplated it now. More to the point, he considered the most expedient means of dealing with Lacy herself. She might have been elusive this morning, but he was not about to let her dance away from him, no matter what the reason. He would ascertain what was bothering her before the night was out.

Unfortunately, his resolve was no match for ill timing and fate. They contrived to keep Lacy out of the house as she helped deliver a baby to one of the slaves. It was nearly seven the next morning when she finally returned to the manor house.

Seeing her exhaustion, Jared did not have the heart to press her for explanations as to her behavior. Patiently he bided his time, deciding they could discuss the matter after she had rested.

He did not count on Lacy's sleeping well into the afternoon. Annoyingly, he and Travis left for a scheduled meeting with Travis's lawyer long before Lacy emerged from her bedroom. Once again, the matter of her unfriendly disposition had to wait.

The appointment with the attorney stretched into

dinner, followed by hours spent in the masculine appreciation of brandy and cigars. While Jared found the company entertaining, he did not in any way abandon thoughts of Lacy. If anything, as the night progressed, he became increasingly resolute in his conviction to speak with her.

Yet, once again, time was a dogged hindrance. The clock in the main entry way of Swan's Watch was chiming one in the morning as he and Travis made their way up the stairs. Speaking with Lacy would have to wait until morning.

Only one thing kept a firm rein on Jared's frustration, and that was his determination. Once he set his mind to something, he normally dispatched any irritating obstacles with quick efficiency. That had not been the case in confronting Lacy, and his tolerance was beginning to chafe at the entire matter. It was with a definite sense of purpose that he left his room the next morning to find her.

Gaye was busy polishing the cherry tables in the front foyer when he descended the stairway. At his inquiry as to Lacy's whereabouts, the young servant proclaimed that Lacy had gone off to the weaving house to inspect some newly woven cloth.

It was only a matter of minutes before he strode past the vegetable garden situated behind the kitchen. From there, purposeful strides carried him to the weaving house at the edge of the wooded grove.

The door to the shop stood open and he entered soundlessly, sweeping the cluttered interior in one all-encompassing look. He found Lacy in the far corner beside a flax wheel, sitting alone, a length of fabric stretch across her lap. At the sight of her, some

142

of his frustration died, to be replaced by a warm contentment.

Seated in profile, her head was bent slightly over her task. She had not noticed his presence yet, and he used a few moments simply to look his fill.

She was perfection. There was no other word to describe the fine-lined contour of her brow and chin, the delicate curve of her cheek or the rare hue of her eyes. The silvery strands of her hair caught and held the sunlight streaming in through the windows, making the soft mass glimmer with a shining radiance.

Throughout all of his travels about the world, he could not remember finding any woman who appealed to him as much as Lacy. She possessed a beauty all her own, a loveliness that was as irresistible as her tender heart and devoted manner. All combined now to draw him toward her.

She raised her head at the sound of his boots on the random planked floor. Instantly, her eyes widened, her lips parting in surprise.

"Jared." His name escaped her lips on a whisper.

He noted her reaction with a slight sense of vexation. Mixed with the shock he saw on her features was a flash of panic, and that strange, enigmatic restraint intended to keep him at arm's length.

Slowly he crossed the small space between them. Now that he had finally caught up with her, and time and circumstances were not conspiring against him, he took his time in broaching the subject that had had him puzzled for days.

"I didn't mean to startle you."

Lacy grasped the length of cotton tightly, searching her soul for a poise she was far from feeling. She was still trying to come to terms with her heartache. To have him here only made the burden all the more impossible to endure.

Remembering to smile, she replied, "You didn't startle me . . . not really." The corners of her lips strove valiantly to maintain the upward curve. They failed the second Jared came down on one knee beside her.

Bowing her head over the yards of cloth once more, she bit her lower lip, trying to evade the magnetic pull of his eyes. She could feel their gray depths coursing over her face as though searching for her innermost secrets.

"I've missed you these last few days," he murmured gently, clearly reading her unease and wanting only to alleviate it. "We've been like two ships on the same ocean, passing each other, but only at a distance."

It was in Lacy's mind that she would have preferred it to go on in that way, with Jared at a far and very *safe* distance. In her own way, she had tried her best to insure that very thing.

"I suppose I am still catching up with all the chores. You know how hectic things can become once you get behind. It never seems to end, seeing to the laundry and cleaning and cooking." She knew she was rambling, but she couldn't seem to stop. "And of course there's the added excitement of the LaRue's ball tonight." How she managed to remember that just now was beyond her.

"Are you tiring yourself out again?"

The concern in his voice speared straight into her heart. "No, not at all," she choked out.

His hand cupped her chin and raised her face toward his. "Then why are you so pale?"

The touch of his fingers was a tortuous bliss. Instinctively, she started to rise, unable to bear the treasured warmth of his hand. But the pressure of his fingers, his very proximity held her in place.

"Lacy . . . ?" His brow furrowed at her reaction.

She kept her gaze lowered, but she felt her composure slip precariously close to tears. Turning her head aside, she freed her chin from his tender grasp. "I'm sure you're mistaken about my coloring. I am . . . quite . . . well."

A muscle ticked along Jared's jaw. Why was she so insistent on feeding him such obvious lies? Irritated by her continued resistance, he stated, "No, you aren't. You haven't been for days. I come near you and you quit the room as fast as you can. I touch you and you try to flee." He surged to his feet, planting his fists on his lean waist. "You won't even look at me."

The edge in his voice stung her pride. Squaring her shoulders, she stared directly up at him.

"Well thank you for at least that much," he commented tightly. He heard the sarcasm in his voice and ground his teeth at his own exasperation. He did not mean to berate her, but she was proving to be extraordinarily stubborn.

In a bid for patience, he scrubbed a hand across the back of his neck, then tried to reason with her again. "Lacy, I'm sorry. You'll have to forgive my annoyance, but you have me worried. You have not been yourself."

"Yes, I have."

"No, you have not. Last week I held you in my arms, we shared more than a circumspect kiss." He ignored the sudden rush of color that stained her face. "You welcomed my touch."

She could not deny the truth of his words. She *did* welcome his touch, and so much more. But it was cruel of him to use that against her when she was so helplessly vulnerable to him.

Coming to her feet, she clutched the cotton yardage to her chest like a feeble armor. "You have no right to throw that in my face."

He started in disbelief. "What the devil do you mean by that?"

"I mean that I am not accustomed to the kind of . . . the kind of . . . goings on in which you are so well versed."

Narrowing his eyes, he concentrated on following her logic. "I am well aware of that."

"Yet you persist with your game."

"What game?"

"The kind of game that only the wordly understand." It was humiliating to have to stand there and explain. But she refused to shrivel up and give into such weakness. "You are not to blame for carrying on as you have. I can only fault myself for allowing you to do so. But from now on, I would appreciate it if you would please turn your attentions elsewhere and leave me in peace."

Jared waded through her indignation to what he thought was the root of the matter. "Are you saying that you believe I have been trifling with you?"

"Haven't you? Isn't that exactly what you've been

doing?" Just saying it aloud broke her tenuous hold on her self-control. Tears flooded her eyes.

The fabric fell from her cold fingers and she surged away, but Jared's hands grasped her by the arms and hauled her back before she could take even a single step.

"Damn it, you're not going to run away from this." Every line of his face was taut.

"Let me go," she cried.

"Not until you've explained what this is all about."

"I already have."

"All you've done is babble on about games, and accuse me of falsehoods."

"Babble?!" Anger joined her embarrassment. "How dare you insult my honest emotions?"

Jared's jaw tightened. "Yes, let's talk about honesty. Tell me why, after weeks of melting in my arms, you suddenly find my attentions unwanted."

She stilled, steeling herself against the love she felt for him. Through her tears, she searched his angry gaze. She couldn't tell him, she could not confess that she had melted in his arms because she loved him. Not when it was all meaningless to him.

Her throat was clogged with tears and misery. Nonetheless, her voice held an unmistakable dignity. "Please, let go of me."

The pain in her voice was like a slap in the face. Instantly, Jared loosened his grip, but he didn't relinquish his hold entirely. His hands hovered above her shoulders while he scrutinized every inch of her face as though he would find sound reasoning there.

"What has happened?" The pain in his voice was reflected in the gray of his eyes.

Emotions spent, only a sadness remained to engulf Lacy. "Perhaps you should ask that of my sister. I'm sure you'll be able to find the answer from her."

She turned then and left the shop, a fresh wave of tears blinding her vision. Stunned, Jared could only stare at her retreating figure, wondering what in the devil she meant.

It came to him in the next pounding thud of his heart. She had accused him of playing games, and now he comprehended exactly the kind of game to which she had referred.

Somehow she knew about Marriette kissing him in the garden. Either she had witnessed it for herself or her sister had boasted of it to her. Either way, Lacy believed that he had been a willing participant.

He swung about, the frustration he had felt earlier a mere pittance compared to what he experienced now. Damn it all to hell, no wonder she couldn't stand the sight of him. In her eyes, he was nothing better than a philandering cad, eagerly pursuing her and then trotting off to snatch kisses from her sister. She believed herself betrayed. The little fool.

He turned on his heel and stalked to the door, intent on going after her and telling her the truth of things. Yet, he stopped, some part of his mind realizing that in his temper, nothing would be accomplished. She was already unwilling to listen to him, and he was sorely tempted to want to shake some sense into her. He could just imagine the impasse they would reach.

Grinding his eyes shut, he exercised all of his self-restraint in an effort to gain control. If he was going to win her back, he needed to be patient and collected. And he needed to give her time to calm down enough to listen to him.

He gave them both until the ball that night.

Chapter Nine

"I can't remember the last time I've been to a ball as grand as this," Marriette sighed excitedly. Practically floating into the LaRue's ballroom in a gown of pink *gros de Naples*, she gave Jared an expectant look, her smile as glittering as the thousands of candles lighting the crystal chandeliers overhead.

Jared acknowledged her glance with a brief nod of his head, but offered no comment. He had nothing of any consequence to say to Marriette. His attention was riveted on Lacy.

Standing beside Travis, she was a breathtaking vision in white silk, and he was entranced by the picture she presented. Her shoulders were bared by the low scooped neckline of her dress, the wide lace edging allowing a tempting glimpse of the shadow between her breasts. The trimness of her waist was accentuated by the pointed bodice and full crinolined skirt. Two deep flounces of lace were charmingly caught up with turquoise roses, a complement for the rose of matching color tucked into the intricate twists of her silver-blond hair.

Jared gazed at her in frank appreciation. He didn't have to scan the room to know that she was the most beautiful woman present, despite the lack of color in her cheeks and the sober line of her lips.

His own lips pulled into a sedate alignment. Since leaving the weaving shop that afternoon, his frustration had dwindled to ashes, the remnants giving rise to a steady, unrelenting conviction. By the end of the night, Lacy would be made to understand *exactly* how things stood between them.

Lacy steadfastly kept her eyes focused straight ahead, studiously ignoring Jared's open regard. Silently she wished to be some place private where she wouldn't be bound by the pressures of polite society to behave as though absolutely nothing was wrong. Instead, she was among hundreds of people, and she was already tired of pretending that her heart was in one solid piece.

A dull ache pounded behind her eyes. Nonetheless, she fixed a pleasant smile on her face, refusing to wallow in self-pity. If this night was to be a trial, then it was her own just desserts for so foolishly allowing herself to fall in love.

Clamping her gloved hands together to keep them steady, she turned to Travis. "I see Jeanne Gail and her parents by the musicians. I think I will pay my respects now."

"If you'll allow me to accompany you, Lacy," Jared proposed, not giving her time to make good another escape.

Her gaze flew to his at the same instant as Marriette's. Neither sister could believe her own ears, but for entirely different reasons. Marriette could not imagine why Jared, after the kiss in the garden, would knowingly wish for Lacy's company. It was incredible, not to mention inconvenient, since she fully intended to use this night to advance her pursuit of the man. Lacy, on the other hand, stood incredulous because she thought she had made it perfectly clear that afternoon that she did not welcome his attentions.

She drew a breath to refuse his offer, but he forestalled her objections. Placing a hand to her elbow, he staked a blatant and irrefutable claim. "I would appreciate your introducing me to our host and hostess."

The fine blue lines of her eyes darkened in a silent testimony to her inner turmoil. Why did he persist in this matter? She did *not* want Jared at her elbow, exuding that powerful aura of masculinity that ate at her senses. She would prefer that he leave her alone . . . that Marriette or Travis make the presentations. But how could she politely refuse him?

Oblivious to her discomfiture, Travis commented, "By all means, Lacy, take Jared on over to meet the LaRues. I'll be along as soon as I hunt down a bourbon." He paused, with a teasing grin, to add in a conspiratorial whisper. "Be warned, Jared, don't let Jeanne Gail waylay you. She's been known to talk a person silly."

It was all Lacy could do to keep from hitting her brother over the head with her fan. Left with no choice but to accept Jared's escort, she clamped her teeth together and headed for the other side of the ballroom, taking the full brunt of Marriette's lethal glare.

Her spirits sank. Everything was going from bad to worse. It wasn't enough that Jared was being perversely stubborn, but Marriette was now horribly angry with her. Any hope that this night might have been enjoyable evaporated.

"It is not necessary for you to retain your hold on my arm, Mister Steele," she forced out quietly. "I will not abandon you in this crush."

Jared peered about the crowded room as though he hadn't noticed her formal use of his surname. "You do have a tendency to run off at times."

His reply provoked her. "I do not run away, sir, I simply do not remain still for folly."

"That's a biased observation. It's a known fact that 'one man's folly is another man's fortune.'"

The line of her back stiffened abruptly. Over her shoulder she gave him a quelling look. "Do not quote your adages to me, sir, not when you would twist them to your own advantage. I suggest, Mister Steele . . ."

"Jared."

". . . *Mister* Steele, that you . . ." But Lacy's suggestion that he go cite his pretty phrases to another woman was cut off by Carter James.

"Well, hello, Lacy," he announced.

She whipped her head about toward Marriette's suitor. It took several seconds for her to clamp down on her ire and focus in on Carter's lean, handsome face. But when she did, she was immensely happy for his presence despite the fact that he was not one of her favorite people.

"Hello, Carter." Try as she might, she could not keep the sigh of relief from her voice.

153

Carter's brown brows arched at the restrained inflection he detected. "As always, it's a pleasure to see you." His almond-shaped eyes crinkled at the corners with a smile.

"It's good to see you again, too, Carter." The steady pressure of Jared's fingers could not be ignored. As angry as she was with him, she could not give into that anger by being rude to Carter. Courtesy dictated that she introduce the two men. "Please, Carter, let me introduce you to our guest, Jared Steele."

Jared extended his hand and found it firmly grasped. "A pleasure, Mister James."

Carter nodded pleasantly. "I've been hearing impressive things about your shipping firm, Mister Steele. Perhaps you and I should sit down one day over a glass of port."

"At your convenience, sir."

"That's the way I like to do business," Carter averred around a deep-throated laugh. "With an emphasis on accommodation and leisure." He chuckled again, studying Jared with renewed interest. "I'll drop around to see you some time next week." He glanced to Lacy. "With your permission, Lacy, of course."

"By all means," she replied. Anything that would keep Jared Steele occupied and away from her suited her just fine.

"Good, then, it's settled." Carter's interest quickly turned to more urbane distractions. "Tell me, Mister Steele, do you play cards?"

Jared smiled readily. "If the stakes are right."

The ease with which Jared replied pricked Carter's

attention. "I believe we could find a game or two in progress right now, if you're of a mind."

It was Lacy's fervent wish that Jared would very much be of such a mind, but it wasn't meant to be.

"Perhaps another time, Mister James," came Jared's decline. "Lacy has been generous enough to agree to squire me through the social amenities."

Lacy was incredulous enough to choke. She shot Jared a damning look. He made it sound as though he had given her a choice in the matter.

"Do not stand on ceremony for me, Mister Steele," she suggested. "I would not dream of keeping you from seeking your amusements where you would." Her eyes darkened tenaciously. "In fact, I insist on it."

Her meaning was crystal clear to Jared. She was all but ordering him to leave her alone, but he wouldn't have thought she would use such a public forum to voice her views. Part of him applauded her bravado in serving up her double-edged edict, but another, less understanding part of him wanted to wring her sweet little neck.

His eyes narrowed slightly. If she was bent on this game of words, then he would make certain she understood the consequences of what she had started.

"Oh, you won't be rid of me that easily." He chuckled, boldly smashing her innuendo with the truth. "Besides, you will no doubt provide me with all the 'amusement' I need."

If they had been standing anywhere other than in the middle of the LaRue's ballroom, Lacy would have slapped his face. *Never* had she been as furious as she was right then. How dare he?! How dare he

155

trifle with her emotions.

A boiling strain began in her chest and spread outward in all direction, making her limbs quiver. She would *not* provide him with any amusement of any kind. Exercising every bit of self-control she possessed, she avowed, "You can only wish, Mister Steele."

Then not caring who she offended, or what either man might think, she jerked her arm from Jared's hand and twirled away, having no idea where she was headed. All she knew was that if she didn't put a distance between them, she would surely erupt into a thousand pieces.

From beside the punch bowl, Marriette observed her sister's progress through the crowd, carefully hiding a malicious smile. Then, one curse after another shot through her mind, damning Lacy for not only snaring Jared's company, but Carter's as well.

Her gaze sliced back to the men. She did not understand the workings of their minds. What could possess either of them to pay Lacy even the slightest notice? It just did not make an ounce of sense. But then, men were horribly ridiculous creatures.

In any event, it wouldn't do for them to be together for too long. She didn't think Jared was the type to kiss and tell, but Carter wasn't always so circumspect. One innocently spoken word . . . from either man . . . could easily jeopardize her plan.

She scrutinized Carter carefully. What was she going to do about him? He was still waiting for her answer to his proposal of marriage. Of course she would have to turn him down, but only after she was assured of marrying Jared. Still, if the unthinkable happened and Jared did not offer for her hand, then her answer to Carter would be yes.

Timing. That was what this all came down to. It would be crucial if she was going to emerge from this scheme victorious.

To her peace of mind, she watched Carter move off toward one of the anterooms, no doubt in search of a game of cards. He did have a penchant for gambling. So be it, if that was what he liked. He was certainly rich enough to play with his money the way he did. She was just glad that he had parted company with Jared.

Her cheeks took on a radiant glow as she glided from her spot. Jared was already striding off in Lacy's direction, and Marriette moved so that her path would intercept his. Graciously she nodded to acquaintances that would detain her, but offered no more than that. In a short moment, she was at Jared's side.

"Has Lacy deserted you?" she lamented sweetly, shaking her head in mock dismay. "I'm sorry, Jared, really I am. You'd think Lacy would have more sense than to leave a guest unattended like this."

The first strains of a waltz floated over their heads as Jared replied, "There is no harm done, Marriette."

"You are so understanding. But I promise you that not all Flemmings are as lacking in manners as Lacy." Her face brightened suddenly. "Why, I refuse to let you stand here by yourself. You shall have my first dance."

Jared's grunt of frustration was nearly audible. Staring hard at Marriette's hand poised in invitation, he was once again caught by the dictates of politeness.

Damn it all to hell, he thought angrily. It was just this type of manipulation by Marriette that had caused his break with Lacy. He looked off to where he had last seen her, but she was no longer in sight. His irritation escalated. Irascibly, he decided that Lacy wasn't the only Flemming sister who needed to realize the full consequence of her actions.

His bow a study in decorum, he took Marriette's hand and led her to the dance floor, but the smile curving his lips did not reach his eyes.

"Isn't this lovely?" Marriette cooed, as Jared swept them about in time to the music.

He ignored her query for a question of his own. "What do you do for an encore?"

Not understanding his meaning, she blinked up at him coyly, tilting her head to one side to afford him a better view of her neck. "I beg your pardon?"

"I asked what you do for an encore."

She still couldn't make sense of his remark, but whatever she was supposed to have done had put a glint in his eyes that was thrilling. An excited shiver skittered along her nerves, turning her smile sultry. "What would you like me to do?"

The laugh that escaped Jared was wholly without humor. "You're good, Marriette." He shook his head, his lips twisting into a snide line. "You're damn good."

Marriette's smile cracked about the edges. Somehow she got the feeling that they were having two different conversations. "Is there something wrong?"

"Nothing that I can't handle. So you like to dance,

158

do you?''

His quicksilver shift in topic put Marriette off her step for an instant, but it was long enough to cause her to flounder slightly. It was only Jared's strong arms that prevented her from stumbling awkwardly.

"Careful," he warned lightly. "I wouldn't want you to make a fool of yourself."

Marriette didn't know if she had just been insulted or not. And Jared's inscrutable face gave her no clues. Hating to think that he was annoyed with her, she let his comment roll off her back. "I love to dance and normally I am much more graceful than I seem to be tonight." Her seductive smile came back full force. "But then, I've never danced with a man who distracts me the way you do, Jared."

"I assume I am supposed to take that as a compliment," he mocked, maneuvering them into the middle of the dance floor.

Marriette leaned closer than was seemly. "That was how it was meant."

He nodded slowly before answering. "Good. I wanted to be certain I understood you properly. I don't want there to be any misconceptions between us."

There was a wealth of promise in the deep, serious tone of his voice and the solemn look in his gray eyes. Her heart lurched excitedly. "I think we finally understand each other perfectly, don't you?"

A brittle smile creased Jared's face as he stared down into the blue of her eyes. Without warning, he stopped dead in his tracks and dropped his arms away.

"We do now." Not giving her so much as a nod of

his head, he turned and left her in the middle of the dance floor.

Marriette felt only shock for the space of a few seconds, and then a vicious, furious anger took hold. Color surged into her face, her hands clenched into shaking fists. He had abandoned her . . . for all to see, while couples twirled about giving her curious looks and amused glances. It was a monstrous insult. And she was not accustomed to being insulted . . . by anyone.

Embarrassed and enraged, she stared around her, damning the sight of knowing smirks and gossiping whispers. It was too much to hope that word of this wouldn't spread like wild fire. She would be the laughingstock of the entire Tidewater. She could well imagine the contemptuous retelling of how Jared had literally deserted her.

Her gaze shot to his retreating back. That *bastard!* That low-life excuse for pig scum! He had ruined all her plans, stealing her dreams of untold wealth and then rubbing her nose in her loss by publicly humiliating her.

Blood pounded through her, glazing everything in sight with a crystalline red. She would not let him get away with this. If she did nothing else on earth to her dying day, she would make him suffer.

With as much dignity as she could muster, she flung her head high and marched toward the edge of the room. Behind her, she thought she heard someone snicker, but she mentally cursed the fool. Let them laugh, let them all laugh. Before she was finished, she would leave them crying in the dust.

Her color high, her fury reduced to a fine

trembling of her limbs, she entered the small parlor off the ballroom. She spotted Carter at once, seated at a table with a group of men playing cards. Making her way past milling couples, she reached the table, just as the men were throwing down their cards.

"I thought I would find you here, Carter James," she complained prettily, smiling an equally pretty smile.

Carter glanced up in surprise. At the sight of her voluptuous figure straining against the fabric of her dress, his look of surprise turned to one of bold appreciation.

"Marriette, you're looking lovely this evening."

She flipped open her fan and waved it teasingly. "I've been waiting all night to hear you say that." She pushed her lower lip into a becoming pout. "But you've been playing cards instead of filling my head with your flattery."

Her quip drew chuckles from the men. "If it's flattery you're after, Miss Flemming," one suggested, "I would be more than happy to oblige."

She demurred coquettishly. "That is such a sweet suggestion, but I really had my heart set on Carter."

Not a man at the table could resist Marriette's playful entreaty. They exchanged knowing glances as Carter pocketed his winnings and rose to his feet.

"Gentlemen, if you will excuse me," he intoned, his smile blatantly smug. Placing a hand to Marriette's elbow, he led her toward the ballroom. But short of entering, Marriette stopped and laid a hand against his chest.

"Oh, Carter, I don't want to go back in there," she pleaded sweetly, dropping her gaze to his mouth in open invitation. "I've had about all the music and crowd I can take for a while. Can't we find some place . . . private?"

Carter's brows flicked upward. Her suggestion, combined with the sensual cast of her features, sent his blood pounding. "Whatever you wish, my dear," he murmured.

They exited the room through a side door, skirting the main entrance hall by following a short passage to a servant's entrance. Moments later, they were outside on the far side of the formal gardens, all but concealed by the shadows of towering elms.

"This is just too wicked," Marriette began, but her words were stemmed when Carter pulled her against his chest and crushed his mouth to hers. His tongue forced its way between her lips, snatching her breath and filling her senses with the taste of the brandy he had been drinking.

"Carter," she exclaimed, dragging her mouth away. The wet texture of his mouth sent a shudder of revulsion through her, but she tamped it down, forcing herself to cling tightly to his shoulders. "Oh, Carter, you're making my head spin."

As though he hadn't heard her, one of his hands lowered to the small of her back, pressing her against his swelling hardness. His other hand grasped the fullness of her breast.

"That's what you wanted, wasn't it?" he muttered thickly. "For me to make your head spin and your bones melt." He brought his mouth to hers again, sealing off the low moan that came from her throat.

It was what she wanted, but it wasn't happening. There was none of the giddy rush she felt in Jared's arms, the exciting tingling that turned her whole body to liquid. All she had now was an appalling hardness pressing into her belly and the revolting touch of Carter's hand pulling her bodice aside.

She clenched her jaw, hating the feel of his fingers capturing her nipple. An overwhelming urge to shove him away swamped her, but she steadfastly resisted, reminding herself of his wealth. It would all be hers, down to the last penny and grain of corn. And then there wouldn't be a person alive who would dare laugh at her. And that included Jared Steele.

She freed her mouth, gasping for breath. "Oh, Carter, Carter, I love you. I was such a fool not to have agreed to marry you right off."

His head came up, his brown eyes riveted to hers. "Then you'll marry me?"

"Yes." She nodded, forcing her features into a semblance of delight. "Yes, I want to marry you more than anything else in this world."

An obscene grin split Carter's face. "It took you long enough to make up your mind." He ground his hips against her softness, assuaging only a small portion of his need.

"Only because I wanted to be certain. I'm not going into this marriage lightly, Carter." She paused, drawing out the effect of her words. "I want to make you happy."

"You have done that, my sweet." His fingers squeezed the soft flesh of her breast. "You have most certainly done that." He fastened his mouth to her neck, riding the aching wave of pleasure that coursed through him.

Marriette clenched her eyes shut, blocking out the

163

sight of Carter's body looming over her. She'd let him have his way for a moment or two longer before she put a stop to his pawing. She might have agreed to become his wife, but that did not mean she was going to consummate the marriage right then.

Marriage to Carter. The reality of it sank in all at once. She was going to live the life she had always wanted. A beautiful mansion with a housekeeper and servants just waiting to do her bidding. New clothes and expensive jewels. No more Swan's Watch, no more Travis going on about every dime they spent. And no more Lacy, with her sickeningly righteous air.

A smile actually worked its way to her lips. Stupid little Lacy. She would spend the rest of her life in servitude to the Watch, and have nothing more to show for herself than a broken back and a face lined by the years.

The thought was too delicious for words.

Standing near a screen of tall potted plants, Lacy stared at Travis beside her. She couldn't help but worry about his flushed face and too loud voice. Her gaze dropped to the glass of bourbon he held loosely in one hand.

She wasn't keeping track, but he had had two drinks in the short time they had been standing here, and there was no telling how many he had had before that. Her brow creased slightly. This wasn't like Travis. He usually handled his liquor, imbibing moderately and for purely social reasons. But now, from the look of him, he was well on his way to getting drunk.

"Travis, is there something wrong?" she asked quietly.

His head swerved toward her, his gaze following sluggishly behind. Only by blinking repeatedly could he focus clearly on Lacy. "What could possibly be wrong?" he questioned in return, thinking he was damned clever to have heard her correctly.

"I don't know, Travis, but I've never seen you drink like this before."

"Haven't you?" He thought about that, looking for all the world as though he was pondering the meaning of life. "Yes, I suppose you're right. But then again, I've never had good cause to overindulge to any extent."

Turquoise eyes filling with concern, Lacy asked, "What gives you cause now?"

He replied with a laugh of self-mockery. Lifting his glass, he toasted himself. "I give you Travis Flemming, the man who will long be remembered as the Flemming to ruin Swan's Watch."

As soon as the words left his mouth, his derisive humor died, the lines of his face falling into a despondent mask. He glared at the amber liquid in his glass, but he saw only his own sense of impending failure. "I've ruined everything, Lacy."

Lacy stared at her brother in a mixture of alarm and denial. "Travis, you haven't ruined anything."

He turned his face away, rejecting her words. "You know as well as I do how badly things are going. And God only knows how much worse it will get once I lay out the money to buy more slaves."

"But that doesn't mean we'll lose the Watch," Lacy reasoned. "We'll just have to work harder this year than most, that's all."

"But what if the crops fail, what if we're struck by another sickness?" He brought his anxious gaze back to hers. "We can't afford more losses of that kind."

"No, we can't. But neither can we go on saying what if, making assumptions about what may or may not occur." She laid her hand on his forearm in a silent gesture of support. "The Watch has never let us down, Travis. There is no reason to think that she will now. You have to have faith, both in the land and yourself."

He gave a chuckle that was laced with scorn. "I wish I had your faith and your strength." He gazed sadly into her shining eyes. "You always were the strong one, believing undoubtedly, unconditionally."

His despair made her heart ache. "I believe in you, Travis."

"Do you?"

"Yes," she said in all honesty. "But you're too hard on yourself. If the crops fail it won't be through any shortcoming on your part. And if we run out of money, it won't be because of your management. You've always tried your best."

Seeing the trust so clearly visible on her face, he could almost believe her. He wanted to believe her. "You're a rare woman, little sister," he avowed, letting his doubts be erased temporarily by her confidence.

"I don't know about that."

"Well, I do. And you're right." He squared his shoulders, realizing that nothing would be gained tonight by crying into his glass. "We'll take each day

166

as it comes and do the best we can."

"That's all we can ever do."

Nodding, he shoved away from the troubles hanging over his head. "Come on, why don't we see if we can enjoy the rest of this ball."

They strolled along the perimeter of the room until they joined a group of friends. Enthusiastic greetings and jovial rejoinders beckoned them into the amiable circle. Still, Lacy's mind was far from settled and she listened to the easy banter with only half an ear.

It disturbed her that Travis was so uncertain of his own abilities. She had always assumed that he was as confident as he appeared. It was also upsetting that he was so unsure of the Watch.

"I hope that frown is not directed at me, Lacy," N. Douglas commented lightly.

Lacy snapped out of her private musings, smiling apologetically. "I'm sorry, N. Douglas, my mind was busy with something else."

Colin Wentworth, one of the owners of the local bank, lifted both hands in a shrug. "I would say then, Miss Lacy, that you need to occupy your mind elsewhere, for you are far too pretty to be going about looking so glum."

"You are indeed looking especially pretty tonight, Miss Lacy," Lt. Aaron Cole confirmed. "It's a good thing that Fortress Monroe is on the other side of Hampton Roads, or else I might be found derelict in my duties."

Lacy peered at the familiar faces about her and felt her cheeks pinken for the first time that night. She was not comfortable with the flattery, and an embarrassed laugh escaped her lips. "Lieutenant, Hampton Roads is a considerable body of water to cross. I would not have you making such a trip on my account."

Jeanne Gail rolled her eyes, giving her limp brown curls a flamboyant toss. "Well, I would be absolutely tickled to have a soldier sailing all that way just for me."

"Soldiers do not sail," Colin corrected teasingly. "Soldiers march about on land."

"That's right, Jeanne Gail," N. Douglas added. "It's the sailors who do the sailing around."

Jeanne Gail waved all their talk away with a delicate hand. "Oh, enough of all this military talk. This is a party, gentlemen."

Lieutenant Cole pulled sharply on the cuffs of his blue uniform. "Well spoken." Turning to Lacy he nodded. "Miss Lacy, if I may have this dance?"

A deep voice sounded from behind him. "I'm afraid this dance is already claimed by me, Lieutenant."

Lacy stiffened, her gentle smile dropping from her lips like a lead sinker. She spun on her heel and stared straight up into Jared's ruggedly handsome face.

Why was he doing this? She had not thought him mean-spirited or dull-witted. Then why would he not leave her in peace? Was it nothing more than stubbornness, or was it simply that he could not admit defeat where she was concerned? Whatever the reason, she was not going to allow him to bully her about anymore, not when her feelings were being stomped on in the process.

"I do not remember promising this dance to

anyone, Mister Steele," she averred soundly, her voice backed by every ounce of indignation coursing through her.

One side of Jared's mouth quirked with a tight grin. "Then perhaps I should refresh your memory." And with that, he clamped her wrist in an unbreakable hold and pulled her away to the dance floor.

"Oh, my." Jeanne Gail sighed, watching Jared stride off, Lacy firmly in tow. "Did you see that?"

"Lacy didn't appear very pleased," N. Douglas observed worriedly.

But Jeanne Gail silently disagreed. It was just too romantic for words, the way the tall Yankee practically swept Lacy off her feet. Oh, what she wouldn't do to be in Lacy's shoes right then.

Lacy's satin shoes were at that very second dragging across the highly polished floor. As surreptitiously as possible, she tried to extricate her wrist from Jared's grasp, but all she managed to do was strain her hand.

"Let . . . me . . . go," she demanded in a furious whisper.

His answer was to swing her about into the imprisoning circle of his arms. "Smile, Lacy," he commanded, his voice as dangerous as his expression was light. "You don't want to create a scene."

The room spun around her as Jared swept them into the headiness of the music. But the magical strains were lost on Lacy. All her attention, every fiber and nerve coalesced into a white-fire anger.

"*Who* do you think you are?" she ground out.

He grinned down at her. "Smile."

Her lips curved upward in a frozen mockery of

humor. "I do not want to smile at you. I do not want to dance with you. I . . . do . . . not . . . want . . . to . . . talk . . . to . . . you."

"Fine, then you can listen," he returned, unperturbed.

Anger, hurt, frustration all collided in Lacy's chest. She tried to snatch away from his hold, but his hands tightened about her.

"Oh, no you don't," he muttered in her ear. "There are a few things we need to settle between us right now."

Breathing heavily, she declared, "We settled everything this afternoon."

"The only thing that was settled was the fact that you're too stubborn to listen to reason. And that I was a fool to let you go before you heard the truth."

Her blood pounded furiously, alternately flushing her body with heat and then dousing it with ice. She knew what the truth was. She had seen it with her own eyes, and it was a pain she would live with for the rest of her life.

"You have no right to speak of truth, not when you go about proclaiming your devotion to me and in the next breath hold my sister in your arms for your kisses." She hadn't meant to blurt it out that way, so plainly that her indignation was vanquished before an unrelenting agony of the heart.

The strength of purpose that had carried her thus far was rapidly evaporating. "Let me go," she whispered desperately, unable to look anywhere but at his shirtfront.

Jared swore under his breath at the tearful catch in her voice. Beneath his hands he could feel her trembling and he knew that she was losing control. Swiftly, he directed their path to where there was a thinning in the dancing, then strode up to the LaRues, never once releasing his hold on Lacy's arm.

Dismally, Lacy knew she should be protesting for all she was worth. But she was too busy fighting back stinging tears to object to his high-handedness. She silently listened to Jared make their excuses for leaving so early, claiming Lacy was not feeling well, before he drew her through the opened doors and along the brick path that circled to the front of the house. All the while, she concentrated on gaining her composure for the argument that was sure to come.

Head lowered, she didn't take note of their whereabouts until the sound of horses captured her attention. Startled, she looked up and discovered that Jared was heading straight for their closed carriage.

"What are you doing?" she asked, her voice underscored with panic.

Jared's reply was an ominous tightening of his fingers on her elbow. In three long strides he gained the vehicle and before she could utter a sound he lifted her easily and deposited her inside.

"Miss Flemming isn't feeling well," he told the waiting driver. "I'm seeing her home."

With wide disbelieving eyes, she watched Jared climb in and sit opposite her. In seconds, the carriage lurched forward.

Moonlight seeped into the space between them, gilding the taut lines of Jared's body and the unyielding planes of his face.

"Now," he said in a distinctly quiet voice. "Let's talk about the truth."

Chapter Ten

Lacy swallowed the knot of fear that was lodged in her throat. Jared's fixed stare was daunting in its ferocity, filling her with a cold dread.

"Jared." She managed to get his name out past trembling lips. "What . . . what are you doing?"

"I'm taking you back to Swan's Watch," he replied in concise, hard tones.

"But you can't," she declared, shaking her head. "You can't do this."

Leaning forward, he impaled her with a dangerous look. "You think not?" One black brow rose slowly, the subtle gesture telling her more eloquently than words what he thought of her denial.

She sat back in dismay, too stunned to do more than stare back in confusion and mounting ire. His effrontery was beyond anything she had ever dealt with, and she wasn't certain what to do. A very conscious part of her mind considered screaming for Thomas, the coachman, to stop at once. But she was equally of a mind to yank open the carriage door and jump to freedom.

Reasonably, she didn't think that either move would be very effective. Jared had a way of turning every situation to his own advantage. This one was no exception. He would most likely thwart her efforts as easily as he had arranged their exit from the LaRues' home; as easily as he had captured her heart . . . and then blithely destroyed it.

Her chin came up. "What precisely do you intend to accomplish by abducting me this way?"

Jared noted the stubborn set of her jaw. At any other time he would have admired her show of spirit, but his patience was stretched far too thin for him to indulge in such a tolerant concession.

Folding his arms across his chest, he stated, "Enough of your injured air, Lacy. I know you think you have just cause, but you don't."

"I have every right to be angry," she shot back, eyes blazing. "You have accused me of being stubborn, sir, but you could teach the meaning to a mule. I have told you repeatedly to leave me alone, yet you won't. Instead, you embarrass me in front of my friends, provoke me before my family. And now this!" She flung a hand wide to indicate her present circumstances. "I want you to stop this carriage right now and take me back to the party."

"No."

That single word had all the effect of an iron fist crashing through fragile porcelain. Lacy's anger fractured into ragged shards of fury. Clenching her fists, she cried, "Let me out of this carriage at once. You have no right to treat me like this. I may have been a fool to have let you sweep me off my feet, but I will not let you humiliate me any more than you already have. I will not . . ."

In one sure, swift lunge, Jared took hold of Lacy's shoulders and waist and dragged her from her seat, hauling her across his lap. Her words ended on a startled cry, changing to a gasp when his arms clamped about her, holding her prisoner against the immovable wall of his chest.

"You're right, you are a fool," he ground out. Then with no warning, he lowered his head and captured her lips for a scalding kiss of burning intensity.

For all of three seconds, shock held Lacy still. But her benumbed brain quickly responded to the feel of the backs of her thighs pressed intimately to his lap, and to the warm insistent pressure of his mouth on hers.

She pushed at his chest, straining away, but to no avail. His arms held her as securely as bands of steel. "Don't," she choked out, turning her head away.

"Hold still, sweet fool," he muttered. One hand rose and took hold of her chin, angling her face back up to his.

A low groan of dismay sounded deep in her throat. She couldn't bear to have him kissing her, not when it meant nothing to him. "Let me go," she demanded, twisting uselessly against his powerful body.

"Not until I've told you what you need to hear."

"I don't need to hear anything from you."

"Not even that I love you?"

The turquoise of her eyes darkened to indigo as she searched his face. That he would taunt her so cruelly

174

speared her heart with pain. "That is nothing but a convenient phrase, intended for your own gain. Although why you continue to plague me I will never know."

In a bid for control, Jared ground his teeth, reminding himself that he would never make her see reason if his temper got the better of him.

"Lacy," he began again quietly. "I love you."

She made another attempt to free herself but Jared's arms tightened. "How can you say that when I saw you . . ."

"You saw Marriette kissing me."

"You're playing with words."

"You saw *Marriette* kissing *me*," he repeated, drilling his gaze into hers. "But you never saw me thrusting her aside and walking off, wanting nothing to do with her." The fingers at her chin gentled to slip back along her jaw and into the silken strands of her hair. "What could I possibly want with your sister? She is a shrewd, selfish woman, bent on finding the richest husband available. She would no more know how to love than she would know how to fly."

Lacy drew in one labored breath after another. He sounded so utterly sincere. And the fierce lines etched into his face were evidence of the intensity of his feelings. Frowning, she gazed silently into his glittering gray eyes, afraid to hope.

Jared read her doubt and confusion as he would an open book. "Lacy, my sweet little fool, think. Think back on all those moments I held you in my arms, think on each and every kiss we've shared, and trust your instincts." He held her closer, fitting her soft

175

curves into perfect harmony with his solid muscles. "I never played you false. From the moment I first saw you, I've wanted only you."

She had always trusted her instincts . . . until she had witnessed the scene between him and Marriette in the garden. Until that moment, she had believed that Jared truly cared for her, maybe even loved her. Until that moment, she hadn't had any reason to think that he was capable of deceit.

But she knew that her sister was.

"Jared?" Her heart beat thunderously. "Is it true? You love me?"

He shook his head as though to clear it of some enigmatic bewilderment. "Do you think I would bother myself trying to explain all of this if I didn't?" The gray of his eyes burned with a fiery light. "Do you think I would even give your feelings a second thought if you weren't the most important person in my life? I love you. Do you understand, you impossibly stubborn, ridiculously sweet little fool?"

He tenderly brushed his lips over hers, coaxing her response as he coaxed her acceptance of the truth. The touch was butterfly light and as honest as the moonbeams filtering through the windows, bathing them in a silvery luster.

Lacy's breath mingled with his, a warm exchange that enchanted and soothed and laid bare the disillusionment she had carried within her. It had all been a mistake, her heart cried. A horrible, painful mistake.

"Oh, Jared," she whispered against his lips. "I'm so sorry."

His mouth slanted over hers, and she gave herself

up to his embrace. All the love she had been holding inside burst free, filling her with the most wondrous need to draw him near. She had never thought to hold him so again, to have her heart beating against his. She had cried into her pillow at night, mourning the loss of the splendor to be found in his embrace.

"I love you, Jared," she whispered.

He gazed at her adoringly, drinking in the sight of her flushed cheeks and rosy lips. She was so beautiful and loving that his chest tightened in an aching clench. The last days had been an agony and he silently cursed the deceit that had nearly cost them their happiness.

"Say it again," he prompted.

"I love you." She sealed the vow by pressing her lips to his.

Her innocent ardor sent a flood of desire streaking into the pit of his belly. He gathered her closer and reveled in the feel of her breasts pressed to his chest. The womanly softness enticed his senses, inflaming him with a purely masculine need.

Lacy's breath caught in her throat as his hand captured the fullness of her breast. Helplessly, she arched against his hand, unable to contain the sigh of rapture that escaped her lips. His touch bewitched her, making her insides turn to liquid while her skin felt too hot to bear. Shivers raced through her and collected deep in the core of her.

Jared felt the tremors that shook her and gloried in her ardent response. From the very start, he had sensed a passion in her that had lain dormant. Now the elemental maleness in him needed to set that passion free.

He kissed the slim column of her throat, pausing to gently bite the flesh where her pulse beat frantically. All the while, his fingers unerringly released her breast from the fabric of her gown and teased the pink nipple to a hardened bud.

"Jared," she exclaimed softly, gasping at the sensations that emanated from beneath his palm. She clung to his shoulders, holding on as though her world would spin away.

"I love you, Lacy" he murmured hoarsely against the curve of her shoulder. With every fiber of his being he loved her as he had never loved anyone in his entire life. His mind was consumed with the essence of her, the generosity of her spirit, her strength, her enticing femininity.

He lowered his head and drew the nipple into his mouth, savoring the feel and taste of her. She was perfection, like the finest wine to be had. And like that enticing wine, one taste only created a desire for one more sip and then another and another. Urgently his fingers kneaded the swelling flesh for his tongue's caress, his body and mind pleasured by the intrinsic womanliness to be found in her lush bounty.

A shimmering flame curled deep into Lacy's stomach. In an unconscious gesture, she reached up and gently cradled his face between her hands, unwilling to relinquish the intimate feel of his mouth. Instinctively, she offered herself up to his touch, and in doing so, offered herself up to the man himself. The bliss he was making her feel was unlike anything she had ever known and she wanted it to go on forever.

She gave a small inarticulate cry when he raised his

head. But his lips found hers again and a different kind of bliss emerged when his tongue caressed hers. He stroked and explored the velvety interior of her mouth, and she gave without restraint. Desire eroded her senses, and she returned the silken foray, gasping when Jared groaned and twisted his mouth feverishly over her own.

Her innocent responses inflamed him to new heights of passion. Against the softness of her thighs, he was hard and pulsing with white hot need, and each and every move of her body only increased that need tenfold.

His tongue plunged into her mouth, retreated then plunged again in a rhythm that was in itself an assuagement for the molten ache in his loins. But the relief was short-lived and once again he was claimed by the necessity for more.

His hand curved over her hip and eased the yards of dress and petticoats away. Through the thin fabric of her drawers he could feel the heat of her flushed skin, beckoning him like a moth to a flame. Gently he parted her thighs and slid his fingers through the opening in the underwear, finding the moist heat of her most delicate flesh.

For the space of a heartbeat, Lacy thought she would die from the most glorious pleasure imaginable. Any shock she might have experienced at so intimate a caress was overridden by sheer desire. Her breath caught in her lungs and her senses swirled with tension so luxurious that it was frightening. She curled in on herself, her head sliding from Jared's shoulder into the crook of his neck. The scent of his tangy cologne engulfed her, just as his body surrouned her with heat and strength.

Her lips parted as his fingers skillfully explored her hidden secrets at the apex of her thighs. A yearning built with each passage of his probing fingers and instinctively she raised her hips, seeking something she couldn't even begin to define.

Driven by passion and love, she sought his mouth with her own, running her tongue along his lower lip. Her breathing became his, his heat her own. A little incoherently, she realized that they were melding into one person . . . until Jared stiffened suddenly and yanked his head away.

Startled, Lacy stared up at his taut bearing, wondering what was wrong. But before she could even voice her question, he levered her off his lap and onto the seat beside him.

"Damn," he muttered under his breath. With deft movements, he adjusted her bodice into a neat and modest order, arranging her breasts back into the confines of her dress.

Her eyes wide, every muscle and nerve trembling, she whispered, "Jared, why did . . . what . . . ?" Words failed her.

Not trusting his voice, fighting back a near desperate need, Jared ground his teeth and gave her the only answer he was capable of giving. He took hold of her chin and turned her face so that she could see out the window. At that point she realized that the carriage was pulling up to the front door of her house.

Thomas brought the horses to a stand and Jared stepped down. He turned and grasped Lacy by the waist, lifting her down beside him, but her legs refused to hold her. His arms caught her and swept her high against his chest.

"Take the carriage back for Mister Flemming," he told Thomas over his shoulder as he strode up the front steps. Adroitly, he managed the door before kicking it shut behind him.

The entryway lay darkened, the blackness alleviated by a single brace of candles on a side table. It was all the light Jared needed to cross to the stairs and ascend to the second floor, carrying his precious burden close to his heart. He made short work of reaching his room and stepping within.

The glow of a low fire in the grate cast the room into a muted blend of grays. The silhouette of the four-poster bed stood a silent vigil as Jared let Lacy slip down the length of his body. Her breasts came to rest against his chest, the soft curve of her belly snuggled to his hardened flesh.

He sucked in a strained breath. His blood had not been cooled by the untimely interruption. If anything his craving to make her his had only increased. Yet he hesitated to continue, wanting to prolong this moment and commit every subtle nuance to memory.

He held her tightly in his embrace, and wondered how he had ever been so lucky to have found this rare woman. She was a fascinating combination of femininity and strength, laughter and seduction, pride and modesty. And extraordinary beauty and ingenuous passion.

He lowered his head and kissed her fervently, pressing the small of her back to his hips and letting her know the extent of his hunger. She responded by arching upward, entwining her hands about the

181

corded muscles of his neck and drawing his head closer. The kiss deepened, intensified and then suddenly spiraled out of control.

Their tongues met in a feverish play that left them both breathless. Their surroundings became meaningless, their clothes a hindrance, and the only thought that was of any significance was that they end what they had started in the carriage.

Jared released the buttons on the back of her gown as he trailed a line of kisses down her neck. With his mouth, he eased aside the straps of her chemise, exposing her satiny flesh by small degrees. Only when her corset became an obstacle, did he loosen his hold and step back.

He parted the front of her corset much as he had done once before. The fastenings were released quickly and then corset and dress were allowed to drop softly to the floor. Nimble movements saw chemise and petticoats join their companions. And in only a matter of seconds, whisper-thin drawers also pooled at Lacy's feet, leaving her covered only by the radiant glow of the fire's embers. And Jared's boldly masculine gaze.

Slowly his eyes traced every curve and hollow of her body, and for a moment he thought he would drop to his knees. He had spent too many sleepless nights imagining what treasures lay hidden beneath Lacy's clothing, but nothing in his dreams had readied him for the splendor he now saw.

Trim shoulders gave way to the lush fullness of her breasts. A graceful curve fashioned her waist and gently flared hips. A thatch of blond hair nestled at the juncture of her thighs, and below were thighs and calves whose contours were finely shaped.

Blushing fiercely, Lacy felt Jared's gaze like she would his hand stroking over her body. The gleaming gray stare rested on her shoulders and her skin burned; it lowered to her breasts and her nipples hardened; it coursed below her belly and her insides melted with the most luxuriant heat. Instinct made her want to raise her hands and shield herself from view, but a new, budding sensuality that she had never ever felt gloried in her standing naked before the man she loved.

She closed the small space between them and tilted her face upward. Jared needed no more invitation than that. He crushed her to him, slanting his mouth hungrily, searchingly across hers, plunging his tongue into her mouth even as he picked her up and stepped to the bed. He laid her down with the most infinite of care, never once relinquishing her lips.

As he braced himself above her, a low groan lodged in his throat. He wasn't prepared for her unabashed response any more than he was prepared for the feel of her skin. At every turn she surprised him, enticed him . . . and made him want her as he had never wanted another, until he thought he would go mad if he didn't bury himself in her heated softness.

He reared up off the bed in one lithe move. Lacy's muted cry of disappointment floated about him as he stripped off his clothes. But it was to the sound of her contented sigh that he returned to the bed and lowered himself atop her.

His heart stopped for an infinitesimal fraction of a second. Along every inch of his body he could feel her curves boring into him, and he had to grind his eyes shut to keep from losing control. He forced himself to take several deep, steadying breaths before he opened his eyes. When he did, Lacy once again provided him with a sense of wonder.

"You look like you have just been granted your fondest wish," he murmured in a husky voice, amazed by the contented smile that graced her lips.

"I think I have," she whispered back, awed and pleased by the feel of his body pressed to her own. The differences between them fascinated her and she contemplated each in its turn. The thick mat of black hair on his hard chest, the steely breadth of his shoulders, long sinewy legs entwined with her own, and a boldly aroused hardness. They were all foreign to her, but all combined, they created a natural compliment to her body.

Her discovery widened her smile.

"What is so amusing, sweet little fool?" he asked, flicking the corner of her lips with his tongue.

"Nothing," she breathed. "I just never knew what it would be like." His tongue teased the other corner. "I like the way you feel against me."

Her words made his heart wrench within him. Quickly, all thought of talking and teasing was laid asunder. The tormenting play had given way to an urgency that could no longer be denied.

He brought his mouth fully to hers, tasting her hunger as he tasted his own, while his hand brushed downward from her stomach to the tightly curling hair. Gently, insistently, he parted her thighs and claimed the moist heat that awaited him.

Currents of piercing pleasure raced through Lacy's entire body, drawing a strangled sigh into her throat. His searching fingers charted her sweet territory and helplessly her hips surged upward, seeking relief from the coil of tension that built inside her. She barely noticed the slight shift of his body as the intimate touch of his fingers was replaced by the hard, heated flesh between his legs.

Jared's breath escaped on a low groan as he lifted her hips to receive him. Fighting off his own rampaging desires, he carefully eased forward and joined himself to her.

Lacy stiffened as he entered her, but the slight pain dissipated rapidly, leaving her with the most incredible sensation of being filled. That she could hold him within her was a wondrous thought and it acted on her senses as effectively as his mouth on hers. Wanting more of the extraordinary feeling, she pressed upward.

Her movement nearly brought Jared to the brink. Muscles clenched in restraint, he moved within her, surging forward and then retreating in deepening strokes, building the tension in Lacy until she was clinging to his shoulders and gasping for breath.

Lacy was helpless against the storm of passion Jared was creating. The coil of tension inside her grew, intensified, throbbed to an aching, unbearable tautness. And when she didn't think she could bear it a second longer, it finally burst apart in a luminous rush of ecstasy. Waves of pleasure cascaded through her, caressing her every nerve, and dragging Jared's name from her lips.

The pulsing of her body around him took Jared to the limit of his control. Kissing her with a tender fury, he thrust repeatedly and gave himself up to molten desire.

Heartbeats slowed and breathing calmed, yet neither moved. Their breaths mingled with the fleeting kisses each gave the other.

"I love you," Lacy finally murmured against his lips.

A wicked, teasing smile stretched the firm line of Jared's mouth. "Considering where I am at this moment"—he urged his hips forward—"I should certainly hope so."

A blush stole up Lacy's neck into her cheeks at the reminder that his body was still tenderly joined to hers. Seeing the proof of her embarrassment, Jared expelled a breath of disbelief.

"Lacy, you're blushing . . . *now?*" After the intimacy of what they had shared, he found it humorous that she would pinken at so harmless a remark. He chuckled warmly. "There is no need for embarrassment. It is misplaced between us."

He smoothed the fine wisps of silvery-blond hair back off her forehead and his expression sobered. Solemn lines etched his forehead as he gazed intently into her eyes. "I love you, Lacy. If I died now I would be a contented man, save for one thing."

"What is that?" she asked, his serious manner making her blink in wonder.

"I want you for my wife."

Lacy's eyes widened enormously. "You want to marry me?"

He gave her an incredulous look. "Did you think I would take you to my bed if I didn't intend to marry you? If I had only wanted your body I could have seduced you weeks ago."

A demure smile came to her lips. "As it is, you seduced me now."

"Only because I had made up my mind that I intended to marry you."

"When did you decide that?"

"When you collapsed in my arms that day I returned from my ship. I carried you up to your bed and knew that I wanted to carry you to my own bed. Not that once, but for always and for years to come."

Lacy looked away, nibbling her lower lip. "And then I nearly spoiled everything by not trusting you."

As much as Jared did not want to discuss Marriette, he knew that it was necessary. Carefully, he eased from Lacy's body and then shifted their positions so that he held her in the crook of his arm and her head rested on his shoulder.

"I'll say this once, Lacy, and then put it behind us. I have never given your sister more than a passing glance. As it is, if it weren't for the fact that she is your sister, I wouldn't even extend her common courtesy." He soothed his fingertips over the curve of her shoulder. "You were a fool to have so little faith in me. I think I have loved you nearly from the first moment I met you."

"But I didn't know that," she said in a miserable voice.

"Which is why you are not to blame for this affair. Unfortunately, before I could tell you how I felt, Marriette enacted her little ploy and all this trouble ensued."

Lacy sighed raggedly. "I am sorry for not trusting you."

He rolled to his side, bracing his weight on his

187

forearm. "It's over and done with," he vowed. "And I won't waste another minute thinking about it. I have more important matters to tend to."

Glad to have the misery behind her, Lacy gave herself up to the happiness coursing through her. Tilting her head to one side, she slid her hands up his chest to his neck.

"What important matters?" she queried.

"To start with, you didn't say if you would marry me."

A full smile burst forth on her face. "Yes," she cried. "Oh, yes," She laughed for the pure joy of the moment and hugged him fiercely. "I don't think I have ever been as happy as I am right now."

"And if you die this instant you will be a contented woman?" he teased, rejoicing in her bliss.

"Yes, except for one thing. I want you for my husband."

"The sooner the better." He kissed her lingeringly. "I hope you aren't planning a prolonged engagement. I can tell you I will go quietly insane waiting to make you my wife. I want to know that you belong solely to me and I to you." He couldn't suppress his one-sided grin. "Now set a date for the wedding or I will do it for you, but make it soon. I wish to be married before we return to Connecticut."

"Connecticut?"

"Yes, you know that little state somewhere north of here."

A ripple of cold ran down Lacy's spine. She hadn't thought about where they would be living. But somewhere in the back of her mind she had sensed that it would not be Connecticut.

188

"Lacy?" Jared searched her grim face. "What is it?"

"I . . ." She couldn't get the words out. In truth, she didn't know what to say. "You want . . . want to live in Connecticut?"

"That's where my home is."

Of course, he was right. His house and parents and siblings were all there, as well as his business. It was only natural that he would want to live there.

Perhaps it was ridiculous on her part, but she had never thought of living anywhere other than the Watch. She had never sought the attention of men, so marriage had always seemed only a vague possibility. And she had been content with that, for she loved Swan's Watch. It was part of her life. It was part of who she was.

A streak of anguish shot through her. How could she leave? She had cared and loved and nurtured the Watch as though it had been her own child. And at the moment, that child was in need of help. The finances were less than secure, the crops were in jeopardy, and Travis lacked the confidence to see it through and set it all to rights.

Yet Jared expected her, and rightly so, to live wherever he did. And that was Connecticut.

"I . . . I need time, Jared. The situation here is not good. I can't just leave Travis to face it all by himself."

"Travis is a grown man. He'll manage."

Two hours ago, before Travis had spilled out his fears, Lacy might have agreed. But she had listened to his doubts about his own inadequacies, and she wondered if he could in truth manage the Watch on his own.

"But what if he can't handle all the responsibilities? Marriette never was and never will be any help. He could lose the Watch."

Jared had to give credit to Lacy's reasoning. It had been obvious to him from the beginning that she was the plantation's real source of strength. But she could not go on forever coming to her brother's aid, sacrificing her own future for his.

"Sooner or later, Travis is going to have to deal with problems on his own."

"I know that, but if I could just help him through the problems the Watch faces right now, I would feel better."

His black brows slanted into deep diagonal slashes. "All right, what if you do stay and help him through this crisis? I can be that patient and wait. But you know as well as I that any plantation or business is nothing but one crisis after another. What will you do then? Wait to solve that problem and then the next and the next?"

Some instinctive part of her responded to that. She *would* want to stay. And she would want to continue caring for the land and all that was on it.

Her stomach twisted sickeningly. Miserably, she sat up and draped her legs over the side of the bed, dragging the end of the sheet to her breasts. She was caught. No matter which way she turned, there was no hope for her. Jared had become as much a part of her as the land. And now she was expected to choose between them. And she couldn't.

"Could . . ." Tears flooded her eyes as she saw her happiness dissolving. "Would you . . . consider liv-

190

ing here?'' Even as she spoke, she knew what his answer would be. This was not a home of his making. Swan's Watch did not belong to him. Living here would be an insult to his own sense of self-worth.

She lowered her head and let the tears flow freely. Behind her, Jared cursed viciously. There really was no other answer. Just a cursing of the fates, a damning of an impossible situation.

She rose quickly and bent to haphazardly gather her clothes. Feeling as though she had lost everything, she blindly fled to her own room.

Chapter Eleven

Travis grabbed his head to still the pounding that had dragged him from a deep sleep. Irritably he cursed and tried to regain the numbness of slumber, but the sound of his own voice only brought him that much closer to full wakefulness.

Cautiously he opened one eye, peered about the darkness of his bedroom and tried to gauge the hour. No light filtered in around the curtains, but for all he knew, he could have been asleep for hours or it could have been mere minutes. Either way, he damned well did not want to be awake. Not with a skull that hammered like a son of a bitch.

Rolling to his side, he sat up and planted his booted feet squarely on the floor. His elbows came to rest on his thighs and his head dropped into his palms as though they alone would keep his head from dropping off. Somewhat belatedly, he realized that he hadn't removed his clothes before he had fallen into bed.

"Damned bourbon," he muttered sourly. He

couldn't remember the last time he had gotten so drunk. But he had been driven by the devil last night; disgusted with the plantation, angry at himself. The liquor had helped lessen the strain that had begun to eat away at him daily. At least for a few hours, he had been able to forget the obligations gnawing at his insides. Only now he was paying dearly.

He came to his feet, staggered slightly then righted himself awkwardly. Crossing to the dressing chest, he lit a candle with hands that visibly shook before he glanced at himself in the mirror.

Damn, what a miserable sight. Puffy, red-stained eyes stared back at him. Strands of hair shot out in all directions, and his neck cloth was twisted up beneath his ear. Irritated, he turned away from his reflection, refusing to look at the proof of his idiocy.

Tugging off his jacket and cravat, he stepped to the washstand and poured a stream of water into the porcelain bowl. As accurately as he could, he washed his face, dragging wet hands back through his blond hair in an attempt to restore some order. His efforts were moderately successful and by the time he dried off, his head was feeling somewhat better. Which was to say he was reasonably assured that it wouldn't split open. When it would cease pounding was another matter entirely.

From the top of his dresser, he picked up his pocket watch. It was at least another hour until dawn and he was now wide awake. And hounded by thoughts that he would just as soon not have to think about. His mouth drew into a thin line. It always came down to that. Regardless of the time of day or location, the Watch hung over his head like some oppressive

193

encumbrance that he could not shake.

He closed his eyes and sighed wearily. Just once, he would like to go back to those days when he hadn't felt the constant weight of it all. The land had seemed so benevolent and sustaining. For a full day, he would like to be as carefree as he had been years ago, and not have to worry constantly. But more than anything, he wished he could feel about the Watch what he had felt then: satisfaction, commitment, and pride.

That was all gone, buried with his father. Yet still the land remained; resolute in her need, unrelenting in her demands.

He rubbed the tension at the back of his neck, hating himself for a resentment he could not control. Not for the first time, he wondered how Lacy could be so strong. Where did she get that inner fortitude that allowed her unqualified faith and determination? Never once had he seen her love for the Watch waver even the slightest bit. She put him to shame with her resolve and conviction.

An enervating frustration set his hands back through his hair again. In the pit of his stomach, a sharp pressure twisted mercilessly, while the walls of the room seemed to close in on him, mocking him for a fool.

He turned on his heel and crossed to the door, having no doubts or illusions as to his destination. He needed Rose. He needed to be buried deep inside her body, for it was there within her embrace that the rest of the world was kept at bay, and he could grasp, if only for a brief flash of time, all that had somehow been lost to him.

His silent path was quick and direct. Moments later, he pushed open the door to Rose's cabin and stepped inside. Predawn light outlined her form as she lay sleeping. Curled on her side, she had one hand tucked beneath her cheek, while the other disappeared beneath the thin blanket.

Travis pushed away from the wooden panel and made his way to the cot. "Rose," he whispered.

His voice roused her instantly. She opened her eyes and came to her elbow at the same time, startled by his presence. For one frantic moment, she thought the dark shape standing beside her bed might be Syphron, sneaking in for more of his talk of running . . . and marriage. But with only a blink she recognized the shape as Travis, and she sank back to her pillow with a ragged sigh.

"Massa Travis?" There was no disguising the uncertainty her fear had put in her voice.

He sat beside her, laying a possessive hand on the curve of her hip. "Who else would it be?" he returned with dubious humor.

"No one," she averred hastily. "I just . . . I guess I was just sleepin' sound. I didn't hear you come in."

His hand made a long sweep from her hip to her knee and then up to her waist. "Well, I did come in and you aren't sleeping any longer." The soft feel of her was a balm to his soul. Unconsciously, he exhaled slowly, deeply, as though he had run an arduous course and had finally come to rest. Responsibilities and burdens slipped away, leaving in their wake only a profound pleasure and a soothing contentment he had come to associate with his Rose.

As always, her presence eased his spirit. As always, he accepted that without delving too deeply into the reasons. The implications were too critical to contemplate.

"It's going to be light soon," he murmured.

Rose nodded. Not saying a word, she pushed the blanket aside and stripped off her thin shift. She knew what was expected of her. Mindless acceptance, unrestrained passion. Yet Syphron's words echoed cruelly through her mind. *You ain't nothin' but his whore.*

She watched Travis remove his clothes.

Don't you want some kind of life other than spreadin' your legs for him?

She moved aside to make room for Travis beside her.

He's usin' you like he uses one of his horses ...

She bent one knee, making herself available as Travis had taught her.

. . . Only difference is when he rides you, he don't need to use no harness.

Her jaw tightened as a single tear trickled from the corner of her eye.

Travis pulled her into his embrace, frowning slightly at the stiffness of her body. "Are you cold?" he asked.

Words stuck in her throat and all she could manage was a shake of her head.

"Well, you feel like a board." He chuckled. In the dimness of the cabin, only the vague outline of her features was detectable. But he found her mouth unerringly as he gathered her against him. Her young, full breasts bore into his chest and all thoughts but one vanished. He levered himself over her, bringing his weight to bear on his forearms. Eagerly, he undulated his hips against hers.

Rose lay unmoving, cradling his body with her own, numbly absorbing the familiar intimacy. Her arms crept about his shoulders, not out of the longing and ardor she had once felt, but because it was what Travis expected of her.

His hands circled her breast, stroking the fullness to a taut peak.

You don't have to be his whore.

The sound of his breathing filled her ear as he traced its curves with his tongue.

I want you to go with me. To be my woman . . . And have my babies.

A moan of despair escaped her tight lips.

"Oh, my sweet Rose," Travis murmured, "sigh for me. Burn in my arms." His mouth captured her nipple, teasing the dusky nub with languid strokes. The sensation stirred a reflexive response inside her, but it was dull and feeble.

At the insistent pressure of his hand, she parted her legs. And like the feel of his lips at her breast, the gentle invasion of his fingers within her, coaxing her body's response, was familiar. She blocked it from her mind, even as she felt the stirring she could not control.

Travis brought his mouth to hers, kissing her with a passion that only she could make him feel. His body was hard, demanding, wanting her as he wanted no other woman. Only Rose made him feel so secure in his own right, confident and proud. Only his Rose could make him feel so much like a man.

He rolled over onto his back, taking her with him so that she straddled his hips. The heated softness of her nestled against his pulsing flesh in a promise of the paradise he knew he would find in her body. He lifted one hand to stroke her breast, while his other hand curved to her back and urged her down for another kiss.

His tongue surged between her lips, just as he thrust into her clinging warmth. Grasping her hips, he forced her weight downward, filling her completely as he felt himself fill with a conviction of the heart and mind and soul.

For whatever the reasons, good, bad, or indifferent, he could no longer deny that Rose was the source of his strength. He had known it all along, somewhere deep in his mind. He openly admitted it to himself now.

The admission was like the bursting of a dam. A tide of exhilaration swept through him, infusing him with a heady sense of power. He thrust upward repeatedly in a fierce rhythm, nourishing himself on the essence of her, making her strength his even as he made her body his. He ground his mouth over hers, took her breath, seized her heartbeat and felt a pleasure so rich he thought he would die from the force of it.

Again and again he surged into her, straining for the pulsing release that would make his rapture complete. His arms tightened around her slender form, molding every inch of her to him, and with his every move, his need grew. Sweat glistened on his body, his blood raced wildly until the all-consuming need tautened, expanded and then finally burst forth in waves of shattering ecstasy.

The pinnacle of his passion was staggering. In mind-snatching pulses, he gave himself up to Rose, replete and sated and reassured.

Stillness filled the cabin, the hush calm broken only by labored breathing. Travis thought the tranquility a perfect compliment for his state of mind.

Slowly, he eased from Rose's body and rolled away to stand beside the cot. With amusement he realized that the pounding in his head was gone.

He gazed at Rose, not quite certain what had happened in the past minutes. But he really didn't care. All he knew was that he had reached a very private understanding with himself. It wasn't anything he'd ever dare share with another living soul. It was enough that he accept the truth for what it was, and keep it well hidden.

Feeling an odd sense of satisfaction, he dressed quickly, wishing to be back in his room before the rest of the house was up and stirring. When the last of his buttons was fastened, he bent low and gently brushed Rose's lips with his. Then with a deep sigh, he turned and left.

Rose lay unmoving, giving free rein to the tears she had struggled furiously to hold back. She drew an arm over her eyes as wrenching sobs broke over her lips.

He had called her his Rose. At one time she had thought those words to be a term of endearment, a sign of his affection and possessiveness. But she had been stupid then, ignorantly hearing only what she wanted to hear.

The plain truth was that she was his Rose, just like the plows in the fields were his plows and the pigs in the sties were his pigs. There was no difference, not when he used her body as indifferently as he used those plows.

God Almighty, she wished it weren't so. She wished she was "his Rose." She wished she could be his wife. She didn't care where or how, as long as he could love her.

She curled into a tight ball, wracked by pain that went clear to her soul.

Travis needn't have worried about returning to the house unseen. It wasn't until almost noon that he, his sisters, and Jared met in the same room at the same time.

The dining room played host to the gathering, but unlike those cordial meals that usually occurred at the elegant cherry table, lunch was a strained affair.

"Well," Marriette declared, looking at the solemn faces around her. "This is certainly a cheerful group."

Lacy stared at her plate and nudged a piece of roasted chicken with her fork. Across the table from her, Jared attended to his meal with bleak solemnity. Between them stretched a raw tension.

"I think we are all recovering from last night's celebrations," Travis returned neutrally.

Marriette's delicate blond brows arched with her droll smile. "I would say some of us celebrated more than others."

Her remark was thrown out casually enough, but

there was no doubt in Travis's mind that it was pointed directly at him. He and Marriette had shared the same carriage ride home from the LaRues and she had told him in no uncertain terms what she thought of his foxed state.

At the time, he had drunkenly shrugged off her upbraiding. But the subtle reminder now was galling, especially so in front of Jared. He glanced to his guest for some sign of a reaction, but Jared was thankfully preoccupied with lunch.

He shifted his gaze to Lacy. Like Jared, she, too, appeared to be distracted. Neither seemed disposed to conversation. Neither indicated the slightest interest in their food. And neither looked as though they had had enough sleep. He could identify with the latter, but he at least was making an attempt to eat.

"Lacy, I understand you weren't feeling well last night," he commented lightly, trying to instill a cordial air into the unusually quiet atmosphere. "I hope it wasn't anything too serious."

All of Lacy's reserves were occupied with putting forth a composed face. Loving Jared as she did, it was a torture to her heart to sit as though nothing had passed between them, as though he hadn't asked her to marry him . . . and she had had to decline.

"No, nothing serious," she murmured as steadily as she could. "I was feeling indisposed and . . . Jared . . . was good enough to see me . . . home."

"Yes, I meant to thank you for that, Jared," Travis said. "Thomas did mention that he had driven you both back here."

Jared's mouth was a hard, bitter slash. "It was my pleasure."

201

Travis's brow furrowed with a frown. Jared looked anything but pleased. He shot a speculative look back at Lacy.

"How are you feeling now, sister?"

Once again, Lacy was forced to make a reply she felt incapable of making. The extra effort it took for her to speak tested her capacities to the limit. "I have a headache. I . . . didn't sleep very well."

Marriette scoffed delicately. "Why was that? I would have thought that retiring early, you would have slept like a baby."

A small grimace pulled at Lacy's features. Her composure slipped and she raised her glass to hide her trembling lips. The cool water did nothing to lessen the ache in her throat.

Her unease was not missed by Travis. "Are you sure you should be up, then? Perhaps this is a day best spent resting."

Lacy declined with a shake of her head. "I can't. Marriette and I have to inventory the larders this afternoon."

But Marriette was quick to object. "I can't possibly trudge through the larders today."

"Why not?" Lacy asked. "You promised to help me."

Marriette didn't care one wit for the promises she had or hadn't made. She was not about to count hams and sacks of grain when she had a wedding to plan. "Now, Lacy, there's no need to make a fuss about this. It's not as though you haven't gone through the larders by yourself before."

"You don't have to tell me that," Lacy commented tightly. "But I was counting on your help. Even with

202

the both of us working, it will take the rest of the afternoon.''

"Then it will just have to take the rest of the afternoon," Marriette gritted out behind a sugary smile. "I will simply be too busy to help. As a matter of fact, I am going to be extremely busy from now on.''

"With what?"

"Planning my wedding." Sitting back in her chair, she assumed a regal bearing. "Carter asked me to marry him and I accepted.''

Travis sat back in his own chair, surprise written all over his face. "When did this happen?"

"Last night." She waited for the acclamations, ready to bask in her moment of glory. But everyone at the table simply stared at her as though she had grown a second head. She stared back irritably, mentally cursing them all. Lacy was sitting like a useless lump, Travis was nothing better than a sot and Jared . . . Jared Steele was a bastard. She would be heartily glad to be rid of the lot of them.

"Aren't any of you even going to congratulate me?''

Travis was the first to shake himself from the shock of the announcement. "Yes, of course, Marriette. I wish you and Carter much happiness.''

"Thank you, brother dear." She looked pointedly at Lacy. "And what about you, Lacy? Don't you have any wishes for me?''

Thoughts and emotions tumbled one on top of another in Lacy's mind. She was not surprised that Carter had asked Marriette for her hand. It had been coming for months. But up until yesterday, Marri-

203

ette's behavior toward Jared had been indicative of a woman not in love with the man who was now her betrothed.

Instead of the happiness she should be feeling for her sister, Lacy felt only a deep sadness. If Marriette could flit from one man to the next in a matter of hours, how devoted could she possibly be to her future husband? It was distressing to contemplate the kind of marriage Marriette would have, where little if any love existed. At least on Marriette's part.

Smoothing her hand over her skirt, she tried for a convincing smile. "I hope you and Carter will be happy."

Marriette beamed, privately rejoicing in a heady sensation of having the upper hand . . . at Lacy's expense. "Thank you, Lacy." She glanced coyly to Jared, pouting ever so slightly. "I hope you, too, will wish me well, Jared. I hope . . . I hope we will always be friends."

If Marriette had been able to read Jared's thoughts, she would have never even spoken to him. As it was, his face was so void of emotion as to be chilling. Still, he added his congratulations to the others.

"I'm sure Carter James is a lucky man," he offered smoothly.

Marriette privately believed that Carter was the most fortunate man on earth. "I thank you all," she commented lightly. Folding her napkin, she laid it by her plate. Now that she had said what she had come to say, she could not be bothered sitting through the rest of the meal with these people. "If you will all excuse me. I really have a million things I have to get started on." She rose and affected a slightly bemused air. "I don't even know where to start."

Her exit was accomplished amid a swirl of muslin and a gay laugh. In her wake, the meal came to a stilted conclusion.

"I suppose I should be on my way also," Travis commented, coming to his feet.

His stance as well as his remark drew Lacy's disbelieving regard. "Are you going somewhere?"

"Yes, I thought today would be a good day to ride over and talk to N. Douglas about some of his slaves. He offered to sell several to me."

A bemused frown pulled Lacy's brow. "But I thought you were going to talk with Michael about putting in another garden plot. He's been waiting for days for you to decide where you want the men to plow."

"It can wait another day, Lacy."

She exhaled sharply. "No, Travis, it really can't. From the looks of the sky, it's going to rain before the night is out. If the men don't turn the ground today, it will be days before it's dry enough to work. Another week lost is another week we'll be behind with planting and harvesting and I was counting on storing those vegetables for this winter.

"Damn, you're right. But I can't wait any longer to see about these slaves." He pursed his lips and finally shrugged. "Why don't you decide where you want the garden to go. Any place you pick will be fine with me." Confident that Lacy would handle the matter, he dismissed it at once and turned to Jared. "Would you care to join me? I would welcome your opinion as well as your counsel."

Jared's eyes shone like brittle glass as he also stood. "I will have to decline, but if I may, I will accompany you to town. There is a matter or two that I must see to."

"By all means. I'll have Thomas bring the carriage around." Glad for even Jared's company, Travis excused himself at once and walked from the room.

A horrid silence permeated the dining room, nearly shouting the fact that only Jared and Lacy remained, alone together for the first time since she had fled from his bed. She felt the shiver of grief vibrate over her skin, drawing her nerves to a shattering point. Caught by an utter dismay, she stared at her hands lying limply in her lap, past words, past hope.

Unable to help herself, she looked up to find Jared staring at her. His eyes were glittering gray ice in a face held rigid and unyielding. Anyone else gazing at him would have glanced away in sheer self-defense, but all she could do was continue to look back, wanting him to love her forever.

Tears pooled in her eyes as her heart clenched in her chest. "Do you see what I am facing?" she whispered in an anguished voice. "Can you understand what would happen to the Watch if I left now?" The torment of the answer forced her gaze to her lap again. Marriette didn't care and Travis could not manage on his own.

She rose unsteadily, all the while praying that Jared would say something, anything, to ease her pain. But she walked from the room followed only by the intensity of his brooding gaze.

Chapter Twelve

The much-needed rain that had threatened all day arrived with a vengeance at dusk. Standing at one of the windows of the front parlor, Lacy watched the driving sheets come down, soaking everything that wasn't protected.

Lifting a hand to the back of her neck, she unconsciously rubbed the ache that seemed lodged there. The slight discomfort matched the headache centered behind her eyes, and with a sigh, she wished both into oblivion. It was a useless expectation on her part, she knew, for the cause of her discomfort was an emotional upset that would not be put to rights. As long as she loved Jared . . . and the Watch, there would be no alleviation for her heartache.

She turned from the window and sought what comfort she could find from the small blaze in the fireplace. The last spring shower had brought much needed rain, but it had been swept on to land by a cool sea breeze. The house felt damp and she had ordered fires lit to ward off the chill. Yellow flames danced beckoningly, and she sat in one of the chairs set before the fireplace. Still, neither the heat nor the burning logs provided the distraction she needed and once again, her thoughts turned to Jared.

He had been gone since the midday meal, but that had not kept her from thinking of him continually. As she walked the grounds with Michael Spruill trying to determine the best location for the garden, Jared had been in her thoughts with all the intensity of the rain now pouring out of the leaden sky. When she had begun her inventory of the larder, memories of their night together engulfed her mind until she could almost feel his body surging into hers again, stealing her breath and setting her hands to trembling.

Just the thought of what they had shared was heady bliss. A faint trace of color stained her cheeks, but it was overshadowed by the anguish that dulled the turquoise of her eyes. How could she be expected to choose between the man she loved and the land that was part of her very being? Yet, what happiness could she expect from a life without Jared? Or a life absent from the Watch? There was no answer that she could see.

The sound of Travis's voice captured her attention, and she turned in her seat to peer back toward the doorway.

"I feel like a damned fish," he muttered irately, brushing drops of water from his jacket sleeves as he strode to the low side table and its assortment of bottles.

"I didn't hear you return," she said, but her gaze was fastened to the doorway, waiting for the sight of

Jared. He appeared within moments. Hastily, she gave her brother her attention once again.

"Do you need towels?" she asked.

Irritably Travis poured himself a bourbon before he waved her offer away. "No, we're fine." Casting an inquiring look to Jared, he asked, "Can I pour you something?"

Jared declined and approached the welcoming warmth of the hearth at a sedate pace. His face shuttered against any sign of emotion, he leaned against the mantel, but he could not prevent his gaze from resting on Lacy.

It took only one look at her pale, drawn features for him to realize just how thinly her nerves were stretched. She sat with her hands clasped tightly in her lap, her eyes studiously avoiding his. Her tension emanated from her in waves that hit him like a palpable thing.

Mentally he cursed a blue streak, damning the impossible situation in which he found himself. Loving Lacy should have been a simple matter, but it had somehow become all twisted and snarled.

Feeling the weight of Jared's heavy regard, Lacy struggled not to squirm in her seat. She absorbed the frissons of unease created by his all too discerning stare and felt her chest constrict painfully.

"Travis," she commented as levelly as possible, "how did your business with N. Douglas go?"

Travis exhaled sharply, and joined Jared at the fireplace, his reply to his sister a long time in coming. Grim lines pulled at his face, and he lifted his glass for a drink.

"It could have been better," he muttered sourly,

swallowing past the bite of bourbon and the sting of bitterness.

"Did the two of you settle on . . ." She hesitated in continuing, the tautness in her brother's countenance not encouraging.

"Oh, yes, N. Douglas was more than willing to sell me the slaves we needed." A scoff worked its way up his throat, his blue eyes glistening with an angry resentment. "The only problem is that we can't afford to replace the thirteen we lost."

Dread formed a knot in Lacy's stomach. "How . . . how much money are we talking about?"

Travis studied the carpet beneath his boots before he answered. "Nearly all we have for operating expenses."

Lacy's breath escaped her in a single rush. Sitting back, she digested the news. "How many could we afford?"

"Four."

There was no need for Travis to go on. Lacy fully understood the ramifications involved in the situation. Swan's Watch had, at any one time, no more than fifty able field hands. Each man and woman represented tons of harvest. Without a full number of workers, the fields would suffer, and that could not be allowed to happen if the Watch was going to produce a sufficient amount of cash crop. Without a full number of workers, any profit they could expect would be negligible and they would be lucky to break even for the season.

Unfortunately, just breaking even put the plantation at a disadvantage for the start of the next year. The money needed for operating expenses was derived from the previous season's profit. If there was no profit, it would be almost impossible to maintain the Watch for any great length of time.

"What do you suggest we do?" she asked.

Travis shoved his hand into the pocket of his trousers and shrugged. "The only option I see open to us is to sell off some acreage."

Lacy gasped. "Oh, Travis, no."

"What else can we do?" he shot back tersely, not liking the idea any more than she did. "The only person I would consider approaching for a loan is N. Douglas, but things are difficult for him, too. He's not in a position to make a purchase right now. And if we go to the bank for a loan, we'll have to put the land up as collateral, which means in the long run we could stand to lose more than just a few hundred acres."

"But to sell part of Swan's Watch? It's been in the family for hundreds of years."

"Don't you think I know that?"

Lacy dropped her head into her hands. The first Flemming had claimed the land when there had been little more than bands of Indians camped along the river. It had taken years of toil and labor to carve the plantation from *this* land. The bricks that had fashioned this very house had been made with clay from *this* land. Generations had lived and loved, laughed and cried and finally died on *this* land. The idea that they were going to have to sell off a part of that same land was appalling.

But inescapable. Unless they were willing to gamble the entire plantation on the chance that they could turn a profit this year, there was no choice left.

Lacy knew that as a fact. And she hated it.

"Who are you thinking of selling to?" she queried in a shaking whisper.

Travis withdrew his hand from his pocket to scrub at his forehead. "I don't know."

"I'll buy the land." Jared's voice cut into the strained atmosphere with all the effectiveness of a sharp blade. Lacy and Travis stared at him in complete surprise, both wondering if they had heard correctly.

Flustered, Travis said, "Jared, there is no need for you to go to the bother of taking on this problem." He spread his hands wide in apology. "I felt free to discuss this in your presence because I believe you have a right to know how things stand here. But it was never my intention that you should be the one to purchase the land."

Jared narrowed his eyes slightly. "Is there any reason why you wouldn't wish me to?"

"No, no," Travis quickly assured him. "Better you than some men I know. But I don't want you thinking this discussion was for your sake. There is no obligation on your part to concern yourself with our finances."

Jared crossed his arms over his chest. "It makes good business sense to me to concern myself with your finances. Especially in this case, where a serious, but momentary lack of cash on your part could indirectly affect the money we both stand to make in the future from shipping your crops."

A smile slowly came to Travis's face. He liked Jared's reasoning. He liked it a great deal. At least they wouldn't have to sell off to a stranger. The land would be owned by someone who had a vested interest in the property. "You would be willing to buy the acres?"

"Yes. And I'd pay you to work them for me."

It was sounding more and more like a partnership, something Travis had never contemplated. But it was an admirable idea. He turned to Lacy, his brows raised his question, eager anticipation replacing the despondency that had marred his features earlier.

The inquiry was laid at Lacy's feet like a huge sack of raw peanuts. Cumbersome, weighty, it could not be ignored. She looked from Travis to Jared and her insides twisted. If anyone else had made the offer, she could have accepted that with nary a second thought. But the offer had come from Jared and no matter how logical she tried to be, she found herself giving the matter not only second thoughts but third and fourth as well.

She had to wonder why he would want to buy their property. She believed him when he said he wanted to protect his shipping interests. But she could not shake the sensation that his decision had been based in part on the fact that she had gone to his bed.

A glimmer of hope kindled deep within her. His owning the land could tie him not only to Swan's Watch, but to her as well.

She dragged her gaze back to Travis. "I don't know what to say. I am still trying to adjust to the idea of having to sell the land."

"I doubt we'll get an offer as good," Travis coaxed, smiling.

Fingering the muslin of her skirt, Lacy nodded. "I am sure you're right. And if the land has to go to someone, I would rather it be Jared." The thought was strangely satisfying.

"I agree," Travis said, then laughed in utter relief at having his problems rectified so quickly and so favorably. "Well, then," he declared, clapping his hands together, "it's all settled. We can discuss the terms after dinner."

"That's fine," Jared remarked.

"And we can have the papers drawn up some time next week."

Jared pushed away from the mantel. "I am afraid it will have to be sooner than that. Tomorrow to be exact, because I leave for Connecticut the day after."

Lacy's gaze sought Jared's and her heart wrenched in her chest, the breath catching in her throat. The faint hope she had felt only seconds before crashed about her feet like shards of broken glass.

"What's this?" Travis queried.

"I have had a sudden change of plans," Jared explained, his eyes never relinquishing their hold on Lacy. "There is a packet departing for New York the day after tomorrow. I have booked passage."

Misery swamped Lacy. She tried to still the trembling of her lips, but her efforts were futile, and it was all she could do just to sit there and pretend that she didn't know exactly why he was returning home. There had been no sudden change in his plans. He was going because of her, because she could not marry him as he wanted.

"Well, I am sorry to hear you are leaving so soon," Travis was saying, but she barely heard his voice. All she could hear were Jared's words when he had told her he loved her and wanted her to be his wife.

214

And now he was leaving her.

She surged to her feet, swallowing the tears that clogged her throat. "If you will excuse me," she murmured, looking anywhere but at Jared.

"Lacy?" Travis asked, surprised by her abrupt movement.

Already turning away, she choked out, "I need to see about dinner."

Not sparing either man another glance, she fled the room, fled the house, out into the pouring rain. In seconds, she was soaked to the skin, skirts clinging to her legs, hair plastered to her head. But she didn't care, not any more than she cared about checking on dinner. She ran past the kitchen, heedless of her feet slipping on the muddy path as tears trailed down her face.

Running toward the fields, she called herself ten kinds of a fool for carrying on this way. It was only logical that he would eventually leave. True, she hadn't allowed herself to even think that far, but it was *only logical* that he would do so, especially now when she had refused to share his life.

In one ragged breath she congratulated herself for reasoning it all out, but in the next breath she cursed the pain that accompanied the realization. She didn't want him to leave, she loved Jared and wanted a life with him. But she could no more give up the Watch than she could give up her love for Jared.

Sobbing, she stumbled into the cornfield and immediately tripped over a trough of newly turned earth. In a reflexive action, she flung her hands wide to steady herself, but the bemired earth sucked her feet into its depths, refusing to relinquish its hold,

215

and she dropped to her knees. Hands shaking, legs quivering, she struggled uselessly, fighting the pull of the ground, battling the rain. She tried to lever herself upward, but to no avail, until strong hands caught her and brought her to her feet.

"You sweet little fool," Jared growled, hauling her into his embrace.

With no coaxing, Lacy melted against the solid wall of his chest, welcoming the feel of him, the warmth and strength and power of him. She raised her face to his and he captured her mouth, kissing her with a fierceness born of the frustration and hurt that had been eating away at him all day.

"Tell me you love me," he demanded, taking her face between his hands, pitching his voice to be heard over the sound of the deluge from above.

"I love you," she breathed. Her feet slowly sank into the wet dirt and she grasped his shoulders with muddied hands.

He could barely make out her words, but the movement of her lips told him what he wanted to hear. A low groan sounded from deep in his chest and he slanted his mouth over hers again, his tongue plunging past her lips to taste her sweetness. He loved her, wanted her more than he had ever wanted any other woman. And he wanted her to feel that same consuming love and passion that coursed through him.

"Tell me you love me," he repeated, hands molding her to his length.

Rain cascaded over her face, but she tilted her head back to look directly into his eyes. "I love you." And this time she backed her voice with enough force to be heard.

"Then why are you out here running away from me?"

She pressed her forehead to his chest, her eyes drifting shut to block his fiercely set face from view. If it were only as simple as that. *I love you, yes, I will marry you.* But there was so much more involved.

The red mud seeped up past her ankles, its cold sending shivers up her spine. "Don't make me choose," she implored, lifting her chin, the blue and green of her eyes pleading with him to understand that the Watch was a part of who she was.

Oblivious to the rivulets of water coursing over the chiseled planes of his face, unaware of the mud smeared over him, Jared searched her features. His jaw tightened at her silence, and he knew. Without another word from her, he knew he had her final answer.

His hands dropped away from her and he stepped back. Frigid anger turned his eyes as black and unforgiving as flint. "You've already chosen."

Swaying in the buffeting downpour, Lacy pressed shaking hands to her lips as she watched him turn and walk away, taking with him her love, her heart, her happiness.

She sank to her knees, doubling over in sorrow. Of their own accord, her hands gripped up clumps of soil, but the sodden dirt slipped through her fingers.

"Somethin's wrong."

Syphron looked up at Taloila's proclamation. "With what, Old African?" From where he sat on the

217

wooden floor of the weaving house, he watched the weaver's hands still at her loom.

"Don't know for certain. Can just feel it in my bones, is all."

Listening to remarks like that, Syphron wondered why he had chosen to come into the weaving house to get out of the rain. He had known that Rose was in the kitchen, so he could have ducked in there to keep from getting wet. Or he could have gone back to his own cabin to wait out the storm. But for some reason he hadn't felt inclined to go to either place.

He bent one leg and braced his forearm across his knee. "You talkin' nonsense again. The only thing you feel in your bones is the rain."

Taloila shook her head as she threw her shuttle once more. "I knows what I feels an' it ain't de rain. Trouble's brewin'."

There was such certainty in the cracked voice that Syphron gave up his contemplation of the wood grain in the floor planks and stared suspiciously at the wrinkled old woman.

"What kind of trouble?"

She heard the too subtle tone of misgivings in his voice and turned an eye his way. "You sound like you already know."

His deep set eyes narrowed slowly. "I don't know nothin' about trouble, Old African."

Taloila scoffed. "I's old, boy, not stupid. An' I ain't blind."

"What you goin' on about?" Annoyance laced his words.

"I's talkin' 'bout you an' Rose."

Syphron's ease fell away in an instant. "Hush up

218

about me an' Rose."

She kept her silence only because it pleased her to do so. To her way of thinking, if she had something to say, she was damn good and well going to say it. But she also knew that it would be only a matter of minutes before Syphron took up the discussion exactly where he demanded it be left off.

Content to move her feet over the treadles and slide her shuttle from hand to hand, she couldn't suppress a smile when Syphron tired of stewing in a fix of his own making and surged to his feet.

"What you want to know about me an' Rose?" he asked, coming to stand beside the great four harness loom.

One of Taloila's thin shoulders hunched into a shrug. "Don't want to know nothin' more dan I already does, an' dat is you is headed for big troubles if you keep on de way you been."

Rolling his eyes in disgust, Syphron leveled her with an impatient look. "And what way is that?"

"You been sniffin' round her like she was a bitch in heat, stirrin' up yo' insides 'till you can't think wid nothin' but dat thing 'tween your legs."

"Hell, Taloila." He thrust a hand back through his hair. "Is this the trouble you 'feel in your bones'?"

"You could answer dat better'n me."

He muttered a curse beneath his breath. He didn't need to be harped at by some old woman. He knew what he was doing, but it was damned unsettling the way she was hinting about at things.

"Has Rose been talkin' to you?"

"Dat girl don't say nothin' but to tell me to mind my own business."

"Well, that's a fair piece of advice." To his surprise, Taloila burst into peals of laughter. His thick brows lowered over sharp, irritated eyes. "You's crazy, woman."

"Could be a fact," she agreed, chuckling, "but I's alive. I got me a notion dat's more'n you're goin' to be." All traces of her humor disappeared in a flash. Her hands fell to her lap and when she raised her eyes to Syphron, a deep, troubling dread dulled the brown orbs. "You goin' to try, ain't you?" she whispered.

A ripple of fear skittered up his spine, clenching his chest along the way. "Do what?"

"Run."

One by one, all the lines in Syphron's face tautened until his face was a harsh mask. "How did you know?"

A huge sigh passed over the weaver's wrinkled lips before she replied. "I seen dat look before. Seen it on my man's face before he ran. Dat look got him killed."

A piercing jab stabbed at Syphron's gut. He knew of the risks involved, but still he vowed, "I ain't goin' to get killed."

Taloila's mouth worked for several seconds, forming words that seemed lodged in her throat. "I hope not, boy. Dey would drag you back here for certain, and den Lord only knows what would happen."

"I don't care," he growled.

"You takin' Rose wid you?"

It was Syphron's turn to struggle with his words. He hesitated in telling anyone his plans. "Don't know," he muttered.

The crooked contour of the old woman's shoulders slumped. "You don't lie worth hog spit, boy. And you is beggin' for a heap of sorrow. Massa finds dat girl gone, you goin' to pay wid yo' life."

"As long as I stay here, my life ain't worth shit."

"You sound just like my man did."

"Your man had it right."

"My man's dead."

Syphron bowed his head. "There's some thin's worse than dyin'."

She sat and considered his words. There was no answer that she could possibly make. Taking up her shuttle again, she straightened her shoulders. "When you goin'?"

He shook his head. "Don't know for sure. Soon."

"Got you a plan?"

"Workin' on it."

The shuttle flew from her left hand to her right. "You come see me when you got it all thought out."

Chapter Thirteen

As naked as the day he was born, Carter James stepped out of his bedroom on to the second-story balcony of his house. Blazing, morning sunshine bathed his muscular form, touching on the hard muscles of his arms and shoulders. Idly he scratched at the thick mat of brown hair on his chest before he lowered his hand to ease an itch in the thatch of tightly curling hair below. His lips quirked up at one corner when his hand came away wet.

Over his shoulder, he glanced back toward the bed. Opulent curves created a sensuous landscape of white sheets and dark green coverlet. Only moments ago, he had broached the soft, succulent terrain hidden by the bedclothes, and he was now feeling extremely satisfied with life.

He looked out over the fertile fields of Bellehaven, and drew a deep breath. Yes, life was damn good just then. The crops were in fine standing, the price of corn had only the week before gone up again for the third straight month, and if it continued, he would make a fortune come harvest. Add to that the fact that Marriette had agreed to marry him and it was no wonder he was feeling so content this morning. Hell, even yesterday's rain had left behind a sweetly pungent scent in the air. Yes, life was definitely good.

And it would get even better once he and Marriette married. With her luscious beauty and regal manner, she would make the perfect centerpiece for the plantation. A mistress for the land as well as his bed.

His pulse tripped just thinking about the feel of her breasts. Damn, but she was ripe. And he was going to be hard-pressed not to pluck her like some juicy cherry before they were married. Maybe with a little coaxing on his part, she could be convinced to have their wedding night sooner than the wedding itself.

A one-sided grin stretched his lips. It was a worthy prospect, but also one that he wouldn't pursue. Marriette might be prime, but she was also as tight-assed as they came. She had protected her virtue like it was some king's treasure, despite all the coy teasing on her part. Oh, he had recognized her little game for what it was, a means of keeping him and every other man she chose on a short leash. He had tolerated it because her efforts had been so amusing. And because she stirred his blood like no woman ever had.

But come their wedding night, he would make dead certain that she understood that the game was ended. She could go on and pretend that she had the upper hand, if that was what she wished. But he was master of all around him, and that included Marriette Flemming. It would be interesting to see just how easily she accepted the idea that if anyone was on a leash it was her.

He strode back to his bed, pulling the covers away with a single flick of his wrist. The brown of his eyes gleamed with a sultry passion at the sight of the two naked figures lying so passively. Still, he couldn't suppress a sudden laughter.

Damn, what he wouldn't give to have Marriette see him now. No doubt she would be horrified that he was bedding not only one of his slaves, but two at the same time. He could just imagine the fire and anger that would course through her. And he could just as easily imagine himself taking her while she fumed with that rage.

Sprawling between the two dark-skinned beauties, he crossed his arms behind his head and smiled up at the ceiling. "Make me happy, girls," he murmured thickly.

Hands and mouths caressed his flesh, broadening his smile. Yes, but life was *damn* good.

If there was one thing Marriette could not stand, it was having to wait. For anything. And having to wait first thing in the morning was even worse. She discounted the fact that it was going on eleven o'clock. Making plans for her wedding had kept her awake until all hours the night before. Rising any sooner than she had had simply been impossible.

She eyed the papers spread out before her on the dining-room table and cursed the fact that she had asked for breakfast almost ten minutes ago, and Gaye had still not managed to get it to her. The only thing that kept her from giving in to her temper was that she had more than enough to keep her occupied this morning.

Picking up one sheet of paper, she scanned the list of names she had compiled last night. Her brow puckered slightly as she considered whether two hundred and fifty was an adequate number of people to invite to the wedding. After all, she intended her wedding to be *the* social event of the year. That simply could not happen if there was a shortage of people present.

A satisfied smile dissipated her frown and she turned her thoughts to more complacent matters. She would be the envy of every woman from here to Richmond, maybe even as far north as Washington and as far south as Charleston. It was a known fact that Carter James was the most sought-after bachelor in the entire Tidewater. Some even said the whole commonwealth of Virginia, and she, Marriette Flemming, would soon be his wife.

That had a delicious ring to it. Marriette James. She could hardly wait to move into Bellehaven, with its tall columns and wide marble steps sweeping up to the mahogany doors. Of course she was going to want to refurbish most of the rooms to suit her own tastes. After all, she could not be expected to live with furnishings that Carter's mother had selected.

And she would see to it that she had a proper house staff, with a housekeeper and a personal maid and perhaps a driver of her very own. She had every intention of visiting the neighbors with great regularity and a personal driver could very well become her trademark as the area's most prestigious woman.

There was no hiding her glee as she scooped up her papers and rose. Her mood was so ebullient that she even dismissed breakfast, and concentrated instead on the millions of things she had to tend to. The first thing was to get Travis to agree to her ideas for the wedding. Penny-pincher that he was, he would probably pull out his hair when he heard that she absolutely had to have a lily pond constructed in the formal garden out back. And he would no doubt plead poor to her need to have real pearls sewn into the bodice of her wedding gown.

Exercising what she thought was admirable patience, she sought and found her brother in his study. She didn't have the time to waste searching for anyone, least of all Travis. Finding him as readily as she had was a boon to her already light mood.

"There you are," she declared, coming to stand at his desk.

Travis sat back in his chair and regarded Marriette's obvious joy with ill-concealed curiosity. "What brings you in here, and what is all of that?" He gestured to the papers she carried.

"*This*," she indicated, rattling her endless lists, "is my wedding, and I have come in here because we need to discuss the plans I have made."

"Is that so?"

"Yes, and I think you need to understand that I am adamant about what this wedding will entail."

Narrowing his eyes, Travis read between the lines of her statement. "What you are really here for, Marriette, is to tell me how much money you intend to spend."

Not bothering to deny it, she cocked her head to

226

one side. "Since you insist on being so crudely blunt about it, yes. I want to discuss money."

He sat forward in his chair and returned his attention to the account books in front of him. "Well, you can demand all you want, but you'll have to be satisfied with considerably less."

If she hadn't been expecting him to take this route, Marriette would have given vent to a few choice words she had been saving for her brother. But she had known all along that he was going to be miserly.

Her chin came up as her shoulders squared. "I'm not asking for money, Travis, I am demanding a share of what is rightfully mine."

Travis's head snapped up, an almost comical look of disbelief settling on his face. "Demanding?"

"Don't look so surprised. Father left the plantation to the three of us equally."

"That's right."

"And so I am entitled to at least a third of the money that is spent around here."

Incredulous, Travis could say nothing for several seconds. He had honestly thought that there was nothing Marriette could do to shock him, but he had to give her credit on this one.

"Where do you think to get this portion of your money?" he scoffed. "From the new fences we put in last month or from the paint that went onto the walls upstairs? Be realistic, Marriette, you know as well as I that all our money is tied up in the plantation itself. You can't separate your third from mine by counting sheep or barrels of corn."

"You're not talking to an idiot, Travis," she returned, losing the edge of her patience. "I know good and well how things run around here. I have had to live with the deplorable state of affairs ever since Father died. But we have money available and you know that as well as I."

"Most of that money," he stated succinctly, "is gone."

"*What?*"

"You heard me, the money is gone. Or it will be as soon as I finalize my dealings with Jared."

The start of a torrid rage surged into Marriette's chest, making her blood pound through her veins and her blue eyes glint with anger. "What in the hell does that *Yankee* have to do with our money?!"

Travis ignored her outburst and double-checked his figures in the ledger. "That Yankee, as you put it, has just saved this plantation from ruin."

"I don't give a damn what he did," she sneered, caring even less about the plantation. "I want to know what he has to do with our money."

It was the tone of Marriette's voice that finally made Travis give up on his accounting for the time being. He had listened to her enough to know that there would be no dissuading her from discussing this in excruciating detail.

He flung his pen aside and gave her as tolerant a look as he could. "Perhaps you have forgotten that thirteen field hands died in the past weeks, but Lacy and I haven't."

"Of course I haven't forgotten."

"Well, if we spent every spare penny we have, we could have replaced four, five at the most." Coming to his feet, he shoved his fists onto his waist. "Do I need to tell you what that means, or can you figure it

228

all out by yourself?"

Marriette tossed her papers on the desk and matched his sarcasm word for word. "Let me just think about that, and while I'm at it, I'll pray for deliverance from my own stupidity." In a mocking gesture, she aped her brother's stance and planted her hands on her hips. "Of course I know what that means. Without enough workers, we'll never be able to make the harvest."

"Right. So in order to raise the extra money we needed, we've decided to sell off the bottom five hundred acres to Jared."

"Sell to *Jared?!*"

"That's right."

"Who made this decision?"

"Lacy and I. We didn't see any other option open to us. With his money, we'll be able to replace all thirteen workers, and still have enough money left over to see us through the season."

Marriette's anger climbed another notch. "You and Lacy. Why wasn't I consulted in this decision?"

Travis's sarcasm came back full force. "Because, bride-to-be, you were too damn busy with your wedding plans to be disturbed. And even if you hadn't been, when did you ever give a damn about how things worked around here?"

Planting her hands firmly on the top of the desk, she cried, "I have always cared about the Watch."

"Only to the extent that it provided you with enough money to buy what you wanted."

That was true enough, but she was not about to admit it, least of all to Travis. "I have worked myself to the . . ."

Travis threw his hands into the air, cutting her off. "Spare me, Marriette. I am trying my best to keep this plantation operating. The last thing I need is to listen to your fantasies."

The rage that had been escalating by the second exploded in Marriette. Whipping up into a rigid stance, she spat, "You greedy, sanctimonious, excuse for a man! I will not let you ruin my wedding with your parsimonious notions about money."

"Shut up, Marriette."

"Go to hell!" she spat. "And while you're at it, take that little black slut of yours with you. I've had just about all I can stomach of your sneaking off to fuck her silly."

Only one thing saved Marriette from the full extent of Travis's anger and that was the desk that stood between them. Infuriated past reason, he grabbed up the papers she had carried in with her and flung them in her face.

"Keep your filthy tongue off Rose," he roared, clenching his jaw just as he clenched his fists.

Marriette stood as unaffected as though the papers slapping against her cheek were nothing more than a gentle spring breeze caressing her skin. A slow satisfied smile curved her full lips upward.

She might not have gotten the money she had come seeking, but she had gained something far more important, the satisfaction of stabbing her brother where he was most vulnerable: his pride.

Her smile turned into a lazy chuckle. Raising one blond brow, she mockingly asked, "What's the matter, brother dear, don't you like to hear the truth that you're trotting off to one of the slaves? Or is it that you don't like the fact that I know about it?"

Not waiting for an answer, she bent to pick up her lists. Then in a twirl of muslin, she crossed the room, her trill of laughter floating behind her.

The interior of the small carriage that carried Jared away from Bellehaven was stifling hot. In a concession to the June temperature, he shrugged out of his dark blue jacket and loosened his stock. Still, there was little relief to be found and he resigned himself to an uncomfortable ride back to Swan's Watch.

His gaze scanned the passing scenery, but for all the intensity found in the startling gray of his eyes, he saw little of the deep verdant forest. It was much the same with the long, carefully released sigh that escaped him. He exhaled slowly, but he wasn't aware that he had kept the breath locked within him.

His movements studied, he rolled back the cuffs of his shirt, and wondered why, after all these weeks, he should be so affected by the heat. It wasn't as though this day was that much different from any other day. The air was even stirred by an occasional breeze. Yet today he felt as confined and restricted by the sun's rays as if he had been relegated to a closet.

Irritably he cursed his own lack of tolerance. The day had been a success for him. The hours spent with Carter James had resulted in yet one more contract, and he should be pleased with that. Carter had even been willing to do business on a handshake until all the legal papers could be arranged.

But Jared wasn't pleased. And he knew damn well why.

He cursed soundly, dragging in on the anger and disbelief that ate away at him. If the situation weren't so pathetic it would be laughable. But there was nothing remotely humorous about Lacy's refusing to marry him.

Another curse came to mind and this one he directed at Lacy. Proud, stubborn, beautiful woman. He had no doubt that she loved him. But he was equally convinced that the plantation had a choking hold on her that would never be broken unless Travis or Marriette relieved her of the burden. Considering her family, that was not about to happen. A sister who could see no further than her own immediate wants, and a brother whose best efforts were less than adequate did in no way constitute a rescuing force. And Lacy, with her sense of honor and commitment, would never desert her land or her heritage.

The firm line of Jared's mouth twisted to one side. He found it morbidly ironic that he had fallen in love with Lacy for the very same qualities that now kept her from marrying him. Her compassion, honor, and sense of commitment had appealed to him from the very start. Yet now they were more than inconvenient.

The carriage coursed up the Watch's winding lane, drawing Jared's attention from these thoughts. Despite his owning several hundred acres of this land, there was little likelihood that he would ever return here. Knowing this could very well be the last time he viewed the plantation, he studied the impressive picture it made.

His perusal was exact and penetrating, but much to his surprise, he discovered more than rows of crops and standing structures. There was a serenity here that could not be pinpointed in any one aspect of the plantation. One did not view the reddish-brown earth or the rows of green corn and feel a calmness. Nor did the dependencies, crisp and white in the brittle sunlight, exude a sense of ease. But taken all together in combination with the splendor of the brick mansion, one could not help but experience a certain peace of mind that he had only ever associated before with the sea.

Narrowing his eyes slightly, he considered his reaction and came away shaking his head. He had to admit that the land was beautiful.

The thought lingered for the rest of the day, dogging his movements as he and Travis finalized their transactions, hovering on the edge of his awareness as he made arrangements for his trunks to be delivered to the ship. And when it came time to bid farewell to Lacy, it slapped him cleanly across his face. Swan's Watch was beautiful, as beautiful as its mistress.

He found her in the parlor, staring out one of the windows. Only weeks ago, he had sat in this very same blue and yellow room and seen Lacy for the first time. It was somehow fitting that he would garner his last look of her in the same setting.

Quietly, he came forward, making little sound. Still he knew exactly when she became aware of his presence. Her shoulders sagged even as she turned to face him.

Lacy swallowed the misery clogging her throat as she watched Jared approach. Exercising every ounce of self-control she possessed, she kept her tears from

233

surfacing, but the strain cost her dearly.

"Gaye tells me that your trunks have already been sent on ahead," she choked out.

Gray eyes glittering, Jared nodded. "The ship leaves tomorrow at first light, so I thought it would be best if I was aboard tonight."

Unable to meet his piercing gaze, she murmured, "It would be no trouble for you to have dinner with us."

"I'm sure, but it's best this way."

He was right. It would be best for him to leave now, before the pain of his departure ripped her into little shreds. She clamped her hands together, sucking in a shaking, quivering breath. "God's speed home, then."

He came to stand before her and her gaze sought his, telling him to get out while she still retained what little she had of her pride . . . imploring him to take her in his arms and never let her go.

The blue and green warring in the shining orbs reflected her conflicting emotions. To Jared, it was a sight as damnable as the battle that raged within her.

His hands curved about her arms and he pulled her against him. Unerringly, his mouth found hers in a tempestuous kiss that did nothing and everything to alleviate their anguish.

Lacy clung to his broad shoulders as if doing so would bind him to her forever. Yet she knew that this would be the last time he would hold her so, the last time she would feel his lips on hers. She absorbed the strength and warmth of him and committed their memory to the safekeeping of her heart, dying a little inside because these memories would have to last her a lifetime.

The tears she had so bravely held in check streamed down her face while words balanced on the tip of her tongue. But when he lifted his head, only silence fell between them. It was past time for entreaties and gentle urgings. He could not beg her to marry him, and she could not ask him to give up the life he had built for himself and love Swan's Watch as he loved her.

Lifting a hand to capture a tear on his finger, Jared gave her one last long look then turned. Chased by the sound of Lacy's sobs, he strode from the room.

Chapter Fourteen

August blazed down on Swan's Watch with a sweltering moisture that heated the ground as well as the air. Windows were left open in the house and every outbuilding in hopes of catching the slightest breeze. Sleeves were rolled up, kerchiefs applied to sweating brows and every hand that could wave a fan did so as often as possible.

Yet for all the thickness of humidity that hugged the tops of the trees, Lacy felt a chill inside her that no amount of heat could dissipate. At any given moment, a shiver would race up her spine, a subtle but inescapable memento of the pain that had captured her heart.

She had thought she understood the meaning of the word *pain*. When she had been nine, she had fallen down the stairs and dislocated her shoulder. Having the bones pulled into place had been so excruciating that she had lost consciousness.

The deaths of her parents had been another kind of pain. Though not physical, it had wracked her insides with an anguish that had been as real as the agony she had suffered from her fall.

In both cases, the pain she had experienced had been like a raw wound that devoured the body and the soul. But both were nothing compared to the pain she felt at losing Jared.

She had not known what to expect in the wake of his departure, so she had been unprepared for the overwhelming sense of loss that seized her in a vicious grip. The wretched grief that resulted stretched her nerves thin and made her days a struggle for composure. During her waking hours, she managed as best she could, but the nights found her defenseless against tears that wracked her slender form.

Lying behind the gauzy bed netting, sweat glistening in the hollow between her breasts, her sobs were a muffled sound that went no further than her pillows. Sleep came only as an afterthought to exhaustion, and waking in the morning was a test of her resolve.

Neither Travis nor Marriette noticed that she smiled only infrequently or that she seemed preoccupied. Travis had been possessed of a foul mood ever since Jared's departure, while Marriette could not think beyond her rapidly approaching wedding.

But while brother and sister seemed oblivious to Lacy's restrained manner, her heavy sighs and lackluster gaze did not go unnoticed by others.

Besha stood by the worn table in the kitchen, her tall, round figure an imposing presence in the room. Early evening sun cast the last of its light in through open windows and bathed her bulky form until sweat glistened on her broad brow, and the thin muslin of her dress clung to her ample curves in damp patches.

From all appearances, she seemed intent on trimming just the right amount of fat from the mound of ham hocks before her. But the glances she threw Lacy belied her interest in seasoning the butter beans for that night's dinner.

"You sure you feelin' up to sorts, Miz Lacy?" she asked, noting the faint blue shadows beneath the turquoise eyes.

Lacy looked up in question from the sack of flour she was inspecting, her face flushed from the kitchen's excessive heat. "Of course I'm feeling fine," she answered just a little too quickly.

Besha nodded, her paring knife slicing with deadly accuracy. "You don't look so fine to me, no, ma'am, you sure don't. You look like you could use you a tonic of mine."

There was no elixir on earth to cure what ailed Lacy, but she was grateful to the woman for her concern. "I think it must be the heat. I'm probably wilting just like everyone else."

"If you says so, but I got me some eelskins to tie 'round yo' wrists if you's taken up wid de cramps."

The mention of the female malady thinned Lacy's lips. Her one night spent with Jared had not resulted in a baby. Like clockwork, her body had continued its normal routine, complete with the minor discomfort of cramps.

Her hands paused in their task and she looked unseeing at the white coating of flour that dusted her arms. She could not deny a longing to bear Jared's child. A little boy with his dark good looks, or perhaps a little girl with blond hair.

It was a foolish dream on her part. And she should count herself lucky that she would not have to bear the social censure of being an unwed mother. Still, the yearning was there in her heart.

A small smile pulled at the corner of her mouth. "I don't have cramps, Besha. But thank you for worrying about me."

The rotund cook shrugged her heavy shoulders. "Somebody got's to worry 'bout you now dat Mister Jared gone back to his home."

Lacy's stomach lurched within her. The blood draining from her face, she whispered. "What do you mean by that?"

With seeming nonchalance, Besha replied, "Just what I says. Dat Mister Jared kept his eye on you, which is more dan I can say fo' some folks 'round here dese days."

A quivering sigh slipped past Lacy's lips. Jared *had* been concerned for her welfare, but it served no purpose to think about it now. "Travis and Marriette have better things to do than worry about me."

Flicking her wrist, Besha tossed one of the ham hocks into a waiting kettle. "Don't know 'bout dat, but Miz Marriette goin' 'round like she got on a pair of blinders and de Massa don't got a good word for no one no more."

Lacy returned her attention to the finely ground wheat. "It's a busy time for everyone, Besha. And this weather doesn't help matters at all."

Besha paused only long enough to cast a speculative glance out one of the windows to the early evening sky. "How many days since it rained?"

"Forty-three." It was a number Lacy easily kept in

her mind. The last rain had fallen on that day in June when she had run into the cornfield and Jared had caught up with her.

Nodding with a sure widsom, Besha vowed, "I'm goin' to have to hang me some dead snakes over de bushes if de sky don't open up soon."

Lacy brushed off her hands. "I'm sure that will make it rain."

"Course it will."

"Well, perhaps you might want to wait until after Marriette's wedding. We'll have enough on our hands without the inconvenience of rain."

"If you says so, Miz Lacy. But 'tween you and me, I don't think Miz Marriette is goin' to last until de weddin'. I know it's only two days off, but if she gets any more wound up, we're goin' to have to unscrew her from de ceilin'."

For the first time in weeks a smile of genuine amusement came to Lacy's face. Marriette's incessant badgering about anything even remotely related to the wedding had become very irritating. Lacy pictured her sister with her head in one of the bedrooms and her feet dangling into the parlor.

Powerless against a spurt of irreverent humor, she pressed her hand to her mouth, but there was no stopping the laughter that erupted. She gave in to the merriment and laughed out loud.

"Now, dat's what I like to hear," Besha crowed in satisfaction. "Ain't heard nothin' so sweet in weeks."

"Oh, Besha, I shouldn't be laughing about this," Lacy declared, still chortling helplessly.

"Don't see why not. If anyone deserves a good laugh 'round here, it's you. I swear, I ain't never seen nobody work as hard as you."

Drawing a deep breath, Lacy said, "We all work hard, Besha."

The cook disagreed heartily, but she kept her opinion to herself. "Well, dat ain't here nor dere. I'm just glad you had you a laugh to clean out yo' insides."

Lacy had to admit that the laughter did have the effect of reaching into the dark corners of her mind and cleaning out the cobwebs of discontent. The pain was still lodged in her heart, but at least the urge to cry had been dissolved.

"I don't need any of your eelskins, Besha," she told the cook, her gaze filled with genuine fondness.

"I know dat, Miz Lacy." Besha tossed another ham hock into the kettle. "Now I got me a dinner to fix, or Miz Marriette goin' to twist one notch tighter."

No further inducement was needed for Lacy to be on her way. She left the cook to her preparations and strolled back toward the house. After the increased heat in the kitchen, the air seemed only pleasantly warm. It was an effect Lacy knew would wear off in a short moment, but she savored it nonetheless.

Her gaze wandered and she caught sight of Rose beneath a nearby tree. The girl's hands were fully occupied with carding raw wool.

"Hello, Rose," she offered.

"Evenin', Miz Lacy," Rose replied.

"Shouldn't you be finishing for today? That can wait for tomorrow."

"Yes'm." Smiling courteously, Rose watched Lacy walk past. It was easy to like the youngest Flemming sister. She always had a kind word for everyone, always treated people fairly. Unlike the older sister.

Scoffing to herself, Rose glanced up at the big house, a reflexive reaction to thinking about Marriette Flemming. The woman was as mean as they came, and selfish to boot. Nothing pleased her and she had a way of making a person feel too small to even notice.

It was a nasty, sorrowful trait, Rose thought. And she recognized it for what it was because she had seen it often enough in Travis. Brother and sister alike had no qualms about using whatever came their way without so much as a blink of an eye. It didn't matter if it was a rock the good Lord had set down in the ground or if it was a person's body.

She tossed the brushlike pads into her basket and rose to her feet. Impelled by an anger that had been steadily growing inside her, she made her way past the kitchen and laundry until she came to the rows of cabins just beyond. Children scampered about, and adults lingered in open doorways, yet she didn't care who saw her. A quick knock at one of the doors and then she stood waiting.

Syphron swung the panel open, expecting anyone other than Rose. Shock widened his eyes, but only for as long as it took him to fully comprehend her presence.

Furtively, he gave the area a scanning look, noticing that more than one set of eyes watched with curiosity. It made little difference to him, and he reached out and pulled Rose into the cabin. A well-placed heel shut the door while he spun and stared at her in a mixture of pleasure and wonder.

"You sure chose a fine time to come callin'," he

remarked, smiling broadly.

Her nose elevated primly. "I didn't think you would mind none."

"Not a lick, girl, but you was the one harpin' on about us not bein' seen together. Would have thought you would have come by after dark."

Rose fingered the basket slung over one arm, her gaze turning uncertain. "Well, I been doin' a lot of thinkin'."

"'Bout what?"

"'Bout what you said . . ." She paused to lower her voice. "Our runnin' off."

The smile dropped from Syphron's face. "And?"

Swallowing with difficulty, Rose whispered, "And I think maybe I would want to come along with you."

It was almost too much for Syphron to take in. His dream had been to leave this place with Rose at his side, but part of him had honestly doubted that she would ever be able to go through with it.

"You for certain?" he asked, his liquid brown gaze searching her face.

She nodded, but there was no hiding her fear. "I don't want to live here no more. I want to have me my own babies and my own life."

"With me?"

Deep regret shadowed Rose's face. For so long, she had wanted Travis to love her. She had pictured herself having his babies as her own some day. "I don't hardly know you, Syphron. But I figure you got to be a good man if you want to live you a free life. You know I ain't comin' to you half as fine as what you deserve."

Lifting a gentle hand, Syphron stroked the curve of her cheek. "I know that. And nothin' that's happened to you is your fault." His fingers cupped her chin. "Not any of us is to blame for the ways things is."

His reassurance went far in allaying her doubts. "Will you give me some time, Syphron? I mean to get to know you some."

More times than not, he forgot that she was barely sixteen. Her hesitancy now made him remember that inside that very womanly body of hers was a young girl. "Much time as you need."

"And you promise that you won't ever lift a hand to me? I don't think I could live with no man that hit me."

He gave her a pained look. "Girl, I ain't never hit no woman, ever. But you thinkin' I could is 'nough to rile me inside."

Rose did her best to overlook the angry slant to his brows. What she was about to do would take all the courage she possessed. She had to know right from the start that she could come to care for Syphron, that she could lie with him and have his children. She couldn't do that, she wouldn't even leave here if she thought that he would hurt her.

"Promise me, Syphron."

He slid his fingers from her chin to cup the back of her neck. Slowly, he lowered his head and brushed his lips over hers. "You ain't got nothin' to worry 'bout with me. I promise."

The soft touch of his mouth brought her fingertips to her lips. No one other than Travis had ever kissed her. It felt strange to feel another man's lips.

244

Flustered, she stepped back.

"I got to get back before Taloila misses me."

"I'll come by tonight," he said, hating to let her go.

She shook her head emphatically. "No." But there her words choked off. Somehow she could not just blurt it out to the man she was intending to run away with that the man who owned her would more than likely come to her cabin to bed her. "It . . . it could be dangerous," she stammered.

Syphron's jaw hardened at the meaning implicit in her few words. Mentally he swore, then vowed that he would see an end to the situation as soon as he could.

"All right," he muttered darkly.

"Don't come near my cabin," she insisted a little frantically.

"I just said I wouldn't," he snapped. "So I won't. But it kills me inside to know . . ."

Rose looked down at her toes peeking out from beneath the hem of her dress. "I got to go." Having said as much, she hurried from the cabin. But with every step she took she felt as though eyes were watching her from every direction.

As quickly as she could, she left her basket with Taloila and then rushed back to her own cabin. A wild kind of energy coursed through her veins, so that the progression of dusk into night took on a strange distortion. The shadows that came with the moon's light appeared eerie and every sound that floated on the night air seemed sinister.

Vaguely she realized that she was waiting for Travis. And just as vaguely, she understood in her own mind that she would never let him use her again.

Her hands trembled, and she prayed that she would get through this night.

She was fully prepared for Travis to step into her cabin. It wasn't anything that hadn't happened hundreds of times before. Still, when he did, her stomach clenched and she forgot to breathe. Standing as still as one of the ancient elms by the house, she stared at his handsome face.

He noticed her unusual rigidity at once. "What are you standing there like that for?" he asked, sauntering toward her.

Her breath came out in a sudden rush. "No reason."

"Are you feeling all right?"

She started to nod, but caught herself in the last minute. "No, not really."

Travis came to stand before her, his blue gaze taking in the tension about her eyes and the slight trembling of her lips. "Rose?"

"I ain't feelin' good," she blurted out. "Got me my monthly time."

A crooked frown puckered his brow. "I thought you dealt with that mess the week before last."

Unable to meet his eyes, she sidled away, rubbing her abdomen for good measure. "I did, but it weren't normal this time. I think . . . I think maybe somethin' was wrong with the potion Besha fixes me." Unthinkingly, she started to sit on the bed, but she quickly changed her mind and sat in one of the wooden chairs. "I got cramps in my belly."

Jamming his hands on his waist, Travis heaved an irritated sigh. His day had been long and tiring. He had wanted nothing more than to renew his strength in Rose's arms.

"Damn," he muttered to himself, but the curse shivered over Rose's nerves.

Once again, she swallowed nervously. She could only hope that he would accept her excuse. If he didn't, he would learn all too quickly that she had lied to him. That was something she had never done before, but she sensed that he would *not* take kindly to the matter.

"I should be fine in a few days," she offered.

"All right." He sighed in resignation. But he continued to study her closely. For the first time, he considered what he would do if anything were to happen to Rose. Almost despite himself, he had come to think of her as being part of his life. The thought of her becoming ill and dying made the hairs stand up on his arms.

In retrospect, he realized that she could have been one of the unfortunates who had not survived the illness of weeks past. It was something that he had not even thought of at the time, but the reality of it struck him that second, and it was so sobering that he stiffened in silent self-defense.

"Are you sure there's nothing else the matter?"

Quickly, she replied, "Nothin' more than bad cramps."

"I want to know if you're not feeling better in a day or two."

Fidgeting under such intense scrutiny, she agreed. However, in the back of her mind, she wondered what would happen when an acceptable number of days had passed. How was she going to keep him away then?

Long after Travis had returned to the big brick house, and she lay on her bed, she prayed with all her might for an answer to her problem. The only one she could see would be for her and Syphron to leave before the end of the week.

Chapter Fifteen

"I am the most beautiful bride the Tidewater has ever seen," Marriette vowed. She made the declaration to her reflection in her mirror. Not that she wouldn't have rather told someone else, but Lacy was in the great room seating guests and every maid who was worth anything was busy running about like a chicken without its head.

A pretty shrug dismissed her disappointment, and one last time she observed herself critically. The curls of her hair were threatening to droop in the heat of the late morning. Thank goodness the coronet of her veil held the blond strands in place. Her cheeks were becomingly pink, again a result of the August heat. But if she weren't careful, the rosy blush would soon turn into an outright flush.

She snapped open her fan which dangled about her wrist from a delicate cord and waved vigorously. All the while she continued her visual critique. Her gown was lovely, even though her bodice lacked the pearls she had once envisioned being there. Nonetheless, the ivory satin was the absolute best that money could buy.

Turning away from the mirror with a smile, she reminded herself to tell every woman present that the lace in her veil actually came from Belgium. She wasn't exactly sure where that place was, but it certainly sounded impressive.

Impatiently, she glided to one of the windows to check if there were any late arrivals. This waiting to be summoned below was damned annoying. She would just as soon get on with the entire affair. The sooner she married Carter, the sooner she could leave Swan's Watch forever. And once she left, she would never look back.

As far as she was concerned, Lacy and Travis could have the place. That was, of course, unless there ever came a day when they decided to sell off part and parcel. She didn't think that would happen, but if it did, then she would naturally expect to be included in whatever profit resulted.

Almost idly, she thought about what she would do with her share of the money. She was still immersed in her musings several minutes later when Lacy came to tell her it was time for the ceremony to begin.

"Carter is waiting," Lacy told her, handing her a bouquet of blood-red roses.

"Are there many people?" Marriette queried, excited at the prospect of making her grand entrance.

"Nearly everyone who was invited."

Marriette's blond brows shot up. "Who isn't here?"

"Jeanne Gail couldn't make it. Her mother says that she's taken to her bed with a terrible headache."

Heaving an exasperated huff, Marriette declared, "She's just jealous. Everyone knows she's been pining away for Carter for years. Now that I'm going to marry him, she can't even face me."

"That's not true," Lacy objected. "If Jeanne Gail has had her heart set on anyone, it's been N. Douglas."

Marriette liked her version of the truth far better. "Well, I will not waste another second thinking about it. Who else isn't here?"

Lacy named several neighbors who were absent, only to have their names dismissed with a negligent wave of her sister's hand.

"Oh, they don't count for anything anyway," Marriette commented offhandedly. "I just wanted to give them a thrill at being invited."

For the sake of the day, Lacy held her tongue.

Unfortunately, she found herself having to do that repeatedly throughout the afternoon. The ceremony itself was beautiful. Carter made a handsome groom, especially standing beside Marriette. They seemed perfectly suited to each other, and to anyone making a casual observation, the bride seemed absolutely smitten with her new husband. Yet more than once, Lacy overheard snatches of Marriette's conversations, and it was readily apparent to her that her sister was far more concerned with impressing the guests than she was with her status as a new bride.

"I have always thought Bellehaven to be the most magnificent house I have ever seen," Marriette murmured to a group of ladies. "Isn't it a shame that everyone can't live in such grand surroundings."

The comment elicited raised eyebrows and simpering smiles. Lacy was hard-pressed not to clap her hand to her forehead in dismay. It was not that she was surprised by Marriette's avarice, she was just shocked that her sister would so tactlessly voice her personal ideas in public. It was not something Marriette ever did.

"Travis, do you sense something unusual about Marriette?" she whispered, watching their sister glide away to the buffet table.

Standing beside Lacy, Travis also watched the bride's passage across the room. "You mean something more than her customary nastiness?"

That earned him a sharp, considering look from Lacy. For weeks he had been as caustic as she had ever known him to be, and always his target had been Marriette. "Well, I suppose you could put it that way. She's always been arrogant."

"You're being too kind," Travis scoffed.

"Perhaps, but this marriage to Carter has made her overbearing."

Travis shrugged. "Well, she's Carter's problem now. Let him deal with her."

He strolled away to leave Lacy still puzzled. It might be an easy task for Travis to ignore the matter, but Lacy could only wonder what had taken hold of Marriette's manner.

She asked herself that same question later that evening when N. Douglas approached her after dinner. "Lovely party, Lacy," he commented amiably.

"Thank you, N. Douglas. But most of the credit should go to Marriette. She planned every detail down to the flowers decorating the banister. She has a talent for such things."

"That will stand her in good stead, then."

"How so?"

N. Douglas shrugged as though he was about to tell her the obvious. "To listen to your sister, she has great plans for Bellehaven. New furniture, new decorations."

This was not something Lacy had heard. "Oh? What does Carter have to say about it?"

A one-sided grin accompanied N. Douglas's chuckle. "Nothing, as far as I can tell. I would say that he doesn't even know yet. Marriette's probably waiting for a better time to tell him that she intends to spend a great deal of his money."

Knowing her sister, Lacy privately agreed. She gazed at Marriette deep in conversation on the far side of the parlor, and shuddered to think what the woman was saying even then.

What Marriette was saying, and what she was actually thinking were miles apart. With Carter at her side, she was forced to keep her more pointed comments to herself. Beyond that, she chafed at having to stand there and pretend an interest in some neighbor's hog farm.

Talk of hogs! At her wedding. It was enough to make her grit her teeth. And if she had to keep the smile on her face for one more minute, her mouth was going to crack and fall right off her head.

Though still appearing to hang on every word uttered about breeding sows, she decided that she had had enough. There was no reason for her and Carter to remain any longer. She had dazzled everyone who was capable of being dazzled. She had impressed every woman who had an ounce of good sense. Frankly, she was now bored to tears.

Laying a languorous hand on Carter's arm, she politely interrupted his discussion. "I don't mean to complain, Carter dear, but I am beginning to tire." A coy smile drifted to her lips.

The promise in the seductive curve drew Carter's immediate attention. "It is about time we left." He bent his head and whispered in her ear, "I'm more than anxious to get you alone."

The edges of her smile faltered, but she turned away before it became apparent to Carter that his remark set her nerves on edge.

They began their exit, stopping to bid farewell to guests and friends, tarrying to accept final congratulations and well-wishes. But when they would have paused to say goodbye to Lacy and Travis, Marriette glided out the front door, leaving Carter to face his in-laws by himself.

For an awkward moment the three stared at each other, held still by perplexity and embarrassment. Then Lacy came to her toes and pressed her cheek to Carter's. "The best of luck to you, Carter."

He nodded his thanks in return then grasped the hand Travis extended his way. In a moment, he joined Marriette and helped her into his closed carriage.

The last rays of sunlight had faded an hour before. Only muted grays filled the carriage. Nonetheless, Carter openly regarded his wife sitting opposite him.

"I always knew," he began mildly, "that you did not see eye to eye with your brother and sister, but was that necessary?"

254

Marriette blinked in confusion. "Was what necessary?"

"Slighting them the way you did."

"Did I do that?" she asked, putting just the right amount of consternation in her voice.

Carter laughed unperturbed. "You know damn well you did, Marriette, but don't explain on my behalf. How you feel about your family is your own business. Personally, I happen to like Travis and Lacy."

The endorsement was provoking, but she hid her anger with a pout that rounded her bottom lip. "You like them because you have never had to live with them." She shook her head dismissively. "Now I don't want to talk about them anymore."

Carter had no objections and let her have her way. Personally, he didn't think her capable of any great mental processes, so he honestly didn't care what she thought. As long as she pleased him in bed, he was willing to be lenient with her out of bed.

Mental images of her lying in his great four-poster teased him all the way home. She was beautiful enough with her clothes on to make a man ache where it counted. The promise of what he would find waiting for him beneath the layers of satin and lace was as potent an aphrodisiac as any oyster he had ever eaten. Already he could feel himself hardening. The night stretched out before him with beckoning pleasure.

Marriette felt only an odd trepidation about the hours to come. As the carriage drew her closer and closer to her new home, she nibbled on her lower lip and gave serious thought to what was to transpire.

Oh, she knew what to expect. No one grew up on a plantation without becoming aware of the nature of things, so she knew what went where and how everything was achieved. She just didn't think she was going to like it very much. After all, Carter's kisses did nothing to instill passion.

It was a private complaint that lasted only until she entered Bellehaven on Carter's arm. The grand foyer with its lavish and obvious evidence of prosperity reduced her qualms about the marriage bed to mere triflings. And the sight of an honest to goodness housekeeper waiting in attendance made her want to throw her arms about Carter's shoulders and kiss him soundly.

"Naomie, you know Marriette," Carter said to the aging black housekeeper. "She's my wife now."

Naomie's smile was toothless, but it stretched from one side of her face to the other. "Welcome, Miz James."

Marriette was already turning away, studying the house that was now hers. Unfortunately Carter cut short her examination.

"Naomie will show you up to your room." His hand lingered on the small of her back. "I'll be up shortly."

The gentle push she received from behind focused Marriette's attention back to the immediate. In her glee at finding herself mistress of the manor, she had nearly forgotten that this was her wedding night and Carter had every intention of claiming his husbandly rights.

She remembered to give him a dimpled smile before she followed Naomie's waddling passage up the wide stairway and into her bedroom.

"This here was Miz Lily's room," Naomie announced proudly. "She was a fine woman, Miz Lily was."

Strolling over the highly polished wood floor, Marriette made a great show of scrutinizing the room. Everyone and his brother knew that Carter's mother had been a fine woman, but she had had an absolute penchant for the color green.

Marriette rolled her eyes in disgust. Green everywhere, and not a deep vibrant hue, but a dull, moss tone that was revolting. It was beyond enough. She could not be expected to sleep under a coverlet that reminded her of molding grass. It would have to go. And the canopy and carpets, too. They looked to be a hundred years old and she wanted everything to be new and bright. Pink suited her. As did red.

The furniture was acceptable, but only because she was partial to cherry. The intricate carvings on the bedposts were most appealing. And the cabriole legs on the chaise were certainly stylish enough. But the tapestry on the piece needed to be replaced, as well as the upholstery on the settee by the fireplace. The floral stripes were too much of a reminder of the wallpaper in her bedroom at Swan's Watch.

Standing in the center of the room, she turned a complete circle and nodded in satisfaction. The room would be beautiful once she had made her changes; a true reflection of the style and grandeur she intended to bestow on Bellehaven.

That decided, she allowed Naomie to assist her out of her gown.

Thirty minutes later, she was sitting in the middle

of Carter's huge bed, nibbling on her lower lip again. The unease she had felt earlier in the carriage had returned and increased with each layer of clothing she had removed. By the time she stood in nothing but her chemise and drawers, she was positive that being a bride was highly overrated.

Her room adjoined Carter's and as soon as she had changed into her frilly night rail, Naomie had ushered her through the connecting door. Now, she waited for her husband with a mixture of dread and annoyance vibrating through her veins. She would have much preferred to have waited in her own room. At least there, she could have occupied her mind with redecorating. But here, she was left with nothing to do except stare at the masculine surroundings and anticipate the night ahead.

She did not like the male aura that permeated the room. The heavy furniture seemed to boast of absolute power and the dark green and black fabrics exuded a sense of unconditional authority. The effect was disconcerting and made her feel helpless. That was not a feeling to which she took kindly.

Patience had never been hers. Lack of that particular virtue nipped at her composure, sharpening her annoyance to a near pique. It was horribly uncivil for Carter to keep her waiting this way, especially since she wanted to have the whole thing done and behind her. She had half a mind to return to her own bed and teach him a few lessons from the very start.

Whatever she intended became irrelevant at that moment. The door swung open and Carter strolled in, his neck cloth loosened, his waistcoat and jacket

258

nowhere in evidence. At the sight of Marriette sitting against the brace of pillows in his bed, his brown eyes darkened to near black.

"I see you have found where you belong," he murmured, coming to stand at the foot of the massive four-poster.

Her nerves already on edge, Marriette bristled. "You make it sound as though you expect me to grow roots to the mattress, Carter."

A sultry smile stretched the line of his lips. "Not a bad idea." He could think of no place more fitting for her, sprawled flat on her back with her legs spread for him. He gazed at the fall of blond hair cascading about her shoulders, following the sinuous curves downward over her breasts. There he openly stared at the swells hidden by her gown.

Idly, he began to unbutton his shirt, making Marriette blink. Seeing her start, Carter chuckled and asked, "Did you think I was going to mount you with my clothes on?"

Her brows slanted into a frown. His phrasing was crude, and not at all what she expected of him. "I'm not a brood mare, Carter."

"Ah, I see I have offended your sensibilities." He tugged his shirt from his pants, revealing the broad expanse of his chest with its mat of brown hair. "Then you had best cover your eyes, because you are probably going to be more than offended in a second or two."

"And I am not some simpering miss," she retorted. Still, when he dropped his shirt to the floor and reached for the fastenings of his pants, she busied herself with an intense examination of her cuticles.

259

Not even his rich laugh or the shift of the bed receiving his weight drew her gaze upward. She kept her eyes studiously glued to her hands, knowing he was naked beneath the covers beside her.

Before she could take a steadying breath, his hands closed about her shoulders and he pushed her flat on her back. In one sure move, he covered her with his own body and planted his mouth over hers. His tongue parted her lips and swept into her mouth in hungry strokes.

Marriette's breath left her in a single rush at his sudden and fierce claiming. Clenching her eyes shut, she waited for some spark of passion to kindle somewhere inside of her. But all she felt was the thickness of his tongue jabbing at her own.

Cruelly her mind dragged up memories of Jared. The kiss in the garden had been short, but it had made her nearly giddy with excitement. The feel of his mouth had been firm and warm, a stark contrast to the wet smoothness that was now ravishing her lips, plundering as though her mouth was some bastion to be stormed and conquered.

She barely suppressed a groan of disgust as Carter's hands moved in much the same manner, capturing hold of her hips, seizing her waist to draw her near. The sheer possessiveness and dominance in his manner was as appalling as it was nauseating, and she felt very much like she was nothing but owned flesh waiting to be claimed by its owner.

Struggling for a breath, she turned her head away. Unfazed, Carter spread kisses down her neck, biting the white skin where her pulse beat rapidly. Her strangled moan of protest seemed to excite him, and he locked his fingers into the neck of her nightgown and yanked the fragile muslin away.

The sound of tearing fabric made her go still for a second. Whatever she had thought this night to be, it had never included having her clothes ripped from her.

"Carter . . ." But that was all she could utter, for his hand closed about her breast, squeezing the flesh into a pouting mound for his mouth. Teeth and tongue explored at will, and it was all Marriette could do not to shove him away.

The weight of him made her feel trapped and his fingers kneading her flesh made her skin crawl. When he yanked the hem of her gown above her knees, she had to swallow heavily.

His palm settled possessively over the thatch of tightly curling hair at the apex of her legs. Lifting his head, he stared down into her darkened eyes and smiled. With no warning, he thrust his hand between her thighs.

Marriette arched away from the intimate touch of his fingers, but his heavy leg held her thighs to the bed and stayed any movements she might have made. Her struggle brought Carter's mouth back to hers.

"Open your legs, Marriette," he breathed against her lips.

"I don't like this," she ground out breathlessly.

"You're not required to like it, only to make sure that I do." He shoved one finger and then a second into her tight warmth and murmured thickly, "Don't worry, you'll get used to it soon enough."

That was the last he said on the matter. He forced her mouth open with his tongue while his knees slowly but relentlessly spread her thighs.

Again, she squeezed her eyes shut, as though blocking out the sight of his face could block out the feel of his hard probing flesh. But the second he surged inside her, the sharp pain snapped her eyes wide and she saw reality for what it was; Carter thrusting into her repeatedly, his mouth ravaging hers, his sweat coating her skin.

When he lifted her hips and pressed her closer, she offered no resistance. When a groan was ripped from his chest, she let the vibrations shiver through her. When he emptied himself in the depths of her, she let out a sigh of relief.

But as soon as he withdrew, she shoved to the far side of the bed, pulling her sleeves back into place, holding her bodice closed across her breasts. Uncomfortable twinges marked her movements, but she ignored them in her haste to return to her own room. Rolling to her side, she sat up. Immediately, she was tugged backward.

Propped up on one forearm, Carter regarded her with undisguised humor. In his free hand, he held the end of her torn gown. He gave it another tug. "Going somewhere?"

"Yes, back to my own room." Her blue eyes flamed with a passion that had nothing to do with desire. Fury fairly sizzled in every nerve ending, making her limbs tremble.

He shook his head, liking the mutiny flashing in her eyes. "It wasn't that bad."

"No, it was worse."

"That's because you were a virgin. Believe it or not, it does get better. And when you learn to participate, you might even get some enjoyment from it."

He was so blasé, she wanted to slap the grin off his face. "And until then, I'm supposed to be content just knowing that you're enjoying yourself."

"That's the idea." He lay back against the pillows, ignoring her infuriated screech, and sighed in deep satisfaction. "Now, you rest for a bit and then I'll see about teaching you how to please a man."

If she had believed for one second that she could leave this bed and gain her own room, she would have run for the door that instant. But she was no match for his strength or speed.

"Teach me . . . ? I've done my duty." She grabbed the shoulder of her gown as it started to slip down her arm. "I've let you paw and grunt all over me. I have *learned* everything I intend to learn."

Carter eyed her thoughtfully. He didn't doubt for an instant that he would make her comply, so she could rant and rave all she wanted. If the truth be known, he preferred her anger to her complacency. The notion that she was not all together willing was a challenge that was extremely stimulating.

Nonetheless, there was one lesson she did need to learn, and she needed to learn it right now.

His hand snaked out and closed about her arm. Before she even knew what was happening, Marriette was hauled onto her back and held in place by his weight. Belatedly, her arms came up in defense, but she found her wrists grabbed and pinned painfully to the bed on either side of her head.

"I know this is still new to you," he commented in a voice that was brutally mocking. "But just in case you've already forgotten, let me remind you that you're my wife." To prove his point, he shoved one knee between her legs and positioned himself firmly against her softness.

Marriette struggled with all her might, but only succeeded in increasing the contact of their bodies. "Let me up, Carter," she demanded.

"Oh, no. I'm going to plow some fertile ground and plant my seed."

"I'm your wife," she spat, "not some piece of land."

"There's no difference between the two." Bringing his mouth back to hers, he muttered, "I own you both."

Chapter Sixteen

"I'm scared," Rose whispered barely able to see Syphron in the blackness of his cabin.

Syphron felt around under his crude bed and snatched a laden burlap sack. Quickly, he stood and slung it over his shoulder. "Ain't nothin' to be 'fraid of, Rose. The weddin' today has everyone goin' five ways at once. Party still goin' on up to the house with no signs of lettin' up. Ain't no one goin' to notice us gone for hours. There won't never be no better time for us to leave."

"But what if Travis comes for me tonight?" She dreaded even to think what was going to happen when he found her gone. Thank the Lord above that she would be far away by then.

Syphron sent her a patient look. "I told you already, Taloila seen him drinkin' hard. He ain't goin' to be able to climb the stairs to his fancy bed, much less think 'bout comin' for you."

Rose wished that she could be as sure. Travis had left her alone for the past several days, believing the excuse she had given him. But nature being what it was, the pretext would only work for so long and Travis would be expecting to be between her legs again. With all her heart, she prayed that tonight was not the night he decided to demand those rights he believed were his.

"What else did Old African say?"

"Only to follow the river north. And to never stray far from the water."

It was still a shock to Rose that Taloila had involved herself with their plans. But the old weaver had, and to the point of gathering up as much food as she could and hoarding it until tonight.

"We got to go," Syphron urged.

Rose nodded and picked up her belongings, all neatly rolled into the bundle she had fashioned out of her shawl. Everything she possessed on this earth was held in one hand. It was a pitiful thing to say about a person. "I'm ready," she vowed.

"Stay right beside me. Don't say nothin' 'til we's well past the fields."

Heart pumping with raw energy, Rose dragged in a calming breath. Slipping like a shadow into the night, she left Syphron's cabin and hurried close behind him. His path took them straight for the concealing trees that ran the length of the plantation. She neither stopped nor looked anywhere but ahead until they had gained the relative safety to be found in the forest.

Only then did she pause, and almost against her will, she turned and looked back at the house. The windows were aglow with light, the sound of voices carrying to her on the southerly breeze. One of those voices could have belonged to Travis.

The reality of what she was doing struck her hard and emotions, strong and relentless, overwhelmed her. There were too many ifs to even think about. And wishes, whether made on the first star of the evening or not, never ever came true. But if she could have put a name to the one desire that had burned within her, it would have been for the time and the place and the circumstances to have been different. Given that, things might have gone another way for her and Travis.

Another burst of laughter came to her out of the darkness.

She turned and followed Syphron into the moonless night.

Jared stared up at the moonless sky and took a deep swallow of his wine. He let the pungent flavor rest on his tongue, before he lowered his glass and breathed deeply.

There was a crispness in the air. Even this late in the summer, he could feel a telltale chill that never seemed to leave Connecticut. The days might warm up, but once the sun set, the cold that permeated the rocky earth made the night cool.

It wasn't something to which he had ever given a great deal of thought. But he did now. And he found himself missing the steamy heat that filled the air at Swan's Watch.

He looked down at the wine in his glass and swore.

Voices, joyous and loud, sounded from behind. But instead of returning inside to his family, he leaned a shoulder against one of the pilasters on his parents' porch and gazed out toward Wethersfield's cove in the distance. Partially hidden by trees, the water appeared inky black, still and remote. The spot suited his need for solitude just then.

His gaze scanned near and far, and he viewed the landscape with a sense of familiarity. Yet, as though he had been gifted with new sight, the area seemed subtly different. The thick pines appeared incorrect to his eye, the ground too mounded and rough. And the breeze that came off the river lacked the scent of hickory and newly turned earth.

"Jared?"

He shifted his weight to glance over his shoulder. His mother's petite form was silhouetted against the light emanating through the doorway.

"Are you all right, son?"

Lifting an arm in invitation, he cocked his head to one side. "Getting reacquainted."

Bethany Steele stepped into her son's embrace. Sliding her thin arm about his back, she glanced up to his shadowed face and gave him a full smile.

"I'm glad you're back. We all missed you."

"It's good to be back." For the most part, Jared meant what he said.

"Things go well in Virginia?"

"Very. My business there was quite profitable. Stephen and I will have our hands full for the next two years just trying to manage the deals that were struck."

"I'm happy for you, dear. And I am very proud of you."

"Make sure that you include Stephen in your

praise. The firm is as much his as it is mine."

"I am very proud of you both. Your father tells me that if things continue as they have, the company will rival any shipping firm in the world."

Jared shrugged. "Father might be somewhat biased."

A very maternal smile pulled at Bethany's lips. "That is a father's prerogative. But there aren't many sons who would have been able to have done what you did. You've worked hard to build a virtual empire from nothing." Studying his face in the meager light, she added, "Sometimes I think you work too hard."

Jared's mouth took on a crooked curve. "Something only a mother would say."

"Then it shouldn't surprise you." Though they were lightly spoken, a wealth of concern underscored Bethany's words. Her eldest child had been back for several weeks and his manner had been just tense enough to give her occasional pause. "You've been awfully quiet since you returned home."

It would have been impossible for Jared to have missed the worry his mother was trying to conceal. "I suppose I've been tired."

"We didn't expect you back for a month at least."

Jared's brows shot up. "Is that a complaint?"

Bethany's arm tightened for a quick hug and she smiled. "What do you think?"

"I think," he remarked on a heavy sigh, "that you are doing your level best to ask questions you know I won't answer."

"Jared," came her shocked reply. But she could not hold on to her mock surprise and glanced sheepishly

269

to her feet. "Was I that obvious?"

"Afraid so."

She raised her eyes to his once more. "It's only because I worry about you."

"There is no need." He drained the last of the wine in his glass and forced a smile. "Why don't we go in."

Bethany knew that of all her children, Jared was the most difficult to reach. But she also knew, from long experience with the man, that there was nothing she could do to change that situation. If and when Jared wished to confide, he would. Until then, she would have to be content with his assurances that all was indeed well. Of course she didn't believe him for a minute, but the fact that he wished to join the rest of the family did ease her mind to some small degree.

They entered the parlor as a pair and came face to face with the entire Steele clan. Jared's brother, Stephen, stood with an arm about his wife, Lilith. Their fourteen-month-old daughter played contentedly nearby. Second brother, Eric, sat beside his wife, Jane, who was pleasantly rounded with their second child. Their first, a chubby little fellow all of the age of two, was happily ensconced on his grandfather's lap.

Jonathan Steele glanced up from his grandson's dark head at the appearance of his wife and eldest son. One had only to look at the gentleman to know from whom Jared inherited his chiseled good looks. Both shared the same lean jaw and gray eyes, and although Jonathan's hair was completely gray, it was as thick and full as his son's.

"There you are," Jonathan averred, giving Jared a

chastising smile. "I was getting ready to send out a search party."

"Taking in the night air," Jared explained.

"Well," Mary Steele declared, rising from her chair and twirling her way to Jared. "I was going to come out and fetch you myself." The youngest of Bethany and Jonathan's children, Mary was a vivacious sixteen-year-old who, like her mother, was petite and fine boned. "You haven't finished telling us all about Virginia."

Eric moaned in exaggerated dismay. "Let it rest, little sister. Give Jared a moment's peace."

Almost in unison, Mary and her three sisters strongly protested. "There, you see?" Mary announced. "We all agree, Jared. You were gone for weeks and all you have told us so far is that it was, to use your words, 'blasted hot.'"

Bethany pressed a hand to her forehead and took her place next to her husband. "Mary, please mind your manners."

Jared chucked his sister under her chin. "I have told you far more than that."

Rachel, Mary's older sister by eighteen months, piped up, "What is the plantation house like?"

Crossing to the only spare seat in the room, Jared sat in a large wing-back. Before he could even settle himself comfortably, Stephen's daughter wobbled her way to his knees and lifted her arms in a demand to be picked up. Jared gladly accommodated the plump little version of her mother and sat her on his lap.

"The house," he replied, picturing the Watch's brick manor with fondness, "is large, beautiful. To look at it, one would never know that it is nearly two hundred years old."

"And what river was the plantation on?" Jane wanted to know.

"The Pagan."

Eric chuckled and waggled his dark brows. "Produces an evocative image of heathens and sultry summer nights."

"For the most part," Jared returned, "it is all quite civilized, quite peaceful." In truth, there was a certain serenity he had discovered at Swan's Watch that he had never found anywhere else. Not even at sea.

"Oh, who cares about houses and rivers," Mary proclaimed, her eyes alight. "I want to know about the women. Are they all beautiful? Are they all Southern belles?"

Jared's gaze dropped to his niece sprawled over his chest, exploring the folds of his cravat with surprisingly strong fingers. "Some are most beautiful," he averred solemnly.

"And what do they talk like?"

A hard glint came to the glance Jared lifted to Mary. "What?"

"Do they have accents?" Batting her eyelashes, she affected her version of a Southern twang. "Do they awl sound lak thee . . . is?"

Jared's jaw tightened. "No, it's more of a soft drawl than an accent."

One voice in particular haunted his mind. Smooth, sweet, it accompanied a face of flawless beauty. Damn her. *Damn her.*

He was still cursing an hour later when he let

himself into his house. The evening with his family had come to a stilted conclusion for him. He had lingered for the sake of his parents, but most of the joy of his evening had been stripped away, reduced to a fine tension by the unshakable memory of turquoise eyes.

He tossed his key on the side table in the foyer and lit the lamp standing at the ready. His movements strained, he turned for his study and the distracting promise of work.

The room lay in deep shadows, the wood-paneled walls giving off only a hint of their warm umber color. Still, he did nothing to add more light to the room. Sitting behind his desk, he found the neutralized hues a perfect complement to his state of mind. Impartial, disinterested, he struggled to focus his attention on the stack of papers, and suddenly all his intentions to keep his mind occupied crumbled like so much old parchment.

Leaning forward, he rested his elbows on his widespread knees and let his hands hang loosely in between. His gaze dropped to his fingers and all he could see were his palms filled with long strands of silver-blond hair.

Damn. Would he never be free of her memory? She invaded his every waking hour until he was at constant odds with himself. He buried himself in his work in the hope that he would not have time to even think about her. But no matter where he looked, he saw the perfection of her face.

His nights were little better. She intruded into his sleep, the remembered sound of her laughter tormenting his senses. More times than he could count, he would awake, fully expecting to have her in his arms. Yet all he would find was the loneliness of his empty bed.

Jerking back in his seat, he dragged a hand through his hair in pure frustration. He wanted to hate her. He wanted to condemn her for putting him through this hell, but God Almighty, he couldn't. If anything, his love for her had grown with each day that had passed.

That love ate at his insides now, tightening his jaw. He had half a mind to sail back that very night and make love to her until she was capable of nothing except agreeing to marry him. Unfortunately, sadly, he recognized the futility of such an action, for Lacy was tied to Swan's Watch in ways he was only beginning to understand.

To some degree, he could identify with what she felt. Strangely enough, the essence of the plantation had somehow become instilled deep within him. He felt it at the oddest times. Like some tender shiver racing over his skin, he was seized by a yearning to feel the red earth beneath his feet.

His stay had been brief, but in those weeks, the attachment had been made. He could only imagine that after a lifetime spent on that same ground, how great Lacy's bond to her home must be. He sensed it was a bond unlike any other, and unique solely to her.

He had known all along that she was the strength behind the plantation, but he was coming to realize that like a circle completed, the Watch itself was the source of her strength. What she drew from the land, she returned, and she was as defined by the rows of crops as she was by the blue of her eyes or her unwavering commitment to her heritage. That kind of connection went beyond a simple bonding. It was a sharing of the land's spirit.

Lacy was Swan's Watch. And they were inseparable.

The moonless night gave way to ponderous morning clouds that hung low over the Pagan River. The air smelled heavily of rain, and Lacy prayed that this day would see the greedy sky relinquish some of its moisture.

Her hands worked steadily to roll back her sleeves as she made her way to the weaving cottage. It was barely seven o'clock, but the heat and mugginess were already making their presence felt. For some odd reason, the effect seemed exaggerated this morning. In the excitement of yesterday's revelry, the still humidity had barely been noticed. Now, with Marriette's wedding past, the sultry air seemed almost too thick to breathe.

Just thinking of the wedding caused Lacy to sigh deeply. She hoped that Marriette had at last found some measure of happiness. Her sister had certainly never been content with her life to that point. Perhaps being married to Carter would bring her the satisfaction she had so desperately wanted.

Lacy gained the cluttered weaving cottage and stepped within. At the sight of Taloila bent over her loom, her thoughts turned to more utilitarian matters.

"Good morning, Taloila."

Taloila nodded, her feet moving over the loom's treadles, her gnarled hands throwing the shuttle back and forth.

"How are you today?"

Again, Taloila merely nodded, her eyes fastidiously set on her hands.

Lacy stopped to peer at the wool fabric that had been wound on the cloth beam. "How many yards do you expect?"

Taloila's lined mouth twisted tightly to one side. "Ten yards from dis here piece."

Calculating the number of winter shirts that could be fashioned from the single length, Lacy's brows rose in pleasure. "Good. As soon as you're finished, we'll have Rose launder the material." Curiously, she looked about. "Where is Rose?"

"Ain't seen her dis mornin'."

"Well, when you do, she needs to get started on boiling those onion skins for dye. Besha has them ready for her."

"Yes'm." Taloila's mouth twisted again, snagging Lacy's attention.

"Taloila, are you feeling all right?"

"Yes'm."

A puzzled frown settled across Lacy's brow. "Are you sure? If you aren't well, the fabric can wait."

Under the pressure of the concerned blue-green gaze, Taloila's hands stilled. "Dere's some mornin's I feel old, Miz Lacy. And dere's some mornin's I feel like a sweet young thin'. Today I feel like de Old African dat I is."

Lacy rested a hand on the woman's thin shoulder. "Why don't you rest for the day." Her suggestion met with an emphatic, negative shake of the head. "Then perhaps you should lie down, for a few hours at least."

"I'll be fine, Miz Lacy. I wouldn't know what to do wid idle time on my hands." Immediately, she resumed her work, hands and feet moving in perfect harmony. "Just feelin' my age, is all."

If anyone was entitled to feel her age, Lacy admitted it was Taloila. The woman was nearing eighty, and still worked harder than women scores younger.

"All right," she relented, "but you are to stop and rest if you begin to tire."

"Yes'm."

Lacy left it at that, but as she made her way to the kitchen, she decided that it was time to increase Rose's responsibilities in the weaving cottage.

The scent of frying ham reached Lacy long before she entered the whitewashed kitchen with its huge fireplace. Even this morning, a full fire was blazing away as Besha worked over her iron trivets and pans.

"You would think" Lacy said with a chuckle, coming to stand at one of the chopping blocks, "that after all the food I ate at the wedding yesterday, I would never again be hungry. But, Besha, I swear I could eat every bit of that ham you're cooking."

The rotund cook beamed a smile. "Dat sure was some party goin' on last night. I ain't heard no such ruckus 'round here since you was born and your daddy had him a party to celebrate."

"Excuse me, Miss Lacy," Michael interrupted from the doorway.

Hushpuppy in hand, Lacy turned to the overseer.

"Good morning, Michael."

The burly man tipped his hat and regarded Lacy solemnly. "I don't mean to trouble you, ma'am, but is your brother up and about yet?"

Lacy nodded. "Yes, but barely. I'm afraid he enjoyed himself a little too much at the party last night. I'd give him another half hour."

Michael's brows slowly descended, his face taking on a pained expression.

"Is there anything I can help you with?" Lacy inquired.

The overseer scrubbed at his chin, swallowing a muttered curse. "Ma'am, have you seen Rose this morning?"

"No, I haven't." His tension brought Lacy to the doorway.

"What about you, Besha? Have you seen the girl?"

Besha straightened from stirring a kettle of grits and faced the man with troubled eyes. "No, sir, I ain't seen her."

"Why, Michael?" Lacy asked.

An angry grunt preceded his reply. "I think she may have run off, Miss Lacy."

Lacy's eyes rounded. "What?"

"No one has seen her. And "—he paused to grit back another curse—"Syphron is missing, too."

Lacy stood as though rooted to the spot, barely able to take in what he said. "Are you sure, Michael?"

"Damn near sure," he averred, giving up trying to watch his language. "He's supposed to be in the south fields right now, but no one has seen him since last night. I checked his cabin and most of his things are gone."

"And Rose?"

"Her clothes are missing."

Fingers trembling, Lacy shoved her right hand deep into her dress pocket and held fast to the ring of estate keys. "I'll have to tell Travis at once." Oh, but God, she wished she didn't have to. He would never consider allowing the pair their freedom. He would track them down. "Are you absolutely positive, Michael? Perhaps they're somewhere about the place, somewhere you haven't looked."

"I wish that were a fact, Miss Lacy. But they're gone."

In her heart, Lacy knew it was true. Michael would have never said a word unless he was certain.

Numbly, she nodded. "I'll go find Travis now." Dreading every step she took, she returned to the house, any hope that she could postpone the inevitable dashed away by the sight of Travis coming down the stairs.

"I do believe the house has a different atmosphere to it this morning," he said, meeting Lacy at the bottom step.

"Travis . . ."

But he stepped all over her trepidation. "Not that I wish to speak ill of our sister, but she has been trying at times."

"Travis, I need to speak with you."

He placed his hands on Lacy's shoulders, too content to allow the strain on her face to affect him. He felt better this morning than he had in weeks. Thanks to Jared, money was not a problem. They had replaced the workers who had died, and with the exception of a minor drought, the situation on the plantation was as good as could be expected. And now, Marriette was gone.

A weight lifted from his shoulders every time he thought of it. From that moment weeks ago when she had spewed out her venom about Rose, he had been hard-pressed not to throttle that lily white neck she prized so highly. A sad admission, not one of which he was necessarily proud, but undeniable nonetheless.

"All right, little sister, what is it that you must discuss with me?"

Lacy swallowed with difficulty. "Michael thinks there might be trouble."

"Oh?"

"He says that Syphron has run off." The words slipped past her lips in a rush.

Travis jerked his hands away, grinding his teeth at the sudden anger that gripped him. "Damn it all."

"Travis, please . . ."

"That bastard has been brewing trouble for too long. I should have known he would try this." He stalked down the hall toward the back door.

"Travis, wait." Lacy hurried after him. "What are you going to do?"

Not bothering to stop or even look back over his shoulder, he spat, "What do you think I'm going to do? I've got to go find him and bring him back."

Lacy stretched out a hand, an instinctive gesture meant to prevent him from following through with his plans. "Oh, Travis, listen to me."

Already down the brick steps, he strode toward the stable. "I don't want to hear any of your pleas, Lacy. There are no choices in a matter like this. I have to bring him back."

Frightened of what course her brother's anger would take, she cried, "Don't hurt them, Travis."

He came to a dead halt and swung back to his sister. *"Them?"*

Dragging in one ragged breath after another, Lacy stared into the cold blue of her brother's eyes and felt her heart drop. "Rose is gone, too."

Chapter Seventeen

He was going to kill her. When he got his hands on Rose, he was as sure as hell going to kill her!

Travis's knees gripped the sides of his lathered horse, his hands brutal on the reins. Just up ahead, he could see one of his neighbors, Jake McPherson, running his hounds on leads. Their baying signaled the dogs's success in tracking, scenting, running Rose and Syphron to ground.

Viciously Travis cursed, his voice joining the sounds of the horses crashing through the underbrush of the forest that bordered the James River. In a vague manner, he was aware of Michael off to his left, riding silently, precisely, always certain to keep McPherson in sight.

They rounded a marshy bend in the river, and grappled their way over ground mired with tar and grasping vines. The rotten-egg stench from the pitch joined the afternoon's stifling dampness and unrelenting heat in a combination that sent the bile into Travis's throat. Fiercely he choked it down, and cursed Rose to hell and back.

She belonged to him . . . in ways she couldn't even begin to comprehend. When he caught up with her, he would . . . *Damn it all!* A part of him wanted to kill her, to grab her neck in his hands and squeeze until he wrung the last breath from her body. But just as wildly, he wanted to take that same sweet body and bury himself within the softness of her. He wanted to take her again and again, until there would never be a shred of doubt that she belonged to him, body and soul, heart and mind and spirit.

The constant howling of the dogs subsided, then dwindled to nothing more than confused whimpers. Travis rode toward Jake and reined in at the river's edge to find the hounds running in impatient circles.

"What the hell is going on?" Travis demanded, dragging his shirtsleeve across his forehead to catch the sweat dripping into his eyes.

Jake McPherson shook his head, then spat out a stream of spittle stained brown from the wad of tobacco jammed against his tongue.

"He's sly, I'll give 'im that."

"Who?"

"That runaway of yours. He knows no hound can pick up a scent through water, so he made sure they took to the river for a while."

Michael rode up, pulling his horse to a stand. "Did you lose the trail?"

McPherson slapped at a mosquito that buzzed at his neck. "Only for the time being. But we'll find 'im." He loosened the slack on the leather leashes and ran the dogs farther up stream. Noses to the ground, the three canines yapped and sniffed, darting in one

283

direction and then another.

Travis wiped at his forehead again. They were nearly twenty miles from home, and if it weren't for McPherson's dogs, he would never have thought that anyone could have made it this far on foot. But McPherson owned the best dogs in the county and once they had latched onto the scent, they had followed the pair northward from Smithfield clear to the James River. Now, they were headed west, following the southern banks toward Richmond.

A piercing howl rent the air.

"Found it!" McPherson called back.

Travis ground his heels against his horse's sides. In pursuit again, he sent his mount through the tangle of trees and shrubs. His blood pounded in a thundering cadence, obliterating the sting of branches whipping against his shoulders and arms, blocking out the feel of his sweat-soaked shirt stuck to his skin, obscuring everything from conscious thought but the obsession to find Rose . . . and make her his again.

Rose's breath came in labored gasps as she struggled to wade through the murky river water. Her sodden skirt clung to her legs, hampering her movements. The trudging stride she was forced to endure taxed her waning strength until her pulse raced.

Inside her stomach, noises rumbled while her head felt close to bursting with fatigue. Her arms and legs ached clear to the marrow of her bones, and more than anything, she wished Syphron would allow them to rest. But he had told her early on that they needed to put as much distance between them and Swan's Watch as they could.

She swallowed past a parched throat and glanced quickly back over her shoulder. Only darkness met her gaze, but she fully expected to see Travis materializing out of nowhere, his body looming over her, his face contorted with rage. It was the stuff of nightmares, a horrid anticipation that sent a shiver through her. Redoubling her efforts, she clung to her small bundle and fought off her fatigue.

Night sounds echoed over the water, and everywhere Rose looked, she saw nothing but a deep, dark gray. The water that encompassed her to her waist seemed like a cold, lead-colored blanket swirling out of a near-black sky. The trees on the shore appeared like indistinct hulking shapes, and the form of Syphron ahead of her was made up of nothing but shadows.

For what felt like hours, she had been surrounded by that shroud of gray. Last night's gloom, then the clouds of afternoon and now the moonless night. She wished that come tomorrow, the sun would shine through if for no other reason than to lift her spirits. They had been running for nearly a day, and her world had been reduced to putting one foot in front of another and staring off through trees whose colors had been stripped away.

"Syphron," she whispered between panting breaths. "Please, we got to stop, for just a minute." In the concealing dimness, she heard more than saw Syphron halt and then close the distance between them. The swish of water marked his movements that brought him to her side. Gratefully she laid her hand against his chest to steady herself. "I got to stop. I got to rest."

Syphron heard the weariness dragging on her every word. He took hold of her elbow and strained to see her face clearly in the dimness. What he saw must have convinced him to slacken the pace he had set for them, because he expelled a soft curse and led her up the sloping banks and into the forest.

"You should have said somethin' sooner, Rose," he admonished gently.

Dropping to her knees, Rose hugged her arms about her waist. "I don't want to hold you back none," she murmured.

Her words brought him to his haunches before her. "Hush up 'bout that. You ain't holdin' me back."

She wished she could believe him, but she knew that every time they had stopped it had been for her sake. "If you was by yourself, you would be miles away by now, you'd be doin' more runnin' than walkin' and you'd stay clear of the land more." His hand cupped her cheek and she looked up into his eyes. "I'm slowin' you down, Syphron."

"You ain't. You're doin' fine . . . we come a long ways."

That much was true, if the tiredness inundating her was anything to go by. "Where do you suppose we are?" She gave the area a nervous look.

Syphron's gaze followed hers. "Don't know for sure. Taloila just said to keep followin' the river 'til it ends, and then keep headin' north."

"How did Old African know this?"

The line of Syphron's shoulders rose with a shrug,

and he wiped the sweat and water from his face. "She didn't say much on it, but I 'spect her man told her . . ." His voice stopped abruptly, his body tensing. He shot to his feet and cocked his head to one side.

Rose frowned in concern. "Syphron? What is . . ."

He sliced a hand through the air to silence her. Holding her breath, Rose stared wide-eyed at the night, listening, waiting, fearing.

And then she heard it; the distant sound of dogs howling.

Her gaze jerked back to Syphron. "Do you think it's them?"

"I don't know."

Heart pounding, Rose came to her feet. The baying was already closer.

Syphron grabbed her arm and hauled her back to the relative safety of the river. "Run," he grated out.

Legs straining against the water, feet struggling for purchase on the slick river bottom, they fought their way along the curve of a secluded cove. The far side seemed miles and miles away, a distance too far to reach. The bundle Rose carried became burdensome and she let it sink away.

Behind her, the barking came louder than before.

"Oh, God," she gasped out, exercising every ounce of strength she possessed. Still, her skirt hampered her efforts, twisting and dragging at her legs. Only Syphron's firm hold on her arm kept her from falling.

Dread ate her from every direction. Her lungs burned and her throat clenched tight. The muscles she had thought too tired to work before, throbbed and convulsed as she scrambled through the water, battling to keep up with Syphron.

"Oh, God," she groaned again. Frantically she stared about her. There had to be some place safe, some place they could hide.

They reached the marsh grass that ringed the cove and she chanced a quick look over her shoulder. Through the dense thickness of the forest, she spotted the flickering lights of torches held high and coming toward them.

"Syphron . . ." She choked on her own breath. "It's them, it's Travis."

But Syphron wasted no time in considering possibilities. He gained the shore and pulled her out beside him. Fighting to fill his lungs, he forced Rose to keep pace as he broke into a run.

"Syphron, what are we doin'?" she cried. "They'll be able to follow us if we leave the water, the dogs will track us down."

Legs pounding over the soggy ground, he got out, "It ain't no use . . . they followed us this far." An unseen branch whipped out of the darkness to slash across his chest, but he ignored the searing pain that resulted. "Only thin' left for us is to run. . . ."

The dogs barking echoed through the forest, seeming to reach down from the trees above. Skirt clenched in her hands, Rose ran as though the hounds of hell were following her. And all the while she prayed, prayed that it not be Travis following them, prayed that she and Syphron somehow find a place to hide.

They ran blindly, leaving the river behind, following a path that had no direction other than away from those following them. But the torches approached at a frightening speed, and the men holding those torches quickly came into view.

"There they are," a voice called.

The words struck Rose's mind with brutal terror. She was going to die. Travis was going to catch her and kill her. Sobs congealed in her throat.

Underbrush tore at her legs, the rough ground cut through the thin leather of her soggy shoes. Syphron's grasp on her arms tightened to a death-grip, but she refused to stop. They had come so far. For a few precious moments, she had actually been free.

And oh, dear God, it had been sweet.

It was the last thought she had before the night erupted around her. Through eyes glazed with panic she saw a rider before her, his face cast into demonic relief by the light of the torch he held. She whirled away only to come face to face with the dogs, snarling, leaping, held in restraint by leads that seemed too fragile.

Again, she turned . . . and stared straight up at Travis.

The barking became frenzied. Horses sidled and danced in high agitation. The eerie torchlight cast long fearful shadows. But all Rose could see was the stabbing gaze of Travis's eyes upon her.

There was death in those blue eyes, a rage so lethal that she was buffeted by unrelenting terror. Her entire being seemed to liquify and flow straight down to her feet, leaving her coldly hollow and dead inside. Already she pictured herself buried beneath the ground.

Her hands flew to Syphron and gripped him tightly.

Face drawn into an iron mask of rage, Travis swung down from his horse. Never once did he release Rose from his pinning gaze, yet he reached to the scabbard on his saddle and withdrew a pistol from the fine leather. Her whimper of fear was like so much debris, and he ignored the sob as he slowly came toward her.

He stopped within arm's length of the couple, and stood. There he grabbed hold of her arm and wrenched her out of Syphron's grasp. She wheeled away, crying out in pain and fear as she tumbled to the ground.

In morbid gratification, Travis smiled, watching her crumple at his feet. Still, he made no other move to touch her. Instead, he turned back to Syphron. Ever so slowly, almost casually, he raised the pistol he held and aimed it directly at Syphron's head.

"No!" Rose screamed. Crawling and scrambling to right herself, she knelt in the dirt, her hands grasping Travis in supplication. "Oh, God, Travis, don't shoot him!"

Like her sobs and cries, he ignored her plea.

"Get her out of here," he ordered.

Michael dismounted and jammed his torch into the dirt. Long strides carried him to Rose, but she clung desperately to Travis's leg.

"Please, Travis, please . . . I'm beggin' you, don't kill him."

In one powerful surge, Travis swung around and brought the back of his hand across her face with punishing force. Lights exploded before her eyes, pain burst in her head threatening to obliterate reality. Still, part of her mind functioned and she sensed Travis coming down on one knee beside her. Instinctively she tried to shrink into herself, but he grabbed her up by the front of her dress and shook her like a rag doll.

"Open your mouth again, and I won't think twice about leaving your corpse here to rot with his." Shoving to his feet, he dragged Rose with him, then thrust her at Michael to take her away.

There was no part of Travis's mind, no fiber of his body that was not devoured by rage. When he turned his gaze on Syphron, every ounce of that fury shone with virulent intensity.

"I should have killed you long ago," he muttered. "The first time you looked at Rose, I should have strung you up."

Syphron stood straight, unflinching before Travis's hate, unwavering in the face of death. The only movement was that of his chest, heaving from his exertions.

"Do it then. Get it over and done with."

As though Syphron had said nothing, Travis demanded over his shoulder, "Michael, you and McPherson get out of here."

The overseer exchanged a troubled look with Jake.

"Go on," Travis repeated. "I've got some private business to settle with Syphron."

Michael shook his head in confusion, but tightened his hold on Rose and led his horse back into the thickness of the forest. McPherson followed close behind.

"Now, it's just you and me." Travis's voice was a

whisper cut from ice. He raised the gun again, jamming the cold steel up under Syphron's jaw. "I want you going to your grave thinking about this. I want you dying, knowing that Rose is mine. Never yours, Syphron, *mine.*" He nudged the pistol. "Think about that on your way to hell."

Syphron gritted his teeth. "I'll be thinkin' . . . and laughin' that she'll curse you to her dyin' day."

"I don't give a damn what she thinks."

"No? She's had her a taste of bein' free. You think she's goin' to just take up where she left off?"

"She'll do what she's damn well told to do." Travis's lips curled into a snarl. "And that includes spreading her legs for me."

The thought stiffened every muscle in Syphron's body. "She'll lie down for you, but only 'cause she won't have no choice. You can plow her 'til judgment day, but you won't get nothin' more than a body." A satisfied smile twisted his mouth. "She ain't never again goin' to be yours, 'cause you stole her freedom."

Travis's hand clamped around Syphron's neck in the next second, strangling off air . . . strangling off words too contemptible to contemplate.

"Shut up. . . ."

"Kill me," Syphron choked out, prying at the fingers locked at his throat, "and she'll hate you with every breath she takes."

A blind wrath tore through Travis, glazing his sight with red, urging him to squeeze the bastard's life away, compelling him to pull back on the pistol's trigger and send blood and brains flying all over the surrounding trees. His body shook with the compulsion, but Syphron's words devoured his reasoning.

Into his mind, came the vision of Rose, her arms raised in welcome, her smile easing his troubles, her body offering a comfort that reached into his very soul.

He blinked, and focused on reality. Syphron had gone to his knees, straining against the vise of fingers.

Kill me and she'll hate you with every breath she takes.

The words could not be avoided, their meaning as inescapable as the loathing that would forever more fill Rose.

Cursing, Travis lunged back, dragging in deep breaths to steady the battle raging within him. He watched Syphron collapse forward, gulping for air.

For long moments, the only sound to accompany the fading torchlight was the labored breathing of the two. Coarse and harsh, it filled the space between them, and mocked Travis for a fool.

"Get up," he snarled.

Swallowing past the pain in his throat, Syphron reared back on to his heels. Defeat pulled at his shoulders, slumping the line of his back, but pride, honest and true, brought his chin up.

"No. Kill me here. Kill me now, but I ain't goin' back with you." Respect for himself, for past generations that had lived and suffered and died before him polished the brown depths of his eyes. "I ain't goin' to be no man's slave no more."

It was a statement of fact. Not a threat or a ploy, and it hit Travis square in his chest. The man was dead serious. He would rather meet his end this instant than continue on.

Automatically, Travis raised the pistol and leveled the barrel at Syphron's head.

Kill me and she'll hate you with every breath she takes.

His thumb cocked the hammer back.

Kill me and she'll hate you . . .

His finger pulled the trigger. The blast of powder and ball split the night open.

The silence that followed was thunderous. And in that startling hush, Syphron realized that he was still alive, his life spared by the infinitesimal levering of Travis's hand to one side. Confused, uncertain, he exhaled in one huge gasp of relief and stared at Travis, trying to make sense of a world that had gone completely mad.

Travis stood rooted, unable to move, barely capable of rational thought. The implications of what he had just done were beyond thinking.

"Get out of here," he spat, his face contorted by pain and an abhorrent chaos that twisted at his entire being. "Run. As far and as fast as you can." His body shook as the words tumbled without restraint. "But if you even come near Swan's Watch, you so much as show your face anywhere near Rose and I swear by God Almighty that I will finish what you began tonight."

Comprehension penetrated Syphron's mind with shocking clarity. He was being allowed to go free. Fighting for understanding, he came to his feet, his thick brows lowered over nonplussed eyes.

"You just goin' to let me go?"

294

Travis's reply was a grinding of his teeth.

"Why?" Syphron breathed. "Why you doin' this?"

It was something Travis refused to answer, either to Syphron or himself. He turned and strode away, never once looking back; to do so would be tantamount to facing his actions and he would not, could not do that right then. Perhaps tomorrow when he was back at the Watch, when the normalcy of life had returned he might be able to think. But not now. All he wanted now was to return home.

Chapter Eighteen

"Miz Lacy, riders comin'."

Lacy stepped out of the hen house at Old Oliver's proclamation, her heart in her throat. She scanned the lane leading up to the house and saw her worst fears realized.

Travis was astride his horse, Rose perched behind. The horse's gait matched that of Michael's, a slow, exhausted plodding toward the house. There was no sign of Syphron. Anywhere.

Hastily, Lacy handed her basket to Oliver and rushed across the rolling lawn. But even as she neared, a horrible alarm assailed her. Travis's expression was grim, hostility barely contained. And Rose looked as though an insignificant puff of wind would topple her.

She gained the back steps just as Travis drew his mount to a halt. Fearing to ask, wanting to help in some way, she lifted a hand toward Rose, but to her horror, Travis shoved the girl to the ground.

"Travis!" Lacy cried, coming to the girl's aid.

"Leave her be," Travis barked.

But Lacy crouched by Rose and put her arms protectively about the girl's thin shoulders. The trembling weariness she felt in Rose tore at her heart. "Oh, Rose," she murmured, trying to soothe the girl's pain and fear.

"I said let her be," Travis growled, swinging down from his horse.

"You can't just dump her here."

"I can do anything I damn well please."

Lacy's trepidation increased. She stared at her brother in a mixture of dread and confusion. She knew he had been furious about the entire incident, but the emotions she witnessed on his face transcended fury.

"Where is Syphron?" she whispered, only to have her words cut off by a choking sob that broke over Rose's lips. Frowning, Lacy regarded her brother carefully.

"Where is he?" she repeated.

Travis refused to answer. His movements taut, he flung his reins to a waiting stable boy before crossing to the two women.

Every nerve in Rose cringed at his approach. In horror, she grabbed fistfuls of Lacy's dress, her eyes filled with alarm.

"Please, Miz Lacy, don't let him kill me."

Almost numbly, Lacy shook her head. "He's not going to kill you."

"He will . . . he will, just like he killed Syphron."

"What?" Stunned, Lacy exhaled sharply. "Travis . . . ?"

"Stay out of this, Lacy," he ordered.

297

"No. No, I won't stay out of this." Terror and loathing clenched at her stomach. This couldn't be true. Travis could not have killed Syphron. Swallowing against the bile that threatened, she demanded, "Tell me what happened."

It wasn't Travis who replied, but Rose. "He shot him, Miz Lacy. He said he was goin' to kill Syphron and he did. I heard the gun." Tears pooled in her brown eyes and trickled over her smudged cheeks. "He killed Syphron and left him there. That's why he ain't here." Words spent, Rose collapsed into Lacy's arms, weeping in a misery of the heart and soul.

Lacy gathered her close, too shocked and hurt to do anything other than hold Rose and offer what little comfort she could. But over the girl's head, she leveled an accusing glare at Travis.

The sight broke the fragile hold he had on his restraint. He lunged for Rose, reaching past Lacy, and hauled the girl to her feet.

Over her hysterical shrieking, he spat, "You're lucky I didn't kill you."

His violence was something Lacy had never before witnessed. When she came to her feet, she did so purely out of instinct, a reflexive action meant to spare Rose from whatever might befall her.

"Travis, let her go!" Her hands wrenched at his arms, trying to extricate Rose from his brutal grasp. "I won't let you hurt her. Let her go!"

Rose's panic only increased, her voice rising to a shrill cry. "I can't do it no more, Miz Lacy." She twisted frantically to escape. "I can't be his whore no more. I'll die if I have to lie down again for him. I'll die . . . I'll die!"

In one overpowering rush of realization, Lacy's eyes flew wide, her breath knocked from her lungs. Jolted down to the core of her, she looked at her brother in vile, disbelieving abhorrence.

"Travis?" She wanted him to deny the accusation. She wanted him to tell her that the very notion was a lie, but he didn't. He stood there with his hand wrapped about Rose's arm, the truth etched into every line in his face.

"How could you?" she whispered. "How could you do this?" When he remained silent, his eyes forsaking none of his anger, she tore at his arm, furious, ashamed, oddly wounded, and planted herself firmly in front of Rose. "You bastard." A rage to match his surged within her. Blindly, she swung her arm in a wide arch and slapped him full across the face. "You bastard!"

The sound of flesh meeting flesh echoed off the bricks of the house. The reverberation joined the sizzling tension with enough force to shove Travis back a step, and then another. For an endless second he was held utterly still, glaring at his sister, glaring at Rose, and then he spun on his heel and stalked toward the house.

Rose's weeping dogged his every step and Lacy's stare bored a hole into his back. Swearing at the damning effects of both, he slammed into the house and made his way to the bourbon in his study.

A healthy shot downed, a second and then a third. The smoky liquor brought a grimace to his face, but the bite felt good, distracting him. He waited for the numbing outcome, but it didn't arrive soon enough. Behind him, he could detect Lacy entering the room, crossing to stand within several feet.

"How could you have done such a thing?" she queried in a stiff, hushed voice.

"Don't pass judgment on me," he muttered, keeping his back to her.

"Someone should. What you have done is . . ."

"Wrong?" he cut in. Swinging about, he leveled an implacable look at her. "Come down out of that sanctimonious cloud of yours."

Lacy gritted her teeth. "We're not discussing my character, Travis. We're talking about you keeping Rose as your . . . whore. You had no right."

He slammed his glass onto the cabinet. "I had every right."

"Why? Because you *own* her?"

"Exactly."

"That accounts for nothing," she railed, her eyes glinting with anger. "Rose is a human being, yet you have treated her worse than dirt."

"I treat her well."

"You treat her as best suits your own purposes, your own lusts. She didn't come to you out of her own free will. The very nature of your status never allowed her to have a choice in the matter."

It may have started out that way, Travis knew, but what existed between Rose and himself had grown beyond that paltry arrangement. Scoffing, he jammed his fists on his waist and stared at the ceiling.

The plain truth was that he loved Rose. The realization of that had hit him as he had walked away from Syphron. He had known then what all his rage had meant. He had been furious, not so much because the two had tried to run, but because Rose

300

had chosen to leave him and he could not picture his life without her.

He loved her. But how could he admit that to Lacy. He could hardly admit it to himself.

"Are you quite finished?" he sneered, returning his gaze to his sister.

A slow shake of Lacy's head preceded her words. "No." She faltered, clenching her eyes shut for a brief moment. "Tell me . . . tell me what happened to Syphron."

"More of your moral judgments?" But he didn't need to ask. He could see her condemnation as clearly as he could see the filth that encrusted his clothes.

He threw back his head and laughed. "This is rich. The one . . . how would you put it? The one humane thing I do and my lips are forced shut."

"What do you mean?"

"I mean I didn't kill him." At her sigh of relief, he added, "That's right, I let the bastard go. I set him free."

"Thank God."

"Oh, yes, let's offer up our gratitude. And while we're at it, let's serve my head on a platter."

Confusion tilted Lacy's head to one side. "What? I don't understand."

"It's not that confusing."

"Rose thinks you killed Syphron."

"Of course she does. And so do Michael and McPherson, because I let them believe it."

"Why?"

"Because I don't have a choice. Can you imagine the outcry that would go up if it was to be known that I actually let a runaway go free? I would be lucky to have people even spit in my direction." He laughed again, but it was wholly without humor. "So you see, little sister, I am caught in a neat trap of my own making. But it should reassure you that I am not totally without conscience. I at least spared the man's life."

Lacy clasped her hands tightly, feeling drained of all energy. "What do you intend to do with Rose?"

"It's none of your business."

The flash of ire came back to her eyes, and her chin came up. "It is my business. I won't stand for you using her."

"*You* won't stand? Since when do I have to answer to you?"

"Since Rose pleaded with me to protect her from you."

"Rose does not need to be protected."

"She doesn't need to be raped!"

Fury surged through him. "It isn't rape!"

"It is nothing better if she does not want you."

But he wanted Rose. More than life itself, he wanted Rose, and now circumstances had taken her from him. And Lacy's interference only made the matter all the more bitter.

Frustration and anger mixed with fatigue. He was defenseless, against Lacy, against the dictates of society, against the Watch. And suddenly, he didn't care. About any of it. He did not have the energy to continue, nor did he possess the strength to maintain any kind of commitment.

"All right," he choked out, throwing his hands up in defeat. "You handle this. You handle everything.

302

The slaves, the house, the fields. I don't care anymore."

Lacy blinked in concern. "What are you saying?"

"I'm saying I'm tired. It's bad enough to have to fight the sun and the rain without having to fight you. How you go on, I don't know, but I can't." He stalked away, heading for the door.

"Travis, where are you going?" she called, following in his wake.

"I don't know. Away."

Lacy's heart lodged in her throat. "You're leaving?"

"Yes."

"For how long?"

"God, I wish I knew."

If Marriette hadn't heard the gossip with her own ears, she wouldn't have believed it possible, but rumor had it that Travis had left the Watch two days ago.

Settling back in the carriage that bore her away from Smithfield, she pondered the news that had all the tongues wagging. First there was that business of Syphron and Rose taking off the way they had, and then Travis killing Syphron. Now her brother had actually packed up and left. Richmond was the consensus of most of her friends, but no one was really sure where he had gone.

Not that it mattered. She really didn't care what Travis did, or didn't do. Not any more than she cared what Carter did. Her skin crawled at the thought of her husband.

Married only six days and she had already begun to dislike him. It wasn't surprising since all he ever wanted to do was take her to bed. All that pawing and sweating. The man was insatiable, as well as disgusting. He had an absolute fixation with breasts. She wished she had known that before she had ever agreed to marry him. She might have seriously considered forgiving Jared for his insults if she had been warned that Carter would be so demanding.

It was too late now. There was nothing she could do to keep him from claiming his rights, but she intended to exact payment in return. Hence her trip into Smithfield today.

A satisfied smile toyed with her lips. Carter might very well use her body like some rutting boar, but at least when he tossed her skirts up about her waist, those skirts would be the very best money could buy.

She had settled for nothing less when she had chosen the fabrics from Mrs. Miller's shop. The dressmaker had been thrilled, promising to complete the new wardrobe as quickly as possible. Wouldn't Carter be surprised when he saw the bill.

The carriage made its way up to the front doors of Bellehaven before Marriette finished her contemplations. Still, she shrugged and turned her thoughts from clothes to furniture. Her eyes taking on a renewed gleam, she entered the house.

"Miz James," Naomie said, holding the door open.

Marriette offered a slight tilt of her head in response to the gray-haired housekeeper. "Is my husband about?"

Naomie's wide, toothless grin stretched her face.

"That he is. Playin' that billiards ball in the library."

Billiards. This was another thing she wished she had known about Carter before she had married him. He was practically obsessed with the game. All that fuss over tapping those ridiculous balls into the proper pockets. And if that weren't bad enough, he insisted on betting money on the game's outcome.

Just last night, he had had some of his friends over and they had spent the entire evening and most of the morning wagering themselves into a drunken stupor. Of course, his preoccupation with his gaming had spared her his groping, lusting attentions, but she had been left to entertain herself.

Pouting and rolling her eyes at the same time, she sincerely hoped Carter's head was splitting open that very second.

To her disappointment, she found him very much a sober, collected man when she entered the library.

"There you are," he commented lightly, not looking up from the shot he was trying to make.

"Yes, here I am," she declared, removing her gloves.

"Did you have a nice ride into town?"

"No, that carriage is a disgrace, Carter. The cushions need padding and something has to be done about its lurching."

"I never thought it was particularly bad."

She was tempted to tell him that with the exception of choosing her for his wife, his standards left a great deal to be desired. "Well, I won't ride in it ever again. I feel bruised all over."

"Suit yourself." He wielded his cue with disarming accuracy, sending three balls into three separate pockets. "Did you visit anyone while you were out?"

"No, but I did stop by the dressmaker's."

"Is that right?" He sauntered around the table, contemplating his next move.

"Yes, I saw to having a few dresses made up."

"Well, you will just have to see about having them canceled."

"Canceled?" Eyes wide, Marriette stared at him in disbelief.

"I do believe"—he paused to tap one cue ball against another—"there is an echo in here."

"Carter, I can't cancel the order."

"Why is that?"

"Because I need those dresses," she huffed, as annoyed by his dictate as she was by his ignoring her.

"You have a closet full."

"But those are dresses I had before I married you."

"And you think being my wife requires new dresses?"

"Well, of course it does."

Carter straightened, trying to see the logic of her reasoning. He studied the beige-striped muslin dress she had on and flicked one brow upward. "What you have on suits you well. What you have in your closet suits you well."

Marriette swallowed the oath she wanted to hurl at his head. "Carter, most of my clothes are years old. I cannot be seen wearing the same thing season after season. People will think that I'm nothing better than poor white trash. Is that what you want everyone saying about me? About us?"

Carter laughed. "No one needs to be convinced of anything, Marriette. Save possibly you."

"What do you mean?"

Laying his cue on the table, he strode forward. "You're the only one who sees the necessity of impressing the neighbors."

"I do no such thing."

He laughed again. "Of course you do, but don't try to deny it for my sake. I've been aware of this little trait of yours for some time, and I still married you."

She drew herself up proudly. "You make it sound as though you did me a huge favor by marrying me."

"Didn't I?" Not waiting for her reply, he laid his hands on her shoulders and smiled down at her. "You and I both know that we wanted certain things from this marriage, so don't waste your time pretending otherwise."

This was too much honesty for her to tolerate. "I don't know what you're talking about."

The taut cast to her face in no way deterred Carter. "You wanted the status that came with being my wife. And I wanted this."

He pulled her to him and kissed her fiercely.

"Carter, don't," she protested, turning her head away.

"But I want to. Right now." His hands lowered to the curves of her derriere and fondled the softness through the layers of her clothing.

Marriette tried to free herself from his grasp. He had already had his way twice that morning. She could not go through with it again this soon. "Carter, we're in the middle of the library. The door is wide open."

"So?" He captured her earlobe between his teeth and bit down just hard enough to make her react.

"Stop it," she demanded, her irritation quickly escalating to anger. But her objections were useless. He planted his mouth over hers before she could utter another word, his hands hiking up the striped cotton of her dress.

Marriette's mind struggled to comprehend the fact that he actually intended to take her right there where anyone could just walk in and see them. Spurred by a burst of ire, she shoved away, but managed only to free her mouth.

"Carter, you can't do this."

Backing her up toward the billiards table, he said, "I can do anything I damn well please. You know that."

She did, indeed, much to her fury. "But I don't want . . ."

"I don't care what you want, wife." His movements sure, he levered her back until she lay flat on the cloth-top table, her legs parted and dangling over the sides. In seconds, he had her dress and petticoats up about her waist and her drawers loosened and down about her knees.

Feeling the air on her exposed thighs brought a flush of rage to Marriette's face. "Get away from me," she hissed, struggling to right herself. To her horror, he stood at the apex of her legs and unfastened his pants.

Cursing, she swung one hand in the direction of his face, but he caught her wrist and pinned it to the table by her head.

"Now, Marriette," Carter breathed, excitement

glistening in his brown eyes. "That isn't any way to treat your husband."

"This isn't any way to treat your wife. You're a beast."

"And you're about to be taken by a beast." Brutally, he yanked her drawers completely away then shoved her legs wide. "Just think in terms of bargaining, my dear."

"Bargaining?"

"That's right." His fingers sought and found the hidden warmth of her. "You want a few dresses. I want to take you. It works out rather well, don't you think?"

He had all but reduced her to a whore, forcing her to sell her body for the price of new clothes. Blue eyes glazed, she spat, "The only thing I can think of is that I hate you."

"You're not required to like me, just to lie there and be available." With his free hand, he delved beneath the neckline of her bodice. "Of course, I would be tempted to be more generous if you could manage to accommodate me to some degree."

The feel of his hand groping at her breasts, the pressure of his flesh pressing intimately to her own made her shut her eyes in disgust. Yet even behind her closed lids, she could picture herself sprawled out like some two-bit whore. It was enough to make her gag, and she might have even given into the urge if his words hadn't played through her mind.

It would behoove her to let him do as he pleased. He was going to have her whether she agreed or not. If she could profit from 'accommodating' him, then she would just have to bear it.

Breathing deeply, she stopped struggling. The second she did, Carter plunged himself into her body. She arched upward at the sudden invasion, hating him with every ounce of her being.

"Now, that's a good girl," he muttered in her ear.

She kept her eyes closed, even when he grabbed hold of her legs and positioned them about his waist, even when he grunted and thrust repeatedly inside of her.

And all the while, she imagined a life free of Carter, a life where her revenge would be sweet and oh, so rewarding.

Chapter Nineteen

There would be no corn crop.

Lacy stood on the edge of the field and admitted that fact to herself. The stalks which should have stood taller than she, barely reached her shoulders. What little fruit had managed to grow, was small and dried out.

The peanuts were in better condition, but not by a great deal. The lack of rain had produced an undersized yield that would fetch little on the market. If they were lucky enough to have a harvest at all. If it didn't rain soon, every crop on the plantation was going to wither and die.

Dispiritedly she removed her wide-brimmed straw hat and ran her hand across her forehead. The heat had not let up at all during the past weeks, nor had the moisture clinging to the air become any less tenacious. The conditions made for an odd combination that had the dust from the bone-dry earth hovering over the land like a heavy shroud.

Replacing her hat, she took the reins of her waiting

mare and tiredly mounted. She thought to check on the south fields, but, knowing she would find more of the same, she headed back toward the house.

It came into view from behind a line of elms, and she couldn't help but think that the structure was the most beautiful she had ever seen. Even in the distance, it emanated a sense of welcome and permanence. How Travis could have ever left it all behind, she did not know.

Her spirits dropped further at the thought. He had been gone three weeks now. And not a single word. She had heard in town that he was in Washington, but she suspected that was as much hearsay as anything else. In any case, she worried about him. His frame of mind had been frightening when he had stormed from the house, refusing to talk or listen to her. It had been as though he could not quit the place fast enough, leaving in his wake bitter words, a seething resentment of the land. And of course, Rose.

Reining in at the stable, Lacy dismounted with a heart that ached for the poor girl. To have been used so callously was an outrage that Lacy would never be able to justify in her mind.

"Miss Lacy," Michael called, riding up to the paddock fence.

"Hello, Michael," she returned, glad to be distracted from her musings. "How are things going with the peanuts?"

The overseer lifted his hat, raked his fingers back through his sweat-dampened hair then set his hat on his head once more. "As well as can be expected, Miss Lacy, but even that isn't saying much. That's what I come to tell you. The stretch of land just beyond the spit is useless. We'll get nothing from it."

"Are you sure, Michael?"

"Yes, ma'am," he murmured.

It was all there in his voice. Lacy heard every bit of his regret and some of the hopelessness she wasn't ready to acknowledge. Little by little, she was losing the crop, and there was nothing, absolutely nothing she could do to prevent it. It was a horribly frustrating situation that made her feel useless.

Searching for clouds, she knew nothing would or could be gained by hoping for the sky to open up that second. Nor would anything get accomplished by lamenting the drought that had reduced the land to dust. All she could do was prepare for next season as best she could. And keep faith with her father's words to be true to the Watch and in return, the Watch would provide.

She scanned the peanut fields that should have been abounding, and sighed wearily. "All right, pull up the vines and we'll get started on drying them out now. At least we'll have winter feed for the cattle."

"Yes, ma'am."

Arms folded almost protectively across her waist, she stared at the ground directly in front of her. "And the wheat? Will there be enough to mill?"

"For profit, no, ma'am, I'm sorry. But for use here, there will be more than enough to keep everyone in bread for the year."

She nodded, having no choice but to be satisfied with that. There would be enough fodder for the livestock, and grain for the slaves.

"Well, make sure we keep the gardens worked. If we want to eat more than ham and greens next year, we need those vegetables."

"We just emptied another forty barrels of water on the beans."

Lacy mentally offered up thanks for the fresh water spring that supplied the plantation with its drinking water. It had bubbled up from the earth for hundreds of years and showed no signs of stopping. It was that water that had been used to irrigate the gardens and keep them producing.

"Is there anything else, Michael?" she asked, almost afraid to hear his answer.

"What did you want done in the cooperage?"

The sigh that passed over Lacy's lips was slightly strained. Hundreds of barrels had been manufactured for a shipment of crops that would never be. At least not this year.

Wearily she rubbed at her temples and sought the most logical solution. "Do you think we can sell the barrels?"

"Possibly," Michael said with a shrug. "Although there isn't anyone in these parts who could use them. You might want to store them until next year."

"But I can use them as a source of income now. Will you look into that for me, Michael? Perhaps one of the ships coming into port or leaving would be willing to buy them, or take them in trade for sugar or salt. We could use the salt to cure out more hams."

"All right, Miss Lacy. I'll ride into town tomorrow."

"Thank you."

Michael nodded, but hesitated in riding off. "Miss Lacy?"

His gentle tone drew her up short. "Yes?"

"You're doing the right thing by tilling some of the fields now."

That he would trust in her judgment so readily caught her by surprise. It also touched her deeply that he would express such confidence in her. "Thank you, Michael. That means a great deal coming from you."

He lifted a finger to the brim of his hat as he turned his mount and rode back to his duties.

Grateful for the encouragement she had just received, Lacy crossed the rolling lawn and made her way toward the kitchen and a cool glass of apple cider. But as she neared the slave quarters, she caught sight of Rose heading toward her, arms full of skeins of cotton thread.

The girl had recovered from her physical ordeal of running off. The scratches and bruises on her legs had healed, as had the blow to her face that Travis had given her. Just the thought of Travis striking Rose turned Lacy's stomach, and not for the first time, she cursed her brother.

"Afternoon, Miz Lacy," the girl offered hesitantly.

"Hello, Rose. How are you today?"

"Fine, thank you."

Lacy wondered at the truth of that. To look at Rose, she appeared well. But she sensed a tension in the girl that was unmistakable, as though Rose expected something dire to befall her at any moment. It had been this way ever since Travis had caught up with her and brought her back.

"Are you sure, Rose? You're not ill are you?"

"Oh, no, ma'am," Rose hastened to assure her.

But Lacy detected the nervousness in the declaration and scanned the pretty features that were drawn tight. Something was wrong.

"Rose," she began on a sudden, dismaying thought. "Are you . . . that is, did Travis leave you pregnant?"

Rose's eyes rounded enormously. "No, Miz Lacy," she breathed out. "Oh, no, ma'am, he didn't. I promise."

Greatly relieved for Rose's sake, Lacy patted the girl's shoulder to calm her obvious fears. "It's all right, Rose. I just wanted to make sure there was nothing wrong with you."

"I ain't 'cpectin', Miz Lacy."

"Then what has you so upset these days?"

Rose gathered her skeins close to her chest. "Nothin', Miz Lacy."

"But I think there is something."

There was more than something and try as she might, Rose could not keep her apprehension from showing.

Lacy frowned at the anxiety she saw shining in the brown orbs. "What is it, Rose?"

Dread clogged Rose's throat, and she wished she could be anywhere but standing there, having to confess. "I'm scared, Miz Lacy," she whispered.

Surprised, Lacy asked, "Scared of what?"

"Oh, Miz Lacy, I wish you wouldn't make me say."

"If you're frightened, I want to know about it. Now what is it?"

Rose nibbled on the inside of her lip, shifting from one foot to the other. She took a breath to free up her words, but her gaze fell helplessly to her feet. "I'm scared of what he'll do when he comes back."

"Travis?"

Unable to reply, Rose nodded in earnest.

"Why are you afraid?"

Alarm brought Rose's chin up and her words spilled out in a rush. "He killed Syphron. There ain't no tellin' what he's goin' to do to me."

That Rose should live in such doubt of her own safety made Lacy's heart sink. "Rose, my brother is not going to kill you."

A fine trembling seized Rose, causing her hands to shake. "But he was so angry with me."

"Not angry enough to kill you."

"Only because you stopped him, Miz Lacy. That's why he didn't raise a hand to me. But when he comes back, no tellin' what he'll do."

Lacy laid a calming hand on Rose's arm and stared hard into the girl's eyes. "I did not prevent Travis from killing you. I agree that he was furious, and that I might have spared you his verbal wrath, but you have to believe me when I say he was not going to murder you."

"How do you know that?" Rose wailed, spiraling on her own anxiety. "He done killed Syphron, he . . ."

"He didn't kill Syphron," Lacy interrupted.

Rose blinked, her lips parted in shock. "What?"

"Travis did not kill Syphron. He let him go."

All manner of emotions flashed over Rose's features. Shock was quickly followed by relief and then confusion. "I don't understand, Miz Lacy." Trying to find reason, somewhere, anywhere, she looked away. "Why?"

"Why didn't he kill Syphron? My brother might be

317

many things, but he isn't a killer."

"Why did he set Syphron free?"

No matter how many times Lacy had asked herself that very question, she could find no answer. Nonetheless, what Travis had done helped restore some of her faith in her brother.

"I don't know why he let Syphron go."

Her face somber, Rose gazed steadily at Lacy. "Why did he bring me back? Why didn't he let me go, too?"

"I wish I knew, but only Travis can answer that."

A silence fell between them, but in the short space of time, Lacy could see Rose's apprehension dissipate like ice melting under the sun. In its place was a healthy bewilderment.

"I'm sorry I didn't even think to tell you this earlier," she explained kindly. "If I had known that you were so frightened, I would have told you the truth of it weeks ago." But she hadn't, and partly for Travis's sake, twisted as that logic might be. And, too, she had been so completely absorbed in the Watch, she hadn't had time to think of the consequences of Travis's lie. Least of all how it might have affected Rose. "I don't want you to worry."

"Yes, ma'am," Rose murmured.

But Lacy knew Rose would fret over the matter nonetheless. Given the circumstances, it would be difficult for anyone not to wonder and question.

Knowing Rose needed time to sort through all she had been told, Lacy gave her a reassuring smile and made her way up to the house, grateful that her arduous day was finally coming to an end. But as she climbed the brick steps, she set her mind to one last chore she needed to complete. It was a task she had put off for far too long, but there could be no delaying any longer.

The book-lined study was cool, and out of the eerie quiet, an emptiness seemed to rise up and engulf her. The silence bore down on her from all sides and only enhanced a longing of the heart she tried so hard to keep at bay. Pursued by a full-blown reluctance to do what she knew she must, she sat at the desk and took up pen and paper.

Yet for several long moments the vellum remained an unmarked, pristine white. Staring at her pen, Lacy fully realized that of all the letters she had ever written, this one was the most difficult to compose. Not because of its contents, but because the letter was to go to Jared.

She sat back, giving up for the time being. The letter *would* be written, for Jared had to be told of the state of affairs on the plantation. He had left the land fully expecting it to produce a profit. What he owned right then was a few hundred acres of useless corn.

It was not the best of tidings that could be imparted, but that was not what stilled Lacy's hand. Contacting Jared for any reason was to force her memories close to the surface where she dearly wished for them not to be. She was only so resilient in dealing with the sorrow that had resulted from his parting. To write to Jared seriously diminished her ability to cope with that sorrow.

Part of her success in maintaining her composure day after day was due to the fact that he was truly and forever gone; out of sight, with no sound or touch of him to remind her of all that might have been.

Breaking with this, even through the written word, was tantamount to reaching across the miles that separated them and tenderly laying her hand along his lean jaw. It was a contact that would dredge up all the hopes she held close to her heart.

She surged to her feet, as though she could walk away from her anguish as easily as she could the desk. But the sadness followed close on her heels and caught up with her when she came to stand at one of the windows.

In her mind, she tried to picture Jared at that moment, tried to imagine what he was doing, what he was thinking. Part of her hoped that his thoughts were turned to her, and that those thoughts were not too denouncing. She would like to think that he held in his heart some small token of the love she gave him. If that were so, he might understand why she hadn't been able to marry him. And perhaps someday he might be able to forgive her.

"Miz Lacy?"

She looked up to the doorway at Gaye's quiet interruption. "Yes, Gaye," she replied, turning away from the window and her thoughts.

"Besha wants to know if you're wanting your supper now."

It was only going on six o'clock, but ever since Travis had left, she had gotten in the habit of eating early. Still, she had no appetite just then. "I'm not at all hungry, Gaye. Please tell Besha that some cold chicken will do for tonight."

"No, ma'am," the house girl avowed determinedly, "I can't tell Besha that."

Lacy's brows arched. "Why not?"

Nodding as though all the wisdom of the ages were hers to relate, Gaye said, "You ain't been eating right, Miz Lacy, and we're all getting plumb worried about you, working from sunup to way past dark. Besha says it ain't right that you got to run this place all by yourself."

The concern behind the gentle reprimand brought a smile to Lacy's lips. "Thank you for worrying about me, Gaye, but I'm fine."

Gaye looked dubiously at the faint blue smudges beneath Lacy's eyes and the cheekbones that had lost some of their gentle curve to strain. "I don't think so, Miz Lacy. Besha don't think so either, and she told me not to come back to the kitchen unless I had your promise that you're going to eat proper tonight."

It was blackmail, pure and simple. Lacy understood at once that she could fight it or accept it graciously. She opted for the latter because she didn't want people worrying about her unduly. But also because she simply did not have the energy to resist.

"All right, Gaye, tell Besha that I will have a full dinner in a half hour." She glanced to the desk and the letter that awaited. "I have a matter I need to see to first."

"Yes, ma'am."

Lacy returned to the desk and did what she needed to do. But each word she wrote brought her nearer and nearer to tears.

The following morning was a replica of the previous, with the exception that Lacy began her morning feeling all the pressures and responsibilities weigh heavily upon her shoulders. The fatigue she had been so successful in ignoring over the past weeks seemed to sap her strength, making rising to the predawn light an ordeal in itself. Still, she faced her day resolutely, refusing to give into the ache that settled behind her eyes.

Her routine was as always; to the kitchen, the dairy, and slave quarters. But it now also included a stop at the barn and the stable before she sat down to a quick breakfast. That done, her trek over the land took her into the orchard, the gardens, the southwest fields, and past the pond with its wood and stone dam that contained the river.

She took her lunch beneath a lacy-limbed willow, much to Besha's disapproval, and then it was the better part of two hours spent supervising the making of soap. By the time she left the women over their steaming vats, she was more than ready to leave behind the scent of lye and instead breathe in the aroma of curing hams in the smokehouse. If time were hers, she would have lingered in the fragrant dependency, but the east fields beckoned relentlessly.

Like a spoiled child who had been given too much and was brazenly thankless, the acres of peanuts stretched out lazily, demanding, selfish, but horribly dependent. Adjusting the wide brim of her straw hat, Lacy surveyed the land.

"I'm doing everything I can for you," she murmured, her soft words underscored with apology. She knew in her heart that she was. Still, it wasn't enough, and she knew that, too. And seeing such obvious proof in the plants struggling to survive only increased the weariness that had become

322

so much a part of her life of late.

She turned for home, and the account books that waited, but she found herself following an unconscious urging that lured her to the river. Allowing herself the respite, she made her way through the bordering trees until she emerged at Flemmings Creek and the sloping banks where the swans came each winter.

The Pagan's water flowed past, its journey taking it to the James River and the Chesapeake Bay beyond that and finally to the ocean itself. The timeless ease of the course was soothing somehow, and Lacy allowed its effects to sink into her senses. She sat in the shade of the trees, her thoughts drifting as freely as the water.

It was an unguarded moment, her defenses down, and helplessly her mind was filled with Jared; the image of his smile, the sound of his deep voice, the remembered feel of his body against hers. Her insides warmed and for a few precious seconds, she allowed herself her memories and hugged them close.

Removing her hat, she drew her knees up to her chest and wrapped her arms about her legs, missing Jared more now than she ever had. Time had done nothing to diminish her yearning. Each day that passed only increased her longing to be held in his arms, to feel his heart beating against her own, to look into his gray eyes and see her love returned.

The bittersweet reverie sent her to her feet. Choking back a sob, she paced to the water's edge. She had known this was going to happen. The letter she had penned the night before had breached her carefully constructed defenses and left her vulnerable to her own heart's desires. Now she was left to face her own misery. Jared was gone and she would spend the years ahead yearning for that which would never be hers.

Her shoulders sagged. The peacefulness of the secluded spot lost the edge of its beauty. In looking about, she doubted it would ever appear the same to her, and in that second, she wanted only to be gone.

Spinning about, she turned for the trees, but pulled to an abrupt stop, her eyes widening in disbelief, her heart beginning to pound in a furious cadence.

"Jared?"

"Hello, Lacy," he said.

She exhaled sharply, then struggled for another breath. Jared was there, standing not more than ten feet away beneath the trees. She tried to make sense of it, just as she prayed that this was no dream. Jared . . . with his boldly masculine smile, his long, powerful form, his piercing gray eyes. Almost mesmerized, she stared at his white shirt, a startling contrast to the trees behind him, and his gray pants blending into the neutral forest tones. She had lost track of the number of times she had wished and hoped that he would someday return. But she had never, never believed . . .

But now he was here. And it didn't matter how or why. All she knew was that she loved him.

Her feet carried her across the short space separating them, and he moved to meet her. She went into his arms with all the ease of the river flowing in its natural course. His hands crushed her to him, and when his mouth captured hers, she clung to his shoulders, holding on as though she would never let him go.

Joy, warm and fluid, washed through her. Months of anguish melted away before the onslaught of his lips on hers. His tongue sweeping into her mouth, his hands gathering her closer still, blocked all thoughts but one from her mind. He was back. Dear God in heaven, he had come back.

"Jared," she breathed against his mouth. "What are you doing here?" Her hands roamed over his chest, his shoulders, down his arms, as though she needed the tactile reassurance of his presence.

"I couldn't stay away." He kissed her again, fiercely, drinking her sweetness like a parched man. "My days were useless, my nights an agony." He yanked her closer, needing to feel every inch of her or lose his mind in the wanting.

His tongue plundered her mouth, taking all she had to give. Not an hour had gone by in which he hadn't ached to hold her so. Days awash with memories, nights riddled with desire. There had been no aspect of his business, no comfort of family and friends that had been able to compensate for having her in his arms. And in the end, his life to that moment had meant nothing. All that mattered was that he return to this woman whom he loved to the depths of his being.

He cupped her face between his palms and searched her features. Her happiness was shining brightly, but tempered ever so slightly by the signs of her fatigue.

His brows lowered in concern. She was thinner than he remembered, her countenance as beautiful as ever, but pale and tired.

"You've been working too hard," he scolded tenderly.

She shut her eyes briefly, not wanting to bring reality into her bliss so soon. "You sound like Besha." Coming to her toes, she brushed her lips over his again. "How did you find me? I didn't even know I was coming here until I found myself headed for the river."

He threaded one hand back through her silver-blond hair. "I could say that I read your mind, but the truth is, I spotted you just as you left the fields." His face sobered, the line of his mouth grim. "Things don't look good, Lacy."

Hearing the truth hurt her more than she would have thought possible, and she did not have the strength to combat the results. Her emotions were in a turmoil, her body exhausted. The utter helplessness that forever circled her determination, eroding it little by little, swamped her now.

She leaned her forehead against his chest as tears welled into her eyes.

Jared stared at the top of her head in regret. Almost too late, he had come to realize Lacy's unique attachment to the plantation. For her to stand by and watch her land wither before her eyes had to be a torment that ate at her soul. And he had not been there to lessen her burden.

Along the length of him, he could feel the quaking of her body as she cried softly. He held her gently, running his hand along the curve of her spine, giving her all the time she needed to assuage her pain, giving her his strength and love.

Her tears at last subsided to quivering sighs, but neither moved. Lacy was too content to remain wrapped in his embrace, and Jared was not ready to relinquish holding her near.

"Are you all right?" he asked at length.

"Yes." She felt better than she had in long weeks.

"I'm sorry. I didn't mean to upset you."

She looked up, her blue-green eyes still glistening. "It was not your fault. You didn't tell me anything I didn't already know. I think I was just too tired to hear it."

Mention of the exhaustion that was so evident brought Jared's hands to her shoulders. "Let's go back to the house. Whatever needs to be done, your brother can tend to it."

Lacy's brows arched as she blinked rapidly. "Travis is gone."

She explained all that had occurred since his departure as they walked back to the house. Jared listened attentively, not saying anything about Marriette's marriage, or Rose's running off with Syphron. His jaw remained fixed as he heard every word Lacy said about Travis's leaving and the drought and the failing crops. His hand at her elbow, he silently escorted her across the sloping lawn and up the brick steps, until she finally concluded her accounting. Only then, in the quiet of the parlor, did he finally make his reply.

"Damn it all, Lacy," he gritted out. "You've been here all by yourself, doing an impossible task, working yourself sick while that worthless brother of yours is off playing? Why in the hell didn't you write to me?"

From her place on the settee, she watched Jared pace before the cold fireplace, not quite sure what to make of his anger.

"I did write to you."

He halted in his tracks. "When?"

She glanced down to her lap. "Yesterday." When she looked back up, he was pinning her with an accusing stare. "I thought you needed to know about your crops."

"To hell with my crops." He jammed his fists on his waist. "You should have sent word that you needed help."

How many times had she wished to have him by her side, if for no other reason than to have his strength to lean on? But they had parted because of her inability to marry him, and she had had no reason to think that he had not come to hate her.

"I didn't think to send for you."

"I would have come back sooner."

Her gaze dropped to her lap again, and when she spoke her voice was a sad murmur. "I did not know that. I didn't think I would ever see you again."

In one stride, he stood at the settee. He took hold of her arms and pulled her to her feet. "Well, you thought wrong," he muttered darkly. "I am back, for now and always."

Uncertain of his meaning, she shook her head. "What?"

"Do you think I sailed back for some little jaunt?"

"I don't know why you're here." In truth, she hadn't wanted to examine the reasons for his presence too closely. She had simply let herself be swept along by her own happiness.

"I love you, Lacy. I always have. That should tell you a great deal."

"But you walked away . . ."

"And I have regretted my actions ever since."

A tiny bubble of hope burst in Lacy's heart. "I never wanted you to leave, Jared."

"Good." His arms slipped about her, holding her prisoner against the unmovable wall of his chest. "Because I intend to marry you, and this time, not you or anything you say is going to stop me."

"But . . ."

"But nothing. In case you have forgotten, I own several hundred acres of this land. And if I choose to build a house on that land, then I shall."

It had come out of the blue, this declaration of his, and her mind tripped along as it tried to come to full comprehension. "You're going to move here? To Virginia? To the Watch?"

"Yes, to all three."

"But what of your business?"

Just the feel of her went far in defusing his ire. Settling her curves more comfortably to the fit of his body, he explained, "My brother Stephen is willing to buy my portion of the firm. But I'll keep what ships I need for the Watch's purposes."

"But the shipping firm has been so much of your life. How can you simply give it up?"

The answer was simple enough, although the process of arriving at the answer had been wretched. When he thought back on the trial his summer had been, he exhaled deeply.

"I poured all my energy into the company for years. But I don't want that for the rest of my life. I've

329

sensed it for months now, even before I was first contacted by your brother last year. Part of the lure of coming to Virginia was to ease a need that had been growing inside me."

He remembered the restlessness that had driven him south. The first time he had looked up the Pagan River, some of that discontent had dissipated. His sense of satisfaction had only increased in his time spent at the Watch.

He let his gaze tour her face, before he stroked the satin of her cheek with a knuckle. "I found what I had been looking for. Only I didn't realize it until I was back in Connecticut and nothing seemed right. I knew then that I had been searching for you. And I am tied to you, just as you are tied to this land." He brushed his lips over hers. "Returning just now was like coming home."

Never in all her imaginings did Lacy ever think this would happen. She was stunned; her knees threatened to give way and her heart pounded furiously.

"Say yes," Jared prompted, effortlessly taking her weight against him. "Say you'll marry me."

Her face aglow, joy infusing every fiber of her being, Lacy clasped her hands around his neck and smiled radiantly. "Yes. Oh, Jared, yes, I will marry you."

Chapter Twenty

His mouth crushed hers in a rejoicing of the hearts. Too long had he waited for this moment, and his body reacted with all the pent up desire of months of frustration.

He slipped a hand to the small of her back and urged her against his thighs. The pressure of her softness cradled him and in one searing moment, he was hard and aching. His breathing ragged, he tore his mouth from hers.

"God, but I have missed you." He claimed her mouth again as she slid her arms about his neck, trailing her fingers up through the strands of midnight hair. Murmuring low in her throat, she gave herself up to the magic he was weaving about them both.

Jared gloried in her response, but it was a teasing evocation of the memory of the greater passion they had once shared. He had been a fool to think that he could return to her, even look at her and not want to experience again the raging fires of desire they had once created together.

He deepened the kiss, his tongue feverishly caressing hers, tasting, loving, until Lacy's breaths were escaping her in broken little sighs and her hands were clinging tightly to his shoulders.

"Jared." Her voice was a husky murmur that tantalized his senses.

He looked down into her slumberous eyes, his own eyes asking a silent question. The look she returned was all the answer he needed.

"Come." Taking hold of her hand, he led her from the room, but at the stairway, her steps faltered.

Self-consciously, she ran a hand over her hair, mussed from a day spent at chores. Her fingers trailed across her cheek and down her neck while she glanced at her dusty gown.

"I'm a terrible sight," she whispered.

Jared's eyes glowed with a potent male possessiveness. "You are the most beautiful woman I have ever known."

His words sent trills of excitement up her spine, but she could not contain her uncertainty. She did not want to go to him looking as she did, fresh from the fields. "I'm a mess, Jared."

He found her doubt adorable. Gathering her back into his arms, he told her, "Order up a bath, and we'll see to making you look less of a 'mess.'"

Her eyes widened in shock, but it took only one scalding kiss to convince her that a bath was indeed in order.

No more than ten minutes later, she faced Jared from across a tub of warm water that had been hastily arranged in her bedroom. She silently blessed Gaye for her efficiency, for she doubted Jared could have waited in the parlor another second.

At the smile that drifted to Lacy's lips, Jared asked, "What amuses you, love?"

"The thought of you biding your time downstairs while the bath was made ready."

A determined, wolfish gleam darkened the gray of his eyes. "I'm no longer downstairs."

His expression made her heart thud in her chest, and when he strode toward her, it was all she could do to draw an even breath. He stood before her, tall and indomitable, pure masculine power overwhelming the intrinsic femininity of her. Irrevocably drawn to that virile force, she rounded the tub and slid her hand up his chest, her move bringing her body flush with his.

The contact was electrifying, making him want to forgo baths and gentle teasing. But he reminded himself of her inexperience, that she was practically still a virgin. Exercising more control than he thought he would ever possess, he released the row of buttons that ran down the front of her bodice, noting the slight flush that stained her cheeks.

In fascination, Lacy watched his fingers drift from one button to the next. In seconds, he was slipping her sleeves over her shoulders and down her arms. Her dress fell to the floor, followed quickly by her single petticoat.

The flush on her cheeks deepened as she watched his hands release her corset and then her chemise. But if he noticed her blush he gave it little thought, for he caught her fingers in his own and urged them to the buttons on his own shirt.

Caught off guard, Lacy hesitated for a moment. The idea of undressing him was startling. Yet it was also appealing, temptingly so and she followed his lead wholeheartedly. The front of his shirt parted and little by little a wedge of darkly tanned skin and a crisp mat of hair was revealed to her eyes.

Unable to help herself, she pushed the fine white fabric aside and ran her hands over the sculpted planes. At her touch, he drew in a sharp breath, his muscles flexing, his eyes clenching shut.

"Jared?" Her low query hinted at confusion.

Slowly he opened his eyes, his breath locked in his lungs. "Do you have any idea what you do to me?"

She didn't, but she wanted to know. Their one night together had been shrouded by a darkness that had concealed his body from her view. Now in the bright light of day, she was captivated by the elemental differences between his body and her own.

Her fingers roved again, finding the flat male nipples. She grazed the nubs and felt her insides clench when they tightened under her palms.

Jared groaned low in his throat. Her touch was taking him to the far ends of his restraint much too quickly, and it was all he could do to concentrate on removing her clothes. Clamping down on the desire that speared from his chest to the pit of his belly, he tugged on the drawstring of her drawers.

He lowered himself to his knees as he eased the muslin over her hips and down her thighs. The garment drifted from his fingers to pool at her feet, leaving her in nothing but her stockings and garters.

The sight was more than even Jared could withstand. Her breasts were full and tempting above the small indentation of her waist. The flat of her belly curved into the gentle flare of her hips, while a thatch of silver hair nestled at the apex of her legs. For months he had had to sustain himself on the memory of her perfection. To have her before him now as he had so often dreamt acted on his senses in an unrelenting demand.

Unable to help himself, his arms came about her, pulling her to him as he leaned into her softness. His mouth closed over one nipple, caressing the rosy crest with slow strokes of his tongue. Long fingers traced her spine, slipping upward and then forward, claiming the lushness of her even as his mouth did.

The dual assault of his palms and lips wrung a low moan from Lacy. Pleasure radiated out from her breasts to warm every nerve in her body. The sensation collected deep inside her, turning her bones to liquid and her blood to fire. She clung to him, circling her arms about his head and shoulders to hold him closer and closer still.

Trembling, she feared her knees would buckle beneath her. "Jared," she gasped.

His head came up, his gaze capturing hers. With near surprise, he remembered the waiting bath. In one lithe surge, he came to his feet and shed his boots and clothes. His moves concise, he rid her of her stockings, then stepped into the tub, taking her with him.

A startled gasp parted Lacy's lips as she found herself sitting astride Jared, facing him as he sat in the tub full of warm water. Her position was just shocking enough to bring the stain of a blush back to her face.

"I take it you have never bathed in quite this manner," Jared teased, knowing full well that she hadn't.

"Of course not," she exclaimed. They were intimately seated; her breasts resting against the iron of his chest, her inner thighs caressing the outer edge of his, the core of her womanhood snuggled over his rigid maleness. His arms were around her, one hand between her shoulder blades, the other cupping her bottom, insuring the snug fit of his body to hers.

From all directions, she felt him hard and unyielding. The sensations that resulted quivered through her until the hands she laid on his chest visibly shook.

"I didn't know bathing such as this existed," she managed to get out.

In answer, he reached for the bar of scented soap on the low stool set beside the tub. The promise in his gaze told her that her definition of bathing would forever more be changed. In seconds, she understood that all too well when he spread an abundance of lather across her breasts.

His fingers caressed languidly, drawing her nipples into pouting buds, teasing, circling, stroking. She fought for breath as hot pulses raced through her and of its own accord, her body arched in response.

Still, his hands were relentless. They lathered up her neck to the back of her shoulders. With wonderful expertise, he massaged the tense muscles at her nape before dipping below the water to knead his way down to the small of her back. There his hands became more insistent, shifting her bottom rhythmically.

Lacy felt her insides melt. The sure pressure of his hands rocked her most vulnerable flesh to his most demanding, and in a flash of a heartbeat, she was hungry to know again the staggering pleasure he had given her months ago.

She lifted her mouth to his, slanting her lips in a sweet assault that ignited fire in his limbs. The groan that worked its way up from deep within him got no further than his lips before she snatched it away and made it hers.

Emboldened by his response, she cupped his face between her hands and traced the firm contours of his lips, relearning the feel and heat waiting within his mouth. It was a heady, almost dizzying discovery that caused her blood to pound and throb low in the core of her, making her ache with a wild desire to have him inside her. Unconsciously she sought the union and when her hips pressed forward, Jared's arms tightened about her uncontrollably.

He cursed raggedly, her unrestrained ardor taking him by surprise. He scooped up handfuls of water and rinsed her body, trailing his fingers over the slope of her breasts again and again then letting his mouth rain kisses over her heated, scented skin.

Hot, demanding desire ripped at his insides. He was desperate to join his body to hers, but he was loathe to end this sweet torture so soon. Months of wanting warred with the insatiable need to prolong the pleasure for as long as possible.

And it was exquisite pleasure that he wanted for her. For them both. He slipped one hand over the curve of her belly, ever downward to the pale hair between her legs. Unerringly, he found the heated softness of her.

Lacy thought she would dissolve at the touch of his hand. Her insides twisted restlessly, melting about the insistent intrusion of his fingers into her clinging warmth. Her entire body strained forward, seeking more, needing everything he had to give.

"Jared, please," she gasped frantically.

Her plea was his undoing. He came out of the water, taking her weight effortlessly. In three strides, he was at the bed, laying her down, and then plunging into her as though all his tomorrows waited for him inside her small, perfect body.

She cried out in a torrent of wild, turbulent pleasure. Driven by passion and love, she arched up as he thrust into her repeatedly, driving into her fiercely, ravenously, until her body convulsed furiously around him, taking him to his own shuddering release.

For long moments, only their labored breathing could be heard. And then the silence was broken by Jared's deeply satisfied sigh. Levering himself up to his elbows, he placed a tender kiss on her lips.

Lacy gazed at him with all the love bursting in her heart. "I love you."

A crooked smile pulled at his lips. "I should hope so after what we just shared."

An answering smile graced her lips. "I didn't . . . ever think . . ." She stuttered to a halt, somewhat embarrassed at how unreserved her response had been.

"What is it?" he coaxed.

338

"It was . . . too wonderful for words."

Still intimately joined to her, he eased forward just a bit. "You are too wonderful for words."

His slight move sent ripples of pleasure up her spine and down her legs. He felt them against him and lowered his head to brush his lips over her.

"Will you stay?" she whispered.

His dark brows shot up. He wasn't certain of her meaning. "In what context am I to take your request?"

She looped her arms about his neck. "I want you here in the house. I don't want you returning to your ship."

As reserved as Lacy was about some things, Jared knew that she did not speak lightly. "We would be alone here. Proprieties being . . ."

"I don't care about proprieties, not when it comes to you. I love you, Jared. I can't be parted from you again."

He had no desire for that either. "Then yes, I'll stay here."

"And here?" She lifted her hips to his.

The gray of his eyes turned smoky. "Most definitely, here."

Lacy wasn't certain what woke her, but she started from her sleep in one abrupt instant. Fully awake, curious to the point of feeling a slight nervousness, she took in all the obvious and subtle nuances of the room.

Jared lay sleeping on his stomach, a well-muscled arm curled about her, his breathing a steady rhythm.

By the last fading rays of light that filtered in through her windows, he seemed larger than ever, especially lying within the delicate framework of her bed. But there was nothing about him that would have jarred her awake so suddenly.

Her eyes scanned the room. From the clock on the mantel she learned that it was nearing eight o'clock. That didn't surprise her. After Jared had made love to her a second time, they had fallen asleep in each other's arms, only to awaken and turn to each other in passion again. And yet again.

She noted the tub still full of water, and her clothes lying scattered about with Jared's. Her ring of keys rested on her dresser. All was exactly as they had left it hours ago.

All was as it should be.

Calling herself silly for her imaginings, she relaxed back in the curve of Jared's arm and turned her attention to him. A rosy blush stole into her cheeks when she thought of all they had shared. Jared Steele was a bold, compelling man. If she had not known that before, she was convinced of it now. She had no experience by which to judge, but she suspected that he was a most ardent lover.

A very feminine smile came to her lips at the thought of a lifetime with such a man.

Careful not to disturb his sleep, she slipped from bed and donned a dressing gown of pale blue. If it was eight o'clock, Gaye would be wondering about her. And Besha would want to know what to do about dinner.

Tying her belt loosely about her waist, she moved toward the door when Jared's voice came to her from the shadows beneath the canopy.

"Running out on me so soon?"

Her gaze met his. "I didn't mean to wake you," she said, crossing back to the bed.

"You didn't." He reached out and took hold of her hand. "Where are you off to?"

"To see about dinner. I thought you might be hungry."

A wicked curve twisted his lips. "I feasted earlier, but I could use some food now."

She gave him a shaming look, but it dissolved with her laughter. "You are too bad, Jared Steele."

He curled a hand behind her neck and urged her downward. His lips against hers, he asked, "Are you complaining?"

"No," she breathed. The mere touch of his hand and she could feel tingles of delicious anticipation kindle deep inside her.

"Good." He closed the infinitesimal space between them and kissed her in a slow, languid mating of lips and tongues. When he released her, Lacy had to struggle to breathe let alone think about dinner.

"I'll . . ." She swallowed hard. "I'll go . . . see about dinner."

"If you wait for me to dress, I'll come with you. I need to send word to my ship not to expect me back." He threw off the covers and swung his long legs over the side. "And I will need my things sent over."

Lacy marveled at the play of muscle and sinew. Even in the muted light, his strength and power were evident as he bent to retrieve his pants. By the time he pulled them on, her gaze seemed glued to his fingers working the fastenings and her mouth was dry.

"Would you rather I take them off?"

His deeply drawled query jerked her gaze to his, and she realized that he had been watching her watch him. Her cheeks flamed.

"But I warn you," he continued, "if I take them off, you'll have to forget dinner for a while."

"Oh, dear," she lamented. She was only just coming to discover this passionate side of her nature. She was not at all certain what to make of it.

Leaving the placket on his pants partially unfastened, he moved to stand before her and take her in his arms. "I can be very accommodating."

One black brow arched rakishly over eyes that darkened rapidly. One hand slipped low to rest on the curve of her bottom, while the other toyed with the belt of her dressing gown. He was in the process of spreading the front of her gown wide to search out the satin fullness of her breasts when the bedroom door slammed open.

Lacy gasped even as Jared's hands gripped her arms protectively. In unison they looked to the doorway. And Travis.

In horror, Lacy stared at her brother, his face contorted with rage, his hands fisted at his sides, and she didn't know whether to be shocked or angry at his sudden appearance. His words made it easier for her to define her feelings.

An imperious finger raised at Jared, Travis swore viciously. "You bastard. I ought to kill you right where you stand."

"Travis, no," Lacy cried.

Jared remained unmoving, giving no evidence that he had even heard Travis other than a slight narrowing of his eyes. He stared at his future brother-in-law for long, tense moments. Only when he had apparently seen his fill did he move.

With deliberate care, he closed Lacy's dressing gown and retied the sash. Then with equal care, he turned and faced Travis squarely.

"This is none of your affair, Travis. But I'll grant you your supposed concern for your sister and tell you this much. Lacy has agreed to marry me."

Brother looked to sister for confirmation, and gradually the anger and disbelief in his eyes lessened. Finally, he exhaled and shook his head in an odd mixture of self-disgust and self-righteous satisfaction.

It was a strange combination of emotions which tugged Lacy in separate directions. She could well imagine her brother's desire to exercise his rights as her protector. But she could also plainly see just how foolish he felt just then.

She let her gaze tour his features. He looked tired. That was something with which she could identify. "I didn't know when to expect you back."

Travis thought that was painfully obvious, but under Jared's unrelenting stare, he kept his mental comment to himself. "It was time to come home."

No one said that it was about time, but the feeling was felt all around. Instead, Lacy said, "I was just about to check on dinner. Would you care to join us?"

Travis's jaw tightened. It was almost absurd being invited to his own dinner table. But in light of his absence of the past weeks, and the present circumstances, absurdity was not so unwarranted.

"All right." Then not giving either Lacy or Jared another look, he strode from the room.

The line of Lacy's shoulders sagged slightly. The telltale gesture did not go unnoticed by Jared.

Taking her chin between his thumb and forefinger, he tipped her face up to his. "Are you all right?"

"I think so. It's rather strange having him back. We did not part on good terms."

"He should never have left in the first place."

A troubled frown creased her brow. "Please don't be critical, Jared. He's back. That counts for something."

Not liking the distress he saw on her face, he ground his teeth. But he would do nothing to increase the tension he knew she was feeling. Gathering her close, he gave her the love and support she had needed for so long.

Chapter Twenty-One

Rose was scared. She tried to tell herself she wasn't, but deep down inside, she was.

Travis had returned the night before, and despite Miz Lacy's assurances that he would not explode in anger, Rose was not convinced. Any minute, she expected him to walk into the weaving cottage and then God only knew what would happen.

She stared at her hands and saw her fingers tremble. Instantly she clenched her hands into her lap, the flax wheel rotating slowly to a stop. She was having trouble enough spinning thin, even threads. Having the shakes was making her job all the more difficult. Taloila would not be pleased.

Her gaze shifted to the old woman at the loom, then shot to the doorway once more. She wished he would just step in so the waiting would end. At least then she wouldn't have to sit and fret. The not knowing was making her stomach clench.

"Keep yo' mind on yo' work, girl," Taloila ordered without looking back toward Rose.

Rose released a pent-up sigh. "I'm tryin'."

"It's early. He probably ain't eatin' his breakfast yet. He'll get here when he gets here."

Perhaps at one time, Rose would have pretended not to understand what Taloila meant. But too much had happened and Rose was far too nervous to play games.

"That's what's got me worried."

"Worryin' a matter to death won't change de outcome none. What's goin' to happen, will. Best you can do is set yo' mind to other matters."

Good advice, to be sure, but Rose did not find it all that helpful. Ever since she had learned that Travis had not killed Syphron, the only matter her mind seemed to want to dwell upon was why Travis had brought her back.

Why? It didn't make any sense at all. She didn't see herself as holding any great attraction for him. And there were plenty of other girls on the plantation he could have as his whore. So her being special in any way was not a good, sound explanation.

There was always the fact that he flat out owned her as his property. But then, Syphron had been his property, and he had set Syphron free. If Travis had been so all fired worried about keeping what was his, he would have brought Syphron back, too.

But something had pushed Travis into tracking her down. She just wished she knew what it was. Just as she wished she knew why he hadn't killed Syphron.

That took a powerful amount of thinking. And no matter how she pondered the matter, she did not understand. Still, the fact that he hadn't killed

346

Syphron gave her a definite feeling of relief. It did her heart good to know that despite his selfish ways, there was good inside the man.

The constant shifting of the harnesses of the loom stilled and Rose glanced up from her lap to find Taloila staring at the doorway. In one horrible second, Rose discovered Travis standing just inside the room.

Her heart lurched into her throat, every muscle tensed. Part of her wanted her to get up and run, but there was nothing for her except to see this through.

Travis lifted a hand in Taloila's direction. "Go rest for a while, Taloila."

The old weaver slid from her bench and did as she was told. All the while, she nodded silently, never once giving Rose a single look.

In the absolute silence that had descended, Travis shut the door and leaned back against the panel. But unlike the weaver who had studiously kept her eyes focused away from Rose, Travis could not look elsewhere.

Mentally he issued a string of curses, and would have laughed aloud at his own folly had he been in a laughing mood. But he wasn't. He was tired down to his bones, and as far from feeling humor as he had ever been.

A scoff collected in his chest when he considered the past weeks. He had tried to put her from his mind, to purge himself of the hold she had on him, but it had been useless. Days that were nothing but a hazy bourbon blur had diffused his anger. And nights climbing on top of one whore to the next had satisfied a base need to restore his sense of self. Yet he hadn't been able to run from the love he felt for her. Not in Charleston, or in Norfolk.

And here he stood now, and still he wanted her as he had never wanted anything in life.

He scanned her face, looking for any changes that might have occurred during his time away. "Have you been eating right?" It was a ludicrous thing to ask, but she had grown thinner. And damn it all, he didn't know what else to say.

Rose swallowed, her eyes wary. "Yes."

Without warning, he pushed away from the door and she shot to her feet. The suddenness of her move tightened his jaw.

"I'm not going to hurt you," he ground out.

But she wasn't convinced of that, especially with his look turning black. For what little protection it could provide, she stepped behind the flax wheel.

"I said I wasn't going to hurt you," he snapped, "so stop hiding behind that damn thing." Irritated as much with himself as with her, Travis raked a hand through his hair and muttered, "If I was going to beat you, I would have done it by now."

He strode to one of the windows and looked out, more for something to do with himself than for any real interest in the lay of the land. The failing crops held his attention for only a second or two before he turned back to face Rose.

Again the silence stretched, this time with the insidious ability to strip away all pretenses. He detested the caution he saw on her face. He wanted the Rose of a year ago, the one who had looked up at him as though he was her whole world. The woman before him now was the woman who had run from him. And from the only position society allowed her to have in his life.

Unable to help himself, he crossed to where she stood. His face lined with tension, he traced the contour of her cheek, the same one he had hit so ruthlessly in his rage. The smooth skin showed no sign of injury.

"I shouldn't have hit you," he whispered, his voice as raw as his emotions.

Rose held her breath, her confusion as evident as her surprise.

He smiled ruefully, sadly. "I won't bother you anymore, Rose." His finger continued to stroke her cheek, his steady hand betraying none of his inner turmoil. And then abruptly, he stepped away and walked to the door.

With every step he took Rose's bewilderment grew. He was not going to punish her, nor was he going to force her to share his bed.

"Travis?"

His hand on the door latch, he regarded her closely.

"I don't understand." Her voice barely carried across the room. "Why did you bring me back?"

Travis knew he could fabricate any number of explanations. He could also state the law as it pertained to slaves, or he could simply walk out the door without another word. But he didn't have the heart for any of those options, and whether it was because the entire situation was so damned galling or because of Rose's look of vulnerability, he realized that he wanted her to know the truth.

"I brought you back because I couldn't let you go."

"But you let Syphron go."

His blond brows lowered fractionally. "I see my sister has been talking to you."

"She told me you didn't kill him."

"No." He glanced down at the floor. "I didn't."

"You gave him his freedom." *But not me.* The unspoken declaration hung in the air between them.

Travis looked up, and for one unguarded moment, all his emotions flashed across his face. But just as quickly, he yanked his feelings back into place. "I couldn't let you go, Rose. God help me, I should have, but I couldn't, because I love you."

"Love . . ." Rose gasped the word, her hands clenching at her chest.

"For all the good it will do either of us." He wanted her with a desperate need, but he wouldn't force her. She deserved better than that.

The voice of his conscience argued that it was within his power to give her what she did deserve, a free life away from Swan's Watch, far from Virginia. But the thought of living a life without her chilled him all the way to his soul.

Disgusted with himself, he left the cottage, unwilling to face the situation as it existed. Perhaps in time, he would be able to gain whatever strength it would take to do the right thing. For now, he had to live with the knowledge that he was a weak man.

The fields seemed to reiterate that sentiment. If it were at all possible, he wouldn't even look at the crops, but the drying acres stretched out all around, making him feel powerless. Realistically, he knew that even if he had not left, his presence could not have changed the condition of the land. Only the weather could do that. Still, he felt a fierce frustration gnaw at his gut, especially with the sky as blue as ever.

He glanced up. Not a cloud anywhere, but a strong wind was kicking up out of the east. The river would be sure to rise, and with high tide, swallow up the banks.

Pausing, he stared out past the peanut fields to where he could just make out the structure of stone and wood. The dam had always meant safety for the fields. This year, there wasn't all that much to keep safe from the briny river water. In a way, he was glad of that. He didn't have the energy it took to worry about the land. Perhaps next season he would regain the inner strength to care again. God, he dearly hoped so.

With no destination in mind, he headed back for the house. And Lacy. A spurt of incredulity tightened his chest. Finding her with Jared had been a shock, and in retrospect, he considered it a good thing that they intended to marry. He did not like the idea of holding a gun to Jared's head to insure a wedding, but he would have done so to guarantee his sister's honor.

For the first time since his arrival, a smile crossed his lips. He liked the idea of Lacy marrying Jared. And of the two of them living on Jared's portion of the property. It was surprising that Jared would give up his business, but it was a pleasing notion, and also necessary if the man planned to work his land.

Travis gained the back steps and followed the sound of voices that emanated from the dining room. Lacy and Jared were already seated side by side at the table and for the next half hour, they all enjoyed an amiable breakfast. Unfortunately, it was cut short by the arrival of Marriette.

She sailed into the room in a cloud of white muslin and azure velvet ribbons. At the unexpected sight of not only Travis but Jared as well, her steps faltered slightly. But only for the second it took for her to regain her composure and remember the purpose of her visit. She had wanted to have her discussion with Lacy alone, but perhaps this way would be best.

"Well, this is an estimable group," she quipped as she came forward. Her blue gaze flicked to Jared before it settled on Travis. "So the prodigal son returns."

Travis gave her a withering look, but his voice was carefully neutral. "I see marriage has not improved your disposition, sister."

"About as much as your little sojourn has improved yours."

Trying to avoid any unpleasantness, Lacy interjected, "Will you have breakfast, Marriette?"

The elder sister settled into a chair next to Travis and made a great show of arranging her new dress and crinolines. "No, I already had the most wonderful breakfast at home. In bed." She gave a coy smile, then added, "You should try it some time, Lacy. It's such a luxury."

Travis did nothing to contain his scoff. "Marriage has also shortened your memory, Marriette."

"Has it? Why, I believe you're right, Travis. My life has taken a turn toward the extravagant lately, and I simply forget how things are here." Her brows inched upward, and as though the crops at Belle-

352

haven were in any better condition, she said, "From what I can see of the fields, 'things' here could be better."

Travis gritted his teeth, but Lacy again intervened for the sake of keeping peace. "How have you been, Marriette? We haven't seen you since the wedding."

"It's no wonder. You've been slaving away here as usual, Lacy, while Travis has been off to heaven only knows where. And"—she turned to Jared—"and you, Jared, left for Connecticut long before my wedding actually took place." Her lips turned upward at the corners. "You did miss a joyous occasion."

Jared tipped his head in acknowledgment. "I regret that my departure in June was so untimely."

"Yes, well, business oftimes interferes with plea-sure." Her eyes narrowing, she studied him closely. "I did not expect you to return. What brings you back to our fair county?"

"Lacy." He stared straight into Marriette's eyes. "And marriage."

"Marriage?" The gasp was past her lips before she could temper her reaction.

A purely male grin stretched the line of Jared's lips. "That's right. Lacy has agreed to become my wife."

Marriette's surprise escalated to rage in seconds, and it was all she could do to keep the signs of her anger from showing all over her face. She had not anticipated this. She had been counting on Lacy's being tired and vulnerable and weak. To have Travis back to lend Lacy support was bad enough. To have Jared adding his strength as well was contemptible.

"Well, well. When did this little turn of events occur?"

Jared and Lacy exchanged a loving look. "Yesterday," he answered.

"And you're going to rush off to Connecticut, no doubt?"

Lacy replied with a shake of her head. "No, we'll live here at the Watch until our house is built."

Feeling very much in the dark, and not liking that in the least, Marriette bit out, "What house?"

"Jared is going to build on the property he bought from us in June. We'll live there."

Marriette straightened. "But what about the shipping company?"

Jared leaned back in his chair. "I sold it."

"You sold . . . ?" She was too incredulous to speak further.

In horrid disbelief, she stared first at Lacy and then at Jared. She had more than a vague idea of what his company was worth. To have sold it outright had to have brought him a huge, no, an *astronomical* amount of money.

Her face paled. He was rich beyond her wildest dreams, possessing a degree of wealth that Carter would never attain. And he was going to marry Lacy. *Lacy!* . . . that sniveling, self-righteous martyr of a sister.

With considerable fortitude, she managed the semblance of a smile. "I suppose congratulations are in order, then." But it was obvious to all that she was not pleased with the news.

Uncomfortable with her sister's reaction, Lacy tried to maneuver the conversation toward a less upsetting topic. "What brings you here, Marriette?"

A chilling gleam frosted the blue of Marriette's eyes. "Business," she blurted out.

"Since when do you concern yourself with business?" Travis asked.

"Since this drought has reduced the Watch to dust."

"What the devil are you talking about?"

A lethal load of determination hardening her face, Marriette slowly announced. "I am talking about selling Swan's Watch."

"What?" Travis exclaimed.

"No!" Lacy declared simultaneously.

Marriette's chin came up. "You both should listen to reason on this matter."

"I will not listen to anything you have to say about selling the plantation," Lacy avowed, then shook her head. "You have had some corkbrained ideas, Marriette, but this one is ridiculous, even for you."

"Not any more ridiculous than hanging on to a piece of worthless property."

Lacy came to her feet at this. "The Watch is not worthless!"

"Have you looked outside the window lately?" Marriette took great joy in asking.

"The crops are struggling."

"The crops are nearly dead."

"That doesn't make the Watch worthless."

"Of course it does. Without the profit from this year's yield, how are you going to manage next year?"

"We'll manage."

"What about taxes?"

355

"We'll manage," Lacy stubbornly repeated.

"How? You need money, Lacy, and you won't get any from the Watch, not without a cash crop from this year. Oh, you'll be able to buy seed, but how are you going to keep up with operating expenses?"

Lacy could not believe her sister was talking about this. Swan's Watch had weathered bad times before, and never had there been a thought of selling.

In pure frustration, she turned to Travis for help. "Make her understand, please, that this is our home. That we will *not* sell it."

Travis looked from sister to sister, and surely felt caught between a rock and a hard place. He had had too many doubts about his own abilities to manage the plantation for him to completely ignore Marriette's suggestion.

"What is this all about, Marriette? Why is it suddenly so important to you what happens to the Watch?"

She smoothed a hand over her skirt. "Because I own part of this plantation. And I see no reason for us to keep sinking good money into a losing venture."

"One season does not make a losing venture."

"It does if money is as tight as it has been. You have no guarantees that next year will be any better than this."

"We have just as much chance that it will be better." At least he hoped it would. He didn't think he could bear up under another season as bad as this. Frankly, he had no desire to do so.

"But I am not willing to take that chance. I want us

to sell now while we can be certain of a good price."

Disgusted, Lacy threw her hands wide. "This is just like you to 'want' this little scheme while you languish in luxury at Bellehaven. Well, you can want from here to eternity. I will never agree to sell Swan's Watch."

"But money . . ."

"Will never be a problem," Jared quietly interrupted.

All eyes turned his way. In the heat of the moment, Travis and Marriette had both forgotten his presence. Not so Lacy.

"What do you mean?" she queried softly.

He gave her a patently indulgent look. "I mean just what I said. While I own part of the Watch, it will never want for anything. That means the entire plantation, and not just my acres."

Lacy had had no time to consider to what extent Jared's involvement with the Watch might be. She had her answer now, and her heart turned over in her chest. "Thank you," she murmured.

"Do not thank me, love. I told you last night how I feel about the plantation." Lacy and Swan's Watch were inseparable, and he was devoted to both. He turned to Marriette and skewered her with a frigid look. "We will not sell."

Marriette gritted her teeth and dragged in a breath. She was outnumbered to an insurmountable degree. Standing, she forced her shoulders back and arched one brow disdainfully.

"Damn you all." With that, she stalked from the room and out of the house. To her waiting driver, she snapped an order to take her home. In seconds, she

357

was lurching and swaying her way back to Belle-haven.

She stared straight ahead, an almost feverish light illuminating her eyes, her mind mired on one thought. *So be it*. The sound of her laughter filled the carriage. They chose to fight her on this, then so be it. The time for them all to pay was long overdue.

Chapter Twenty-Two

"Where is my husband?" Marriette threw her inquiry at Naomie with a voice that was just short of agitated.

"He's below, Miz James." The housekeeper continued to turn down the coverlet of Marriette's bed. "With them gentlemen, playin' them cards."

"Gambling as usual," Marriette muttered to herself.

"Come again, Miz James?"

"Nothing, Naomie." Stepping to her mirror, Marriette studied her reflection with a preoccupied air. For once, she was all in favor of Carter closeting himself with his cards and his billiards and whatever else it was he did with his cohorts. Tonight it suited her purposes perfectly.

She swung back to Naomie. "Leave that for now."

Naomie paused with coverlet in hand. "But I always turns down the bed, Miz James."

"I'll do it myself."

"All right," Naomie murmured. Frowning

slightly, she asked, "You feelin' a headache comin' on, Miz James?"

"No."

"I can fix you up some powders if you're feelin' poorly."

Marriette's blue eyes blackened with her glare. "I said no. Now, get out and leave me alone."

Eyes rounded, Naomie hurried for the door.

"And I don't want to be disturbed," Marriette added.

The housekeeper nodded her way out of the room.

The door no sooner closed than Marriette hastened to her armoire. Rifling through her assortment of dresses, she discarded one after another until she found what she sought. Of dark blue muslin, the dress was one she had intended to discard weeks ago. She was glad she had held onto the old thing, at least for tonight. Tomorrow she would be glad to shred it into rags.

She donned the dress, forsaking all but one petticoat. If she could have maneuvered her waist into the bodice, she would have left off her corset as well for the sake of agility. As it was, she would have to accomplish her goal as tightly laced as ever, and not worry about keeping her breath.

As quietly as possible, she slipped from her room, taking the servants stairway instead of the grand stairs leading into the foyer. Her lower lip clenched between her teeth, she made her way unseen out of the house.

Dusk had passed an hour before. Still, she carefully kept to the shadows as she hurried to the stable. The wind that had blown all day had increased with each

360

passing hour, until it now blustered with enough force to catch her skirt and whirl it out about her.

"Damn wind," she whispered to herself. It was just one more problem with which she was going to have to contend. Riding out to the Watch was going to be difficult enough itself without adding the wind into the entire matter.

As she knew, the stable was empty. The slaves were all having their dinner, which gave her the chance to act in secret that she wanted. In the back of her mind, she wished she could have had someone saddle a horse for her, but she didn't trust anyone enough to engage their help. No, this was one time she was going to have to take care of matters completely on her own.

By the time she had the sidesaddle in place, and she had stuffed a burlap sack with all she required, a fine sweat dotted her forehead and upper lip. The urge to curse soundly was overwhelming, but she exercised every bit of patience she possessed. Too much was at stake for her to give into her temper just then.

Leading the horse from the stable proved easy enough. Remaining within the shadows was more difficult. Twice, as she headed for the forest, she was forced to hold her breath and pray that a passing slave did not glance too closely at the shrubs and trees. Only when she reached the thick copse did she mount and ride for Swan's Watch.

Her blood began to pound with the impending sense of victory. Never again, she told herself. Never again would she be at her husband's command, forced to serve his lust like some cheap whore, forced to barter her body for ribbons and lace.

Never again would her wishes count for nothing. She would never again be ignored by anyone, and that most especially included Lacy and Travis. And Jared.

Damn him! If he hadn't shown up, she might have been able to convince her brother and sister to sell the plantation. But back he was, and with enough money to thwart every one of her plans.

Well, she would take care of that. When she was through, there wouldn't be enough money on earth to salvage Swan's Watch. The only course of action that would be left open for Lacy and Travis would be for them to sell the property. And a third of that money would be hers.

And that money would mean her freedom from Carter.

Lacy gazed at her bed with a sense of longing. Memories of Jared lying there sent a rush of warmth through her veins. She wished he could spend all his nights there, beside her, holding her close, but with Travis present in the house her sleeping arrangements were as virtuous as ever. As much as she chafed at the delay, she was going to have to wait until after she and Jared were married before they could spend the entire night in each other's arms.

The howling wind distracted her from her thoughts. The gusts swept through the willows and elms surrounding the house with enough force to create an eerie stirring of branches and limbs. With the darkness of night as a backdrop, the effect was almost unsettling.

Lacy laughed off her uneasy notion, and viewed the wind with a sense of optimism. Sooner or later it *had* to sweep the rain in from the sea.

Her bedroom door opened quietly behind her, surprising her. Jared stepped into her room.

"I was just thinking about you," she averred, smiling.

"Good thoughts, I hope."

"Yes and no."

Her crossed to stand before her and slid his hands up her arms. Amusement lurking in the smoky orbs, he regarded her with exquisite care. "Are you going to explain that?"

She settled comfortably against the muscled length of him. "I was just thinking that I miss you sleeping in my bed."

His black brows climbed slightly, giving his face a devilish cast. "I think we can remedy that if we try hard enough."

Startled, but also extremely intrigued, Lacy began to ask exactly what he meant when a cry of warning sounded from outside. Her words died on her lips as she left Jared's embrace and crossed to the window. One look at the night's landscape beyond the barn and horror froze her blood.

"Oh, my God!" she choked out.

Jared came to her side and in an instant saw the cause for her alarm. The fields were ablaze, orange flames whipping up to illuminate the sky.

"Stay here," he ordered, but Lacy was already heading for the door.

They raced down the stairs, down the hall and out the back door. From ground level, the fire seemed

363

worse. Flames arched and twisted, choking smoke poured over the land. A strange roar thundered up from the ground and seemed to spew sparks from field to field.

Cries of alarm sounded from all directions; slaves ran from their quarters frantically. Somewhere in the distance, the peal of the plantation bell rang out its warning.

Jared grabbed Lacy's arm and propelled her toward the dependencies. "Get as many slaves as you can. Send them out to the fields with hoes, rakes, shovels."

"What are you going to do?" she cried, staring back at him even as she ran in the other direction.

"Try and stop the blaze before it reaches the stable and barn." It was all he said before he disappeared into the night.

Heart in her mouth, Lacy sped toward the quarters, issuing orders to everyone capable of lifting a shovel. Besha appeared at her side and together, they gathered frightened children.

"Have you seen Travis?" Lacy demanded above the frantic cry of a baby she held.

"No, ma'am, I ain't."

Lacy swallowed a knot of fear, her gaze darting about desperately. "Keep the children here," she told Besha. "If the flames make it as far as the barn, gather them up and head straight for the river." She thrust the baby into the cook's arms. "Don't stop for anything, Besha."

The rotund black woman took a fierce hold of Lacy's elbow. "Where you goin', Miz Lacy? You can't run out into dat fire!"

"I can't stand here and watch my home burn down around me." Not giving the woman time to say more, Lacy ran across the sloping lawn toward the stable. All around, sparks flew past on the wind, littering the sky before falling dangerously to the parched ground.

A piercing scream rent the night. Chills streaked up Lacy's spine, but still she didn't stop. The livestock had to be freed. Now.

As though out of some bizarre nightmare, Travis emerged from a billowing cloud of smoke. Face smudged with soot, he dashed to her side, words spilling out in a wild torrent.

"I just passed Jared. He's taken the men to the west fields."

"Besha has the children," she gasped out. "The horses . . ."

"I was on my way there."

The sounds of frantic horses met them long before Travis tore open the stable doors. Panicked by the smell of smoke, the animals needed little urging to flee their stalls and instinctively head for safety.

Cattle and sheep came next. By the time all the animals were set loose, Lacy was coughing, eyes stinging from the fire's fumes. She hung her head, bracing her hands on the fence to catch her breath. When she looked up, a low moan of despair emanated from deep within her.

In the time it had taken them to tend to the animals, the flames had spread wildly. With the wind whipping, it would be only a matter of time before every building was set aflame. And Jared was out there trying to battle the blaze.

"Oh, God," she cried.

Travis staggered up beside her, his gaze following hers. It was out of control. Despite the efforts of every man and woman risking his or her life, there was no stopping the fire.

Rose. Sickening fear twisted his gut. Rose was somewhere in the middle of that danger. Swearing viciously, he turned and ran straight for the blaze.

Buffeted by the wind, Marriette stood in the shadow of the bordering forest and watched her handiwork with a sense of satisfaction. Every stalk of corn, every grain of wheat, every cow, every building would be nothing more than ashes. It would take years . . . and more money than even Jared had . . . to rebuild. Lacy and Travis would *have* to sell.

No one person in the area could afford to make the purchase. The land would have to be divided, parceled out. But money was money, whether it came from one transaction or a dozen. Marriette didn't care, as long as she got what was her due.

Having seen enough, she skirted the cornfield that was only now beginning to smolder and catch. She needed to find her horse and return to Bellehaven before she was missed. More than likely, Carter was still playing cards, but she did not want to take any chances on his finding her gone. As far as everyone knew, she was in her bed asleep.

Smoke rose up suddenly in her path, and she stumbled to a stop. In a flash, the underbrush caught fire. Frightened, she reared back, blinking and murmuring in astonishment.

Spinning, she retraced her steps, intending to bypass the rapidly expanding inferno in a wide arc. But a rain of sparks flew overhead and with terrifying speed, brittle, dry brush and limbs erupted in a blast of heat and flames.

She whirled about, and found fire everywhere. It had happened so fast that she could barely take in the reality of the danger she was in. Only seconds ago, she had been safe.

Scorching heat seared her skin, smoke was thick in her nostrils. A terror that chilled her to her bones squeezed her lungs, constricting her throat painfully. Eyes dilated to near black, her wide gaze darted about, seeking some avenue of escape, but there was nothing but a wall of glowing, rioting flames.

"There has to be a way," she sobbed. "I can't get caught in this. I can't!" Desperate, she lunged toward a break in the underbrush, only to be shoved back by a gust of heat.

"No!" she screamed, but her voice was carried away by the wind, drowned out by the crackling and rushing of a burning world.

From a distance, Travis thought he heard the sound of a woman screaming, but he shoved the impression away. His mind, his entire being was focused on finding Rose.

Curse after curse came to his mouth and he spat each out with a vengeance. He had to find her, he could let nothing happen to her. Dodging a stretch of burning cornstalks, he ran toward a group of women shoveling dirt onto the flames. Whether their efforts were successful or not, he didn't care. All he wanted was to find Rose.

But she wasn't among the women. Frustrated, shaking with a soul-wrenching alarm, he spun about, dragging in gulps of air as he scanned the area.

Through the concealing screen of shifting smoke, just beyond a burned-out supply shack, he could make out the shapes of another group fighting the inferno. Forsaking all thoughts of his own safety, he plunged headlong toward the source of the heat.

Frantically, he stared from one woman to the other. "Rose," he shouted, but his voice could not carry against the sound of the fire. He glared about him, searching, this time toward the river . . . and he spotted her. Silhouetted against burnished yellow and brilliant orange, her figure was bent over a rake.

"Rose!" Once again, his voice was all but swallowed up. He sprinted across the field, his gaze never relinquishing its hold until he came to her side and grabbed hold of her.

The suddenness with which she was caught wrung a startled cry from Rose. Finding herself in Travis's arms only added to her fright.

"Travis?" She looked up at him in question and doubt.

His fierce gaze toured her face, touching reverently on each feature. "When I realized you were out here . . ."

"What are you doin'?" She could not make sense of his presence. Especially *now*.

"I had to find you."

"Me? Why?"

"Don't you know?" Even though he knew she was safe, he couldn't suppress his fear for her. "I love you.

If anything happened to you, I'd die."

Stunned, she lost her voice. Twice in a matter of hours he had proclaimed his love for her, but she was no more sure how to handle that now than she had been that morning in the weaving house.

"You really . . . love me?"

Ignoring all about him, Travis gathered her close and vowed, "More than anything on earth."

Jared dragged his arm across his forehead and viewed the scene before him. People all around him worked frantically, digging trenches, and throwing dirt on the flames in an attempt to snuff them out. But the wheat was gone, the corn destroyed. In a very short time the peanuts would be consumed also.

And given the direction of the wind, the fire was headed straight for the house.

His every muscle clenched at the thought. The Georgian structure epitomized the best of everything the Watch had to offer. Grace and beauty, harmony of the mind, and a generosity of the spirit. Yet nothing stood between the structure and total ruin.

"Damn it all to hell," he ground out in a frustration that ran clear to his soul. He could not allow it to end this way. There had to be some means, some way . . .

His head jerked to one side, his gaze shooting to the dam. The wind had pushed the river surge to a precarious level, flooding the banks by feet. The water held in check by the dam was near to overflowing. If it could be released, it would flood the peanut fields that lay between the fire and the house. The worst of the blaze would be extinguished.

The salt water would also ruin the fields for years to come.

He stared back at burning crops. If they worked quickly . . . if he could get enough men to release the dam's wooden supports . . . they just might be able to stop the progress of destruction here.

"Jared." Lacy's cry came to him from out of the smoke seconds before she stumbled into his arms.

"Are you all right?" His voice was hoarse, barely recognizable.

Held in a shock that precluded tears, Lacy managed to nod.

"Good; take the women and get back to the house."

She stared up at him in desperation. "What . . ."

The wind gusted fiercely, blasting heat and smoke in their faces. Jared shoved Lacy behind him, turned to hold her to his chest in order to shield her with his own body.

"We have to break the dam."

Her eyes flew wide. "But that's river water. The fields will be useless."

"It's the only way, Lacy. If we don't, we'll lose everything."

"But . . ."

Urgency lent his voice a brutal edge. "The house, the barn, the dependencies will all burn, Lacy. Now go." He gave her a shove to speed her on her way.

There was no choice. It was the one thought that repeated itself over and over in Lacy's mind as she scrambled up the smoldering lawn.

The land had to be flooded. It was the only logical thing to do. She told herself that as she gathered the women around her by the kitchen.

The most fertile fields, cleared by Flemmings centuries ago, had to be sacrificed to spare the rest of the plantation. That was her litany as she stood and waited. And waited.

It was the sound of rushing water that reached her first. Her gaze fixed on the burning acres, she held her breath, afraid to think or move. Part of her prayed, although she didn't even know for what. And then she saw the water gush out across the land, dousing fire in its path in much the same manner that the flames had consumed the crops.

The stench of acrid smoke was thick. The night sky slowly lost its orange glow. And with the exception of the howling wind, a deadly silence settled over Swan's Watch.

Slowly, as though unable to make her limbs work with any precision, Lacy made her way to the house. There, her body refused to work and she sank to the ground.

She stared at what had once been the glory of generations past. Her ancestors had suffered and toiled in the belief that the land would reward their love and sacrifices with a bountiful life. Her father had told her that, just as his father had told him and his father before that. It was what she had always believed. It was a cornerstone of her life. Yet there she sat and the truth hit her like a painful blow.

She had believed in the land. She had given, gladly so, of her entire herself. She had nurtured and cared and truly trusted in the land, never giving up hope. And for what?! God in heaven, for what? All she had now was a smoldering waste.

Pain of the heart and soul ripped into her, and she double over as tears cascaded down her smudged cheeks. She grasped handfuls of dirt and hugged them close to her chest. But still, the hollow sense of betrayal she felt was excruciating.

She had no idea when Jared finally joined her. She became aware of his presence only when he lifted her to her feet to hold her close. And even then, it took long moments for her sobs to subside.

"There is nothing more we can do tonight," he told her.

A weary sigh passed over her trembling lips. "Is anyone hurt?" Her words were muffled against his chest.

"I don't know how we managed to be so lucky, but no one was hurt. A few burns, but nothing serious."

She digested that before she asked, "How . . . how much did we lose?"

He hesitated in answering. "Almost all the crops."

"And the peanut fields . . ."

"It couldn't be helped, Lacy." He cupped her face in his hands and stared down into her despondent eyes. "It will be all right. In time, it will be all right."

She wanted to believe that. She needed to believe that. But she couldn't. Not tonight. Perhaps never again. For tonight, she would let Jared believe for her.

Chapter Twenty-Three

An oppressive silence hugged Swan's Watch. No birds called their early morning song, no trace of the howling wind stirred the trees. The land lay sadly, pathetically still.

That more than anything ripped at Lacy's heart. Standing in what had once been a field of peanuts, she viewed the blackened debris around her with a hollow, aching sense of loss, and longed for the abundant signs of life. Instead, tendrils of smoke curled up from the charred earth.

The feel of Jared's arm slipping about her shoulders caught her off guard. She had not heard his approach. But she welcomed him beside her and leaned into the solid strength of him.

"It looks so terrible," she whispered.

"For now. By next season the fields will be green again."

"Not all of them."

Jared did not need to be told how useless the washed-out tract of land would be for growing crops.

"In time, Lacy. It will all work out in time. Nature has a way of healing itself."

She silently wished nature would do something to alleviate the anguish inside her. She could not help but feel as though she had lost a part of herself.

Jared's arm tightened reassuringly. "Come back to the house, love. Nothing can be gained by standing here."

With a sense of resignation, she turned away from the acres of ruin. Her eyes sought out the house and as always, the sight of the structure lent her a measure of calm. The feeling was as appreciated as Jared's presence.

They gained the path in silence. Lacy felt no inclination toward further discussion and Jared gave her the quietude she needed. It wasn't until Travis emerged from the house and joined them at the bottom of the brick steps that the morning hush was broken.

Travis gazed over the land. "I thought it would look better this morning than it did last night. How bad is it?"

"Bad enough," Jared returned. "But not irreparable, given time and enough patience on our part."

Bitterness twisted Travis's mouth. "Damn. What a mess."

"I've seen worse."

"Then you've been to hell and back." Travis's jaw tightened, his face contorting with a mixture of emotions.

Seeing his upset, Lacy laid a comforting hand on his arm. "Are you all right?"

Her brother's reply was not immediate. Words seemed to be stuck in his throat. At last he muttered, "I'm better than I've been in a long time. Better than I have a right to be considering how miserable everything is right now."

The harsh edge to his voice drew Lacy's frown. "What do you mean?"

Again, Travis struggled for speech. He stared at Lacy, his blue eyes filling with pain . . . but his expression also conveying an odd tranquility. "Hell, I might as well tell you now and have done with it." He glanced to Jared briefly. "I've decided to leave."

"Leave?" Lacy echoed.

"Hell of a time to tell you, I know, with everything as bad as it is, but I can't go on pretending any longer."

"Pretending what?"

"That I'm Father. Or Grandfather. I realized last night that I don't have the mettle it takes to live here. You have it, Lacy. You and Jared both. But I don't." He paced a few steps away, then turned to face them, his hands shoved deep into his pants pockets. "I don't care about the Watch the way I should. When everything was going up in flames last night, I realized my life is somewhere else." His face hardened, taking on a wary cast. "My life is with Rose."

Lacy could not contain her surprise, and she could not even begin to make sense of what he was talking about. Travis read her confusion and scoffed in mock humor.

"At least you aren't condemning me on the spot," he averred. "Thank you for that." He sucked in a deep breath as though to do battle. "I love her. I've known for some time, but I tried to deny it to myself. I even tried to walk away from it, but the weeks I spent in the Carolinas showed me how useless that was. And last night only proved I don't want to run from it any longer. I want Rose as my wife."

His words left Lacy a little numb. What he was suggesting was unheard of. But she could see the conviction in his gaze. He truly loved Rose.

She breathed out in wonder as she contemplated her brother's actions of late. This certainly explained a great deal, not the least of which was why he had brought Rose back.

"What . . . what do you plan to do?" she queried.

"Go north." He gave Jared a crooked smile. "Perhaps to Connecticut. Into Canada if necessary." His smile faded. "I just want to find some place where we can live peacefully as husband and wife."

Jared's brows arched upward at the revelations. "It won't be easy. You're sure to find social condemnation no matter where you go."

"True, but I won't even find understanding here, so any chance of acceptance is nil."

"Does Rose know about this?" Lacy asked.

"Yes. But she's scared."

And with good reason, Lacy thought. "And she has agreed to marry you?"

The chuckle that came to Travis's lips was rueful. "She was surprised, I can tell you that. A man doesn't ask one of his slaves to marry him every day. But she knows I love her. And she loves me." All trace of humor left his face. "I wasn't sure she did, especially after all that has happened between us. I thank God

376

for little miracles. We may not have much, but we will have each other. And maybe some land of our own."

"A farm?"

Travis nodded. "But nothing as large as the Watch. It seems my whole life has revolved around this land. I resent that, which is one more reason I won't stay." For the first time, remorse dulled his gaze. "The Watch deserves better than that. She deserves what the two of you are willing to give her."

Lacy wasn't so certain at that moment that she had enough reserves left to offer Swan's Watch all she was going to need. But Jared did, and for that, she was eternally grateful.

"When are you leaving?"

It was not the question Travis had been expecting from her. "You mean you aren't going to try and talk me out of this?"

"Would there be any use?"

"No."

"I know that. I also know that you truly love Rose. I want you to be happy, and that can't happen here."

A genuine laugh brightened Travis's face. "You are a remarkable lady, little sister."

Lacy shrugged the compliment away. "No, not really. But I do understand what it is like to love someone as much as you do." She turned to gaze up at Jared. The look her returned spoke volumes.

It was Travis's turn to ask his own question. "When do you two plan on marrying?"

Jared answered without delay. "As quickly as possible."

"Good. I'd like to be here for the wedding."

From the far end of the lane, the sound of an approaching carriage interrupted. Standing between the two men, Lacy recognized the driver of the small conveyance at once.

"It's Carter."

Travis squinted slightly. "I'm sure he saw the fire from his place. He probably wants to pay his respects."

The carriage pulled to a stop several yards off, and Carter slowly descended. His usually buoyant step was missing.

"Good morning," he commented, his voice taut. Try as he might, he could not keep from looking out at the fields. When he turned back to the three, his face was strained. "I'm sorry about what happened. I didn't know about it until . . ." His voice broke.

He swept his hat from his head. For several moments he studied the black brim, until he seemed forcibly to shake off a tormenting preoccupation. "There is something you need to know. About Marriette."

His distress was so palpable that Lacy's heart constricted. "What has happened, Carter?"

"She . . . there's been an accident." He slapped the hat against his thigh. "It was Marriette who set fire to the Watch last night."

"Oh, dear God," Lacy breathed.

Carter continued as if Lacy had said nothing. "I didn't even realize that she had left the house until it was too late. I saw the glow in the sky from the flames, but even then, I wasn't aware that she was gone. I thought she had retired early. But she hadn't."

Jared's black brows slanted into a fierce angle. "How do you know she was responsible?"

"She confessed as much. Somehow, she . . . she managed to make it back to Bellehaven. One of my slaves found her by the stables." Carter swallowed with difficulty. "She was pretty badly burned."

Lacy pressed a hand to her mouth, but still she could not contain her cry of dismay. "Is she still alive?"

"Yes. But she wishes she wasn't." Carter's eyes filled with regret. "The doctor has been with her most of the night, but there is nothing he can do about her arms . . . her face." He clenched his eyes against the remembered sight of his wife. "She'll be scarred for life." His words stopped abruptly, then began just as suddenly. "She's been delirious for the most part. But there was an hour, before the doctor arrived, when she spoke at length, especially about the Watch."

"Why?" Lacy wanted to know. "Why would she try to burn it to the ground?"

"I don't know exactly. She's rambled on about hating this land, about hating . . . about hating all of you. And me."

As though the telling had exhausted him, Carter's shoulders sagged. "There's not much else to say."

"I'd like to go back with you."

"No, Lacy. I don't think you should see her right away. Marriette is so twisted up with hate and the pain, seeing her would be upsetting for everyone."

Lacy wanted to disagree, but she relented for Carter's sake. This couldn't be easy for him. "You will let us know if there is anything we can do to help?"

"I should ask the same of you, Lacy."

"We'll manage," she assured him. As she watched Carter take his leave, she felt a small measure of doubt about what she had said. She so wanted to believe that they *would* manage.

The setting sun cast its burnished rays on the perfection of Lacy's face as she watched the waters of the Pagan River flow past. Beside her, Jared studied the gentle curve of her brow, the serious tinge to her eyes.

Brushing a stray strand of silvery hair back from her cheek, he asked, "Looking for swans?"

A small smile pulled at the corners of her mouth. "No. They won't be here for another month or so."

"Then what are you thinking about?"

Turning, she rested her head against his chest and gave voice to her thoughts. "I'm thinking about everything that has happened. The fire, Travis and Rose. And Marriette." She sighed deeply. "I feel so sorry for her."

Jared slipped his hands about her waist to hold her close. "Most of your sister's problems are of her own making."

Lacy understood that in her heart. "I know, but it hurts to think of her suffering." A ragged sigh escaped her. "I never knew just how little she cared about the Watch. Oh, she was always temperamental, always complaining about the chores that needed

380

to be done, but I never thought she hated the plantation."

"Not everyone loves the land the way you do, Lacy. It takes a commitment that not even Travis could bear."

At the mention of her brother, Lacy tipped her head back to peer inquiringly up at Jared. "Do you think he and Rose will be able to find the peace they deserve?"

Jared's answer did not come quickly. "I won't lie to you, love, and tell you that all will be sunshine and roses for them. What your brother has chosen to do will be considered by most to be beyond damnable. Even in the North, he won't find any guarantees that society will accept his marriage to Rose." A slow smile spread over his lips. "But I think he'll manage. Any man who loves a woman as much as he does Rose won't let something as paltry as social dictates stand in the way of their happiness." He tightened his arms about Lacy. "Just as I couldn't let anything prevent me from returning to you."

In his face, Lacy saw unwavering faith and determination. The sight was wonderfully reassuring. Rising to her toes, she pressed her lips to his in a kiss that was as fervent as it was loving.

"I love you, Lacy," he murmured, already feeling the stirring effects of her sweet passion. He traced the curve of her lower lip with his tongue. "God above, what would I do without you?"

"I won't give you a chance to find out," she returned in between the small kisses he teased her with. She had waited a lifetime for Jared. She would love him until the day she died, and beyond. Arching against him, she returned his kiss with all the love bursting within her.

The kiss deepened, intensified, and threatened to spiral out of control. When Jared finally lifted his head, a poignantly tender smile illuminated his face. "This is a perfect way to begin our future," he averred, his voice a husky growl. "With you in my arms."

Lacy's brows arched in question at the emotions she saw on his face. There was desire and love, but something else she could not name. "Why are you smiling like that?"

"Like what?"

"Like you know something I don't."

His hand slipped down to caress her stomach, and his smile only widened. "I'm picturing you with my baby within your belly, your body rounded with my sons and daughters. I'm already anticipating the next generation we'll give rise to."

Tears rushed up to clog her throat. He was all that she had ever dreamt of. A strong, honest, caring man who loved her and wanted to spend his life with her. Still, she could not suppress a small shudder that wracked her body. "There isn't much of Swan's Watch to pass on to the next generation."

"Not at the moment, no. But in time, the Watch will be restored."

"I so want to believe that."

"You will, Lacy. Right now, you're too tired to have much faith."

"I am tired. I feel as though the fire took a part of me, a part of my energy."

"You'll heal, Lacy love. Just as the ground will

heal and flourish again. I'll see to that."

"You sound so sure."

"I am as certain of that as I have ever been of anything in my entire life."

Lacy tilted her head to one side and gave him a penetrating look.

"Have I sprouted horns?" he asked, considering her prolonged stare.

Blinking, she shook off the memories that had come so suddenly. "No, I was just remembering something my father said just before he died."

"Advice?"

"To a certain extent. He said that Swan's Watch will pick her own master or mistress. That she would pick the person most worthy to have her."

"And you think she has?"

She nodded slowly. "Yes. She's chosen you."

His black brows elevated over skeptical gray eyes. "What makes you think that?"

"I don't know exactly. It's just a feeling I have that even though the land is scarred, it is at peace at last. It's as though all these months since Papa died, the Watch has been waiting. And now the wait is finally over." Hearing her own thoughts made her shrug self-consciously. "I know that sounds silly, but I suddenly can't shake the feeling."

Jared grinned, an indulgent curling of his lips that originated in his heart and burst forth in laughter.

"What is so amusing?" Lacy asked, startled by his humor.

"Your father was right. Swan's Watch did choose me . . . the day you told me you loved me."

"I don't understand."

"Don't you see?" He cupped her face between his hands. "*You* are Swan's Watch, Lacy. When your father said the plantation would pick her own next master, he was talking about you, whether he knew it or not." His thumbs stroked over the satin of her cheeks. "You are the essence of the land itself, and you chose me."

For as long as she could remember, she had felt a bond with the Watch. But she had never regarded her connection to the plantation in precisely that light. Oddly enough, she sensed Jared was right.

For the first time since the fire, her smile was unfettered. "I'm glad, Jared. I'm glad it's you."

"Are you truly?"

"Oh, yes. Travis was right when he said you have the strength to give the land what it deserves."

"I'll always be beside you, Lacy, to lend you that strength and give you my love." Sweeping her tightly against him, he lowered his mouth to hers.

Caught up in the love they shared for each other, neither noticed the elegant swan that swam into the creek, weeks ahead of the flock. Its presence marked another season past, and heralded years of promise for the plantation called Swan's Watch.